THE REMAINS IN THE POND

ANN SWANN

5 PRINCE PUBLISHING

THE REMAINS IN THE POND

Ann Swann

5 PRINCE PUBLISHING & BOOKS, LLC

PO Box 16507, Denver, CO 80216

www.5PrinceBooks.com

digital: ISBN-10:1-63112-202-9, ISBN-13:978-1-63112-202-6

print: ISBN-10:1-63112-203-7 ISBN-13:978-1-63112-203-3

THE REMAINS IN THE POND. Ann Swann

Copyright Ann Swann 2017

Published by 5 Prince Publishing

Cover Credit: Viola Estrella

First Edition 2017

NOTE TO READERS

Although there is a real Live Oak, Texas, this is not it. The setting in this story is straight out of my twisted imagination, right down to the murky pond on the south side of town.

I wrote this book before the massive Big Sur landslide that occurred on May 23, 2017. I'm not sure when the road will reopen, but I can't wait to go back and see how it's changed.

Hurricane Harvey was also a distant disaster waiting to happen. Too bad we can't control Mother Nature the way we control our fictional settings.

My heart goes out to you all.

Dedicated to my dear readers—especially those who email me and message me and look me up on Facebook or at my few-and-far-between book signings. They invariably ask when the next book will be released. I tell them it's in the works, because it always is. So keep those comments coming, your words are the feedback that feeds me right up until I write The End again.

ACKNOWLEDGMENTS

A heartfelt thanks to my husband, Dude. He is my rock. I never
write a love scene without
his face in my mind.

ALSO BY ANN SWANN

All for Love

Stutter Creek

Lilac Lane

Copper Lake

THE REMAINS IN THE POND

A novel
by
Ann Swann

Rare as is true love, true friendship is rarer.
Jean de La Fontaine

FOREWORD

"We were in love," I said. "I know that's what teenagers always think, but in our case, it was true." I pushed my glasses up and took a deep breath.

The unsmiling detective simply stared at me and pulled out his little notebook. His burnished scalp gleamed under the fluorescents. I wondered if he shined it with a towel, maybe some wax like Reece and his surfboard.

And why wasn't he writing in that notebook anymore? He just held it, as if he found nothing I said worth noting.

The room grew cold and I shivered. Probably a tactic; turning down the temperature to make me uncomfortable. Just like his little waiting game earlier. Waiting me out to make me talk. I'd watched enough crime TV shows to wonder about these schemes. I took a sip of the Diet Coke he'd brought—to make me feel grateful, I suppose—and immediately regretted it because it made me need to burp.

I let the little bubble of gas explode in my closed mouth and began talking again to cover the sound. "We fell in love at prom. We were both with other people. I went with Asa and he brought his cousin, Rose." I sat up straighter in the hard-backed chair and hoped I'd said enough to placate him.

The detective sat motionless, one ankle propped on the opposite knee. I got the impression he might sit that way forever.

I started talking once more. I had to do something to make him stop looking at me as if he already knew everything and because yes, suddenly I *wanted* to tell him. I'd held onto the truth for too long.

I wanted to tell him everything about that night.

1

Senior Prom Nineteen Ninety-Nine

THE BIG SONG that year was Prince's hit, "1999." Naturally our high school cover band, Jaywalking Dead Guys, played it over and over. Each time they did they would mix it up, slow it down, rap it, chop it—whatever—they were as high as everyone on the dance floor, and we were all whirling as rapidly as the spinning planets and stars that highlighted the theme, **The Universe is Ours.** The multicolored lights and the glittery Art Department constellations contributed to the dizzying emotions that the end of senior year always produced.

Add to that the ecstasy and cocaine in the bathrooms and the booze in the punch bowls, it's no wonder we almost had a fatality. Actually, there was one, we just didn't know it until much, much later.

Like I said, it was prom night, my first—and last—dance with Matt.

He came with Rose Lintz, a girl he introduced as his cousin.

She was new to our area, and she attended the private school across town. Everyone thought Matt was amazingly sweet to bring her to our prom since the private school didn't have one. Well, most of us thought it was sweet.

I went with Asa Letter, my best friend. I knew he was gay, but it wasn't common knowledge. In nineteen ninety-nine, in small town Texas, gay high school kids did not simply come out. Especially not when their father just happened to be the most prominent surgeon in town.

Standing in line to have our picture taken in front of the Milky Way backdrop, Asa and I made nervous small talk while observing the antics of the popular crowd making their fashionably late entrances.

I'd already spotted Matt with Rose.

As I watched, he made a beeline toward me, dragging her in his wake.

"Hey, Gabs! I thought you'd be at home doing our homework." He smiled to let me know he was kidding.

"Hey, Matt Brennan, good to see you out from under your rock for a change." Matt was my chemistry partner.

He stepped up and presented the red-haired beauty on his arm. "Gabrielle Kelly, meet Rose Lintz—my cousin. Our dads are brothers."

I had to hide a smile at that last part, as if he had to explain the word cousin. I glanced at her nametag. He'd said her name so quickly I couldn't tell where the first name ended and the surname began.

The girl smiled, but her green eyes continued to scan the room behind my head.

"This is my friend—" I indicated Asa, but before I could finish, she simply turned and walked away.

"*Sweet* girl." Asa's voice dripped venom.

I didn't take the bait. We'd discuss it later, at length, on his father's rooftop deck.

But Matt heard the cut. He tossed his head in that endearing way he had of dismissing things he didn't agree with, or didn't want to acknowledge. "She's nervous." He shuffled his feet. "I had to beg her to come."

Could've asked me, I wanted to say. You wouldn't have had to beg *me*. I wonder if she's really even your cousin.

Asa, God love him, stuck his perfect nose up in the air and turned away. His navy-blue tux made his brown eyes shine, and the tiny blue and white boutonnière I'd pinned on his lapel had given him such joy it made him glow.

"Nice flower." Matt stood in front of me, just to the side of the line, and uttered the awkward segue which, nevertheless, echoed my own thoughts so closely it surprised me.

"Thanks." I fingered the gorgeous corsage pinned to my navy-blue dress with its filmy floral overlay. "Asa had it specially made. We wanted to match."

"So, are y'all like, dating, or something?" He didn't look at me as he said it. He let his gaze wander toward his cousin. She had found a thin, broody senior who appeared to have a flask in his coat.

I swallowed a laugh. Asa hid his sexuality well from those he didn't trust.

"We're just friends." I glanced at my buddy. He'd struck up a conversation with the girl behind us. "We've been friends forever."

Matt's gaze came back to mine. I'd studied his gorgeous face many times, usually from the side while we were in class, but we seldom looked right at each other. In fact, we sort of made a conscious effort to avoid it. "Friends like us?" he asked. "Like you and me?"

I wasn't sure where he was going with that. Friends like us?

What kind of friends were we, exactly? We'd sat near each other from day one but we didn't eat lunch together the way Asa and I did. We didn't go to movies or out for coffee or to each other's homes.

"Yeah, *sort* of like us." I fidgeted, and then took the plunge. What did I have to lose? "Actually, Asa and I really are *just* friends. There could never be anything else between us." No way I would betray my buddy's confidence, but I wanted Matt to know I was free, unencumbered, available. Was that why he'd never asked me out, he thought I was dating Asa? The thought boggled my mind.

Matt jammed a finger in the neck of his dress shirt as if to loosen it a bit. The tux was obviously a rental—standard black with a gold cummerbund, our school's colors—his family wasn't wealthy. His dad worked in the oil field. Matt worked part time at the local landscape nursery on the weekends and in the summer. Although he claimed to love working outside planting trees and pruning bushes, he often belittled his own job saying he couldn't wait until the day he graduated so he could get out of this town and get his hands out of the dirt.

"Maybe you'll save me a dance later," he muttered.

"Sure." My throat clicked and I heard myself struggle to say more. He'd asked me to dance. I couldn't believe it. Cloud nine, all the way.

Matt turned to look for his cousin but she appeared to be deep in conversation with the dark senior.

"Imagine that," Asa whispered. "Save the last dance for me." The disdain in his voice was palpable.

I was a little taken aback. "He didn't say the last dance, just *a* dance. Anyhow, you don't mind, do you?"

Asa stepped forward into the light of the starry backdrop. "Of course not."

The photographer arranged us together, me in front of Asa,

his hand resting lightly beneath my elbow. We made a sweet couple, almost the same height, same coloring, and wearing lovely matching flowers.

After snapping a couple of shots, we were instructed to move on to the information table in order to choose the copy of the photo we liked the best.

"Okay, maybe I am a *little* bit jealous. I mean he is your crush." It wasn't a question; it was a statement, even though I'd never admitted it out loud to anyone.

I shrugged. It felt funny to discuss *my* crush when I had absolutely no idea who his was—if he had one at all. So I changed the subject. "Do you think she's really his cousin?"

Asa waved his hand dismissively. "Where did he say she was from? I never actually caught it."

I laughed, then immediately covered my mouth. He somehow made it sound as if she came from Mars or Venus. "She goes to the private school."

"LCFL—last chance for losers—I got that. But where did she come from before? Lubbock, Dallas, Fort Worth? I mean, why is she even here?"

I looked at Matt looking at Rose and felt a slight twinge of doubt. "I think they moved here to get her away from bad influences in Dallas." Matt had mentioned her once or twice in class, but only as his cousin. I'd had no idea she was a red-haired beauty with big green eyes.

Asa nodded. "Strange girl."

I poked him in the rib with my elbow. "You're one to talk about strange people." I couldn't understand his apparent dislike for Matt's cousin. Sure, she'd slighted him, but his attitude seemed a bit too vehement for that. I wondered if they'd had some sort of dealings before tonight. Is that why she dismissed him when I'd tried to introduce them? Asa did have his secretive side—I always assumed it was because he had to hide so much of himself just to get by in our little town.

Suddenly he grinned and the mood lightened. "You're right. I'm the strange one." He winked. "With the strange name. Too bad I don't have a nice name like she does, but at least I have an excuse. My dad had it planned from the moment he named me. Asa actually means healer. Did I ever tell you that? And since I'm going to be a doctor just like dear old Dad, I suppose I can afford to be a little strange." He grabbed my hand and twirled me across the corner of the dance floor toward the punch tables.

I noted that we were moving away from Matt and his cousin, but before we could get across the floor, the band's current cover of "1999" ended and they went on break. Sneaky John, our high school's only DJ, put on Cher's huge hit, "Believe (Life After Love)". which had the coolest autotuned vocals ever. Asa gave me an unreadable look, dropped my hand, and broke into a spontaneous dance, which can only be described as a hybrid of the twist and the monkey.

I giggled and followed suit.

In moments, the floor was packed with sweating, gyrating dancers high on drugs, alcohol, and youth. Then Sneaky John put on a slow song.

I patted the moisture from my upper lip as Asa tugged me through the maze of dancers toward the refreshment tables. He picked up two pre-poured cups of punch and I had a moment to wonder if someone could have tampered with them. I heard Mom's voice in my head. *Always watch your drink. I've heard such horror stories about that date-rape drug.* But I ignored Mom and took the red Solo cup, gulping the sweet liquid without another thought.

Shiny silver ribbon twirled around the planets and stars and the disco ball hanging from the ceiling of the gymnasium and for once I felt in the middle of things rather than on the outside looking in. That's when I knew, right then, standing in front of the refreshment table with Celine Dion crooning in the background, that this had to be one of those moments that would be forever engraved in my memory. "My Heart Will Go On, indeed," I said sarcastically.

"Good punch." Asa smiled. "Just a hint of Jack Daniels."

I shrugged and held my cup out for a refill.

Asa took it and got back in line.

Glancing around, I spied Matt standing at the end of the photo line with his back to Rose. His face looked like my Grandpa's old hound dog, Jake.

I raised my hands in a what's up gesture and he smiled a slow, crooked smile that stopped my heart. In that smile, I saw a man instead of a boy. A man who might someday remember this night on his way home from work, tired and empty, making a living and wondering where the time had gone.

I saw that smile and it melted me right into the floor. Across the gym, I gave him a brief thumbs up and then felt like a complete idiot. Probably reading way more into it than what was really there. I put my thumb down and felt my face grow warm, but when I looked again, his eyes seemed to stare straight into my mine. Those eyes. It suddenly felt as if we were the only two people in the place, maybe in the whole entire universe.

2

I held Matt's gaze as he threaded his way across the dance floor to where I stood fanning my face and awaiting my refill.

Without a word, he held out his hand.

I gripped his fingers, delighted at the strength I felt there. Matt played football. He had even earned a full ride to our state university. But I didn't like to think of that. It meant he'd be leaving soon.

I planned on going there too, but first I had to get my basics out of the way at our local junior college. It was much cheaper that way. I did not have a full ride in my chosen field, which was art and design; and as a single parent, my Mom couldn't fork over the dough. My living large days would have to wait a little longer.

Matt's fingers were warm. My hand disappeared in his. This was the first time we'd actually touched each other except for the occasional accidental brush as we traded papers and pencils. It felt good. It felt right. I could smell the alcohol on his breath, and when he pulled me close, it became obvious he had already had more than one cup of punch. He seemed much looser than before. In the back of my mind I had the idea that the boozy punch had given him the courage to dance.

But I didn't care. I held onto his big paw like a lifeline. I wasn't sure which of us was more self-conscious, him or me. With the Jaywalkers still on break, we swayed around the floor to another slow song; Whitney Houston this time.

I felt Rose shooting lasers at me every time we passed the table where she sat with her bored-looking friends. I guess there were lots of kids from the private school invited to our prom.

When Matt began humming in my ear along with the song, I forgot about Rose and everything else. His chest was broad, his breath was warm, and when his lips touched the skin below my ear, I felt my knees wobble as if I had just run a relay race.

And then the stupid song ended. He stopped swaying and we stood for a moment, holding one another lightly. The band came back and launched into yet another version of "1999" and we had to break apart or stand there like idiots. He titled my chin up and kissed me gently, not even a hint of tongue.

After that we didn't leave the dance floor again except for occasional refills of punch. Even the fast songs were fun with Matt the Giant as my partner.

Was I rude to leave Asa hanging? Probably.

Was Matt rude to leave Rose with her broody little clan? Maybe.

Were we falling in love?

Definitely.

It had been building all year—I just hadn't let myself believe it. He was such a hunk; tall and kind and built like a young Thor, all gangly muscle and thick wrists and that slow, slow smile. I looked up at him. His arms were lightly linked around my waist and his eyes were closed. I leaned my forehead against his chin, and for a moment I wondered if I could be dreaming or if I had somehow been drugged the way Mom had feared.

If so, I didn't care. I didn't want to wake up to reality no matter what.

Every now and then he leaned down and kissed me again, and when we stood on the sidelines with our cups, I could feel even more eyes upon us. Matt wasn't the prom king, or even Mr. Popularity, but he was a standout on our tiny football-crazed west Texas team, and that gave him a certain mantle of respect which he wore with decided unease.

And me? I was nobody.

I sang in choir and lived for art. I got good grades and had a nice little job after school. Self-confidence had never been my middle name. I wasn't a joiner or sporty type; I just liked music and art. Sometimes I wrote poetry. But Asa was the only one who knew that.

Tucking my wavy hair behind one ear, I pushed my glasses up on my nose and marveled at the fact that I hadn't thought about them once all evening. Usually I felt quite self-conscious about them. I'd worn contacts when I first started high school, but after a couple of years I had developed an allergy to the solution and had never been able to wear them again. So now I was stuck with glasses—and they were bugging the heck out if me because all of a sudden they were fogging up from our dancing and other exertions.

I took them off and swiped my thick hot bangs off my forehead.

Matt glanced at me, and then did a double take. "I like that," he said.

I wasn't sure whether he meant the lack of glasses, or the bangs-off-the-forehead look, so I did what I did best; nothing.

OUTSIDE OUR HIGH school there were several eating areas complete with stone picnic tables and benches. West Texas only has about two months of cold weather per year so that means most of our meals are taken outdoors or at neighborhood fast food joints. Only lower class students are forced to sit in the cafeteria.

On prom night, most of those stone tables and benches were filled with prom goers drinking, smoking, and making out. Chaperones made occasional sweeps with flashlights—even though the areas were lit with strings of multi-colored lights laced through the trees.

Matt pulled me out the side door to one of those twinkly areas after I requested a soft drink instead of punch. My head spun and my stomach lurched. I wasn't a saint, but the punch seemed to be getting stronger and the dance floor warmer.

He grabbed a silvery can out of one of the ice-choked metal washtubs on our way out. I pretended not to notice how he staggered when he turned too quickly, or how he grabbed at the door's push bar handle twice before we made it outside.

We found a deserted bench and plopped down. The coolness beneath the live oaks—which were thick on our campus—soothed us almost immediately.

The lights cast a rosy glow over the gray concrete table. It also cast a rosy glow across Matt's tanned face and dark hair. I couldn't see his blue eyes, but I suspected they were rather bloodshot. I gathered my dress and sat on the tabletop with my feet on the bench. Matt sat beside my silver sandals. I couldn't resist touching his dark brown curls. He sat perfectly still as though I'd mesmerized him with my caress. Then a breeze blew the hem of my dress across his hand and he rubbed the filmy overlay between his thumb and forefinger. "Soft. Like you."

My cheeks grew warm and I trapped a lock of his coarse hair between my splayed fingers.

He smiled and it made me bold.

I tugged his head back and planted a tentative kiss on his

mouth. He groaned and held my face there with a hand on the back of my head. When he released me, I sat up slowly. "Only two more weeks of school." My voice came out husky. "What will it be like, after tonight?"

Matt appeared to think it over. I could almost hear the wheels turning as he tried to understand exactly what I was asking. But instead of answering, he moved himself up onto the tabletop and pulled me into his arms. His kiss was not tentative like mine. It was gentle, but insistent. I believed he was answering my question the best way he knew how.

I loved the taste of whisky on his tongue. I adored the feel of his huge palms on my back. Without reservation, I wound my hands into his hair and took his bottom lip between my teeth.

With a groan, he twisted his body to the side, dragging me onto his lap as if I were no bigger than a child. My heart thundered. It matched the pounding I could feel through his tux.

His breath was hot against my throat. "My truck is right there…"

I nodded, not trusting myself to speak.

He stood and helped me off the table. He still staggered a bit, but I wasn't worried, we weren't driving anywhere. Just going to sit in the truck. Before we got there, we caught sight of Rose getting into a car with her new tribe. "Crap," Matt said. "I should really check on her—she shouldn't be leaving. She doesn't even go here."

I hated the way he hesitated. It would come back to haunt me later. What if I had stopped him? I know I could have; one more kiss, even a tug on his sleeve and I'm certain he would have followed me on to the parking lot where his old pickup truck waited. But I didn't do that. Instead, I encouraged him to go to her. In truth, I felt guilty about ignoring Asa, too.

"Rose!" he called.

The red-haired girl looked back, one foot inside a purple Trans Am, the other still on the pavement.

"Where you going?"

"A party." She tossed the answer over her shoulder. "Don't worry, Cuz. You're off the hook."

He made his way across the picnic area to the curb where the Trans Am waited. "I don't know these people."

Even from where I stood, I could hear Rose's slinky laughter "It's okay, they're from *my* school." She waved a dismissive hand in his direction, her hair fiery in the glow of the lights.

Matt stood uncertainly. "I should take you home. Dad will be furious if I come home without you."

From deep inside the car, Rose laughed again. "No worries, *Cousin*. I will meet you back here at one a.m. We can go home together." And with that, the car reversed out of the parking space and roared away into the soft night.

I looked at my new watch, an early graduation gift from my grandparents in Oklahoma, and noted that it was nearly eleven already. I had serious doubts that Rose would make it back by one o'clock. That just didn't seem feasible, and something about the way she kept calling him Cousin, as if with a capital C, made my skin crawl. What was she trying to do, make him feel even guiltier?

We watched the car until it turned the corner out of sight. Then Matt looked back at me. "I didn't mean to ignore her that way. I feel awful."

Although Rose had completely interrupted my fantasy come-to-life, the fact that my crush actually had a conscience made me like him even more. "Yeah," I agreed. "I feel kinda bad about Asa, too. Maybe I should go inside and find him."

By this time, Matt had crossed the few yards between us.

He swooped me up, stood me on top of his feet, and smashed my breasts against his chest. Then he leaned down and kissed me in a way that told me exactly what was on his mind, and what I might have experienced in the dark cab of his truck. The night was a fuzzy velour blanket. I wanted with all my heart to just be selfish, forget the other two, take Matt by the hand, lead him to the truck and experience all those things I'd read about in books.

"This is what the next two weeks will be like," he whispered. "Tomorrow night we will try out the old Sky-Vue drive-in movie over in Lamesa, and the next night we'll go to Steak and Ale for a real sit-down meal like grownups, and then on Friday we are going to th—"

I held up my hands, laughing. "Wait, wait, what about our jobs?" He worked after school and I had my job as a waitress at The Sandwich Factory sub shop.

He tipped his head back. "You're right—I forgot. We'll just go after we get off; besides, we won't be working much longer, will we? Two and a half months from now I'll be moving into the dorm in Lubbock and you'll be—"

"Stop." I put my fingers to his lips. "I'm going to be right here for another year or two, getting my basics, trying to figure out what I want to be when I grow up."

That shushed him. I'm sure he'd just assumed I'd be going off to college, too. For some reason, I think he thought the two of us were on the exact same path because we were in so many of the same classes. His ego might not have been large, but it was male.

He crushed me to him and found my mouth again. When he turned me loose, he was out of breath. "I don't think that's going to work."

I was a little breathless myself. "What won't work?"

He tilted my chin up with one finger and looked into my eyes. "I don't think you can stay here. You have to come with me. You can get your basics there. We both will."

I didn't answer right away. I was too busy planting kisses on his jawline—the only part of his face I could reach. Finally, I let him go. "You have a scholarship. I don't. I have to get my basics right here at the good old JuCo—where I can continue to work." I stood on tiptoe and pressed my lips to the corner of his mouth.

He made a sound in his throat and hauled me to his chest again.

When I pulled away, my hair caught on his button and we both reached to untangle it. "Ouch." I was tied to him securely.

"Whoa, hold on." He unbuttoned his shirt to free me and I caught a glimmer of silver in his dark chest hair. It was some sort of small medallion on a thin chain.

I touched the medallion curiously. "What's this?"

He hesitated a split second, and then he pulled the thing over his head and draped it over mine. It was long on me. I tilted it up to examine it.

"It's just an old buffalo nickel. It belonged to my granddad but I wear it every now and then." He looked away. "When I need a shot of courage."

I held it up to the moonlight. "It looks really old."

"Yeah. I think he had it a long time—from when he was little —maybe even his dad before him."

I started to take it off, to give it back, but he stayed my hand.

"I want you to keep it. My gramps said it was his connection to me, now I want it to be my connection to you."

"Oh, no. I can't do that—it's special to you."

Matt pushed my hand down so that the necklace lay on my chest. "You're pretty special to me, too." He kissed me lightly. "I'd tell you I was falling in love with you—but that would sound stupid—especially since I think I've been there since the first day you sat down beside me in class. But at least this way, if you're wearing the buffalo, I know I'll see you again."

Asa appeared in the doorway. For a moment, I was reminded

of old photos I'd seen of Victorian parties with ladies in fine dresses and gentlemen in top hats and tails. Asa's tux had the tails, and behind him, in silhouette, I saw girls twirling, their sparkles and spangles glittering beneath the lights. If there had been bustles and parasols I would've sworn we'd been transported back across the pond and across time. Except for the music, of course.

The band was into the grunge set now. "Smells Like Teen Spirit," "Black Hole Sun," "Runaway Train." Every song seemed more depressing than the one before.

When they began to play "Last Kiss," which had recently been re-made by Pearl Jam, and which had taken the entire school by storm, Matt dragged me back inside, right past Asa who held out his hand toward me. I let my palm slide along Asa's arm, and the two of us curled our fingertips into hooks and snagged each other as if it were planned.

For a split-second, he was drawn along with us toward the dance floor. "C'mon," I called. "Come dance..."

But at the last instant, he pulled loose and came to a halt.

As Matt wrapped me in his embrace, I caught one last glimpse of Asa making his way toward the punch bowl and a slender blond boy standing apart from the crowd.

3

One a.m. came and went, and no sign of Rose.

Matt and I danced the hours away as if there were no tomorrow. I think the idea that we had wasted the entire school year—and that he would be leaving for college in a couple of months—had brought us both down to earth.

Several times I thought about his truck sitting, empty, in the parking lot, and though I'd been bold but an hour before, now I was more sober, and more subdued. Dancing would have to do. After all, he'd already promised the next two weeks were ours— and hopefully the next two months as well.

AROUND ONE FIFTEEN Asa found me and asked if I wanted to ride home with him. He'd had all the prom he could stand.

I looked into his tired face. "Of course I want to ride home with you. And if you feel like it, maybe we can stop and get a bite to eat at The Golden Skillet."

Asa rolled his eyes. "I don't need your charity, girl. I just don't want to leave without knowing you have a way home."

I looked around to see if anyone waited for him in the wings. There was no one. "Let me just say goodbye." I tilted my head toward Matt who was returning from the restroom. "I'll meet you at the car."

He nodded and left.

Matt saw Asa going toward the parking lot. "Don't worry, I'll take you home."

I shook my head and tried to think of the best way to tell him I was leaving with the one who brought me. "Thanks. But I feel I've neglected Asa too long already. I think I'd better go home with him."

He appeared somewhat crestfallen. "It's not exactly the ending I'd hoped for. But I understand—I think." His eye held a mischievous glint. "Is it all right if I walk you to the car?"

I smiled and linked my arm through his.

"I need your phone number." His voice was solemn. "But I don't have a pen."

Laughing, I grabbed one from the chaperone's table. "I have a pen but no paper."

Matt held out his hand and I ignored it and pushed up his shirtsleeve. I wrote my number on the top of his wrist. "Just don't go home and wash it off before you call me."

Nearing the car, I could see Asa fiddling with the radio or maybe it was the CD player. Matt pulled me to him for one last kiss. "I'll call you," he muttered against my lips.

"Mmmm," I mumbled.

"I'm glad I got up my courage."

I opened my eyes and looked into his. We were so close I could see the black ring around his blue iris. "Me, too." I trapped his face between my palms and held the kiss a moment longer.

"Goodnight," he whispered.

I opened the car door and slid inside. I didn't want to. I wanted to stay in the warm May darkness, holding on to the most perfect night I'd ever experienced. But I could feel the hurt emanating from Asa as soon as I entered the small space. There's always tomorrow, I thought.

Matt rapped his knuckles on the closed window and I flattened my palm against the glass. He pressed his palm to the glass on the other side.

Asa turned up the music as we backed out of the parking space and drove away. I angled the side mirror to watch Matt as he grew smaller and smaller.

He had one hand stuck in his pants pocket—tux swept to the side, cummerbund glowing in the moonlight—and the other hand raised in goodbye. Tall and dark, thick hair curling over the edge of his tux, he could've been an advertisement in a magazine.

Something pressed into the center of my chest.

I felt as if I'd crossed some line—one of those no-going-back lines—and I had to restrain myself from begging Asa to turn the car around.

What if I never see him again? What if there is no tomorrow after all?

"So, is it love?" Asa's voice wasn't as sarcastic as it could've been, but it was enough to shatter my little pity party into a few million pieces.

I slumped down in the seat and readjusted my mirror. Matt was no longer visible. We had turned the corner. "I don't know. Maybe. We had a great time." I looked at Asa from the corner of my eye. "I hope you had fun, too."

He flipped one hand back and forth in the air as if to say it could've been better, could've been worse.

"Did you meet anyone interesting?" I asked. We had never really discussed his love life in detail. But we each joked about our single status on occasion.

He shook his head. "Same old geeks and fringers, you know."

I nodded. Apparently there weren't any gay guys there, or they were afraid to be in the same vicinity of one another. "Asa," I waited for him to acknowledge me.

After a few seconds, he glanced my way. "What?"

I gnawed the cuticle around my thumbnail. "Do you know any other gay guys at our school?"

For a long time we drove in strained silence. Then at last he said, "I do know one. He just hasn't come out yet."

I nodded. I wondered who it was, of course, but I wasn't going to ask. Not just yet. I figured if he wanted me to know, he would tell me.

Without another word, Asa drove straight to The Skillet. Kids like us made up the bulk of the restaurant's clientele after families went home and before the bars closed. We seldom took in a movie or went to a football game or party that we didn't stop by afterward.

"Burger?" Asa asked.

"Fries," I said. "With cheese."

He nodded and parked, and then we entered together and sat at one of our usual booths near the plate glass windows. Asa ordered for us.

I fiddled with the sugar and Sweet-n-Low packets. "You okay?"

He sat back and loosened his bow tie causing it to hang crookedly on one side of his neck. "Little bummed. Prom. Don't know what I thought would happen. I'm just ready to let go and cut my losses. Was it a letdown for you?"

He always said he wanted to cut his losses when something was beyond his control. I stared at his crooked bow tie. For some reason, it made him seem older—and sexier. It was all I could do not to reach over and touch it. "Not a letdown at all." I glanced up at the window, surprised to see my pink-cheeked reflection staring back. My hair looked wild but it complimented my heightened color. "I actually had an amazing time." I bit my lip after I said it. After all, Asa had been my date, such as it was. "I'm sorry you didn't."

He shrugged, but his eyes were haunted.

I felt even worse. "Oh, Asa. I really feel—"

"Not your fault." He waved a hand at me. "My new friend was there. I didn't expect him to fall all over me, or even try to sneak in a dance or anything like that, but I thought he would, I don't know, acknowledge me in some way. I mean, I haven't told anyone this, but we've been talking on the phone almost every night for the past couple of months."

I wondered if the shock showed on my face. "He was there, at prom?"

It was Asa's turn to fiddle with the condiments. "Yes." His voice grew soft. "He turned away when I approached him."

I held my breath. How cruel.

His eyes were glassy. What would I do if he actually started to cry, here, in public? "That must have been awful." I knew how I would have felt if Matt had turned his back on me. Talk about cutting your losses.

But I needn't have worried about Asa breaking down. He was made of much sterner stuff. He took in a deep breath and composed himself. "Yep." He rubbed the side of his neck with one hand. "He gave me the strangest smile. I think he was terrified I would out him right there in front of God and everyone. As if I would."

I reached across the table and squeezed his fingers. "He just doesn't know you well enough yet."

"Thanks, Gabs." He smiled sadly, his thickly lashed brown eyes looking into mine. "It's even more complicated with him. He... he hasn't been here that long."

"I wish you had come and got me. We could have danced away those blues."

He laughed. "I wouldn't have interrupted you and the stud for any amount of love or money."

I pushed his fingers down on the table and tapped them for good measure. I was about to give him a tongue lashing when the waitress brought our order. "Saved by the food."

He reached over and grabbed some of my cheese fries. "Comfort food."

I nodded. "Are we going to your house?"

Asa took a bite of his bacon burger.

His thick, faux-pompadour reminded me of pictures I'd seen of Elvis.

"I don't think so. Not tonight." He slurped from his straw. "Think I'll go home and fall in the jacuzzi. Nurse my wounded pride."

"You sure?" This was so unlike him. Usually he was all about commiserating. Then it hit me, he was hoping for a phone call.

He looked away, making excuses. "That punch seemed pretty wicked. My head has barely stopped spinning." He coughed and held up his burger. "This should help, right?" He crossed his eyes and leaned sideways as if drunk.

"Jeez Louise, if I'd known you were that wasted I would have made you let *me* drive." I pointed my fork at him. "Shame on you for risking my young life."

Asa placed the back of his hand across his forehead and swooned. "Dahling, I nevah meant to endangah yo young life. I sweah it'll nevah happen again!" He punctuated the southern charm with another tiny cough.

"Getting sick?"

He shook his head. "Spring allergies as usual. Dear old Dad's trying a new medicine on me. Says he's tired of me being sickly all the time. Think he wanted a boy, you know."

I stabbed another fry and popped it into my mouth to stave off a rude reply. I was glad to see my old friend's sarcasm coming back. But he *did* seem to be sick a lot. And the chasm between him and his father also seemed to be widening. I hated that—of course I'd never had a father so I couldn't really compare on that level—but I did have a great mom, which Asa had missed out on. His own mother had succumbed to ovarian cancer when Asa was just a boy.

On the way home, we belted out our own version of "1999." When we stopped in front of my house and turned off the music, the silence was shocking. It seemed to call for something serious to fill the gap.

Guess Asa felt it, too. "Can't believe we're almost done with high school."

I poked him in the shoulder. "Me, either. And you're going to go away to med school and leave me here all alone."

He rolled his eyes, and then straightened in his seat. "Go with me." His tone was serious. "I've got to get my premed courses—"

We had both been earning college credits through the dual-credit program at for the last year, but he was miles ahead of me.

"I'll get there eventually. Just not yet. Gotta save up a little more dough."

He ducked his head. I knew for a fact that his father's wealth often embarrassed him. "I've got my eye on an apartment off campus. I could save you a room."

I leaned across the console and hugged him around the neck, marveling once again at how handsome he looked.

"I wish we *were* a couple," he whispered.

My body froze and my breath lodged under my breastbone as if it had suddenly turned solid. I almost regretted the hug.

Then he said, "It would make everything so much easier if we liked each other that way."

I exhaled shakily. "Yeah, I guess it would." I touched his crooked bow tie gently, the way I'd wanted to do back at the restaurant, and then sat back in my seat.

He climbed out and came around to open my door like a real gentleman.

Hand in hand, he walked me to my porch.

I grabbed him and planted a chaste kiss on his cheek before he could turn away. "Thanks for taking me to the prom."

"Thanks for going." He gave me a sincere smile that could melt the heart of any red-blooded teen. Halfway back to the car, he turned. "I'm serious, Gabs. I'll hold that room for you."

I dismissed him with a wave. I knew he would find someone to share his off-campus apartment. To me, the university seemed massive. By the time I got there, he would be with someone else. In fact, I was sure by then he would actually *be* someone else.

From the porch, I watched as he sauntered back to his car. He opened the door and put one foot inside, waiting, I supposed, for me to enter the house.

I COULD HEAR my phone ringing as I opened the front door.

Dashing through the lamp-lit house, I pounced on it before it could wake Mom. I was surprised she hadn't waited up.

With the cordless receiver tucked between my cheek and shoulder, I slipped out of my silver sandals, and plopped down on the edge of my bed. "Hello?"

Matt's voice was deep and smooth. "I hope it isn't too late to call."

"Not at all." I lay back on my mound of pillows and sighed. "In fact, I just got home."

"I'd call that perfect timing."

"Yeah." I smiled. "It's like you're psychic or something."

4

M att chuckled. "I am psychic. Did I forget to mention it's one of my many charms?"

"Uh. Yeah, actually. You did." I twirled a hank of hair around my finger, picturing his lips near the phone. "Did your cousin make it back?"

He hesitated. "No. And I'm getting really pissed." He stopped and cleared his throat. "I mean. Is she doing this just to get back at me for dancing with you?"

"That thought crossed my mind, too. But I don't really know her so I couldn't say for sure. Is she that type of person, vindictive I mean?"

"She can be, yeah." His mattress springs squeaked.

I didn't know what to say. I didn't think he should waste another second worrying about her, but then I tried to put myself in her shoes. I *had* monopolized her date after all—even if he was her cousin. Then again, we'd put Asa in the same position and he hadn't run away like a spoiled brat. At last I said, "I hope she'll be back soon."

Matt snorted and I heard the pop-hiss of a soft drink can

being opened. I stood, shimmied out of my gorgeous dress, and slipped on a long, purple sleep shirt.

I hung my dress on its padded hanger on the outside of my closet door my little corsage still pinned to the bodice. I took it off and crept into the kitchen where the clear plastic flower box sat on the table where we'd left it. I put the corsage back inside and slid it into the fridge.

"You still there?" he asked.

I poked my head into Mom's bedroom, relieved to see her propped up on her reading pillow with the TV on low. She appeared to be sound asleep. An old black and white movie played across the screen and reflected off the oyster-colored wall behind her head. I knew better than to turn it off. The one time I did, she woke immediately.

It made me feel good to know she had *tried* to wait up for me to get home. Even though I'd never had a father, Mom did have a boyfriend, Joe, whom she'd been seeing for a couple of years. But she worked such long hours at the orthodontist's office that she was often too exhausted to go out. Fortunately, Joe worked hard in his accounting career, too. Between them, they rarely had a lot of free time.

I backed out of her room quickly, keeping my voice low. "Still here. I was checking on my mom. Didn't want to wake her."

He must have understood; he didn't say anything else.

When I got back to my room and closed the door, I told him all was clear.

"I just called to say goodnight again," his voice lowered. "And to let you know how glad I am you agreed to dance with me."

I pictured his gorgeous blue eyes staring into mine right before he kissed me. The image made me shiver. "I'm glad, too."

We talked until I fell asleep—mostly about college but also about the coming days and all the things we were going to do together—and then the next thing I knew it was almost four o'clock and he was telling me to wake up and go to sleep. I told him goodnight and then staggered into the bathroom to remove my makeup and brush my teeth. It felt as if a nest of spiders had taken up residence in my mouth.

The next day, Mom let me sleep in until noon. When I finally straggled into the world, I found her in the living room with her hair in a towel.

I toasted a couple of strawberry Pop-Tarts, poured a cup of coffee, and joined her.

"I want to hear all about it," she said.

I held up my coffee.

"After you're able to communicate."

Mom reached for the remote and clicked on the noon news. We were immediately treated to a blurry picture of a pickup truck crashed up against a tree. The caption below the photo said it all.

Teen in ICU Following Early Morning Crash

Mom turned up the volume just in time for us to hear the pretty, brunette anchor say, "The driver apparently lost control going around the curve. Still wearing his prom tux, investigators are trying to determine if alcohol was a factor in this tragic crash."

I grabbed the remote and hit pause, staring at the picture of the twisted truck.

"What is it, Gabs? Someone you know?"

My Pop-Tart turned to sawdust in my throat. "I'm not sure." I stood, knees shaking, intent on going somewhere, just not sure where.

Mom said something else, but I didn't stick around to decipher it. In my room, I threw on jeans. My sleep shirt hung down to my knees. I didn't care. My head pounded when I bent over—

too much punch—and for a moment I thought I would be sick. *Was* alcohol a factor in the crash? We'd only shared a couple of drinks, but I hadn't been with him the whole night. Just the last few dances. Just enough to fall in love.

I stepped into my flip-flops and grabbed my keys. Even in my altered state of mind I noticed what a perfect spring day it was. The scent of newly-mown grass nearly overwhelmed me. Mom caught up just as I put my car in reverse to back out of the driveway.

"Gabrielle, what's going on?" Her face mirrored my feelings of confusion and concern.

I gulped. The sky behind her head was a perfect sapphire blue, right out of a fresh box of crayons. It reminded me of his eyes. That sky killed me. Or maybe it was the flawless rectangle of sunlight painting its warmth across my bare forearm resting on the open window.

"It's Matt, Mama." I struggled to get the words out. "I'm almost positive."

Mom's face still showed confusion. "Matt?"

"From chemistry. We danced last night. At prom." I inhaled in an attempt to calm my nerves. But it didn't work. I dropped my forehead onto that patch of sunlight on my arm and gave in to the sobs.

Mom shoved me over and drove me to the hospital, but I wasn't allowed to see him. Only family members were allowed into ICU and his folks had never even met me. I skirted the hungover football players assembled in the waiting room, and told his mom I was Matt's chemistry partner and I'd just heard the news.

His dad grasped my shoulder and told me he was "holding his own." His mom sat back down without speaking. "The thing the doctors are worried about is whether they can stop the swelling in his brain." His dad's grasp grew slightly painful. "Apparently, he went through the windshield headfirst."

I nodded. "It wasn't alcohol," I said. "I talked to him on the phone after prom. He wasn't drunk."

His dad pulled me to his chest in a brief hug. "Thank you. Thank you." He wiped his eyes. "I knew he wasn't. No matter what they said."

He released me and I walked away, wondering if I'd said the wrong thing, remembering how Matt had staggered a time or two as we danced. But that had been during prom. Afterward, on the phone, he'd seemed fine. Besides, didn't they do blood tests or something? Wouldn't that tell the tale?

I ignored all the students that kept streaming in. There was no one I wanted to talk to except Asa, but he wasn't one of Matt's buddies. They were mostly jocks. They must have seen the news, too.

I squeezed through the side door.

Out front, the sun had taken over completely. The sidewalk reflected the heat upward and the metal handrail along the ramp was hot enough to blister skin. Spring in Texas. I wobbled. The cement wavered.

Mom saw me. She'd been waiting and pacing, not wanting to intrude.

"I have to sit down." Even my voice was watery.

Mom grabbed my upper arm and directed me to a shaded bench beside the fountain. "I'll get the car. You, don't move from this spot."

I nodded, head throbbing. I could feel tears dammed up behind my lids. I hoped Mom would take her time because I didn't think I could answer any questions. One word, one look of sympathy, and I would fall apart. I closed my eyes and willed the world to be still.

A cool shadow fell across the side of my face. "I can't believe you did this." Venom laced the girl's voice.

I opened my eyes.

Rose towered over me, a black silhouette in the harsh noon sun.

"What?" I must have misheard her.

"You," she spat. "This is all your fault." Her stance took on that of a hawk hovering over its prey.

"I wasn't there," I gasped. "I was at home asleep. I don't even know what happened—"

She moved half a step closer. "He danced with you all night. If he'd been with me like he was supposed to, none of this would have happened. He wouldn't be in a coma."

"Coma?" It was the first time I'd heard that word. Coma was bad. It was the worst.

Rose slid onto the opposite end of my bench with a hiss. "Yes, coma, stupid. His brain is swelling. Oh, he *might* be all right, they *think* they've stopped the bleeding, but now he's in a coma and he might not wake up." Her lips twisted into an evil sneer. "And I was just about to tell him about the baby. Now, thanks to you, he may *never* know."

I looked at her in horror. She had one hand pressed to her midsection.

"Yes..." She ground the words into my ear like fragments of glass. "We are *more* than just cousins. There. No one knows but you. Are you happy now?"

Happy? Shocked would've described it better. No, beyond shocked. I was disgusted, appalled, sickened. *His own cousin?* How could the Matt who had kissed me so tenderly just a few hours ago have done something so hideous?

Her long-fingered hand pressed into her middle. I was positive I could see a definite bump under there. Tears welled up in my eyes. Mom appeared with the car and I stood and stumbled toward the curb, blinded by pain and disbelief.

"Honey?" She hurried around the front of my little Honda and opened the passenger door for me.

My breakfast roiled inside my belly. When I thought of what Rose's shapely hand covered, the strawberry taste came right up my throat into the back of my mouth. I fell into the passenger seat, leaned over, and spat the mess into the gutter. Mom held my forehead with her hand and I retched again and again.

When I glanced up, wiping away strings of nastiness with my thumb, Rose sat where I had left her, palm still pressed to her middle, the tiniest little smile on her lips.

What was that look? That smile? What does she find funny about any of this? She's pregnant—by her own cousin—how could she find any humor in that?

And then it dawned on me. If Matt died, or if he was even incapacitated, perhaps that would ease her burden. Then no one would ever find out what they had done. No, no, no. She said she *wanted* to tell him. She was going to tell him last night at prom. But that didn't mean they were going to tell anyone else. Maybe they would've run away, or got an abortion, or maybe they would have—I don't know. My thoughts spiraled around their dark little secret like dirty water circling a filthy drain. In the back of my mind I heard Asa's voice, cut your losses, he would say. Just cut your losses now, before it's too late.

I leaned back in the seat and allowed my mother to close the door. I flipped the air-conditioner to high and pointed all the vents at my face. I couldn't believe Matt would do something like that, but then, he *had* seemed protective of her. Or was I simply imagining things in hindsight?

And what was he doing out so late? Looking for her? She'd left the dance early with some guy in a purple Trans Am. I'd fallen asleep on the phone and then instead of going to sleep like me, Matt had got back into his truck and left the house. Apparently, he hadn't even taken off his tux. As if he'd known he wasn't in for the night.

Did she call him after we hung up? Had she begged him to meet her somewhere so she could tell him the news? I needed answers. Wanted answers. Wanted to know everything. But he was in a coma, he couldn't tell me anything.

I knew down in my heart that this was all *her* fault. It had nothing to do with me. He'd probably gone out looking for her when she never came home. If she'd met him back at the prom at one a.m. the way she'd told him she would, this probably wouldn't have happened.

But it didn't matter now.

Mom climbed into the driver's seat. "You okay?"

I nodded, tears dried like magic by the thoughts running through my mind. I would go away for a while. Matt and I had shared such a magical night—he'd even said he had been crushing on me all year—just the way I had been on him, and now this. It was too much. And with Rose at the hospital, I wouldn't be able to visit him if—when—he did awake. A nightmare, that's what it was. A nightmare so unbelievable it was almost ridiculous.

To her credit, my mom didn't interrogate me on the way home. She seemed to know I was in shock. In truth, my mind was formulating a plan. I'd never been good at confrontation, had never had to deal with it much. I was one of the original live-and-let-live girls. Rose's evil words had sickened me. And the knowledge that Matt was not the boy I'd thought made it so much worse.

My instinct was to run. Run like a rabbit. Just get away.

But of course I couldn't do that, could I?

I thought back over the past few weeks of school. A representative from the Student Conservation Association had visited our senior class. Did I still have that pamphlet at home? It had sounded very interesting at the time, now I began to think maybe I should look into it seriously.

Leaning my head back, I closed my eyes and willed my mind away from the events of the past few hours.

Once home, I hugged Mom and crawled back into my bed to escape my tormented thoughts.

5

My bedroom phone awakened me around two a.m. Scrabbling around, I located the cordless beneath my pillow and stabbed the TALK button before it could trill again. I'd fallen asleep begging God to let Matt be all right. I imagined him lying in that sterile hospital room, a thick white bandage wound around his poor head, bedside phone clutched in one bruised and battered palm. At this time of night, I just knew it was him calling from the hospital, wondering why I hadn't been to visit.

"Hey, you." I pressed the phone to my ear. "I came up but they wouldn't let me in—"

"Matt's out of the hospital. He wants to see you." The whispery voice was definitely female. "Meet us at South Pond. He asked me to drive him there. He's weak, but he'll be waiting for you. He wants to explain in person."

I held the phone away from my face and looked at the Caller ID.

PRIVATE CALLER.

Was it Rose's voice? I couldn't tell.

I swung my feet over the edge of my bed. South Pond. That was miles away, out in the country. "Rose?"

The tiny screen on my cordless went dark.

I tried calling back, but it's impossible to redial a private call. Should I phone his parents, find out if he's been released? What would I tell them at this hour of the night? They couldn't possibly know about him and Rose, could they?

What Rose told me at the hospital had left me reeling. Is that what the caller meant he needed to explain? It had to be. There was no other possibility. But if Matt had been released, why didn't he call me himself? Maybe he's too embarrassed, my subconscious said. Or maybe he left the hospital without permission. Maybe he *can't* talk—literally. Oh my God. What if he lost the ability to speak, don't some brain injuries cause that?

Heart pounding, I pressed the numbers for the hospital, but the ICU nurse told me she couldn't release any information and I should contact a family member directly. She wouldn't even tell me if he was still a patient or not.

I located my flip-flops and grabbed my keys. There was no way around it. I would have to go. Matt would come on the run if I needed him. At least I thought he would. The boy I had sat beside in chemistry would. That's probably what had caused his accident in the first place. His cousin had needed him and he'd gone out in the middle of the night to help.

I dashed off a quick note to Mom in case she woke:

Going to check on a friend. Home soon. Gabs

I drew a big heart around my name to let her know it was really from me— sort of our secret code—then I stuck the note in her coffee cup and set it beside our ancient Mr. Coffee. Notes were our main way of communicating when our schedules kept us from seeing each other.

The air felt warm even though the clock read three a.m. May in West Texas was always warm, sometimes scorching. Judging by this early heat, I felt certain today would be the latter. My jeans were hot, and my sleep shirt too long. It reminded me of yesterday when I'd thrown on the same jeans and dashed to the hospital. This time, I wished I'd grabbed shorts instead. I turned the air-conditioner on high and then the radio, but I had no idea what songs played. My head was full of the possibility of seeing Matt again. Of finding out the truth.

I drove on through the eerily quiet town. I saw only two cars on Main and I didn't recognize either of them. Hard to believe our entire junior/senior class had been dancing and living it up just yesterday.

What a depressing thought.

I turned the radio up louder, never even wondering if I were doing the right thing. Going simply on instinct and adrenalin. It seemed I would never get there. Live Oak isn't large, but it sprawls like an octopus. South Pond lay on the opposite side of town in a rural area where kids would often go to park and make out, smoke a jay, or bust open a keg. There really is a pond, but it's just an old stock pond that's deep in the spring and shallow in the dryer winter months. I've heard it referred to as a buffalo wallow, which meant that the huge herds of bison that once roamed the plains had probably visited the shallow pond making it wider and deeper as they wallowed in the mud. Now it's one of those bodies of water we all take for granted.

When I pulled into the roadside turnaround that served as a parking area for the old pond, the sky had gone the pale pearly gray of false dawn. The sun wouldn't come up for a couple of hours. But enough moonlight reflected in the water to give it the thick shimmer of molten lead. A spring mist hung above it.

I didn't see Matt anywhere. There weren't any vehicles in the gravel lot. I parked but didn't roll down the windows. Something felt wrong. The night began to feel as opaque as the murky water. If Matt wanted to see me, where was he?

Backing up, I shone my headlights a different direction, then I made a small tight circle and lit up the entire parking area a little at a time. Low mesquites and spindly live oaks bordered one side of the lot. It was the sort of foliage that loved a little water now and then but thrived just as well without it. I saw neither Matt nor Rose.

After a few minutes, I pulled out of the lot and circled the pond as far as I could go. The gravel road didn't loop around the entire thing, only about three quarters of the way, and then you were forced to turn around in the only remaining wide spot unless you wanted to get out and have a picnic beneath the single stand of oaks tall enough to give good shade.

Of course I didn't need any shade now. And I really didn't want to get out of the car. This seemed too weird. I put the car in reverse and executed a careful turnaround. When my headlights picked out the figure at the edge of the water, I inhaled sharply. It was not what I expected to find.

I rolled down my window. "Rose?" I called. "Is that you?"

A branch cracked, a shadow moved, and panic slid between my ribs like a blade. The figure turned toward my headlights, definitely female. She wore her long hair loose and flowing. Under the moonlight, I couldn't be certain if the woman's hair was red or light brown.

"What are you doing here?" No answer. "Where's Matt?" I tried to keep my voice steady, to show her I wasn't afraid. I put the car in PARK and opened my door tentatively, putting one foot on the ground.

She stared into my headlights, one hand shielding her eyes like a sailor looking for land, and then, like a flash, she ran straight at me. Straight toward my little Honda with the window rolled down and the door open. Her hair flew out behind her and it was all so surreal that for a moment, I simply sat there, paralyzed. Then she raised her right hand above her head. In her grip, I caught a glimpse of silver.

I dragged my foot back inside, shoved the gearshift into DRIVE, and let my foot crash onto the accelerator. The sudden acceleration slammed my door shut beside me as I pressed the gas pedal all the way to the floor, heaving the steering wheel hard to one side, but the stupid girl didn't stop. She veered directly into my path. I smashed my foot onto the brake. The car shimmied and the rear end skewed around as the steering wheel twisted out of my grip. I wrestled the car back under control, and then, *Thrumk!*

The sound felt as solid and slushy as if I'd hit a large cardboard box full of water. Rose flew into the air and landed across the road out of view. In the darkness, I thought I heard a splash, but I couldn't be sure. It had all happened so *fast*.

I sat in the driver's seat of the Honda unable to move, unable to focus. My mouth had hit the steering wheel. My little car was so old it didn't have an airbag. Blood salted my lips and I ran my tongue out to taste the damage.

Headlights punctured the interior of my cave and I shrank away from them, shielding my eyes the way Rose had done only moments earlier.

Because I'd just made the turnaround to go back to the parking area, the vehicle drove directly toward me, lights shining on my face. I didn't recognize the car. It was silver.

Asa tumbled out of the passenger side and ran to my still-open window. "Get out of here," he shouted. "Go!" He reached in and squeezed my shoulder to make me look at him. "We saw it all," he said. "She ran right in front of you. Just go. We'll make sure she gets home. We'll tell her what we saw. We'll make sure she knows she has to leave you alone or we will go to the cops."

I looked up into the eyes of my dearest friend in the world and I considered allowing him to take my burden. "But I hit her." My mind didn't know everything, but it knew that much. "I hit her with the car. She flew up." I craned my neck to get a better view. "Landed over there." I nodded toward the water's edge.

"She's okay," Asa said. "I saw her get up. Just go. I'm a doctor, remember." He grinned, his teeth so white in the headlights. "Or will be."

And just like that, it was done. He took my part. My responsibility. Why did I let him do that? Why did he offer?

At the last second, a modicum of common sense tried to prevail. "But that isn't even your car. How'd you know I was here?"

"No. It isn't my car." He glanced backward. "We saw you when you passed us in town." He licked his lips and it made me wonder if he'd seen the blood on mine. "I knew something was wrong. You're never out at this time of night. I made my friend follow you. To make sure you were okay."

I sat still a moment longer, taking it all in. Only later would I have the sense to wonder exactly who he'd been with that night. I assumed it was the "friend" he'd spoken of on prom night, but I couldn't be certain.

Asa bumped my door with his knee. "Look, she's fine. There's not even a dent on your old Honda. Not a new one anyhow." He flashed me another bone-white grin. "Now go home. Let me take care of that red-haired harlot. She's caused you enough trouble, I'd say."

I nodded, relief flooding my senses. "If you're sure..."

Asa squeezed my shoulder again. "Go home." He turned away from me. "I've got this."

But I couldn't simply drive away, not knowing. I was too much of a control freak for that. "I'd feel better if I just saw her." I opened my door.

Asa stopped and huffed, one hand on his hip. I knew that

pose well. It meant I had no chance. It meant I would lose this argument. "Honey, she ran at you with a knife. She wasn't just headed over to say hello. Why'd you come out here anyhow?"

I gulped. So I *had* seen a flash of something silver. Asa waited for me to tell him why I was there. "She called me." My voice came out a whisper. "She said Matt got out of the hospital and wanted to see me, to explain everything."

Asa waved his hand at me. "Oh, God. Get out of here. Cut your losses before I change my mind and leave you to it." He clamped his lips closed and forced his words through them. "He isn't out, sweetie. I've got spies checking on him for you. He opened his eyes a couple of times, that's all."

That decided me, that and the fact that Asa had seen a knife, too. That convinced me it wasn't just my horror-movie imagination.

I closed my door and maneuvered around the silver car. Its headlights were still on, blinding me. I thought it was an Audi, but I couldn't be sure. It was a model I didn't easily recognize. Whoever it was, at least Asa wasn't alone. "Call me when you get home," I said. And then I drove out of there without looking back.

Too keyed up to go straight home, I stopped by the hospital and sat in the parking lot beside Matt's mother's SUV. I recognized it because she had a football decal with his number 33 plastered to her back windshield.

Asa was right. He hadn't been released. It had all been a lie.

In the deepest part of my little black heart, I hoped Rose *was* dead. She had lured me out there with the intention of hurting me. I didn't want to admit it, but what other reason could she have for being there in the middle of the night with a knife? The possibility chilled me and I began to tremble so badly I had to roll up all the windows and turn on the heater even though a few moments earlier I'd had the AC blowing on high.

I drove away from the hospital and made up my mind to carry on with my first instinct, which was to get out of town. They can have each other, I thought. I don't want to be in the middle of this twisted mess anymore.

Halfway home, my mind cleared and I began to worry. If Rose were badly injured, or dead, my dark-heart chimed in, I could be in big trouble. Since I'd left the scene of the accident, everyone would think I did it on purpose. Even though she lured me there to hurt me, I left without reporting the accident, or her. What if I got arrested?

I continued toward home, not knowing what else to do. When I parked in my driveway, I felt such a sense of relief I wanted to cry. In the house, Mom slept on. For the first time I was glad she worked so hard. I'd gotten over my anger at my absentee father years ago. Mom said the bitterness would kill you if you held onto it. I think that was back at the initial Donuts With Dad program when I was in elementary school.

My grandpa filled in for the donut thing, and over the years he filled in at every Dad/Daughter Dance and event he could make until they moved off to Oklahoma, but that didn't mean I wasn't faced with a multitude of questions. After a few years, I began to pretend he had died. It was easier that way.

IN MY ROOM, the one Mom and I had decorated together, I threw jeans and T-shirts in the suitcase Gran had given me for an early graduation present. The irony didn't escape me. She'd intended the large case to carry me to college one day and now, here I was, packing it to run away to her house. College would have to wait. Even my junior college plans were on hold.

After I packed, I lay on the bed beside my phone so I wouldn't miss Asa's call. What could be taking him so long? If

Rose wasn't hurt, he should call. If she was hurt, he should take her to the hospital and then call. Either way, he should call.

Maybe he couldn't find her.

I gave in to my doubts and pressed his home number. He had his own cordless phone just like me. But the call went to his answering machine. I left what I hoped was a cryptic message in case anyone heard it before Asa. "Hey Ace, you home? Just calling to chat. Give me a ring-back when you can."

As soon as I hung up I had a sickening image of the police scrolling though his early-morning messages, listening for evidence. I could easily imagine a detective stopping the tape after playing mine, nodding to his partner, checking his service weapon in preparation for my arrest.

I jumped up from my bed and ran to the bathroom to retch.

My phone rang.

I snatched it up and held it in front of my face. I was certain it was Asa, but I examined the caller ID anyway.

Relief flooded through me. "Finally! You had me so worried."

"I know," Asa said. "I stayed there a long time. She must have had her car parked nearby. We couldn't find her anywhere."

I heard him say something to someone there with him.

"Is that your friend?"

"Yes," Asa admitted. "He just brought me home. I don't know what else we can do."

I closed my eyes. In my head, I could hear the *thrumk* sound her body had made when she connected with my front fender. "It's okay," I mumbled. "Thank you for trying. I-I still can't believe she lured me out there, and—"

"—and then came after you with a knife."

I took a deep breath. "Yeah. That. I knew she was scary outside the hospital that day, but I never dreamed she could actually be dangerous. And I can't even tell anyone about it because I hit her with my car!" My voice broke apart like small waves on fast water. I hadn't known I was on the verge of crying.

"Oh, Gabi. Don't." Asa sounded panicky. "If you cry I'll have to come over there."

I sniffled and tried to get a grip. "No, d-don't come over. I'll be okay. I just need to think. I mean, what should I do? I've got to find out if she was hurt or not. Can you get her phone number? I could call and see if she made it home."

Asa stayed quiet. "Don't forget, sweetie. She came at you with a knife."

I burst into tears. I couldn't contain it any longer. "I know! She lied to get me out there. She *was* going to hurt me, wasn't she? Did you find the knife?"

"No," Asa said. "Maybe she threw it in the pond."

"Yeah. I did hear a splash. At least I thought I did." I chewed at the cuticle around my thumb. "I'm leaving town tomorrow. Going to my Gram's house in Oklahoma. This is too weird for me."

Asa cleared his throat but didn't speak.

"Thank you for looking out for me, Ace." I let the old nickname sink in. "I'm going to miss you." I took a leap of faith. "But I'm glad you met up with your crush after all."

My old friend laughed. It had a dark edge to it. "I'll keep that room for you, Gabs. Don't forget."

"I won't. How can I ever repay you?"

He didn't hesitate this time. "Just put this behind you and come to Tech next year. I'll only be a year ahead. It'll be great."

But I knew it wouldn't be great. It was a wonderful thought, but I knew we would both be different people by then. Maybe even by sunrise today. "That's sweet, Ace. I'll try, I will."

"Love you," he said.

"You, too, bestie. Always."

I pressed the END CALL button before I started to blubber again.

I REMEMBER THINKING if Rose were going to report me, it would have been that night or the next morning. And since no one ever came for me that night or the next day, or even the next, I took the bit between my teeth and started planning a new life. I began by driving myself to my grandparent's farm in Oklahoma. I left behind my mom, my home, my best friend, and the guy I'd been crushing on all year. All because of one innocent night at prom.

It reminded me of that old W.W. Jacob's story we read in Lit class, "The Monkey's Paw." The theme of the story is "be careful what you wish for." After prom, it took on even more meaning.

My mom asked a few questions, and my grandparents asked even more, but they knew it had something to do with Matt's accident. I didn't tell them the truth about Rose; I didn't want my mom to know Matt had turned out to be a creep like my so-called dad who had flown the coop as soon as Mom had told him she was pregnant with me.

I guess that's why I couldn't bring myself to tell her about the pregnancy. I felt tainted by the cousins' ugly secret. Because of that, I didn't want to be there when Matt awoke. I wanted to be far away, someplace I'd never been.

I just wanted to start anew.

Were all men shallow and selfish like Matt and my dad? I was seriously beginning to wonder.

6

When my class walked the stage at graduation a few days after Matt's accident, I was already in Oklahoma. I'd found the pamphlet from school, contacted the Student Conservation Association representative, and signed up to spend the upcoming summer in California helping a crew clear trails in the national forest.

My time with my grandparents flew by in a whirlwind of gathering supplies for my trip: North Face fleece outerwear, silk long johns for warmth, Teva waterproof sandals for fording streams, Timberland hiking boots and wool socks over silk liner socks because we would be hiking miles and miles every day, and last but certainly not least, a Nalgene water bottle and water purifier kit to avoid contracting giardia from drinking fresh stream water.

The supplies were expensive, but my Gram and Gramps bought it all without complaint. They were good that way. I didn't even ask if the money came from them or from the college fund they'd set up for me so long ago. Maybe I didn't really want to know. This was a big leap. The sooner I got out of Oklahoma and on to my SCA assignment, the better.

My life had taken on a distinct spiral pattern that sometimes, in the late hours of the night, felt a lot like freefall. I slept in the familiar little bed—which had been my mom's when she was a girl—and roamed the farm where I had spent so many summers as a child. I accompanied my grandparents everywhere. It pleased them and it made the time pass more quickly for me. Every now and then I felt as if I were on the opposite side of one of those dividing lines, the kind of memory-line that would forever divide *this* from *then*.

At last the day arrived. Gram and Gramps drove me to Oklahoma City to catch my plane to Los Angeles. Our crew leader, Lucy Barnes, would be there to meet me and the two other volunteers that were flying in from different parts of the country.

The Oklahoma City airport was large, well laid out, and noisy. Excitement nearly overwhelmed me. We stood in the ticket line for only a few minutes. When I turned to hug my grandparents at the gate, I felt six years old again. The tears welled up in my eyes and I had to laugh and make a stupid remark to will them away.

Gram seemed to understand. She simply squeezed me a little tighter while Gramps leaned in for a kiss on the cheek. "Call us when you get there. Or call your mom and let her call us. We won't relax until we know you've made it."

I promised them I would, and then I hurried through the gate, my new heavy-duty backpack going with me as carry-on. I stowed it overhead self-consciously. It was so large an older gentleman in the next seat over had to help me shove it in.

The flight was uneventful and it wasn't until we were making our landing approach that I began to worry. What if Lucy wasn't there? What if I got lost in the airport? What if I'd got the date wrong, or the time, or even the airport?

The what-ifs almost got the better of me. But at last, I took a deep breath and practiced counting backward from ten the way

Mom always did when she was angry or upset. I was surprised when it actually seemed to help.

Finally, I managed to enjoy the view from my window. Los Angeles sprawled in all directions. Even just the airport seemed bigger than Live Oak, my hometown.

I told myself if I couldn't find Lucy, I would simply go to one of the staff members at the desk and have her paged. Having even that tiny bit of a plan helped me relax and avoid a full-blown panic attack.

When we deplaned and came through the gate in a straggling crowd, there stood a woman with shiny brown hair holding a large sign that read SCA in bold black letters.

I took to Lucy immediately. The other two volunteers soon joined us. They seemed as nervous as me, but Lucy's bubbly personality soon had us all laughing and feeling at ease.

She led us out to the company van and told us everything we would be doing for the next couple of months. Then she directed our attention to all the points of interest along the way. The towering palm trees and wide, multi-lane highway amazed me.

"Yep," Lucy said in response to my awe. "This is Interstate 405. Better known as the four OR five." She chuckled.

"Why is that?" we asked almost in unison.

Lucy pointed to her speedometer. "We're making good time now, but come five o'clock this evening, the speed on this section of the 405 will be only four OR five miles per hour."

The three of us looked at each other in disbelief. I didn't know whether to believe her or not. Guess we'll find out at some point, I thought. It seemed okay at the moment.

Once we got to base camp, she became all business. The first thing we did was call our folks and let them know we'd arrived. Mom sounded quite subdued, as if she were lonely—though I knew she had Joe—but she promised she would call Gram and Gramps and let them know I'd made it.

After our phone calls, Lucy took us to our sleeping quarters (rows of cots in a large, open room), where we were introduced to our other teammates.

Then she made us show her all our gear. She inspected our footwear carefully. "It's a fifteen-mile hike to our camp on the mountain," she explained. "You won't make it half that distance if you don't have your liner socks under your wools."

We had a leisurely dinner of cold cuts and thick bread in the basecamp break room, and we slowly got to know one another. I was dismayed to learn that Jerenda, the girl from Indianapolis, had been a girl scout and had years of camping expertise.

Stephen, the boy who had arrived with us, had even more experience. He'd spent weeks at summer camp in North Carolina every year since he'd turned ten.

By bedtime, I was feeling quite amateurish and wondering exactly what I'd gotten myself into. I wasn't an outdoor girl.

I tossed and turned all night, certain the others could hear my bed squeak every time I shifted my weight. By the time my alarm went off the next morning, I was a nervous wreck.

We set out at dawn and by hour four on the trail, I realized I'd never done anything so physically demanding or amazing in my life. It took my mind off Live Oak, completely, until I sat down that first night to write a letter to my mom. Even though I had just spoken to her on the phone the night before, at the end of the first day on the trail, I had so many new things to share I just had to write them down. Unfortunately, I was so exhausted I barely had the energy to wolf down half a sandwich before I conked out.

The next morning, I dashed off a quick note to Mom and stuck it in my pack. Lucy said it would take a while to get the letters out anyway, since supplies only came up by horseback every two weeks. She encouraged us to keep a letter going and add to it daily. That way we'd always have one ready to go when the horses did show up.

And so, I did. And each time I wrote, it seemed I had another life changing event to tell her about. Like hiking fifteen miles in one day, learning to avoid attracting bears to the campsite, learning to work as a team even though I had no idea what I was doing, and falling into a rushing stream only to be fished out by two of my cohorts, laughing.

I intended to write Asa, too, but somehow I never did. I assumed he was immersed in getting ready to make the move to Texas Tech University where he would be taking his premed courses in the fall. I still thought I might join him there, next year, after my nine weeks in the wilderness and a few more months at home, saving up my money and getting my head back in the game.

I told Mom basically the same thing in one of my first letters to her, but the truth was, I just didn't feel excited about anything now. If not for the forced atmosphere of this assignment—and being a thousand miles from home—I don't know what I would have done.

Of course, I only got Mom's return letters every few weeks, but since I left, she'd become very busy with her own life, especially after Joe surprised her with a Caribbean cruise.

Joining the SCA was probably the best thing I could have done.

I went in as a city girl who had only camped out in the woods a few times with her grandpa, and within days I became a trail-savvy volunteer who could build a fire, identify poison plants, and hike for miles and miles every day.

Lucy, a decade older than me, had been with the SCA for years. She had worked on mountaintops counting cougars and at inner-city schools teaching kids how to grow vegetables. She had helped dig wells and taught others how to eradicate invasive plants in national parks.

Being so tired each day made it easy for me to put away all thoughts of Matt and Rose, and concentrate on becoming a warrior for conservation like Lucy.

Throwing myself into every single day, and falling in love with the program and with nature, I found myself quickly becoming more mature, more helpful, more self-assured. I seldom even thought about prom. Or the sound of Matt's voice so silky in the darkness of my bedroom the night we'd talked until I fell asleep. The night he went through the windshield.

And if I did wake in the dark sometimes, dreaming about Matt's voice in my ear, I quickly turned over and forced myself to focus on the sound of crickets outside my tent, or the lonely sigh of the wind in the tops of the pines.

I refused to let myself dwell on anything. It was just too painful. I'd gone from the top of the emotional mountain to the bottom of the proverbial sea in the space of a few hours. We'd made such silly plans. Silly now because of what he'd done, how he'd fooled me into thinking he was someone I could respect, someone I could love. Silly because I never even got to say goodbye.

AFTER THE FIRST month with the SCA, my old life felt like a distant memory. My only complaint was my inability to really connect with the other kids. Although I loved being with them in the great outdoors, I didn't allow myself to get too close. There were six of us in all, and every one of them seemed to have more experience and plans for the future. Most were headed to college right after the assignment was over in August. I felt out of place. I found it difficult to get close to anyone besides Lucy.

Was this the new me; wary, suspicious, unable to trust? I didn't like feeling this way, but what could I do? Perhaps this was what the teachers had meant when they talked about growing up. Maybe I *would* grow up a little. Or maybe time—and the SCA—would heal my broken heart. Heal me or kill me, I thought. That's the best I can hope for.

I threw myself into the forest work, ignoring the mammoth mosquitoes that feasted on our sweaty necks, learning to drink plenty of water to stave off the dehydration headaches that plagued us all from time to time, and most of all, learning to rely on my own body and common sense when it came to knowing when to push myself harder, and when to let myself give in and sit down to rest.

Clearing brush was the hardest part of the job. I quickly learned to avoid the oily leaves of poison oak and poison ivy, and my work gloves became my dearest friends (along with Band-Aids and blister-blocking moleskin, that is), but eventually I became able to keep up with the others as we worked. And just when I finally began to feel like an equal, Reece blew into camp and threw me for a loop.

A COUPLE of weeks before the end of our assignment, he arrived out of the blue. Like Lucy, Reece had a few years on the rest of us; in fact, he had already decided to make the SCA his career. He wanted nothing more than to lead teams of volunteers and teach kids all about the outdoors. He also planned on going back to college to obtain his Master's.

I'd never met anyone like Reece.

When he hiked into our camp, the seven of us were busy preparing our evening meal. Lucy squealed and greeted him with a big hug.

"Reece! What are you doing here? I thought you were near the summit."

The tall, curly haired man pushed his black-framed glasses up on his hooked nose and grinned broadly. "I'm just headed down." He lowered a gigantic backpack to the ground. "Headquarters said you guys were camped here, so I thought I would stop in for a hot meal and a cold drink."

Lucy laughed and slapped him on the back. "Gabi, put another pancake on the griddle." She looked up at the lanky hiker. "Better make it more than one. He looks hungry."

Behind her head, the man she'd called Reece grinned and held up five fingers. My heart fluttered in my chest and I almost spilled the entire jug of batter into the fire.

He winked. "Maybe I'd better pour my own."

I smiled and ducked my head. "Maybe you should."

He crossed the camp in three big strides, took the plastic jug from my hand, and expertly poured five silver-dollar-sized pancakes onto the cast iron griddle.

I shook my head. "That's not enough."

He took the spatula from my other hand and flipped them one after the other. The bottoms were golden brown. "These are for you," he replied. "Mine are next." Then he looked up at the other volunteers standing in line with their plates held at the ready.

"Oops," he muttered. "Maybe theirs first."

I laughed. "I think that would be wise. We only had trail mix for lunch."

In the blink of an eye, he had all of us fed and watered and eating out of his hand. We'd grown used to having beef jerky for protein, since we had no way to refrigerate meat, but when those pancakes were bubbling, I could almost swear I smelled bacon sizzling, too.

"What are you looking forward to eating, back in the world?"

he asked the group at large when we were all settled around the fire, resting and nibbling our evening M&Ms.

"Bacon!" I said.

The others echoed my answer confirming what I'd thought earlier. Only one of us said pizza—and that was Lucy.

We all laughed until her face turned pink. But that might have just been the firelight. Too soon the time came to clean up and get ready to turn in. We still had miles of trail to clean and check the next day. It sounds like an easy job, but the reality is a lot different. It entails cutting back bushes, leveling washed-out spots with shovelfuls of earth, and relining the edges of the trail with buried stones. It's a lot of backbreaking chopping, cutting, digging, and hauling.

As I repacked the foodstuff into the bear bag—which we would hang from a tree downwind of camp—Reece appeared.

"Want me to walk with you?"

My heart did that funny little flip-flop again. "Sure, thanks."

We set off down the path, waving at Lucy as we passed.

He stuck out his hand. "Reece Anderson."

I briefly grasped his strong, bony, fingers. "Gabrielle Kelly." I became suddenly self-conscious of the fact that after nearly a week on this particular trail, I'd had nothing more than the luxury of one brief, lukewarm, sun-shower two days ago.

I put a hand to my pony-tailed hair, attempting to tuck a thousand grimy little pieces back into their proper places.

"Looks fine," Reece said from behind me. "Looks great, actually." He reached out and flipped the end of it playfully.

I laughed. Now I was *really* self-conscious.

He cleared his throat. "Sorry—it's just—"

"You've been up the mountain and haven't seen a girl in months?" I tried to make light of his compliment.

"Yeah," he joked. "Something like that."

After that awkward beginning, we began to talk about what

we intended to do after our assignments were over. He let me know right away that he was never going back to the real world except to pick up his Master's degree so he could move up even higher in the organization.

I gazed down at the ground. "I'm thinking about taking some courses out here, too. I've been listening to the other kids, and the ones who are local seem to think California State University at Northridge is better than the Emerald City."

He chuckled. "That's where I got my undergrad degree. It's where I'll complete my Master's, too." He smoothed his crazy-curly hair back with one hand. "I'm not in any big hurry though." His eyes immediately strayed to the surrounding trees. "This is my passion, right here. I'm thinking I'd make a good youth counselor. Combine that with my biology degree. Work with kids in the forest. I can't imagine being stuck in a nine-to-five. Not anymore."

I let my gaze follow his. "Sounds like an amazing plan. I've fallen in love with this forest, too. It's sort of holy, isn't it? Like church in between services."

He looked at me. "Exactly. Out here, you feel the connection,"

"—to everything."

He gazed at the darkening sky. "Everything." He reached out and flicked the end of my ponytail again. "Gabi Kelly, I think you may be my soulmate."

Gooseflesh popped up on my forearms and I rubbed it away with my palms. I didn't know if I believed in soulmates, because if I did, I would have thought mine was Matt. He was definitely the first boy I'd ever fallen for. Regardless of what had happened between him and Rose, he was the only guy I had ever wanted to kiss, and keep kissing. Before him, I hadn't even understood what others were talking about. I'd spent a whole school year sitting beside him in Chemistry, laughing, teasing, trusting, and then one torrid night of promised passion had changed every-thing, and it had seemed right. So very right.

Until the accident. And Rose.

But Reece? Wasn't this a little soon? Maybe he was only joking around. Although I definitely felt an attraction, I didn't know if it was a real *connection*. For all I knew he might act this way with everyone he met. As for me, well, everyone's heard about love on the rebound.

My feelings for him were tempered with wariness. I defi-nitely felt something, but after Matt's deception, I wasn't about to jump into a "love at first sight" thing. Not with anyone. This time I would keep my heart wrapped up like a piece of fine china. Bubble wrap and tissue paper all the way.

"Look out!" Reece reached for me just as my toe found the edge of a protruding tree root.

Caught completely unaware (because I was gathering wood and not paying attention to my surroundings) I tripped over the root and fell down.

"Sorry! I tried to grab you but I didn't want to drop the food." He set the bag down, pulled me up, and began to dust me off.

Embarrassed, I pushed his hands away and swiped at the seat of my shorts. "It's okay," I said. "I'm just a klutz. Thank God for pine needles. They make a pretty soft landing."

We both looked at the huge root snaking across the trail. "You'd think I would have remembered that one." I laughed to cover my embarrassment.

He chuckled. "Knock, knock, Gabi..."

I glanced up. "Who's there?"

"Tree root," he said.

I rolled my eyes. "Tree root, who?"

He grabbed the food bag up and smiled a goofy smile. "Tree root of all evil is the almighty dollar!"

I groaned. "That's awful." I giggled at his silly humor. But then he twitched the end of my ponytail and we set off again, the experience bonding us somehow.

By the time we hung the food bag and started back up the trail, we were in the midst of a knock-knock joke battle that would spill over into the campsite and continue off and on for the rest of our time together.

"Knock, knock."

"Who's there?"

"Dwayne."

"Dwayne, who?"

"Dwayne da baftub, I'm dwowning!"

He chuckled and came right back with one for me.

"Knock, knock."

"Who's there?"

"Boo!"

"Boo, hoo?"

"Aww, don't cry. It's only a joke."

We could have gone on and on, and in fact we did. It became a sort of secret language between us. "Knock, knock, Gabi Kelly."

I would stop what I was doing and reply, "Who's there?"

At first, he would reply with something completely ridiculous, such as, "Jamaica."

And of course I would say, "Jamaica, who?"

Then he would answer with the stock answer, the one that made sense, the one we'd all heard before, "Jamaica your bed this morning?" But after he'd stayed with us for the whole week, his jokes got more serious. "Knock, knock, Gabi."

"Who's there?"

"Reece."

"Reece, who?"

"Reece Anderson, your soulmate."

When he did that, usually out of earshot of the other kids—

but not always, he didn't seem to care who heard—I would dismiss him with a wave of my hand.

He would laugh and saunter off, whistling, not the least bit perturbed.

For two glorious weeks Reece worked side by side with us as we finished up our restoration of this section of trail. He entertained us, cooked us amazing meals, and generally wormed his way into our hearts. He had requested and received a transfer from his previous job—which had finished up early—and he simply moved his gear to our camp and settled in.

At first, the others assumed he stayed because of Lucy, especially after the way she'd greeted him that first day, but as the days passed it became apparent he had stuck around because of me. And if I caught her looking at the two of us from the corner of her eye a time or two, I simply assumed it was to make certain we were following the guidelines about no fraternization between crewmembers.

Could it possibly happen twice in the space of a few months, this true love thing? I couldn't let myself believe it. He's got an ulterior motive, I thought. He wants sex-in-the-woods, that's all. Then our terms will be up and I'll never see him again.

I stood my ground.

I played his knock-knock games, I allowed myself to enjoy his company, I even felt myself falling for the way his crazy hair tumbled over his forehead, the way his heavy glasses slid down his nose when we were pulling invasive plants or digging ditches for run-off water beside the trails. I even liked the way he would toss the curls off his forehead with a shake of his head and shove the glasses back up without thinking, without even noticing.

And I especially liked the way his thin T-shirt clung to his back, molding itself to his lanky work-hardened physique in the heat of the day. I also admired the way his biceps rounded up with each thrust of the shovel into the soft, black soil.

What it would hurt if we had a fling? We *were* in the woods, after all, high up in the Santa Lucia Range. There were bound to be pockets of privacy beneath the heavy trees. He wasn't my supervisor after all, nor even one of our actual crewmembers. He was an anomaly. An add on. Perhaps it would be all right after all.

But, no. I couldn't go there. Not this soon—not after Matt.

And to my surprise, that wasn't Reece's intention after all.

The teasing continued, and he made it plain that he liked me, but that was as far as it went. I was relieved and truth-be-told, a little disappointed. Especially on those nights when we knocked off early and sat around the campfire telling spooky stories and roasting marshmallows (one of our favorite treats since they were so light to carry in our packs). On those nights, I felt him watching me, and I watched him, too. Wondering what it would be like to kiss him, to feel those rock-hard arms clasped around me, pulling me close.

But then Lucy or one of the others would start a game of truth or dare or he said/she said and the moment would pass.

We also played a lot of firelight poker. I learned all about bluffing and betting and standing pat. Marshmallows and M&Ms were often our currency, although playing for chores happened, too.

Before I learned the basics, I wound up doing a lot more camp cleanup than I should have.

In the end, the Student Conservation Association was everything I thought it would be, and so much more. It was by turns scary and terrifying, wonderful, awful, and above all, fantastic.

Having Reece there upped the ante. He made everything brighter, easier, more fun. Except for those nights when nothing I did could dispel the memories of Matt and of the incident with Rose at the pond.

Lucy helped somewhat. She told me again about some of the

programs she'd been involved with and that gave me a lot to consider. I tried to put away all thoughts of Matt and Rose. I tried to become a warrior for conservation like my mentor. I tried and tried, and most of the time, I was successful.

By throwing myself into every single day, and falling in love with the program and with nature, I slowly began to leave that other Gabi behind. I found myself becoming someone different, someone more mature, more thoughtful, more self-assured. I even became able to shut down thoughts about prom and the horrible events of the recent past.

On the rare occasions when I did wake in the dark, certain I'd heard Matt's voice in my ear, I quickly turned over and forced myself to focus on something else, the sound of crickets outside my tent, or the sigh of the wind in the tops of the pines. I couldn't allow myself to dwell. It was too painful. We'd made such silly plans. Silly now because of what he'd done. How he'd fooled me into thinking he was someone I could respect, someone I could love.

By working like a dog, making certain I was too tired to even think, I kept myself busy enough during the day to control my thoughts and memories (Reece helped just by being there, being a distraction), but there was nothing I could do about those few nights when I awoke in a cold sweat, certain I'd seen a flash of moonlight on silver and heard that awful cardboard-box-full-of water sound again, that horrible *thrumk.*

No matter what I did or who was around to distract me, it seemed I could not completely eliminate the memories, or the dreams. It seemed I might never stop re-living that one horrific night—the night at the pond.

7

Finally, the day came when Lucy told us we'd done so well we had earned a week's vacation in Big Sur. We whooped and hollered and danced like fairies in the moonlight. Big Sur was one of the most rugged, most desirable hiking spots on the California coast.

The excitement gave us new energy. We finished up our remaining days and cleared our campground with a bittersweet joy. We'd all grown close, even me, even Reece. Especially Reece and me.

For the past few weeks we had suffered through our own iffy campfire cooking— which had improved greatly with practice and with the addition of Reece—outdoor solar-heated sun showers (plastic bags of water hung from tree limbs, heated by the sun), hard physical labor, and worst of all, outdoor toilets, actually just a hole in the ground that we had to dig, and cover up, each time we had to go.

"One thing I know," I said. "If I ever have to take care of myself out in the wild, I'm confident I'll be able to do that now."

Everyone laughed. I had been the real greenhorn of the group. But as an added bonus of this little expedition, I had learned how to laugh at myself, how *not* to take things so seriously, and by the time of Big Sur, I'd even learned to let some of the others into my heart.

Those first uncertain nights, when thoughts of Matt and Rose would slither into my tent like poison, were almost gone. Hard physical labor turned out to be the best sleeping pill ever invented. And I had no doubt the appearance of Reece had been my saving grace. He, along with the continued hard work and camaraderie of Lucy and the rest of the crew, seemed to be helping me put things back into perspective.

At the end of our assignment, on the final hike from our camp back down to SCA Headquarters, we sang and laughed and practically floated along the trail, blisters and all. At the base of the mountain, the SCA van picked us up and took us to the Lucia Lodge, where we were each promised a chance to phone home on the one public pay phone. The satellite phone Lucy had used for emergencies was way too expensive for simple calls home to mama.

For now, we had to call collect.

While we waited our turns, we enjoyed nice warm showers, and big bowls of ice cream. I couldn't decide which thing I liked better.

Aurelia got first dibs on the phone. She called her mom and dad and talked for nearly twenty minutes.

Then it was my turn.

After punching the square silver zero button, I waited for the operator to come on. I pressed the heavy black handset to my ear and twirled the silver metal cord until she answered, and then I recited my home phone number and asked her to place a collect call to my mom.

I could hardly wait to hear Mom's voice. When she picked up the receiver, I felt a huge weight fall off my shoulders. A weight I'd grown so used to carrying, I'd almost forgotten it was there.

"Mom!" My voice quavered with emotion. This had been the first time I'd ever been away from her—except to visit my grandparents in Oklahoma—for more than a day or two.

"Gabi! It's so good to hear your voice. I've missed you so *much*."

A deep voice piped up in the background. "Me, too!"

I laughed. "Is that Joe? Tell him I missed him, too."

"Did you get my latest letter?" she asked.

I thought back to the packet of letters in my backpack. The last one I'd gotten had come several days earlier so it was possible I hadn't received the latest one yet. "I'm not sure," I admitted. "The last one told about your raise at work." Mom was a dental hygienist who was very popular with her patients.

I heard her inhale deeply. "Well," she began, "I wanted to tell you before you heard it from anyone else."

"What is it, Mom?" I couldn't keep the worry from my voice. Who would I possibly hear any news from out here? "Is it something bad?"

From the background, Joe yelled, "I asked her and she said yes!"

I heard the sound of a playful swat, and then Mom came back. "We're getting married! And I wanted *you* to be the first to know."

Biting back a tiny snippet of something—could it be jealousy? I tried to work up the correct amount of excitement. I'd been gone eight weeks and I'd just come down out of the woods—literally—and she hadn't even asked if I'd enjoyed it, or anything.

At last I found my voice. "Wow, Mom. Congratulations. To *both* of you." I swallowed my feelings. "When's the big day?"

"Oh, well—"

"Just tell her, Suse! She's a big girl, she can handle it."

I'd always been fond of Joe. We weren't super close, he'd

never tried to actually be a father figure or anything, but at that moment, hearing him tell my mom I could handle it, whatever *it* was, I could have cheerfully strangled him. Instead, I said, "Sure Mom, I'm a big girl. Just tell me."

"We're flying to Vegas tonight." She squealed like a teenager. "We're going to get married in one of those little Elvis chapels."

Tears sprang into my eyes, surprising me. My own mother didn't want me in her wedding? Didn't even want me as a witness, or anything?

"Oh, okay. That's *great*."

"Oh, honey. You're not happy?"

I heard the hesitation in her tone and I was immediately sorry. My mom had put her entire life on hold to raise me as a single parent. I'd never want to deny her this bit of happiness, and really, what would I do in Vegas except get in the way? After the last two months spent communing with nature in the gorgeous Lucia Mountains, the thought of being cooped up in a hotel or casino held no appeal whatsoever. In fact, it sounded downright torturous.

"No, it's not that, Mom. I guess I just feel as if I missed out, not being there with you."

"Do you want to come with us? We'd love it, wouldn't we, Joe?" Her voice went away from the phone a bit.

Joe's voice boomed, "Of course we would!"

I rolled my eyes at the over the top merriment. "It's okay," I said. "I still have a week here. We're going to relax and explore Big Sur. I might even get brave and try surfing." I took in a deep, steadying breath. "You should see this Lodge. I got lucky and drew Cabin #10. Mom, it is literally clinging to the side of a cliff overlooking the ocean. You've never seen anything like it. I'm calling from near there now, looking out at the sunset, and well, it's every shade of orange and gold and pink you can imagine." I knew I was babbling, but I couldn't help it. If I stopped talking, I was afraid she would hear the sadness I felt.

It wasn't that I didn't want her to marry Joe. I did. He was a super guy and always kind, but it was just such a surprise. What would life be like afterward?

Of course, it wasn't going to be the same no matter what. An image of Rose with her hand on her belly invaded my thoughts and at that moment, I knew I could never again walk the same streets she walked, or even breathe the same air.

At that moment, I knew I never wanted to live in Live Oak again, so really, Mom's news was a good thing. Now, she wouldn't be alone. Everything happens for a reason. Mom getting married so suddenly seemed to be the ultimate sign that I needed to make my new life somewhere else.

"Honey?" Mom's voice sounded tiny, far away.

"I'm here, Mom. Sorry. Just distracted by this amazing view. We're going hiking tomorrow, all the way down to the beach— did you know some of the beaches here allow you to hunt for jade? Apparently, there's a big underwater shelf and pieces break off and wash up on shore. Our trail boss said the biggest piece ever found weighed 900 pounds! Can you imagine?" Rambling again. I couldn't seem to stop.

"That sounds exciting. I think I'd like to see that place some-time, but right now there's one more thing I want to discuss with you."

I didn't like the sound of that. Mom never *discussed* things with me. Up until now it had been more like, "here's what we're going to do, get on board."

"Ok-a-a-y." I tried to keep the trepidation out of my voice, but no such luck.

Mom dove right in. "Joe has decided to open a branch office in Houston." She hesitated long enough for the implications to sink in. "I think it's a great idea."

Oh. Well. That was not at all what I expected. I felt like a balloon the day after the party. "Wow." I let my breath whoosh out on that one syllable. It was just a subconscious ploy to stall the conversation while my mind played catch up.

"Are you okay?"

I nodded. But, of course, she couldn't see that. "Sure," I said, not sure at all. "It's just a lot to think about. I mean, you and Joe getting married in Vegas, then moving off to Houston while I'm thousands of miles away out here in California."

"Oh, baby, that makes it sound terrible. Does it really feel that way? Of course our home will always be your home—and there are so many good colleges in and around Houston, your choices will be *tremendous*."

I swallowed, hard. "That's right. I understand. And what about you? I mean your job?"

My young-sounding about-to-be-a-bride mother, laughed cheerfully. "Oh, I've already got a dozen interviews lined up. We'll just play it by ear."

"Well, it sounds wonderful, Mom. It really does." I didn't know what else to say.

There was an awkward silence.

"Hey," Mom said. "We don't have to fly out to Vegas tonight." I heard her mutter something to Joe. I could almost see the be-quiet-or-else look she was probably giving him. "You've got another week, right?"

I murmured agreement.

"Well, that settles it. We aren't going to get married until you get home—as a matter of fact—Joe! I just remembered that Gabi has a layover in Vegas on her flight back. How perfect is that?"

I started laughing. I couldn't help it. The magnificent sunset, hearing my mother so deliriously happy, and catching a glimpse —every now and then—of Reece lounging on the cliff side deck, sneaking surreptitious glances at my cabin window, it was all beginning to feel right. As if the world's roulette wheel had just clicked over to my lucky number.

And the fact that I was now going to be at my mom's wedding—that was the best thing of all. Then she took it one better.

"After the wedding, I want you to come to Houston with us to house hunt. Oh, honey, this is going to be fantastic!"

At last, I began to get excited. "Mom, that's the best news I've heard all day." It meant I wouldn't have to go back to Live Oak— ever. It would be a new start for all of us.

Little did I know, by the end of that one magical Big Sur week, I would *never* want to leave California.

8

"I can't believe it. My mom is getting married in Vegas."
I'd just hung up the phone and wandered out of the little alcove to the deck where Reece leaned against the rail. "I hope that's a good thing."

"It is. Mom has always been my only parent—worked night and day to keep me from feeling left behind. She deserves some happiness. I just never thought she'd get married in Las Vegas."

"Sounds like everyone is happy." He pointed out at the deep blue water. "I just saw a whale."

I stared at the spot he indicated. At first I didn't see anything, and then as if in slow motion, something huge breached the surface. It was massive; unlike anything I'd ever seen. It split the skin of the sea and rose above it magically. There was no splash, no tail flap, no crash back into the water. It simply rose in a large gray hump, and then slid back into the depths without a sound.

"Wow. Wish we had binoculars." I don't know why I whispered. It just seemed like the right thing to do.

Reece whispered, too. "Humbling, isn't it?"

"Astonishing." I smiled but couldn't drag my eyes away from

the last spot where I'd seen the creature's back. "Wonder if it was a gray whale or a blue whale."

"Maybe a humpback. Aren't they the ones who breach that way?"

I laughed. "What I know about whales would fit on the head of a pin."

We stood, side by side, leaning on our elbows against the stout deck rail, watching as the magnificent creature frolicked silently in the last rays of the sun, putting on a show seemingly just for us.

"Amazing, isn't it?"

"It is," I agreed. And I *was* amazed. Not only by the spectacle of the whale, but also by the sound of awe in the voice of the gentle man standing beside me. Could he really be all that he seemed? Or was he, like the whale, just putting on a show?

As if privy to my thoughts, Reece said, "This is one more reason I chose the SCA." He hesitated for a moment as the whale finally flipped its tremendous tail out of the water. "When I first started college, I thought I'd go into forestry and become a ranger or wildlife biologist, and then I did my first stint in the Student Conservation Society and I was hooked. There's so much variety."

That got my attention. "What do you mean, variety?"

"Well, while I'm working on my Master's, I can continue working locally. Afterward, I'll be able to choose from duty stations all over the world."

I stood there, quietly taking in what he was telling me. When I didn't respond right away, he continued. "That way, I'll never be tied down too long. And I'll be treated to scenery like this." He indicated the ocean spread out below us with a wide sweep of his arm. "After I get my graduate degree, I will move on up the ladder at my own pace. There are tons of opportunities with this organization." He stared off into the distance. "And the great thing is, it's all about improving the earth."

Something about his plan excited me. "I like what you're saying." I imagined myself living like this for the next few years. "I wonder if I have what it takes to do that?"

Reece looked at me. "If you really want to find out, you can keep volunteering for trail assignments for the next couple months—until the weather gets too bad to get up the mountain—and then you can join me at CSUN and we'll take some mid-winter classes together. I have an apartment near campus, but the dorms there are really nice, too. Once you fill out paperwork for student aid, and you tell them you're with the SCA, you will most likely qualify for grants and various scholarships. Maybe even work-study during the winter months."

"You're kidding, right?" It sounded too good to be true.

He shook his head. "Not at all. That's what I've been doing for the past four years. And by the time you get a few more months of trail work under your belt, you'll know for certain if this is what you want to do."

"Sounds like a win-win."

He grinned. "For me, it will be."

I looked at his angular face to see if there was a hidden meaning behind those few simple words—did he mean his job and education were a win-win, or did he mean it would be a win-win if I came on board and took classes with him in the winter? I couldn't tell for sure. His expression was the same as always. Either he was a master of deception, or I was just too inexperienced to know.

As always when I was unsure, I simply remained silent. The thing with Matt and Rose had left me gun shy. What was the old saying, fool me once, shame on you, fool me twice, shame on me? Mom had often said it over the years. I'd started to notice how her little sayings kept popping up now that I was on my own.

We stood at the railing for a few more moments, watching the evening fog roll in over the water. The air became chilly as the dense moisture encroached. "Want to go inside?"

I shook my head. "We don't have anything like this where I'm from. I want to enjoy every moment of it."

He smiled. "Be right back."

I felt much colder when he was gone, without the warmth of his body beside mine at the rail, and with the sun almost completely gone; but in a couple of minutes, he was back, two cups of coffee in hand.

I gripped the thick white mug gratefully. "Thank you." I inhaled the warm steam escaping the mug.

"You're welcome. The dining room is just down there." He pointed toward a bend in the stairs with his chin. "They have an amazing view, too."

I glanced over, looking forward to dining there later. I noticed Reece had donned a sweatshirt and jacket while he was gone.

He took off the jacket—once again seeming to read my thoughts—and draped it around my shoulders. It enveloped me like a warm hug. I snuggled into it and didn't even think about pretending he shouldn't have.

"That's nice," I said. "I can't believe the weather here. Back home it's probably a hundred degrees."

"THAT'S another perk of this life. Getting to experience things we might never have the chance to if we were tied down to an office somewhere."

I sipped and nodded.

By dinnertime the fog had grown so thick we could no longer see the ocean. We met the others in the dining room and everyone began to chatter like a flock of magpies coming to roost.

After a few moments, someone mentioned the whale. Come to find out, every person had seen it from his or her window or from the deck.

"This is the most beautiful place I've ever been." I gazed out at the fog-shrouded deck. "Doesn't it feel cozy, wrapped in fog like this?"

"Like a soft blanket," Lucy agreed.

All the others murmured their agreement and we dug into our meals. The fish and chips were so delicious I vowed to never eat anything else, ever again.

After dinner, the chef came out and greeted us. He told us how he and his wife were simply continuing a tradition started by his ancestors, one of Big Sur's nineteenth century pioneer families.

"No wonder it feels so rustic," Eduardo said. "It's been here awhile, huh?"

"Yep," the chef said. "So, if you feel a little chill at night in your cabin, or you see a quick shadow shy away into the corner, don't be alarmed. It's probably just one of my ancestors, checking to make sure I'm keeping the place up."

Everyone laughed and nudged each other. Eduardo told Nate, "Now I guess you're *glad* I'm your roomie. Not like on the trail when you booted me out of your tent after mine sprung a leak."

Nate laughed. "I didn't mean to do that. I just didn't like you standing there streaming water on me. Tonight, just make sure you don't scream if your blanket slips off your foot and something caresses your toes."

Eduardo grinned and smacked him on the shoulder good-naturedly. "I'm not afraid of ghosts. You'll be the one squealing like a little girl."

Lucy rolled her eyes, pulled out a deck of cards, and we fell into one of our nightly games, this time, gin rummy. Before the game was through, we were all yawning. It had been a long hike down the mountain and the thought of sleeping in a real bed began to seem more and more appealing as the clock ticked.

Stephen yawned. "I think I hear that pillow calling my name." He was going to bunk with Reece since only two people were allowed in each cabin. Aurelia was bunking with Jerenda, and my bunkmate would be Lucy.

"I'll walk down with you," Jerenda told Stephen. They'd had a close bond almost since the start. Everyone assumed something romantic had sprung up between them, but since that sort of thing was strictly forbidden, no one brought it up.

"I'm about to turn in, too," Lucy said. "I'd feel better if everyone got tucked in before I hit the sack. We are on a cliff, after all."

Everyone laughed uneasily.

"Have there ever been any accidents?" I asked the chef.

His eyes strayed to the fog-shrouded deck that looked out over the cliff. "Only one, and it happened to a family member. Her name was Olivia. We called her Livie, for short." I saw him wink at Lucy, but I didn't know if the others caught it.

"Well, we'll all watch out for poor Olivia, then." Lucy winked back at him.

I had to remind myself that this wasn't Lucy's first rodeo. I don't think she ever said how many times she'd brought teams here, but I assumed she'd been here a few times.

"I'm ready to turn in," I said. "I can't wait to get up tomorrow and check out Jade Cove."

The others nodded, and Reece said, "It's a beautiful place. It's going to be a wonderful trip."

We all thanked the chef/owner for his delicious meal and then we trooped out and headed to our cabins. "I'll be around to check on each of you in a bit. Make sure you're all where you should be." She shot a warning look at Jerenda and Stephen.

Jerenda rolled her eyes. "We're not children."

Lucy chuckled. "Right. So, let's not act like it. Children think nothing of breaking rules, adults know rules are there for a purpose." She didn't smile. "I'll see you in two minutes." She included Aurelia in her comment. "Goodnight, ladies."

A couple seconds later, I caught a glimpse of Jerenda and Stephen in a serious embrace in the telephone alcove. I hurried by, Reece close behind me.

At cabin #10, we stood for a second, looking down the cliff into the swirling fog. "It's like the setting for one of those old horror movies."

"Yeah, one with Vincent Price or that Bela Lugosi guy." He shielded his face with his arm like Count Dracula. "I vant to drink your blood!"

I laughed. "Thanks for walking me up, Drac. If nothing gets me during the night, I'll see you in the morning." I reached for the door but he caught my shoulder and spun me gently toward him.

He touched my hair. "I can't wait until this week is over."

My heart skipped a beat. I thought he would kiss me, but he pulled back.

"Why?" I asked.

He lowered his voice. "I can't kiss you until we aren't co-workers anymore."

I didn't know what to say. Didn't know what to do. I almost pulled him back to me, in spite of the warning. At that moment, I wanted him to kiss me, just like with Matt. Up until then, I'd always just allowed myself to be kissed because I thought it was the expected thing to do. Until Matt, I'd begun to think something might be wrong with me. Now, I felt the same thing with Reece. Maybe even deeper.

I chewed my lip. "I–um, I'm going to Houston after this week. After Mom's wedding in Vegas."

Reece groaned. "Nooo. I wanted to show you L.A." He swiped the unruly curls off his forehead. "I also hoped to help you sign up for the next assignment. I can't pull many strings, but I can pull a couple." He flashed a gleaming white grin in my direction. "I selfishly thought I might be able to keep you near me until you enroll at CSUN."

I stepped back. I hadn't even decided if I *wanted* to do another assignment. Not for certain. I still reeled from the idea of being in my mom's wedding on Saturday.

We heard Lucy's footsteps on the stairs. She never simply walked anywhere, she always tap-tap-tap-tap tapped.

"Hey there, kids." She bopped past. "Glad to see you had an escort, Gabi. It's really dark up here. The fog, I suppose. Blocks out the moon."

I chuckled nervously. Had she heard anything? I didn't want to get in trouble, or get Reece in trouble.

He turned to leave and I heard the squeak of his hiking boots on the moist wood. "See you ladies at breakfast." He gave me a half-salute.

"Goodnight." My voice blended with Lucy's and I stepped aside so she could enter the cabin first. I wanted just one more glimpse of those rakish curls on his way down the stairs.

9

True sleep would not come. When the sun brightened the windows, I felt as if I'd barely closed my eyes. All night long I'd dozed in and out, dreams of unholy tendrils of fog caressing my bare legs. I must have awakened half a dozen times to make sure my limbs were tucked securely under the blankets.

When I finally gave up on sleep, I looked around for Lucy. A notoriously early riser, on the trail she'd often have the fire going and breakfast started before the rest of us had even opened our eyes.

I pulled the slightly-damp-feeling comforter up to my chin. For the first time in ages, I wished I could simply stay in bed and go back to sleep. The memory of Reece on the stair stayed with me. But was it too soon? And what about Matt, lying in that hospital bed? Was he well yet? I'd have to ask Mom when I talked to her again.

And then there was her big news. What a change. My whole life seemed to have hinged on that one night at prom—and even though it had all been completely out of my control, that hinge had allowed a door to swing closed, and another to swing open.

No way I could go back to sleep now.

I sniffled and wiped at my face. Idiot, my subconscious said. So what if Matt wasn't what you thought? You didn't really know him, just because you sat by him and helped him in Chemistry all year. So what if he had turned out to be a user? You're lucky to be away from him. Think of Reece. Think of the future, instead.

But as wonderful as Reece seemed, I couldn't let myself relax. Could I trust him? Should I? Five more days until Vegas. Maybe I'll talk that over with Mom, too, on the way to Houston after the wedding. Wait—what about the honeymoon? Surely they would go on a honeymoon before moving all the way to Houston.

Snappy steps on the stairs. The door burst open and Lucy came in singing "Oh what a beau-ti-ful mor*ning*!"

I pretended to be asleep, glad when she went on through to the bathroom. I didn't need pity for the tears on my face. I needed to get used to the idea that Matt was now just a part of my past, no matter how magical the few hours we had shared. Nope. He belonged to someone else. Time to forget him, completely. I scrubbed my face with the corner of the sheet, and dragged myself out of bed. "Good morning," I called.

The water cut off and Lucy poked her head out. She'd tied her shiny hair back in a ponytail, and she held a toothbrush in one hand. "G'morning sunshine! You ready for Jade Cove?"

I felt my lips begin to grin, in spite of my doldrums. I couldn't be depressed around Lucy. She exuded light. "I'm ready for breakfast."

She laughed and went back to brushing her teeth.

I slipped into my shorts and T-shirt. But with the fog still gripping the cliff, I knew it would stay chilly for a while so I pulled my fleece hoodie and sweatpants on, too. One thing I'd learned about the mountains—always dress in layers. Much easier to take something off when the sun came out rather than scramble to find something to put on when it disappeared again.

Besides, I loved the smell of my fleece outerwear—it was all campfire and wood smoke. I vowed never to wash them, even though I was glad I'd heeded Lucy's advice and kept this one pair of shorts and T-shirt rolled up in bottom of my backpack, clean.

"Hey, Boss, any chance we can tour the Hearst Castle while we're so close?"

Lucy gargled, spat, and ran more water into the sink. "You've been peeking into my brain, haven't you, young lady?"

I laughed. "Actually, I saw the brochure in the dining room last night and just sort of hoped."

"Yes, we will definitely get to tour parts of the castle. It's magnificent. Been there a couple of times. It's amazing what untold wealth can build."

I pulled my spread up and tucked my pillow under.

Lucy was a staunch conservationist. The opulence of Hearst Castle seemed like it would be anathema to someone like her. Me, on the other hand, I wanted to see it just to see if *The Great Gatsby* got it right.

"I've already had breakfast," she said. "But you go on down. It's free so just help yourself. Oh, and check out the gift store when you finish. They've got amazing things made from local jade. You might get some ideas for the treasure you will find on our trip today."

She knew how to get my attention. But I really didn't want to go down without washing my face and brushing my teeth so I lingered on the attached deck, wrapped in my fleece outerwear and my blanket.

The fog had turned downright freezing.

"Hey, stranger!" Reece's voice echoed down the walkway. He had the cabin two doors down from ours.

"Good morning."

"Been to breakfast yet?"

I shook my head. "Going down in a few minutes." I shivered. "It's cold!"

Reece looked down at himself and splayed his hands. He was wearing the same pair of jeans he'd worn for the last week. "Layers, layers, layers." He echoed my own thinking. "I've got my shorts on underneath, and I'm going to wear my daypack to stow my outerwear in, when it gets hot later."

I nodded. "That's a good idea. I'll get mine, too." I turned toward my cabin glad he'd reminded me to bring the small daypack we carried for just such purposes. "I'll be back in a few."

Dashing back inside, I dug my small pack out of my huge one just as Lucy emerged from our shared restroom. "I'm just finishing up, but I've got to make some arrangements for our daytrips so you guys go ahead. I'll be down in a bit."

I nodded and took a quick turn with my toothbrush and hairbrush.

When I opened the cabin door, a breeze had made its way through the fog. The smell of breakfast wafting up from the dining room caused my stomach to rumble. Reece stood with his back to me, hood up, hands in his pockets, gazing out over the cliff.

"Ready?"

He turned, a sleepy grin on his lips. "Ready, willing, and starving."

I led the way down the wet wooden steps with Reece close behind. Just inside the dining room, we spied Lucy on the office phone. She was smiling. Indoors or out, Lucy always appeared to be in her element.

I inhaled deeply. "I think we could almost make our breakfast out of the wonderful smell."

We made our way to the buffet and Reece handed me a heavy china plate. Not too fancy, but very substantial, just like the coffee mugs from the night before. The ambience of the dining room was bright and appealing. A cheery fire burned in the fireplace and the wall of windows looked out on the foggy sea. To further the mood, tiny lanterns burned in the center of each table. They lent a cozy feel to the shiplap-paneled room.

We filled our plates and made our way to one of the small tables. Nate and Eduardo raised their hands in greeting. Jerenda and Aurelia came in and made their way to the buffet behind us.

Breakfast tasted delicious, probably because we didn't have to cook it ourselves. They treated us to such an assortment of pastries, eggs, and breakfast meats I ate as though I'd been on a two week fast. Once, I looked up between bites embarrassed to find Reece watching me, grinning.

"What?" I asked. "You said you were starving, too."

He tilted his wiped-clean plate toward me. "I'm just a little faster than you." He reached for another biscuit dripping with butter.

I laughed and gulped ice-cold milk. I felt like a little kid. Funny how easy it was to enjoy the small things with Reece—like a hot buttered biscuit eaten indoors, out of the weather. "Every person in America should be required to spend a few weeks working and sleeping outside like we've been doing." I took another bite. "It's made me appreciate everything so much more."

He turned his chair toward mine. "If you really think so, then you would probably like to backpack around Europe the way I'm planning on doing next summer."

My eyes might have bugged out a bit. I had never even considered anything so adventurous. "Backpack through Europe? I wouldn't know where to start." I imagined alpine meadows like in *The Sound of Music*. "Although it does sound like fun."

Reece grinned, his eyes crinkling at the corners. "That's what I like about you. Always open to possibilities."

I took a sip of coffee. Was that true? Was I like that? I'd always thought of myself as something of a pessimist or at the very least a stagnant realist. Maybe he was the one who brought out the adventurer in me. "Well, it does sound like fun, even though I have no idea what it would really be like."

"I've been planning my trip for a while. Youth hostels and train tickets all the way. I want to see and experience every country on the European continent."

I halted, mid-sip. "Is that even doable?"

He stretched out his long, lanky legs and laced his fingers behind his head. "Not on my limited budget." He shrugged. "But I like to dream big."

I ducked my head. Dream big, he said. Why not? Isn't that what my mom always told me while I was growing up? *You're only young once, don't waste it.* I often got the feeling she was telling me not to make the same mistakes she'd made. She didn't like to talk about my father, but I sometimes wondered about him—where he was, and if he had another family—but I had never tried to find him because I figured if he didn't want me then, why should I want him now?

"Penny for your thoughts?" Reece's expression was kind, as if he really had an interest.

"Nah. Inflation. Cost you at least a quarter."

He started to speak, but Eduardo ambled over and sat down. "You really thinking of taking some classes out here, Tex?"

I didn't mind the nickname. "Maybe. I think I'm falling in love with this area." I knew he'd like that since he was a native Californian. Most people are proud of their state—except for teens. Teenagers always tend to denigrate their roots. It's like a rite of passage. I couldn't believe I just thought of a group of people as teens. I'm a teen. I'm only eighteen. Wow—this trip really had changed me.

Eduardo nodded. "I'm enrolled there, too. I hope you'll let me give you the grand tour before we all head home this week."

I didn't mean to, but I glanced at Reece to gauge his reaction. He appeared to be studying the view outside the windows. "I do plan on looking things over," I said. I didn't want to commit to anything with Eddie, my nickname for him, but I certainly didn't want to be rude.

A look of confusion crossed the boy's handsome face. "Well, it was just a thought. We can talk more later." He shot Reece a quick, questioning look, too.

I took that opportunity to change the subject to my mom's upcoming wedding. "I can't believe they're getting married in Vegas and then after the wedding, she wants me to go right on to Houston with them to go house hunting."

Eduardo nodded. "Sounds like you've got quite a set of plans already."

I smiled to let him know I wasn't just blowing him off. "Yes, it looks like I'll be getting a new dad, which is great. But I'm a little bit leery of moving—" I thought of never seeing my childhood home again, which I kept thinking I wanted, but then an image of Matt sitting on the picnic table underneath the live oaks popped into my head, unbidden.

Lucy strolled into the dining room. "Everyone about ready to go?"

We all began to stand, chairs scraping and shuffling on the hardwood floors.

"The bus will be downstairs," she said. "Don't forget your jackets and your daypacks."

I turned to smile at Reece, to let him know I found it funny that he and Lucy both thought to remind us "rookies" about the daypacks, but he was looking at the floor and I couldn't seem to catch his eye.

We trooped down to the bus and piled in for the short ride to the beach. There were so many things to see, such gorgeous scenery, that conversation was kept to a minimum.

10

Only nine miles from the lodge, Jade Cove turned out to be unbelievably beautiful and pristine. When we arrived, there were already a couple of people out searching for the precious metamorphic rock. "Don't turn your back on the ocean, kids," an older lady shouted by way of greeting. "She's a greedy thing. She'll snatch you right off the sand."

Oh, no, I thought. There's someone who's losing her grip on reality.

Reece must have seen the look that crossed my face. He leaned down and whispered, "I wouldn't have said it that way, but she's telling the truth. The waves will grab you if you aren't careful." Then, to the group at large, he said, "The lady is right. There are dangerous rip tides in this cove. Rogue waves have sometimes washed unwary beachcombers right off the sand into the water, and into the currents." He smiled crookedly. "So go, have fun. Find jade. Don't die."

Lucy swatted his shoulder playfully. "Listen to Reece, the voice of doom. Stay with your buddy, and always be aware of your surroundings." She shaded her eyes with one hand. "And if you keep heading north, you'll eventually wind up on Sand

Dollar Beach. That's where you'll see surfers, hang gliders, and people parasailing." She shook her finger at each of them. "I don't recommend trying any of those things today—not on my watch—not even if someone offers to teach you."

I didn't quite understand why she would say something like that out of the blue, but after everyone began to wander away, Reece cleared it up. "Last year one of the girls took up with someone she met on the beach and he offered to show her how to body surf." He smoothed one hand over his chin. "She almost drowned."

"Oh—" I began, but Lucy was yelling something across the sand so we had to stop and cup our hands to our ears to hear her.

"Meet me in the Sand Dollar parking lot at two o'clock. I'll be waiting there with the van."

We all waved in acknowledgement, and then we were on our own. Except for Reece, of course.

"Well, you heard the woman," he said. "Stay with your buddy." He winked at me and then dashed ahead to issue a couple more instructions to the rest of the team.

When I caught up to them, he was doling out dollops of sunscreen for those who had forgotten theirs.

Everyone had naturally split into pairs or trios, me with Reece, Jerenda with Stephen, Eduardo with Nate and Aurelia. I smoothed Banana Boat Sunscreen into my skin and the coconut smell immediately took me back to my childhood days when swimming was the thing I most looked forward to every summer.

I rubbed another dab of lotion onto my neck and face, inhaling the summery mixture of sea salt and sunscreen. "I think the smell of this day—and this cove—will stay with me the rest of my life."

Reece walked beside me in silence. Then he took the lotion

and ran a line up his forearm. "It's the best place in the world," he agreed. "I wish I had my surfboard—"

"Would you teach me to surf?" I tried to keep my tone light, but it came out sounding somewhat sarcastic.

"In a heartbeat." He looked out at the crashing surf. "But not here. We'd go out to Malibu or Doheny. Some place slow and gentle. That's how you learn to surf."

I swallowed any other remarks I might have made. I hadn't expected him to take me so seriously.

"Maybe after you're enrolled in a class or two at CSUN, we'll have time to catch a wave." He smiled when he said that, and all at once I could easily picture him on a surfboard, wild blond hair longer, bleached even lighter by the constant sun and sea, and I found myself longing for that, longing for something I'd never even *considered* before.

I gazed out at the ceaseless waves. "I'm glad the fog burned off. This weather is perfect."

He squeezed my shoulder and we walked slowly up the rocky beach, eyes peeled for jade, or sea glass, or any other treasure the ocean chose to throw at our feet. Before we'd gone very far, I spied a gray-green tip of rock protruding from the edge of the water. "Look!" I felt like a little kid on an Easter egg hunt. "That's it, isn't it? That's a piece of jade."

I dug the small flat rock out of the wet sand and polished it against my sweatshirt. Dull green began to give way to brighter green shot through with a couple of tiny streaks of gold. The sound of the surf soon made it second nature to shout at each other. The constant wind whipped my ponytail against the back of my neck and caused me to slit my eyes even behind my Foster Grants.

Reece smiled. "Yep, that's jade all right."

Later I found another, smaller piece, even though I'm pretty sure Reece saw it first. This one appeared jagged, shaped more like a nugget instead of a flat slab. I immediately had the idea to have it polished up for a wedding present for my mom and Joe. But when I voiced my idea to Reece, it didn't sound like much.

"I think it's a cool idea," he said.

"You're just saying that to be nice. It's really dorky, I know."

He shook his head. "Look here." He took the flat piece from me. "What if you had them polished up and had the wedding date engraved on them—one for your mom and one for Joe?" He held the small stones in the palm of his hand. "I noticed a lot of jade already carved right there in the gift store at the inn. I'll bet they could do it right there. Mount them on a stand, add some fancy curlicues or something." He grinned and handed the jade back to me.

I thought it over. "That *would* make it more special, wouldn't it?" I sort of liked the idea. "I'll talk to the gift store when we get back, see if it can be done in time, and if I can afford it." I laughed.

The sun and the smells and the sweet salty taste of the breeze on my tongue suddenly made me feel so alive it seemed as if I'd just been born. Reece made everything fun and easy. Even my best bud, Asa, hadn't been this easy to get along with.

We hiked and hiked and found several more tiny pieces of jade along with a couple of starfish and one magnificent conch shell. After a while, we wound up at the picnic sites at Sand Dollar Beach. Lucy waited there, as promised, with ice chests filled with bottles of water, cans of soda, sandwich makings, and hot dogs for roasting. She even brought the makings for s'mores.

"We can't have a fire on this beach," she said, "but we can build one in the little grills here in the picnic area."

All of us crowded around pulling cold drinks from the ice chests, while Lucy and Reece built a charcoal fire in the iron grill. "I really wanted to treat you guys to a beach bonfire," she continued. "But they just aren't allowed here. Maybe we can make it down to Monterey before it's all said and done. They have the best beaches for bonfires."

Reece seconded that. Then he leaned over and whispered that he already had it on our itinerary when I returned from Vegas.

I didn't say anything. On one hand, I really looked forward to spending more time with him, without the restrictions of mentor-student, but at the same time, I almost resented his certainty that I would be back. I hadn't actually decided what my plans were. Which was a stupid thing, I suppose. We only had a few more days before the assignment ended, and I hadn't made up my mind whether I wanted to return or go on and move to Houston with my mom and soon-to-be stepdad.

Talk about passive decision-making. I felt ashamed of myself. I looked around at the group with whom I'd spent the last eight weeks. We'd all grown and changed and I didn't have a single regret. In fact, I'd never felt so secure in my life. And what did I have to look forward to in Houston? I didn't know anyone other than my mom and Joe. I would have to enroll in college, get a part-time job, and live under my parents' roof. Those were my cons.

My pros for staying were just as many. I loved this area, I already had at least two local friends here to show me the ropes, I had the possibility of a job that I loved, and I could probably get grants and scholarships to CSUN. Maybe I could live in the dorm. Reece had even said I could stay with him. Did that mean rent a room from him? That seemed drastic. Oh well, I could always use some of the college fund my grandparents had set aside for me, if I had to.

If I decided to return, that is.

I sat with my chin in my hand, thinking about my options, reliving my amazing assignment with SCA, considering all my pros and cons about the future until all at once it occurred to me that I was sitting on a picnic bench just like the one Matt and I had shared the night of prom.

I let my hand venture to the necklace Matt had given me the night of prom. I'd taken it off after Rose told me she was pregnant, but the day I left Live Oak, I dropped it in my backpack, and when the hiking got hard, I took it out and put it on. It gave me a shot of courage just the way Matt said it did him.

Resting my hand on the pitted, salty, concrete table, I resisted the urge to imagine Matt sitting beside me. But I couldn't make my mind shy away from the memory of those mind-blowing kisses we'd shared. I'd never felt that overwhelming desire for more—until now.

Several times over the last few weeks, I'd found myself wondering how it would be if Reece held me—and kissed me—the way Matt had done. But, of course, that was out of the question while we were on the job.

Reece snapped me out of my reverie when he plopped down on the tabletop and slid a dollar under my palm.

I looked up in confusion.

"For your thoughts." His hair was unkempt and wild and a vision of him, shirtless, on a surfboard sprang into my head. I'd never been boy-crazy like a lot of my friends, but now I seemed to be making up for it. All I could think about was Matt, and now Reece.

I took the bill, folded it, and slipped it into the netting on the side of my daypack. We'd stripped off our outerwear hours earlier and stowed it in our packs. When Reece had pulled his hooded sweatshirt up and over his head, his T-shirt had come up with it revealing a large band of tanned abs, hardened by surfing and hiking. It had refreshed my interest in seeing him on that board, and had even sparked my own interest in getting on a board.

He nudged my shoulder with his knee. "You're going to take my money and give me nothing in return?"

Oddly enough, he was sitting the way I'd been sitting on prom night, and I was sitting the way Matt had been. I smiled up at his kind face. "I don't really know where to start. My thoughts are going around and around in my head like the blades of a windmill."

He sat quietly for a moment. Then he pulled out his wallet and began counting singles. "How about this much?" He held out a thin sheaf of bills. "Will that cut some of them loose?"

I shoved his hand down as my cheeks flamed. "Put that away, the others will think you're paying me for something."

He grinned. "Favors, perhaps?" He dug deeper into his wallet and pulled out a hundred dollar bill. "Here's my reserve cash. I think this would be more appropriate for that way of thinking." He arched his eyebrows and waved the bill at me.

I laughed out loud and grabbed for the money, suddenly enjoying the game, not caring what the others thought. My mind was definitely not on prom anymore, or Matt. Once again, Reece had figured out a way to cheer me up and get me out of my own head. My decision about the future seemed to be getting easier and easier.

As if reading my mind, he said, "I can't wait until you return from Vegas. We'll go into L.A., look into signing up for the next assignment, and then we'll snag a CSUN course catalog for the mid-winter semester." His voice grew quiet. The others were lying about on blankets or sitting in folding lawn chairs Lucy had brought from the Lodge. Eduardo sat on another picnic table, examining a chunk of jade he'd found.

I dug my own jade pieces out of my pack just to keep my hands off my buffalo nickel necklace. "I think I'd like that." I heard my voice tremble. "If you're sure it isn't too much trouble."

Reece exhaled. "No trouble at all." There might have been a

slight tremble in his voice, too. He nudged me with his knee again. "You think I'm kidding about the soulmate business?"

I couldn't meet his eye.

"Knock, knock," he whispered.

I swallowed and brushed a layer of fresh sand off the table. "Who's there?" I expected him to say "your soulmate," or something like that.

Instead, he said, "Me, the guy you're going to spend the rest of your life with."

Heat flooded my face and almost blew the top of my head off. The world went away, replaced by a low buzzing sound that might have been my red blood cells rushing through my veins at light speed. "Funny, I don't think I've ever heard that one before."

He stood and dusted the sand off his shorts. "You think I'm crazy?"

Crazy? No. I hadn't thought that. But in retrospect, what did I really know about him? And what did he know about me?

"I don't know," I mumbled at last. "I don't have near enough experience to say." After uttering that idiotic statement, I immediately wished I hadn't. If he *was* some sort of nutcase, I might be playing right into his hands.

He walked over to the barbecue and laid two hot dogs on the grill. "I hope you like yours charred. If you don't, better tell me now."

I opened my mouth to tell him I did like mine charred, but a gust of wind blew up out of nowhere and coated my tongue with grit. By the time I'd drunk enough water to wash it away, he was pulling the dogs off the grill and stuffing them down in toasted buns.

Eduardo sat down on the bench beside me.

I gulped and looked up at Reece who stood there holding our hotdogs.

"Would you like to join us?" I asked.

Reece held out one of the hotdogs and said, "Here, bud. Take this one. I'm going to slap a couple more on the grill."

I smiled up at him. "I'll get the chips." Lucy had a big bag of chips and other goodies on her table. She really had thought of everything.

Eduardo smiled and took the hotdogs from Reece.

He was such a nice guy, but I certainly didn't feel for him the way I did for Reece. I was glad he didn't push the subject, and even more glad that Reece didn't seem to mind the attention.

11

A sudden squall blew in while we were eating.

We scrambled to pack up our food and get back on the bus before we got soaked. The fresh rain mixed with the earlier smells of sunscreen and salt water made my head spin. The huge drops of moisture struck the sand with such force they sent up little puffs of dust. They also dotted the entire parking area with dark, mini-splotches, which added to the amazing mix of odors. Wet dust, another smell I will always associate with that perfect day.

By the time we made it back to Lucia Lodge, the squall had become a full out storm. We pulled our hoodies back on and dashed across the parking lot to the dining room.

Through the wall of windows, the thunder and lightning grew more and more spectacular. The rain deafened us, but the blazing fireplace and glowing sconces made the lodge feel like home. We couldn't have asked for a better place to wait out a ferocious summer storm.

Grouped around the hearth, we stripped off our damp sweats, laughing and talking all at once. The manager brought out a deck of cards and a stack of board games. We pulled our chairs up to the tables nearest the fire and chose our games. Tired of gin rummy, I grabbed Monopoly and looked around for players.

Eduardo and Reece chose their tokens.

"We need a Ouija board." Aurelia looked around the group to see if anyone would second her thought. She twirled a strand of dense black hair around one finger, a look of dark glee in her eye. She reminded me of the classic fortune-teller at a county fair.

I shook my head. "Those things scare me."

Aurelia laughed. "It's all in fun. We used to play with them when I was a kid. And this place, the cliff, with this storm churning up everything outside, seems like the perfect time to try it again."

"Sorry." The manager laughed. "That's one thing I don't have."

I relaxed, unaware until that moment that I'd been coiled as tight as a snake. I'd tried the game as a child, too. And the way the planchette had raced across that board in response to the question my friend had asked about her brother—who had died in a car crash—had terrified me. Mom had assured me that my friend's emotions had been the thing pushing the little plastic triangle across the letters, but Mom hadn't been there. She hadn't seen the look of shock on Shan's face when the board said, YES, her brother *was* in the room at that very instant.

I tried to get that image out of my head and concentrate on buying up all the railroads and utilities on the Monopoly board. But when the thunder boomed and the lights flickered, the look on my friend's face reappeared.

The lights blinked out. Someone let out a little scream and we were left in near darkness. Only the firelight and the sconces pushed back the gloom. The memory of Shan's face hanging over the Ouija board would not leave my mind.

"Everything's fine, folks," the manager said. "Generator will kick on in a few minutes. This happens from time to time, as you can imagine." We heard him chuckle. Then he appeared near the fireplace holding a battery-operated lantern, which he placed upon the mantel.

"Well this just gets cozier and cozier." Lucy's voice came from somewhere behind me. "I guess this is a good time to clean up and call it a night." We heard her scraping the cards up and tapping them on the table to straighten them.

The lights came back on and I heard someone giggle in nervous relief. "I'm glad they're back on." My own voice was little more than a whisper. "I didn't look forward to climbing those wet steps in the dark."

"Yeah, me eith—" Reece's sentence was cut off by an ear-splitting bang of thunder and a strobe-like flash of lightning. The wall of windows lit up like a movie screen. I heard several gasps and a few self-conscious murmurs as the lights went off once more.

"Well," the manager chuckled. "That sometimes happens, too." He picked up the lantern and moved through the room. "I've got matching lanterns for everyone. Just give me a moment to dig them out." He walked through the dining room and disappeared into the kitchen where we could hear him opening another door, presumably to a storage room.

He was back in a heartbeat, carrying enough lanterns so that every cabin had one. Lucy took ours and gave each pair of room-mates one to share. "This is almost as good as that awesome little shower we experienced up on the mountain about, what, day four?"

Everyone laughed. The "little shower" to which Lucy referred had washed two of our tents down the mountain and almost drowned us all when the nearby creek overflowed its banks and became—for a few hours—a raging river. I'll never forget scrambling around in the darkness, lightning zapping trees in the distance, stinging rain pelting us as we huddled together for cover under one of the remaining tents.

"Yeah," Eduardo called out. "Remember how we found my tent hung up in a tree the next day, torn to shreds?"

Lucy chuckled again. "Yes, I do. And I recall how everyone pitched in with their tiny little sewing kits and dental floss and stitched it back together—"

"Franken-tent!" I interrupted.

Everyone laughed. "Franken-tent, huh?" Reece asked. "I thought you just had a really old tent." He grinned at Eduardo.

"We never did find mine," Aurelia said. "Thank goodness Lucy let me share hers until we could have another one sent up."

I looked around the room at the faces glowing in the lantern light. With the rain streaming down the wall of glass behind them, and the fireplace crackling off to my left, I felt safe even in the storm. It shocked me to realize I'd somehow connected with these people. They hadn't let me keep them at arm's length after all. In fact, I'd never felt so connected to any group of people in my life—not even in high school.

I finally admitted to myself that I never wanted to leave this place. I never wanted this adventure to end. It felt as if I'd discovered something about myself out there in the forest. Something deep inside that I'd never known existed.

Maybe Reece was right. Maybe I *should* keep working for the SCA if they'll have me. Or at least until I find out if this could be my life's work. I can take some basic classes as I go, part time of course, and before long I'll know if this is what I want.

As soon as the storm hit a lull, we all dashed out, holding our lanterns high as if we were twelve and it was our last Halloween to trick-or-treat the neighborhood.

"I'm going to do it," I whispered to Reece as he escorted me to Cabin #10. "I'm going to do this SCA thing as long as they'll let me. I'm going to take classes and get a degree in forestry or something like botany so I can recognize plants out in the wilderness, and—"

Another rumble of thunder interrupted my little speech, but Reece heard me. He picked me up and spun me around almost dumping us both onto the wet wood of the walkway. "Best news I've heard all day." He gave me a sidearm hug—totally allowable between coworkers—and said, "We'll start making plans at breakfast." Eyes twinkling, he went on, "I'm going back up the mountain in a couple of weeks, but higher this time. We've got brand new trails to check out. A couple of them haven't been tested since they were blazed. Maybe you can get in."

I laughed and allowed myself to hug him back. In the back of my mind lay one niggling doubt—could I really handle six more weeks of working with him every day and every night without getting physical?

We released each other somewhat self-consciously.

"Thanks for walking me up," I said.

He nodded, but didn't linger. After another quick hug, he hurried back down the walk toward his cabin. I was fortunate I got to keep the lantern. Lucy, being the mother hen, got one of her own. As before, she made the rounds, making certain all her little chicks were tucked in before she came up.

I took advantage of her absence, in order to get a quick shower. Then I got myself ready for bed. The storm seemed to be on the way out but the windows still reflected occasional bursts of lightning as it moved away across the water. Every now and then the sound of distant thunder rumbled comfortingly through the darkness. I liked the way the sound grew smaller and smaller as the storm moved on. It reminded me of a song Matt liked—*And the Thunder Rolled*. He used to hum it under his breath while we were waiting for class to begin, or when he was working on a paper.

I pulled the quilt up to my chin and watched the beautiful display in the blue-black window. And the thunder rolled, I thought, as I drifted away.

12

The next morning, I awoke with a scream in my throat. A cold hand had me by the shoulder, shaking me, telling me to get up, a storm was coming. I could still hear the haunting refrain of the old Garth Brooks song in my head.

I opened my eyes. The shaking stopped. No one grasped my shoulder. No one stood near my bed. It must've been a dream. A very vivid dream.

Wondering if I had screamed out loud, a shot a glance at Lucy's bed and found her stretching, looking toward me.

"Are you all right?" I heard concern in her voice. "Has something happened that I need to know about?"

I must have screamed. Plastering a smile on my face, I sat up. "A bad dream, I guess. Someone had their hand on me, shaking me awake."

Lucy kept her cool. "Do you have them often? We've been together for weeks now and I never heard you make a peep—"

I shivered involuntarily. "Actually, that's the first one I've ever had like that. It was so *real*."

She stifled a yawn with one hand. "Do you want to talk about it?"

"I don't think so. It was just more of a feeling, an awful cold hand shaking me, and a feeling of darkness and icy fear."

To my surprise, Lucy laughed. "It must have been the storm over the ocean. Cold dark water, icy fear. It makes sense, doesn't it?" The sound of relief in her voice was nearly tangible.

"That must be it." No way would I tell her the truth that I thought it had something to do with all the talk of Ouija boards the night before. That would make me sound crazy. "I feel like a little girl, full of doubt, afraid of a thunderstorm."

Lucy reached across the gap between our beds and patted my arm. "Are you kidding? That storm was fierce. Besides, I've seen you in action in the darkest part of the forest. You weren't scared then." She seemed to stop and think about what she'd just said. As if the fact that I *hadn't* been afraid in the forest, in a storm, or under any other circumstances made her rethink this episode. "You're sure there's nothing you need to tell me?"

"Not at all," I replied. "Just a silly dream." Now that she'd mentioned it, I had to wonder about it myself. I hadn't suffered anything like this—not in the entire six weeks we'd been gone, not in the two weeks I'd spent with Gran and Gramps, not in a long, long, time—not until I had to decide whether to stay in Cali or go home to Texas. Maybe my subconscious was trying to tell me something, but what?

"Is it time to get up?"

Lucy yawned again. "False dawn." She waved her hand at the window. "I say we should sleep another hour at least."

She didn't have to tell me twice. I snuggled down in my quilt and tried to go back to sleep.

When I woke again, Lucy's bed was empty. She had already gone. I hadn't heard her at all. Soft morning light coated my quilt with the promise of a better day.

Lucy emerged from the bathroom and tossed her damp towel into the basket in the corner. She clapped her hands together. "And how are you this beautiful morning?"

Her optimism infected me. "I'm fine." I shook off the remnants of the dream. "Ready for adventure. What's the plan today? Elephant Seal Beach?"

"Yep! Technically known as Piedras Blancas Rookery—the place that has been instrumental in helping bring the seals back from the brink of extinction. It's situated right near the light-house. Another great tour. And tomorrow I've got our party reserved for a tour of Hearst Castle. It's only four or five miles from San Simeon, where we're going to see the elephant seals. Unfortunately, this isn't the very best time of year for the seals— that would be a few months from now, in the winter—but I think we'll see some of the younger males. They come ashore about now, in order to molt."

"Wow. You know a lot about them. I didn't even know seals molted. I thought that was reserved for birds and snakes."

Lucy grinned. She loved being the teacher. "Actually, many animals have to shed their outer coverings. You see, these seals dive to such incredible depths—the *really* big ones can go down almost a mile—that their bodies divert blood away from their outer layer of skin in order to protect their internal organs from freezing. Because of that, the outer layer begins to die and has to be sloughed off so a new layer can grow."

"Amazing." I couldn't even imagine what it might look like a mile beneath the sea. Of course, being from the deserts of West Texas, I hadn't come in contact with a lot of marine life.

Lucy continued, "I hope we can see some of the big males while we're there. I think you'll see why they're called elephant seals. That long nose is quite strange the first time you see it."

"I hope so, too." I began to gather things to stuff in my daypack, and then I went to the bathroom to brush my teeth.

"Don't rush. There's plenty of time. We've got quite a day ahead of us. And for our last full day together, I thought we would visit the Monterey Bay National Marine Sanctuary. The Coastal Discovery Center is right across the highway from Hearst Castle." She smiled. "Of course, there are a couple hundred miles of beach to explore. It is absolutely outstanding. I wouldn't feel right if I let you desert-dwellers go home without visiting a real marine sanctuary." Her eye held a glint. "Who knows, it may even make you want to stay in our beautiful state. The sanctuary has some excellent educational opportunities, possibly even some internships and fellowships for college kids who want to work and learn."

I spun around, wondering if she'd somehow overheard my conversation with Reece. But she had gone back to her packing. "I uh—I'm sort of at that point already."

Lucy chuckled. "I could see it in your eyes."

"Seriously?"

"I haven't seen too many kids take to this area and this type of work the way you have."

I felt my face grown warm, but it wasn't embarrassment, it was more like a glow that came from having my half-baked ideas validated. "Thanks, Lucy. I have enjoyed it so much. I feel as if I've found my place in the world." I rinsed my mouth and brushed out my fluffy—okay, frizzy—hair. I gave up and decided a braid was my only hope of rescue. The moist salt air had given my mane a whole new definition of volume.

Reece waited for us just outside the dining room. "Diggin' the hair," he said.

I touched my hasty braid and tried to smooth the flyaways that wanted to spring out all over. "Thanks." I ducked my head, embarrassed by the attention.

The rest of the crew soon joined us and we all visited the breakfast buffet before taking our seats. I noticed we all tried to sit in the exact same places as we'd done the day before. Creatures of habit, just like animals.

Lucy went over our itinerary in between bites of biscuit smeared with homemade strawberry jam. Once we were finished, we all piled into the bus, once again taking our customary seats, and headed down the highway toward Elephant Seal Beach.

"I can't wait to see them," I said. "I've never seen any seal up close."

Reece nodded. "They're pretty impressive. The big boys can weigh up to five thousand pounds.

I turned sideways in my seat to look at him, to see if he was teasing me. "No, way. How can they get around on land if they weigh that much? I mean they don't even have legs!"

Barely able to keep the merriment from his voice, Reece replied, "You'll see. They ripple. That's the only way I know how to describe it."

I clamped my mouth shut, in order to keep from making an even bigger fool of myself. "Maybe I'll study them at CSUN. Or maybe my next assignment will be with one of the conservation groups rather than trekking up the mountain."

Now Reece look confused. "You decided to sign up for another spot with SCA?"

I nodded. I hadn't meant to blurt it out that way. "Yes, after discussing it with Lucy, I'm sure it's the right choice. I also intend to take a few classes; find out if it's what I really want to do."

Reece beamed. He couldn't seem to keep a smile from playing across his handsome, open, face. "I have a good idea." He hesitated, waiting for me to take the bait, perhaps.

"Okay, I'll bite. What is it?"

He looked at me closely. "You could share my apartment." He held up three fingers in a Boy Scout salute. "Scouts honor, I'll never make you scrub the baseboards or mow the lawn."

I gasped, and then decided he was joking. I pushed his hand down and waved his words away. "I'll bet you were never a Boy Scout."

"Oh, but I was." He grinned. "Scout's honor."

I couldn't tell if he was serious or not. I gave up trying to figure him out and made up my mind to simply enjoy the ride. While on the bus, we discussed what it might be like to live together. "You'll do all the cooking, while I wax my surfboard and tune my old guitar."

I decided to play along. "Wrong! You will cook *and* clean, while I lie around eating chocolate bon-bons and writing bad poetry."

He shook his head and laughed. "*You* will cook and *serve* while wearing a tiny French maid outfit. I will lie back and demand special attention."

Oh, dear. That was a little too risqué for me. I was only eighteen—and a very innocent eighteen at that. Fortunately, before I could formulate a response (and I had no idea what it would've been), we were there, on another awe-inspiring beach, rough with rocks and littered with lumpy creatures that barely moved.

I could hardly believe my eyes. I had no idea there would be so many. Three or four, maybe five, I thought. But here were dozens of stout bodies lying about, draped over one another like dark malleable chunks of driftwood. I was impressed. They weren't the huge ones Reece had told me about, though. These were smaller, shorter, and scruffier than I'd imagined them to be.

"Yep," Lucy said, "they're molting all right." She pointed to a couple that appeared to have brown strings hanging off their chins.

"They're wonderful." I nearly broke my neck trying to see everywhere at once. "I'm so glad we came." I had definitely fallen in love with everything about the Big Sur area and its wildlife. Of course, the company didn't hurt, either. Reece had turned out to be so laidback, so easy to be with. He never demanded anything, and I never heard him utter an unkind word to anyone. Plus, he wore his sense of adventure like a second skin. And then there were those tanned abs and that unruly blond hair that seemed to beg for smoothing hands. But live with him? Yikes, I could barely wrap my head around the idea.

I forced my mind back to the seals.

Visitors stood and leaned against a three-rail fence bordering a walkway that ran the length of the shallow beach. It seemed the perfect way to watch the antics of the lazy seals. A film crew had just set up. They were filming for the Sanctuary and Discovery Center. We tried to stay out of the way. But at the same time, I wanted to stick around, see how they worked. It fascinated me and made me think perhaps I could work there—or intern as Lucy had said.

Together, Reece and I climbed the hill and waited on the other side of the fence. I sat, content, amidst waving hummocks of sea grass. The salty breeze and the sun on my skin felt like a balm. It completely blew away any trace of doubt left over from the silly dream and the nighttime storm.

After watching a while longer, we finally made our way back to the bus. The lighthouse was closed that day, some sort of repair work going on, so we didn't get to go inside it. I'd really looked forward to seeing the spiral staircase. "Don't worry," Reece whispered, seeing the look on my face when Lucy told us the news. "We'll tour it later, after our next assignment." He grinned at our little half secret.

In the public area near the bus, we set out folding chairs and coolers of cold cuts with fresh avocados and tomatoes and cheese. Our impromptu sandwiches were accompanied by icy cold bottles of water with bags of chips and packs of crackers.

Fresh oranges and containers of dried fruits with M&M's made up dessert.

"That was a feast," I said, wiping my mouth.

Everyone agreed. "Next up," Lucy said, "A little lunch, and then Hearst Castle."

I grinned. Could it get any better than this?

13

After lunch, we repacked the van and headed out.

We could see the historical Hearst mansion gracing the top of Enchanted Hill way before we arrived. "We don't have anything like this back in Live Oak," I mumbled, eliciting laughter from everyone on the bus.

We were allowed to follow a tour bus up to Casa Grande rather than having to park and get onboard with another group of tourists. I know my mouth and eyes were both open wide as we approached the main house with its rolling fields and terraced slopes. "Are those zebras?"

Lucy nodded. "Descendants of William Randolph Hearst's original private zoo." She gazed out the window. "I never tire of coming here. Wait until you see the view from the veranda."

As it turned out, there was way too much to see in one tour. Of course, we were treated to the sprawling Neptune Pool, the elegant theater—which was so cool and inviting I had to force myself not to collapse into a plush seat—and my personal favorite, the indoor pool which had been styled after an ancient Roman bath house.

"I feel like we've stepped back in time," I whispered as we

stood gazing into the tiled pool. "I think I want to stay here, forever."

"Don't worry," Reece whispered back. "We'll come here so often you'll know it like the back of your hand." He winked at me and cleared his throat as Aurelia jostled his elbow to get a closer look at the pool.

Back in the main house, Lucy pointed out all the ceilings that had been brought back from European castles and reassembled here. My neck began to ache from staring upward at all the magnificent artwork.

Too soon, the tour ended and we trooped back to our van for the gorgeous drive back down Highway One.

We stopped at the unparalleled Ragged Point lookout where the black basalt cliffs dove straight down into the deep cerulean blue ocean. The beach appeared deserted.

"Can't we get down there?" Jerenda asked.

"Of course," Lucy grinned. "It's our day trip tomorrow." She told us about the rugged hike beginning at the trailhead sign that warned hikers to attempt the descent only at their own risk.

Everyone loved the idea. "We'll also drive up to Carmel in the opposite direction. Can't let you all go back home without exploring those world famous beaches—not to mention historic Bixby Bridge, and the waterfalls."

Later, back at the Lodge, I began to wish I didn't have to leave at all. Not even for Mom's wedding.

I didn't tell anyone, though. It felt bittersweet, as if I might not be able to get back to the place I'd come to love. For only a split second, my mind wandered toward the idea of going back to Live Oak to see Asa and check on Matt. But I pushed that thought aside. What would seeing Matt accomplish? And what if I got there and saw him and Rose together?

I mentally shook myself. No. There was no real reason to go back to Live Oak except to help Mom pack up the house, and she'd already said Joe's company was going to take care of that.

In the dining room, we all dug in to a seafood dinner. I wasn't the only one who seemed down in the dumps. Jerenda and Stephen seemed especially morose.

Lucy must've been used to the end of assignment blues, she kept up a running patter about all the things we'd done and all the things we would still do tomorrow.

After dinner, we played a few hands of gin rummy, and then we all retired to our cabins to rest up for the last day's adventures.

THE NEXT MORNING, we breakfasted at the Ragged Inn and Resort before starting off on our hike down the bluff. We each carried our own water and snacks for later, when we accessed the beach. I'd slept well the night before, possibly because Lucy stayed in the cabin the entire time, and I didn't have any dreams at all.

In the parking area, we piled into the van in a fog so thick it felt like cotton batting, but by the time we'd driven the few miles back to Ragged Point; it had begun to burn off.

We had no problems hiking down the bluff to the pristine beach where we spent the entire day exploring the cove, the rocky bluffs, and the tide pools.

We ate our snacks then hiked back up the trail to the van and made our way back to Highway One. There seemed no end to the gorgeous turnarounds and lookouts. "We can't see everything before you guys go home," Lucy said. "But we'll cram as much in as we possibly can."

So saying, we drove on past Lucia Lodge to Bixby Bridge and McWay Waterfall. The views were stunning, but the best part came when we had to walk through the short tunnel beneath the highway to access the waterfall pouring down onto the beach. With Reece leading the way, we scurried through the shadows into the sun.

The falls were completely worth it. One of only two waterfalls that empty into the ocean in the U.S., the sound of the water hitting the beach sand from eighty feet above will stay with me forever, filed away in that same memory file as the smells, sights, and sounds from all the other beaches we'd visited so far.

No doubt about it, California had completely captured my heart.

The remainder of the week flew by and before I knew it, we were all at LAX to catch our flights home except for the locals, Lucy, Reece, and Eduardo.

Stephen, Jerenda, and I were catching flights to Vegas. Theirs were both connecting flights with one travelling to Indianapolis, and the other going on to North Carolina, while my flight was my actual destination. Tonight I would be in Las Vegas with my mom and Joe.

I wasn't sorry when my seat didn't turn out to be near Jerenda's or Stephen's. They'd gotten adjoining seats, but mine was much farther back, near the window. I knew they shared a special connection. I didn't want to intrude upon that seeing as how this would be their last couple of hours together.

Besides, I wanted time alone to reminisce about the way Reece had whispered into my ear after breakfast.

His crazy hair had tickled my cheek when he leaned over, grasped my hand, and said, "Don't forget about me. I meant every word I said."

Lucy came bounding up behind us before I could respond. We were on such a tight schedule I never had a chance to track him down and ask him exactly which words he'd meant. Had he meant the part about soulmates, or the part about sharing an apartment, or the words about spending our lives together—or all of the above?

I'd tried to catch his eye in the van, but the emotional energy of the group was so high it was pretty much impossible.

Outside the airport, Reece helped us all with our backpacks —our only luggage—and then he simply looked at me and said, "I look forward to your return." Due to the fact we were parked in a loading and unloading zone, he'd kept our hug brief and businesslike. In fact, we all hugged, a few of us blubbered, and everyone promised to write and keep in touch. Aurelia, like me, had also been entertaining the idea of doing more work for the SCA, although she'd discovered another crew in West Virginia much closer to her home.

Lucy walked us in to our respective gates—had to make sure all her little chicks were in their proper places—while Reece went to park the van in the short-term parking area. It felt strange watching him drive away. As if I might never see him again.

On the one hand, I was excited to be on my way to see my mom, I hadn't realized how much I would miss her, but on the other hand, I wished I didn't have to leave at all.

I settled down in my window seat with a magazine I'd picked up at the gift store, but I couldn't concentrate. Too much had happened. I stared out the window as we took off, then I pulled down the shade, suddenly wanting sleep and nothing but sleep.

14

I stepped off the plane in Vegas and there stood Mom and Joe looking like the happiest couple in the world. They appeared tanned and rested.

"Gabi!" Even Mom's voice sounded younger.

I allowed her to envelop me in a hug. "Mommy!"

Joe stepped up and wrapped his arms around the both of us. "Girls!" he bellowed.

We all laughed and hugged some more. "You guys look fantastic."

Mom held me at arm's length and examined me critically. "Us?" She glanced at Joe. "Honey, look at this girl. She has become a lean, mean, hiking machine."

I laughed self-consciously. "Mo-o-m. Seriously—"

She pulled me to her again. "I missed you so much!" She planted a loud smacking kiss on my cheek and linked her arm through mine. "Let's go find a place to for lunch."

"Sounds good. I'm starved!"

Mom patted my tummy. "I can see why. You look like you've lost ten pounds."

I glanced down at myself. "Maybe I have. There aren't any

scales where I've been."

She laughed and squeezed me again.

The concourse was crowded with people and we were all headed toward baggage claim. It had been awhile since I'd been around so many people at one time. It was really quite disconcerting. On top of that, I hadn't worn any makeup or done anything to my hair—other than a quick ponytail or braid to keep it off my neck while I worked—in three months.

I actually felt like a different person. And in this overdressed, bejeweled crowd, I stuck out like the reputed sore thumb. Even my mom looked like someone who had just stepped off a cruise ship at a tropical port of call. Of course, that's basically what they'd been doing for the past few weeks.

She said Joe actually proposed (for the umpteenth time), on a beach in St. Thomas. I'm surprised they didn't just get married there, but Mom said she'd still harbored some doubts and that it wasn't until they got back home and my room was still empty that she decided it was time to make her own life after all.

As the luggage came around, I spied my filthy backpack—the big one that weighed almost forty pounds—and grabbed it up. I slung it off the conveyor but Joe was quick. He took it from me with a grin.

"Allow me." He winked and hoisted it easily.

I smiled and gave in. If I had to have a step-dad, I couldn't think of a better candidate than Joe.

We walked through the airport gawking at all the sights. Slot machines blinked and dinged and pinged. After the silence of the forest and the grandeur of Big Sur, the Vegas atmosphere seemed garish and overwhelming.

We made our way to the parking area where the taxis waited.

"So, what time is the wedding?"

Mom clasped my hand even tighter. "Day after tomorrow, eight p.m. We've reserved the Pink Cadillac wedding chapel with one of the Elvis impersonators officiating and singing, too. You are our maid-of-honor, ring bearer, and witness all rolled into one."

"I can't wait." I smiled to show I really meant it. "Too bad Gerry couldn't make it." Gerry was Joe's only son. A few years older than me, he had been in the Army since he'd graduated from high school. "Is he still stationed in Germany?"

Mom nodded. "We thought about trying to time it to his leave but he convinced us that waiting would be like tempting Fate. He said there was a chance he might be deployed soon, so it would ease his mind if we went ahead with it and just sent him pictures later."

Joe raised one eyebrow. "He did make us promise to have a huge celebration whenever he *does* get to come home—and we forced ourselves to agree." He laughed and snagged Mom for a quick smooch.

Mom giggled and shoved him away.

He opened our taxicab doors and waited until we were seated before he went around and got in the other side. I appreciated the way he treated Mom—and me—as if we were special. That's what I want, I thought. Someone who will always make me feel special.

My mind went straight back to the night Matt and I sat on the stone picnic table outside the high school gym. He had made me feel very special. All night long I'd been the center of his attention. In fact, he'd made me feel special all that year with his teasing and flirting. Maybe that's why I had such trouble letting go of him now.

I yanked my mind away from those memories and stared out at the Vegas strip. "Where are we staying?"

Mom turned around in her seat, a gleam in her eye. "A brand new place, just built last year... didn't I tell you?"

I knew she had, but for some reason, I couldn't remember

the name. "Yes, you did, it just didn't stick with me for some reason. What is it again?"

"The Bellagio!"

I think she thought I would be impressed, but I knew nothing about Las Vegas other than it was a gambler's mecca.

"It's gorgeous," she continued. "Wait until you see it. We've booked adjoining fountain view rooms that are so luxurious you will never want to leave. And they also look out at the Eiffel Tower."

Mom's enthusiasm was so contagious I began to look forward to being pampered for a change. After sleeping on the ground, or in a damp cabin for the past two and a half months, I couldn't wait to sleep in a fancy room.

"Wait until you see the lobby. It is unbelievable."

She wasn't kidding. When we drove up to the hotel, the illuminated fountains were dancing. It was truly amazing. Beautiful. The taxi driver commented that even he never got tired of looking at them.

The driver had also caught a touch of Mom's enthusiasm. As he unloaded my backpack from the trunk, he kept up a steady stream of patter. "And wait until you see the Chihuly ceiling in the lobby." He shouldered my pack. "I'll take this inside for you. Just so I can look at it again." He grinned.

I had no idea what the man was talking about, but we didn't get ten steps before a porter came and relieved him of my filthy pack.

I might have been embarrassed if I hadn't felt so protective of the thing. It had been with me through thick and thin the past few weeks. It had held my food, my water, my clothing, even my tent. It was my home away from home.

To his credit, the porter didn't seem the least bit put off by it, even though I could smell the delicious smoky odor as soon as it had been liberated from the taxi's trunk.

But that was the last time I thought of my pack because that's when my eye was drawn upward to the amazing sea of glass flowers floating *in* the ceiling.

Every color imaginable seemed to be represented in the huge blown glass blossoms. I stood transfixed, staring upward, all conversation forgotten, trying my best to decide if the blown glass objects were flowers or more nearly jellyfish.

Once inside, the sounds of the strip disappeared and we were left with lights, colors, and greenery. Everywhere we looked there were plants and trees and flowers. Could this really be the desert? I couldn't help wondering where all the water came from. Most people probably didn't even think about it, but I'd just spent the summer in the forest learning about how to protect and conserve natural resources, and in here it appeared they went out of their way to use up every last drop of water and energy allotted to them for the next one hundred years.

We took the elevator up to the seventeenth floor. What a change from the past few months. At first I thought I might be ill. But as we rose higher and higher all my doubts fell away like the floors below us. The further up we went, the more fairytale it seemed.

When we got to our rooms the opulence made me forget all my cares. As soon as I unlocked my door (feeling oh so grown up having my very own key) my eye immediately took in the floor-to-ceiling windows where the half-sized Eiffel Tower replica was framed as surely as if we were on the Champ de Mars in Paris.

"Isn't it wonderful?"

I hadn't realized Mom had come in behind me.

"It's surreal." I felt like a kid at the circus. "Is it finished?"

"Almost. We would've made reservations at the Paris, but the grand opening isn't until September. I've heard the view from the Eiffel Tower Restaurant will be even better than this."

I turned and hugged Mom again. "I thought I would hate

this place, but it's so outlandish I'm sort of in awe."

Mom hugged me back. "I know exactly how you feel. I wasn't sure this was for me, either, but Joe convinced me. Now I'm glad he did. And I can't wait to help you choose a college in or near Houston—big or small, it doesn't matter—I know there will be something for you to love."

I turned from the window and busied my hands with my backpack. "I appreciate the offer, and it sounds like something I *would* love, but I've already got plans to go on another SCA job. It will be a short one—only a few weeks, to check out some new trails on the mountain—and after that, I'm hoping to take a couple of midwinter classes at the California State University at Northridge."

Mom's face registered her shock.

I hadn't meant to spill my news all in one breath that way, but that's me. Open mouth, insert foot. I suppose that's why Mom felt it was a good time to tell me what she'd learned.

"Matt finally got out of the hospital," she said, her voice neutral. "But unfortunately, his brain trauma was such that he's been sent to a rehabilitation hospital in Fort Worth."

I plopped heavily onto the edge of my bed. What an awful piece of information. What did it mean, exactly? "Brain damaged?"

Mom laid her hand on my shoulder. "Sorry to be blunt, but yeah. Pretty severe I think. His mom is one of our clients—I'm not her hygienist, Kammi takes care of her—but of course she told everyone all about it."

I grasped her fingers. "How bad is it? The damage?"

"About as bad as can be."

All my pent-up breath whooshed out of my chest. "That's awful." I remembered how he'd made football look so simple. Such an athlete. And how he'd casually mentioned he'd been promised a full ride to play for Texas Tech.

"I didn't want to tell you that in a letter." She fiddled with a strand of my ponytail. "I thought it might be too upsetting."

"Thanks, Mom." It did upset me, but maybe not in the way she thought. Instead of making me sad, the news made me feel shallow, empty.

To me, Matt would always be the jock who'd held me so strong while we danced at prom, and later, outside on the picnic tables. Since I'd never been able to see him in the hospital, I really had no concept of his injuries. It was what she said next that floored me, left me reeling.

"There's one more thing I think you should know..." She sat beside me, her voice falling into a register that could only be considered grave.

I waited. What could be so terrible? Oh my God, something has happened to Asa. "What is it, Mom? Is it Asa? What happened?" I steeled myself for the worst.

She looped her arm around my waist. "No, no, no. It isn't Asa. I haven't seen him since you left."

"What then?" My patience had run out.

"That girl," she hesitated. "The one outside the hospital that day?"

My mind rushed back to that awful day. "You mean Rose, Matt's cousin? The one who practically accosted me outside on the bench?"

"Yes. That's the one."

"Okay? What about her?" Mom was the dental assistant and yet I felt like I was pulling teeth.

"She's missing."

"Missing?" I spun to face Mom on the edge of the bed. "What do you mean?"

Mom shrugged. "I mean she went missing. Left home one night and didn't return."

My mind spun with possibilities. "How did you find out—"

"Oh, it was all the news when Joe and I set sail on our cruise." She stood and walked across to the windows. "When we got home, she still hadn't been found. The theory is that she took off with one of her boyfriends. It seems she had more than one."

I thought of her hand on her middle, and how she insisted she was carrying Matt's baby. "Her family must be devastated." I didn't know them, but I could imagine how my mom would feel if I disappeared without warning. "Do you know exactly when she went missing? I mean, was it before Matt got transferred or afterward?" I hoped it was after, that would mean she made it home from the pond. "Maybe she went to Fort Worth to be near him."

That seemed to give Mom a moment's pause. "No," she said. "The news said she disappeared while he was still in a coma there in our hospital. In fact, I think it was the day before you left, or a couple of days before, maybe."

My heart sank. "That's a long time to be missing." The sound of a splash crossed my mind. "Surely she just went to Fort Worth... or something."

"One of her boyfriends moved to Montana," Mom muttered. "Maybe she went with him. I'm not sure if they ever located him to find out."

I recalled a purple Trans Am and a dark, sinewy senior. Could Rose be with him? Did Matt's accident spur her to seek another place to live?

Thrumk.

The sound of a car fender hitting a body.

Splash.

The sound of something hitting the surface of the pond.

Did she run away with a boy to avoid dealing with her condition?

Or could it be something much, much worse?

15

That night we ordered room service; club sandwiches and iced tea, with a beer for Joe, and sat around the small table in their suite, catching up. Mom noticed my eyelids trying to close on their own, so after supper and a quick stroll down the circus-like strip, we were all ready to hit the sack.

I took a shower, washed my hair, and then blew it dry with the dryer attached to the bathroom wall. It was the first time I had used a hair dryer since I'd left home.

When I finally climbed in between the blessedly soft sheets —Egyptian cotton, according to the hotel information book on the desktop—I picked up the remote control and flipped on the TV, something else I hadn't done since leaving home almost three months earlier. Funny, I hadn't even missed it.

But right now, I wanted some company no matter how artificial. I found VH1 and watched music videos until I fell asleep. My dreams were as vivid and colorful as the lights outside and they stayed as maddeningly just out of my realm of understanding as the dancing waters of the fountains.

Sometime, in the middle of the night, I awoke to Cher singing

"Do you believe in life after love?"

I immediately recognized her song, "Believe," and it soothed me, but also kept me awake. When Sarah McLachlan began singing "I Will Remember You," the song evoked such a feeling of sadness and despair that I pressed the OFF button on the remote in self-defense.

Lying there, dozing, wishing I'd never heard that last heart-breaking song, I began to think to myself about how much I'd grown. The SCA had definitely changed me. It seemed as if I now felt everything more deeply, more profoundly. As if being part of nature so long had given me an insight I'd never had before.

Drifting back to sleep, I reveled in the feel of the amazingly comfortable bed. But I also missed the smell of campfire smoke and the sounds of the nighttime forest, the wind soughing through the pines, the crickets chirping in the twilight, and the funny little cracklings of brush and dry leaves as small creatures scurried about, looking for food.

After I turned off the TV, the low hum of the AC—which I'd made sure to turn down before climbing into bed, since I wasn't used to the artificial coolness anymore (like television, it was amazing how quickly I had adapted to life without it)—was comforting. I felt at peace, glad Mom and Joe had brought me out after all.

The ringing-purr of the bedside phone interrupted my sleep sometime before dawn. I came awake slowly, wondering for a moment where I was, and why it had grown so cold.

After turning off the TV, the room had been black-velvet dark, not even a nightlight to push back the gloom, but the bedside phone had a small amber light that pulsed in time to each ring. It gave me a place to focus my attention while my mind tried to understand my surroundings. The air had grown so cold I had drawn my legs up and wrapped myself in the blanket like a burrito. I must have mistakenly turned the AC to colder instead of warmer before retiring.

I stuck one arm out of my blankets and dragged the ringing phone close enough to the bed so I could grab it. When I finally wrestled the receiver to my ear, I fully expected Mom to be on the other end—telling me something about the upcoming ceremony—but when I mumbled hello, it wasn't Mom's voice on the other end. It was nothing but the sound of wind echoing through the speaker into my head. Did my missing the sound of the wind sighing though the pines somehow cause the forest to call me? As if in answer, a cricket—far away and very small— chirped three times and fell silent.

I pressed the handset into the side of my head and shivered.

The line went dead. I dropped the receiver to the bed and struggled my way out of the blankets, fumbling for my glasses on the end table. The chill air felt as damp as the inside of a walk-in freezer.

From the bathroom came the sudden sound of the faucet gushing water into the shell-shaped sink.

I pushed the on-off button at the base of the lamp.

Nothing happened.

I felt around for the remote control. The TV would give me light if I could put my fingers on the silly thing, but it must have fallen to the floor during my struggle to free my legs from the blankets.

Keeping one hand on the bed as a guide, I stumbled around until I made it to the windows. In the bathroom, the water cut off as suddenly as it had come on.

I fluttered the drapes searching for the pull cord, but this being the Bellagio, the drapes were operated by remote control just like the TV. There was also a control panel on the wall beside them, though, and when my fingers connected, I smashed the top button with my thumb and the drapes slid apart soundlessly, flooding the entire room with the soft orange light of the Eiffel Tower across the way.

Shadows leapt into corners and I dashed across the thick carpet to flip on the overhead light. The room was instantly illuminated, but it was so cold and damp I could actually see my breath.

The bathroom light came on.

I knew it had been off only a split-second earlier. I thought of calling out for Mom and Joe—there was only that connecting door between us—but now that the lights were on, I began to feel foolish.

Before I could chicken out, I forced myself toward the open door and stood just outside, holding my freezing breath, listening for the sound of the faucet or of someone breathing or moving around.

I heard nothing but the sound of my own pounding heart.

My imagination kept bringing up images of a shadowy form standing just inside the bathroom door—mirroring me standing just outside the door—but I pushed those frightening images away. I hadn't spent the last six weeks busting trail in the national forest without growing a little bit of backbone. At least that's what I told myself.

I sucked in a breath and prepared to stick my head inside the small room, ready for whatever I was about to see—

The lights went out and the drapes swished closed across the windows.

I screamed. My courage disappeared. The darkness felt even deeper than before, the already freezing temperature dropping toward glacial. An icy hand gripped the back of my neck.

On instinct, I turned to run and whammed right into the

corner of the desk chair—a heavy monster I hadn't even noticed before. Down I went like a dead tree in a high wind.

"Gabrielle! What is it?" Mom flung open the door between our rooms and weak light from her side filtered through into mine.

For a moment, I could see icicles hanging from the door-jamb. "Mom?" I sat up, holding my shin where a bluish bruise had begun to swell.

She rushed to my side. "Why is it so cold in here? It's down-right frigid." She glanced back at the doorway, now filled with the rumpled form of Joe tying a hotel bathrobe across his plaid boxers. "Check the AC, will you, hon?"

Joe ambled over to the thermostat on the wall as Mom helped me up off the floor. I sat on the edge of the bed and nursed my wounded leg and my wounded pride.

"I thought I heard someone in the bathroom," I blurted. "Then the lights went out and I banged into the chair." I swiped at my drippy nose with the back of my hand.

"Set on 74," Joe said. "It shouldn't be this cold, unless it has a major malfunction. I'll call the desk." He picked up the phone that had started this whole thing and held the receiver to his ear.

I saw him frown and push a couple of buttons. "Hmm. I can't get a dial tone—oh wait, there it is." Just as he was about to dial the hotel operator, the AC came on yet again.

"What the—?" Mom jumped up, strode over to the wall, and tapped the round thermostat with her fingernail. "Hah! No wonder." She turned to us with a look of triumph. "When I tapped it, the needle jumped. It isn't set on 74, it's set on 47." She made an adjustment on the dial. "There, let's give it a few minutes and see if that helps."

Sure enough, the AC kicked off.

"I think it was stuck," she said. "But I can't imagine the lights going off, too. Unless there's an electrical short in here somewhere."

I nodded. That would explain everything. "Let me just check the bathroom," I said. "I need a cold wash cloth for this bruise." I hobbled over and stepped through the door before Mom could protest. I had to see for myself that no one was in there.

Everything appeared exactly as it should have except for the small puddle of water around the drain in the sink. But that could've been left over from brushing my teeth five hours earlier, right?

I glanced down at it. The puddle of water looked as green as pond scum. I turned on the faucet and grabbed a snowy white washcloth to hold under the flow. The water ran clear and cold. The brackish little puddle disappeared, and I stepped back into the bedroom and sat on the edge of the bed, holding the wet cloth to my shin.

I glanced at Mom. "Sorry I yelled." The room already felt much warmer.

"Were you having a bad dream?"

"No." I thought back to the strange phone call. "At least I don't think so, why?"

Mom looked at me as if I'd spat a spider out onto the bed. "Well, honey, that wasn't what I'd call a falling-over-a-chair yell." She looked to Joe for confirmation, but he looked away, covering his mouth with one hand as a giant yawn overtook him.

"What do you mean?" I wasn't sure I wanted to hear her reply, but of course I had to know.

"What I heard was a bloodcurdling scream. The same kind of scream you let out at the end of the movie, *Carrie*, when that hand came up through the grave and grabbed that girl by the ankle."

I laughed uncomfortably. That was not an image I wanted to take back to bed with me.

Mom leaned over and hugged me fiercely. "I'm going to stay in here with you—"

"Oh God, no. Mom. I'm not ten years old. I'm a grown woman, I've been—"

Mom patted me on the shoulder. "I know, I know, you've been camping out in the deep dark forest for weeks now without a hitch, but hey." She took me by the chin and forced me to look into her eyes. "I know you. And I know what I heard. Something really scared you."

I sighed. And laughed. "Okay, you win. Come and sleep with me. Or better yet, I'll come in there and sleep between the two of you like a little kid, how will that be?"

Joe snorted and coughed, obviously stifling a laugh. "Or we could just leave the connecting door open."

Mom and I glanced at each other and burst into self-conscious laughter. "That's the reason I'm marrying him." She tapped the side of her head and nodded sagely. "Common sense."

In spite of everything, I grinned. It was good to be loved.

WE ONLY HAD three days in Vegas before the two of them intended to go on to Houston to start the house hunt. They insisted they'd already had their honeymoon—the Caribbean cruise—but still, I couldn't believe things were changing so quickly. We all went back to bed, with the connecting door open, and a couple of hours later Mom woke me and we left Joe sleeping in their lush suite while the two of us made plans to explore the Vegas version of Rodeo Drive in search of a wedding dress.

I felt a terrible sense of trepidation when I made my way to the bathroom that morning, but everything appeared normal.

Not a drop of water where it shouldn't be nor a shadow that didn't belong.

Just a dream. Another bad, vivid, dream. Guilt?

I thought of all the stories I'd read over the years in which the protagonist had succumbed to imagined terrors due to nothing more than unrelenting feelings of guilt. Poe's *Tell-Tale Heart* topped the list.

I shuddered and vowed to put the past behind me and get on with my life, or rather, my mom and Joe's life.

AFTER WE ATE a quick breakfast from the complimentary pastry and coffee bar downstairs, we were off to shop.

We found a bridal store immediately. Mom, being the practical sort, wanted something she could wear again sometime. "It's not like I'm a girl in a fairy tale," she said. "Who knows, I might want to wear it to *your* wedding someday. Or to my first grandchild's christening." She winked to let me know she was kidding.

I rolled my eyes, recalling the elaborate weddings I staged with my friends when we were children. We must have wasted a million rolls of toilet paper making our veils and trains.

In the very first store—The Wedding Boutique—we found a lovely rose-colored chiffon dress that floated gently around Mom's knees. It sounds old-fashioned but to give it a modern touch, the back of it consisted of two wide, filmy straps that crisscrossed from her shoulders to her waist. The rose color complimented her dark hair and tanned skin. It made her look even younger than when they'd met me at the airport.

"It's perfect," she said. "But you have to have one, too."

I hadn't thought about that.

Her mouth turned down, ever so slightly. "You don't want to wear your hiking shorts, do you?"

I imagined the wedding picture with Mom in her pretty dress; Joe in his rented Elvis tux (which was included in the price of the wedding), and me in my one pair of decent shorts.

"Yeah, I guess not." I laughed at the expression of relief that flitted across her face. "But nothing too fancy."

Mom waved her hand at me. "Of course not. I wouldn't want to be upstaged by my own gorgeous daughter." She smiled and gave me a brief hug before turning to the row and rows of bridesmaid's dresses.

I thought back to my prom gown. After I'd made my decision to go to my grandparents' house, and then on to SCA, I'd pulled it down off the door—none too gently—and stuffed it in the back of my closet. It would have made the perfect bridesmaid dress. But that was just one more thing about that night that was forever tainted. When I thought that, a tiny voice in the back of my mind scolded me. You're worried about a dress, the voice whispered, when your prom date almost lost his life and his cousin is missing? How selfish can one girl be?

Properly chastised by my own conscience, I began to dig through the racks in earnest. "Here's one that sort of matches yours." I held up a shimmery rose and gold mini dress that was both young and somewhat classy.

"Nice!" Mom said. "Come on, we'll try them on together."

We hurried to the dressing room accompanied by a bored looking clerk. "Let me know if you ladies need anything."

We assured her we would, and then we went into separate cubicles and tried on our frocks. We both appeared in front of the large outer mirrors at the same instant.

"Looks beautiful," I said.

"Yours is perfect," Mom replied. "Can it really be that easy?"

I shrugged. "I guess we're just good that way."

"Look at your legs!" Mom bent over to examine all my scrapes and bruises. "What on earth happened?"

"You already know about this one." I indicated the one from the desk chair the night before, and then touched a long scrape. "And this one was from an incident on the hike at Jade Beach. The others are just from hiking and camping for two months, that's all." I smiled to let her know I wasn't being sarcastic. "And Mom?"

She looked up. "I absolutely love it. I really think I've found my calling." I smiled self-consciously.

"Oh, honey. Are you serious?" She took my hand and led me to one of the plush chairs placed here and there along the wall.

I nodded. Once I'd said it, I realized it sounded kind of... pompous. I rushed to explain. "I absolutely love being out in the forest, and hiking the Big Sur beaches." I stopped to think about what I'd just said. "I guess I really love California."

Mom gasped.

"I'm a traitor, huh?"

"Well, I've heard you can take the gal out of Texas, but you can't take Texas out of the gal. You may get homesick, eventually." She smiled. "But I'm delighted you've found something you're passionate about."

I didn't mention anything about Reece's offer to share his apartment. In the back of my mind, I wanted to keep that to myself for a while. At least until I figured out if he was the reason I liked California so much.

Mom stood. "Let's go have lunch, just the two of us. Let Joe rest, or play slots, or whatever. We'll have a catch-up day. I want to hear all about your new passion." She brushed my wild hair back and planted a kiss on my forehead. "My girl. All grown up." She let out a loud sigh and disappeared behind her curtain.

A feeling of pure happiness enveloped me. It felt so good to have my feelings validated. I am a grown up. I *can* make my own decisions. Reece's face appeared in my mind like a beacon calling me back to California.

16

By the time we paid and made our way back to the hotel, we were both hungry. The Café Bellagio—near the amazing conservatory with its whimsical exhibit of a giant tree house surrounded by all the nuances of perfect childhood pastimes—beckoned us and we agreed to splurge. I started to feel better.

Even in the daytime, the gorgeous lobby blinded like Christmas and New Year's all rolled into one. In the café, the hostess led us to a booth in the back and we both ordered salads. Caesar for me, Cobb for Mom; apparently, we were both thinking of our form-fitting dresses.

The cool, comforting atmosphere provided a welcome respite from the garish hustle and bustle of the outdoors. Mom settled her napkin across her lap. "Now, tell me about your trip, from day one. And the boy."

I almost choked on my swallow of water. "What boy?"

All sweetness and light, Mom paused to sip her own water.

"Mo-o-m. What are you talking about?"

She laughed knowingly. "When I talked to you on the phone,

you briefly mentioned someone named Reece who had recently joined the team."

My mind reeled. I'd told Mom about Reece? How could I not remember that? I scrolled back through my recollection of our recent phone conversation. Maybe I had. He'd been waiting for me out on the deck, maybe I'd been in such a hurry to hang up I'd mentioned his name in passing.

Jeez. I must be losing it. Who has memory problems at my age?

"He's a super nice guy," I said. "He's going to help me get another assignment with SCA and then we're going to look at the course catalog for CSUN. He, uh, he goes there, too. Getting his Master's already." I wanted to bite my tongue. Saying it like that, altogether, made it sound as if he was the only reason I wanted to attend the school. But that wasn't exactly true. I'd already been thinking of it, after talking to Eduardo and a couple of the other locals. I didn't want my mom thinking I made all my decisions based on which boy was in my life at the time—like the way I'd left home because of Matt.

Just then, someone knocked a glass off a table. An exclamation followed the crash just loud enough to bring me back to the present.

"Tell me more," Mom said. "Where will you live, do I need to come out and help you hunt for an apartment or fix up a dorm room?" Her voice took on that let's-start-planning tone. Give my mom a chance and she would organize you right into oblivion.

I laughed. "Not yet. I'll be living in a tent again, at least for a few weeks. Then we'll see." I hoped that would be enough to dissuade her for now. I didn't know if I would take Reece up on his generous offer of sharing an apartment or not. The only thing I knew for certain was that I needed to get to know him a lot better before I committed to anything that drastic.

Wow. That did sound like a grown up.

I sipped my water and began to regale my mom with the funny tale about the storm that had caused the creation of Franken-tent. Eventually we got around to discussing the possibility of my coming to Houston with them to hunt for their new place.

"We're thinking of renting a townhouse until we decide whether we want to live in the city—a big if for me—or in one of the suburbs like Katy or Sugar Land." Mom reached across the table and laid her hand on top of mine. "I hope you'll come with us." Her voice went soft. "It will only be for a few days, until you start your next assignment in California." She grinned when she said it, as if sampling the taste of the words. "Besides needing your input, we both want you to pick out your own room for the times you *do* come home to visit."

I turned my hand up and clasped her fingers with my own. "I'd love to, Mom. I think it will be a lot of fun."

So that settled it. I would go to Houston with them. Just for a week or so, to house hunt. We weren't going back to Live Oak at all. Mom had packed up the personal items. We'd let the moving company handle the rest.

I took another sip of water. "Joe's company must really want him in Houston."

Mom blushed. "They do. He's opening his own branch, you know. He's a very good catch in the field of accounting as well as in marriage."

I laughed. It thrilled me to see my mom so happy.

"So," I said, to fill the conversation gap. "Have you seen Asa about town lately?"

Mom remained quiet for a moment. "You know, we went on the cruise about a month ago. I'm trying to recall if I saw him at all after you left." She clamped her lips together as if to keep something in.

"What? What were you about to say?" I figured it had to be

something about graduation. We had been carefully skirting that topic it seemed.

"A couple of weeks after the graduation ceremony, your diploma came in the mail." She wouldn't look at me.

A lump the size of a golf ball formed in my throat. I had hurt my mom by not walking across the stage. I'd never thought of that. After everything she had done to make certain I graduated —putting her own life on hold to give me everything a two-parent household would have provided—I'd thought nothing of running off at the last minute and depriving her of the joy of seeing me receive it. What a horrible daughter I am. And all of her friends and coworkers were probably talking about it at work the whole time. Such a small town.

"Oh, Mom. I'm so stupid, and so selfish." I covered my mouth with my hand. "I never even thought about how it would affect you not getting to go to the ceremony. I feel terrible."

My mom looked up, her eyes shiny.

"And you never even said a word."

She dabbed at her cheeks with the corner of her napkin. "Honey, I'll admit, it was a disappointment. That's why Joe took me on the cruise, to cheer me up. But you've never disappointed me before. You were always the perfect child—I knew it must've been something terrible to drive you away like that. And I knew it had to be connected to Matt, somehow—"

"Yeah," I interrupted. "Definitely connected to Matt. But probably not the way you think." I hesitated, and then plunged ahead before the window of opportunity closed. I told her about how special he'd made me feel, how I'd had a crush on him all year, and then before I could spill the beans about Rose, she incorrectly read between the lines.

"And then he had the wreck. No wonder you were devastated." She got up from her side of the booth and slid in beside me, arm around my shoulders. "I assumed that's why you left."

"It's still so hard to believe," I spluttered. "First Matt in a coma, now Rose missing? Where's Asa, I wonder why he didn't write me?"

The waiter brought our food. Condensation ringed the table around the bases of our iced tea glasses, and the other patrons went on with their babbling lives all around us.

I picked at my salad, but couldn't seem to start eating.

Mom returned to her side of the table. "What is it, honey? I mean, I know the news isn't great, but there seems to be something more." She waited for my acknowledgement.

I took a deep breath and slid my tea glass back and forth, and then I told her what Matt had said, that I was the one, that he couldn't wait until we were at Tech together, and that he was certain he had fallen in love with me. I told her all that and then I took another drink of my iced tea. Our salads both sat there, wilting.

Confusion clouded her face. "I didn't realize it was that serious." She toyed with her fork, and then plunged ahead. "But... why didn't you stay? Stick by him while he was in the hospital?"

So I told her the rest. I blurted out exactly how Rose had acted at prom and then I relayed the bombshell she'd dropped on me outside the hospital that day.

Mom's face turned as pasty white as our paper napkins.

Now it was her turn to grasp her tea glass in a death grip.

"I remember that day," she said at last. "You were sick to your stomach. I had to drive home. That's when she said it, huh? On the bench beside you?"

I nodded.

"Oh, my God. No wonder you took off. I probably would have done the same thing. And you never even got a chance to see Matt before you left—"

"No, I wasn't family. They wouldn't let me in at all. And then Rose made it sound like he was going to be fine, and that they were going to run off together and live happily ever after."

Mom's mouth became a thin hard line. "That horrid little bitch." She didn't curse often.

For one nanosecond, I debated telling her all of the story. How Rose had tricked me into going out to South Pond and then ran in front of me when I tried to leave. How Asa had sent me home so he could take care of her after I'd hit her with the car; how he hadn't been able to locate her. And now she's missing?

I needed to talk to Asa. I had to talk to him, *soon*.

My hand went to my throat, to the necklace Matt had draped over my head in that other lifetime. I pulled the old nickel out of my shirt. It felt as warm as the night he'd put it there. Once again, I thought of him lying still as stone, trapped in some world between life and death, on the verge, on the edge.

My world shifted to one side as a rogue wave of emotion surfaced beneath me. I rubbed the nickel between my thumb and forefinger subconsciously trying to conjure the past like a genie from a lamp. The coin grew warmer and warmer, but it didn't bring back the past. Of course not. Nothing could.

17

All the way back to the room, I turned the news over and over in my mind. Matt, in a Fort Worth hospital, Rose, missing. Probably missing since the night I'd hit her with my car.

My stomach turned over and over just like the thoughts in my head. Was anyone looking for Rose? If she was considered missing they had to be. Right?

The stroll back through the Conservatory was no less impressive than before. But this time, nothing could capture my interest. Mom remained quiet.

I couldn't wait to get up to my room and phone Asa. Find out exactly what happened, and when. Find out what became of Rose. His complete silence all summer suddenly seemed ominous, a black cloud shot through with lightning.

"I'm sorry," I told Mom. "It seems I just keep ruining your big days. This was supposed to be such fun."

She hugged me, a quick sidearm hug, which reminded me of Reece (who now seemed to exist on another planet), and said, "None of this is your fault." She gave me a tiny smile. "You were right to go."

"Well, that's enough of all that. Now it's time to cheer up and get on with it. We're getting married tomorrow and that's all there is to it. We've already got our gorgeous dresses, and the best Elvis chapel. There's nothing to be done about Matt or Rose." I took a breath and looked up as the elevator doors opened. I wanted to get to my room as quickly as possible.

I'll just call Asa, find out what happened, and that will be the end of it. I held my emotions tightly. Together, we stepped out into the plush hallway. "I'll see you in a few minutes." I knew my voice sounded harsh, but Mom didn't say anything. She simply patted my arm and watched as I unlocked my door.

I hung up my dress and then crossed to the bed and dialed 9 for an outside line. When I heard the second dial tone, I punched in the remaining numbers from memory. Asa's private line rang and rang. I could picture it sitting there on his night-stand. It was a fancy clear Lucite phone, one of those that showed its inner workings. It reminded me of the pictures of human bodies in his medical books, the ones with the clear overlays. The more overlays you peeled away, the more the inner workings of the body were revealed.

If only I could do that. Peel away the layers to see what lay beneath. Did anyone else know I was the last person to see Rose at the pond? What about Asa's friend, the one driving the car? Who was he, anyway? Did he see me hit her? Did he?

The phone kept ringing. Oh, Asa, where are you? Why doesn't your answering machine pick up? Should I call his dad? No, if he isn't answering, there's a reason. Maybe he doesn't want to talk to me after all the trouble I caused him. But he said they couldn't find her, so what was the big deal? He tried to help, but there was nothing to do.

Did he go to college early? Getting his undergrad degree at Tech had always been his plan—then on to medical school.

Perhaps his wealthy father had given him a ski trip or something for graduation. Asa did love to ski.

A new idea surfaced in my mind. What if something had happened to Asa? That would explain why he didn't write me the whole summer. Oh my God, Asa. My fingers dialed Directory Assistance before I even knew I intended to. I got his home number and punched in the buttons.

Mrs. Gomez, the housekeeper, answered. I'd met her a few times, although she was usually gone before Asa and I went up to the roof in the evenings.

"Mrs. Gomez?" I held my breath.

"Si. This Maria Gomez." Her accent reassured me somehow.

I took a deep breath and plunged ahead. "This is Gabi Kelly, Asa's friend from school."

"Oh, si," she said. "I know you."

Relief seeped through me. "Oh, thank goodness. I hope you're doing well. I'm trying to reach Asa but he doesn't answer his phone. And his machine doesn't come on."

Silence.

"Mrs. Gomez?" Maybe I overloaded her. Went too fast. I recalled her broken English.

"Si. Asa gone now. To school. College."

"Oh, okay. I didn't know he'd left already. I've been out of town—"

"Si. He left. You want his nombre'?"

"His number at school? Yes, please."

She laid the phone down. I could picture it on the narrow, marble-top table behind the sofa. In a moment, she was back.

She read the numbers carefully. "555-806-8761. It's in the hall."

"What's in the hall?" This inexplicable bit of information left me puzzled. I couldn't for a moment connect her standing by the sofa, talking to me, with something in the hall.

"The telefono," she said. Her patience must have been monumental. I'm sure she thought me a complete imbecile.

Then it hit me. Dorms. Phone on the wall in the hall. But that didn't jive with Asa's plan. He said he wouldn't be able to concentrate on his studies if he lived in a dorm—didn't he tell me he already had an apartment in mind? I suppose even in an apartment, if he had roommates, they might have only the one phone. Nah, not Asa. He was such a private person I couldn't imagine him sharing a phone.

I thanked Mrs. Gomez, broke the connection, and immediately dialed the number she'd given me. While it rang, I thought of all the things I wanted to say. All the ways I would scold him for not writing to me about Matt, or even about his own early move to Tech.

But just like the one in his old bedroom back home, the telephone simply rang and rang without being picked up. Not even an answering machine. After the twentieth ring, I gave up.

How unlike my old pal. I recalled the way he said he'd been talking—secretly—to his crush every night for two weeks. Maybe they'd gone on to school together and were guarding their privacy. Maybe they were living together there. Stranger things have definitely happened. I could call the boy, if I knew his name. But I had no idea. Asa had been so secretive, and I didn't blame him.

But who could it be?

I thought back to the night at the pond. The silver Audi meant the parents probably had money. Like is attracted to like, after all. Asa's doctor-dad was country club all the way so possibly this guy ran in that same circle and that's why I didn't know him. Although in tiny Live Oak, Texas, I thought I knew pretty much everyone, at least on a superficial level.

I had sometimes wondered how I fit in with Asa's country club life. It had always been a mystery, even to me. Maybe he considered me his guilty pleasure, the token kid from the poor side of town. Or maybe he just kept me around to bug his upper crust dad; they'd never had what you'd call a great relationship. His father was seldom home anyway.

In truth, I knew Asa kept me around because he trusted me with his big secret. I'm just not sure what *made* him trust me. We'd clicked the first time we had whacked each other with the dodge ball in elementary school PE class.

Now that connection seemed a thing of the past. Either he was dodging my calls, or he was dodging the whole world. A sharp worry wiggled its way into my psyche. Could his retreat from the world be connected to Rose, to that night at South Pond?

I pushed the thought away. Ms. Gomez said he'd gone to college. I had no reason to think otherwise. But why hadn't he contacted me? Once Mom and Joe moved to Houston and I went back to California, there would be no way for him to contact me. I didn't have my own address yet, and neither did Mom and Joe. Everything was in limbo.

What a mess. That sharp little worry stabbed me again. I could always try calling Asa again later. I could call and give Mrs. Gomez my new address, my new phone number once I got one. On the other hand, maybe this is Fate's way of telling me to leave it alone.

I believed in Fate. I believed in a higher power. I believed when the tiny voice of the universe gouged you in the ear, you should listen.

With a shrug, I made a conscious effort to get Matt and Asa off my mind. I'd hung my bridesmaid dress—in its protective plastic bag—over the closet door just the way I'd done with my prom dress back home. Now I took the plastic off and looked it over. We'd forgotten one minor detail. Shoes.

My hiking boots wouldn't do.

In a determined effort to save the day from all the depressing news, I sloughed off my shorts and T-shirt and slipped the dress over my head. The smooth fabric slid down over me like cool water. I stepped back into my hiking boots, left them unlaced, and knocked on the door connecting my room to Mom's.

When she opened the door, Mom burst out laughing and pointed at my feet. "Joe, you were right. That shopping trip *was* too quick and easy!"

Joe stuck his head around the edge of the door and chuckled as he pulled his wallet out of his pocket. Holding out his American Express card he said, "The shoes are on me."

Giggling, all thoughts of Asa and Rose smashed down into the back of my mind, for examination later, I bumped fists with my mom, and after changing back to my shorts, we dashed down to the Via Bellagio, the European inspired collection of shops featuring designers such as Prada, Armani, and Gucci. We found extremely expensive strappy sandals for me—gold, something I'd probably never wear again—and tamer, off-white pumps for Mom. I'd never expected to shop in such an outlandishly elegant place. It was both exhilarating and intimidating—especially since all I had to wear into the shop were my hiking boots and shorts.

After we were done, we stopped in the Guess store so I could get one more outfit, a simple skirt and blouse I could wear for our night out after the wedding. We also went to a coffee shop for a mug and a muffin.

Mom asked if I'd been able to contact Asa. When I told her I couldn't, she echoed my idea about calling and leaving our new addresses with Mrs. Gomez as soon as possible.

I nodded. On the one hand, I wanted to forget all about Matt and Rose and everyone connected with Live Oak, just stay here in this fairytale world with my mom and Joe and pretend that nothing bad had ever happened, just look forward to house hunting with Mom and then returning to my new life in California.

On the other hand, I couldn't escape the memories of that night at the pond. Something wasn't right. I felt that in my bones. Especially now that Rose was missing and Asa was not answering the phone.

That was the thing that bothered me most of all. My connection to Asa had been much deeper—and longer-lived—than my connection to Matt. Asa and I had been buddies since grade school. How could he move away without a word?

YOU MOVED ON, my subconscious whispered. You moved all the way to California. He didn't desert you. He took up for you, looked out for you at the pond. To him it probably felt the other way around, like you deserted him.

With a supreme act of willpower, I tamped all the feelings of guilt and confusion back down into their damp little cellars and graced my mom with a wide white smile. I hoped it looked more convincing than it felt.

We took our expensive shoes and rode the elevator back up to our rooms. Joe had left a message that he would be downstairs playing baccarat, craps, blackjack, or roulette. He drew a silly looking face on the note with a large-toothed grin.

Mom laughed. "I just hope he has enough money left to pay Elvis."

We both got into our dresses and shoes and admired ourselves in the mirror. Then we talked each other into making appointments at the hair salon for later in the evening. "I hate to say it, but I think I could get used to being able to shop and get my hair done at any hour of the day or night. It's such a change from where I've been." I thought back over the last few months. "A week ago, I felt lucky if I could even *wash* my hair."

Mom agreed. "Well, then. Want to get our nails done, too?"

I shrugged. "Why not? Then let's see what show we can take in tomorrow after the wedding."

This time it was Mom who shrugged. "How about a magic show?"

"Yes! Let's see if we can get into David Copperfield!"

We looked at each other. I was imagining Mom in her wedding dress sitting at a table watching a magician. Apparently, she was thinking the same thing. At the exact same second we both said, "Nah. After the wedding, we need to go *dancing*."

She grabbed my hand and twirled me around as giddy as a schoolgirl, or someone at their first prom (why wouldn't that darn memory stay down in the cellar where it belonged?). "There's nothing that says we can't try the David Copperfield show tonight. Let Joe gamble, we'll see what trouble we can get into on our own."

Her excitement was infectious. I hurried back to my room, threw on my new skirt and blouse *and* sandals (guess I *will* wear them more than once), and away we went.

Staying at the Bellagio had its perks. We were able to get good seats for David Copperfield's show through the concierge. Mom tried to get me to raise my hand when the magician needed a volunteer for a card trick, but no way. I tried to raise hers instead. Thankfully neither of us was chosen, maybe he had people planted in the audience, but whatever the deal, it was the best show I'd ever seen. We were both stunned by the things he could do; the things he could make appear and disappear. I thought briefly how useful he would've been with Rose, but then I pushed that silly thought away and simply enjoyed the show.

It was over by eleven and after we stopped to watch the last display of the colorful dancing fountains, we hurried back to our rooms to get some sleep. Joe had come to his senses, or the bottoms of his pockets, and was waiting for us there.

We told him all about the magic show—which the program billed as the Greatest Illusionist Act on Earth—and then he dropped a small bombshell on me.

"I'm not really superstitious," he said, looking very embarrassed as he hung his head, "but everyone at my table downstairs said it was bad luck to see the bride on the day of the wedding—until the ceremony, you know?"

I nodded. I'd heard that, too, of course. Probably even played it out in my little wedding scenarios all those years ago. "And..."

He grinned that toothy grin I already knew meant he wanted something; usually something I was glad to give. "I thought maybe I should take your room—just for tonight—and you could stay in here with the bride-to-be."

I quickly agreed. "That's a great idea. We don't need any bad luck to start with, that's for sure."

Mom shook her head. "You two are just alike, aren't you?"

We both nodded in unconscious imitation. "I'll gather my things," I said. "And tomorrow, you can go to the chapel first, and I'll escort Mom in and walk her down the aisle."

Joe grew a little misty eyed. "Ahh, damn. I wish Gerry could be here."

"Should we postpone it? Wait for him to get home on leave?" Mom was serious. I could tell by the tone in her voice.

Joe shook his head. "It's like he said, that might be a while. He could be deployed any time now." He wiped his eyes, unashamed. "I just miss my son."

That made me love my soon-to-be stepfather in a way I didn't know was possible. It sort of made up for the father who hadn't wanted me enough to stick around. We didn't talk about him—ever—but when I was small, and kids wanted to know where my daddy was, I had asked and asked and asked. Mom

would always just say he lived in another town. It was my Grand-
mother who finally told me he'd left as soon as he learned Mom
was pregnant. They'd been juniors in high school. "One of those
old stories," Gran had said, as if I would know what that meant.

Pushing another set of memories to the cellar, I dashed back
to my room and started gathering my things to move to Mom's
room. But my memories wouldn't stay where I put them.
Worries about Asa and Matt (and Rose), and even the upcoming
wedding and move to Houston, swirled around in my head until
I finally dropped to my knees beside my bed and said a prayer to
God to let me go into Mom's room and actually sleep without
interruptions and without worrying her.

It was the first time I'd said a kneeling prayer since I was a
little girl. It felt good. It felt right. And best of all, it worked.
Mom and I watched an old Humphrey Bogart movie—*The
African Queen*—and I drifted off to the sound of her murmuring
into the phone to Joe.

18

Since the wedding ceremony was set for eight o' clock the next evening, that meant we would have the whole morning free except for the scheduled salon visit for hair and nails. I hoped we would have a quick breakfast in the room to save time. In truth, I'd grown anxious to get it over with. I felt guilty even thinking that—I'd ruined so many things for Mom lately—but I couldn't help myself. My entire past seemed destroyed—Asa, Matt, my childhood home—but that didn't mean I should ruin Mom's wedding day.

Once I thought of it that way, and reminded myself of all the things she had given up over the years, it caused a dark shadow to fall over me. That always happened when I thought of the things Mom and I had done without because I hadn't had a father, and she hadn't had a husband.

Naturally, my eyelids popped open and I saw that Mom had gone on to sleep. She had managed to hang up the phone, which I don't remember, so I guess that meant I'd drifted off, too.

But now I came wide-awake.

I got up, went to the bathroom—no murky water in the sink this time—then returned and crawled back in the bed in front of the television. HBO and Showtime were provided free of charge so I clicked around in search of another movie. Mom and I had enjoyed *The African Queen*, but this time I was in the mood for something a little younger. I found *Pretty in Pink*, by John Hughes. It was an old favorite. I'm sure Asa and I had seen it at least a dozen times, maybe more.

It put me right to sleep.

I awoke swaddled in dread.

I'd been dreaming of Matt, but it seemed to be a good dream. We were standing beside his old truck. He'd just slipped the buffalo nickel necklace over my head and the look in his eyes seemed a mixture of lust and something I could only assume might be love. I knew those feelings were real. But then that dread tightened its grip and the world turned as purple as the Trans Am that Rose had stepped into at the curb.

The remembrance of Mom's news about Matt's extensive injuries and Rose still missing crashed down around me like shards of brittle glass. I lay like a corpse, willing myself to get up and start my morning routine.

Mom began to stir.

Reminding me of Lucy, she rolled over and grinned. "I'm getting *married* tonight."

I couldn't help but smile. "How about room service?"

Mom agreed and we took turns in the shower while waiting for our fruit platter. Before long, we were ready for the salon.

We each had our hair trimmed and highlighted and then we let them do our makeup. As a finishing touch, they did my nails in a light, shimmery gold and Mom got a glittery rose color on hers.

I wished Asa could see me. He'd been after me for years to be more girly. We arrived at the chapel right on time and the hostess tucked us away in a tiny room with Elvis playing on the overhead speakers. I recognized "Love Me Tender," Mom's favorite song.

We had pictures made of the two of us in our near-matching dresses, and Mom was given a gorgeous bunch of burgundy star lilies with cream roses surrounded by a cloud of baby's breath. I thought I'd never seen such a perfect bouquet. The photographer took several more pictures.

When the "Wedding March" began to play, the hostess appeared. "Are you ready?" she asked.

Mom nodded, her eyes misty.

I linked my arm in hers and we marched solemnly through the door and down the short, rose-petal-strewn aisle.

Joe stood at the front of the chapel, knees shaking, before Elvis in all his splendor.

To my credit, I didn't laugh when I saw that they really were going to be married by an Elvis impersonator—who turned out to be a real Universalist minister—and once I'd turned my mom over to Joe, I was glad I hadn't. The look they exchanged said more than any vows ever could.

Mom handed me her bouquet, they joined hands, spoke the correct words and answered affirmatively in the correct places, and then Elvis told Joe he could kiss the bride.

When they turned around, Mr. and Mrs. Joe Romano, I gave her back the bouquet so the photographer could snap a few pictures of all of us together.

Then she made me go through the whole who-will-catch-the-bouquet thing in which the hostess and the photographer practically killed themselves getting out of the way, so of course I got it.

After champagne cocktails and shrimp-stuffed avocados we toasted the happy occasion with a final glass of champagne and then traipsed back down the strip to the Club Bellagio where Joe did his best to dance our legs off. We had one more bottle of champagne and I began to feel way too woozy.

When a guy from the bar came over and asked me to dance, I didn't hesitate. I already felt a little like a third wheel where the newlyweds were concerned, so having my own partner made everything easier.

After a couple of dances, Bubba-from-Dallas began to get a bit feely so I cut him loose and told Mom and Joe I was headed to bed. They claimed they were only going to share one more dance and then head upstairs as well.

When I got to my room, staggering only a little, I made certain no one had followed before I opened my door. I hadn't had the foresight to leave on any lights, so the room was dark except for a thin orange blade coming through the gap where the drapes didn't quite meet. I thumbed the switch just inside the door and soft light bathed the lush surroundings. The designers obviously realized no drunk wanted to be subjected to harsh lights upon their return from the bars and casinos.

I locked the deadbolt and laid my key card on the dresser before turning on the TV. This wasn't how I'd expected the night to end. I hadn't had any expectations to begin with, but this aloneness proved quite a letdown. I sat on the edge of the bed and unfastened my sandals. They'd been okay for dancing, but now my feet felt sore and mistreated. I was used to hiking boots and flip-flops, not heels.

I shrugged out of my pretty dress and let it fall to the floor. Then I sighed, retrieved it, and hung it up. Who knows? Maybe I will wear it to a fancy dinner in L.A. once I get settled there.

Tears stung my eyes. I wiped them roughly away and went into the bathroom to wash my face. I hadn't forgotten the puddle of weird green water. All through the day, and even after the wedding, when there was a lull in the action, images of the mossy green edges of South Pond had surfaced in my mind.

I smoothed cleanser over my cheeks and scrubbed off the unfamiliar makeup before pulling on a sleep shirt and crashing on the freshly made bed. The room spun every time I closed my eyes, so I kept them open. I'd forgotten to turn off the overhead light.

Forcing myself back to my feet, I located the remote that controlled everything, and lay back down. With the push of a button, I opened the curtains to take in the view, and then I turned the television channel and found another old black and white movie before clicking off the overhead light. If it hadn't been for prom, my life might have stayed on course. I would probably be at home in my old bed, dreaming of starting college, dreaming of decorating a dorm room, dreaming of dates with Matt in between classes.

If not for prom, would Mom and Joe be married right now? My abrupt exit seemed to have accelerated their courtship. Or was it Joe's decision to move to Houston that had done that? Everything didn't revolve around me. I knew that. Wiping my leaky nose, I reminded myself how my life had recently taken a turn for the better.

The prom night tragedy had been the pivot that forced me out of Live Oak and on to California. Now I simply had to focus on Reece and the SCA and my new plans for CSUN. Asa seemed as gone as Matt, and that's what bothered me most.

Think of Reece, my drunken psyche insisted. Reece in his black Buddy Holly glasses and thin white T-shirt.

I pulled off my own glasses and laid them aside before pressing the off button on the TV remote. A quicksilver image of a face appeared in the black screen.

Champagne and eyestrain, I thought. I might have been more alarmed if my phone hadn't rung just then. It couldn't be Mom. She wouldn't be calling me on her wedding night.

I picked up the receiver and crossed my fingers that it would be Asa returning my call. But the voice on the other end of the line assaulted my ear. It wasn't like anything I'd ever heard before. It sounded like someone speaking through a mouthful of mud.

"What? What did you say?" I jumped out of bed, trying not to panic, trying not to slam the receiver down, but when the watery voice whispered in my ear a second time, I yanked the thing away from my face and stared at it in fear and disgust. My stomach roiled. The room spun. "It's all your fault," the voice gurgled. "I'm in the water because of you." It sounded like a female voice.

I placed the receiver back in the cradle. It took every ounce of willpower in my body not to slam it down as hard as I could.

The second I broke the connection my hands went to my mouth. I wanted to scream, cry, run down the hall to the elevator and rush back to California, pretend I'd never made this trip at all.

The phone rang again. The sound ignited every nerve ending in my body. The off-white receiver vibrated in its cradle. My hand snaked out, snatched it up, and pressed it to my ear, waiting anxiously for the sickening voice to come again. Had it been nothing but guilt? A drunken dream?

"Gabi? Hello?"

Relief flooded me. "*Reece*?"

His laugh answered my prayers. It felt like coming out of a cave into the sunlight. "Oh my God, I'm so glad it's you. How did you find me?"

He chuckled again. "You said The Bellagio. That's not hard to find. So how was the wedding?"

I exhaled shakily. "Nice. Really, really nice." I felt my face break into a fierce grin. "I'll show you the pictures when I get back. Believe it or not, Elvis was quite impressive." The previous phone call tried to crowd my mind. "Hey, Reece. Did you just call and hang up?" I knew I sounded paranoid.

"Nope. Not me chickadee. Why?"

I took a deep breath and sat on the edge of the bed. "Must've been a wrong number. It's a big hotel." I exhaled and clung to the receiver like a lifeline. I was probably dozing; dozing and tipsy. Everything would be okay, now. I twisted the curly phone cord around my finger. "So. How's California?"

"Way too quiet without you. I can't wait until you get back."

I swallowed and tried to relax. "Me, either. You have no idea how good it is to hear your voice."

"Are you okay? You sound a little stressed. I thought weddings were supposed to be happy things."

"Oh, they are, I mean, it is. It's just, well, so many changes I guess." I couldn't bring myself to tell him the truth. About the dreams, and the voice on the phone. All just dreams, right? Or am I cracking up?

"—you there?"

My mind had wandered, my eyes searching the blank TV screen, the half-open bathroom door—was that a sound?

No. It couldn't be. There was no one here but me. Besides, I'd just washed my face a little while ago.

Another small sound came, like the stealthy opening of a door.

"Gabs?" Reece's voice in my ear.

"I'm here. Just had too much champagne, I think. Can you hold on a sec? I've got to go check on something." I felt better having him on the other end of the line, but this phone wasn't cordless. I set the base on the bed and stretched the curly cord as far as I could. It didn't quite reach the bathroom.

No one could be in there; I'd just used it a few minutes ago. But I hadn't used the shower—could someone be hiding there?

Was the door clear, frosted, or the old fashioned kind with a shower curtain?

No, no, way more modern than that—no door at all. Simply a deep walk in area separated from the rest of the bathroom with fat, glass blocks. I hadn't actually gone all the way inside it though.

Could someone be crouched behind those shoulder-high glass blocks awaiting the perfect opportunity to step out with a knife—

I clenched my teeth and balled my hands into fists.

The door stood partially open.

Sudden soft knocking on the dividing room door. "Gabs? You still up?"

Mom. *On her wedding night?*

I looked back at the phone on the bed. "I'm up, Mom. Just a minute." I spun away from the bathroom door, grabbed the receiver off the bed and bid a hasty farewell to Reece.

"I heard," he admitted. "I know you're busy. Good luck and give my best to your mom and new step-dad, and whatever happens or has happened, just know that I am with you there in spirit."

I hesitated a moment, on the cusp of telling him everything, of telling Mom to hold on, go on to bed, something. Instead, I said, "Thank you." I imagined him pushing his heavy frames up on his nose as he held the receiver to his ear. What did his place look like? I hadn't been there yet. I could only picture him on the phone outside cabin #10 facing the cliff, waves salting his skin, watching the whale breach the surface of the sea, looking out over the ocean like an old sea-faring captain, or a near-sighted pirate. "Thank you for calling," I said. "You don't know how much it means to me."

He grumbled deep in his chest. "I did it for me. I miss seeing you, hearing your voice." He paused. "But I'm glad you don't mind."

This time I laughed. "I don't mind at all." I glanced back at the partially open bathroom door and gathered up the last remaining tidbit of my small store of courage. "I can't wait to see you again." I replaced the receiver and floated to the connecting door on a wave of happiness. My earlier trepidation evaporated when I talked to Reece. What was wrong with me?

Mom stood in the doorway with her cotton nightshirt hanging down to her knees. She looked young, disheveled, pretty. "You aren't supposed to be here," I said. "It's your wedding night. You're supposed to be sleeping, or whatever..." I knew I was babbling, but I had to say something to cover my disjointed frame of mind. Paranoia gripped my sandpapered senses.

I opened the connecting door wider. "Don't tell me you guys had your first fight already?" I knew that would get her. Plus, I knew there couldn't *really* be anything or anyone in the bathroom —not *really*. It had to be a draft, an errant breeze through an air-conditioner vent that had caused the sounds. Just like the stuck thermostat before. I'd got a lemon of a room, that's all. *It's The Bellagio*, my subconscious whispered. *There aren't any lemon-rooms.*

Then it occurred to me that the little noises I'd heard had simply been Mom and Joe coming into their room, opening the connecting door. And the rest was, what, just more guilt working its way to the surface of my mind like detritus from the bottom of the pond?

At my mild admonition, Mom grinned. Her voice sounded tinkly, even at this hour. "No fight, of course not. Too much champagne, I think." The joy in my mom's voice made me happy. Nothing could be wrong—not today, not ever. She came in and hugged me. "I thought I heard you talking to someone."

I ducked my head. She'd caught me unaware. "My friend, Reece. He called to say hello."

Mom's face lit up. "Oh, I hope I didn't interrupt."

"No, no. We were just hanging up. Hey," I said, struck by a sudden bit of inspiration. "Is Joe missing his shave cream? I think he left it in my bathroom."

Mom stepped over and pulled open the door. Nothing popped out. Nothing *slithered* out; no one shambled out with a sharply curved knife.

She reached inside and turned on the light. "I don't see it," she said. "Oh. You mean this one supplied by the hotel?"

"Sorry. Is that all it is?"

Mom nodded and fluffed her hair in the mirror before strolling back into the bedroom. "I just wanted to check on you, sweetie." She smiled self-consciously. "I know you're grown and all." She patted my shoulder. "But you're still my baby. I just wanted to make sure you made it back upstairs safely."

I groaned and hugged her. "Only you would worry about *me* on your wedding night."

She sighed. "You'll understand someday, when you have kids of your own."

I pushed that thought away. Kids? Not *even*.

I shooed Mom back to her room—and her new husband— and then I pushed the button for the hotel operator and asked her to re-dial the last person who had called me.

Reece seemed very glad to hear my voice.

"Hey," he murmured. "I can't wait until you return."

I breathed a sigh of relief.

"Me, either. But first I'm going house hunting in Houston with Mom and Joe." I thought of Reece waiting for me and my mind did an about face. Why did I want to go to Houston? I love my mom, of course, but this was her move, not mine. Besides, this third wheel feeling probably wouldn't get any better in

Houston. And I'd already decided to go to CSUN after the next SCA assignment; I really needed to get settled in *my* new town.

Mom and Joe could pick a place with a guest room for me, because that's what I would be from now on, a guest. I closed my eyes and imagined breaking the news to Mom. This might be tough.

19

I made up my mind on the spot. "Reece?"

"Yes?"

"I'm not going to Houston after all. That feels like a step backward. I'm returning to L.A. as soon as possible."

"Well, all right. Have you got your flight?"

"No, but I'll do that now. I'll get the earliest one available"

"Call me when you find out the arrival time," he said. "I'll pick you up."

My heart began to pound. "I was only going to stay because I didn't want to hurt my mom again. But wouldn't this be easier for them, not to have me tagging along like a toddler?"

Silence took root. "Reece?"

He spoke softly. "Don't rush back on my account. I'll be here whenever you come back. I don't want you to hurt your mom. Heaven knows I lost mine when I was twelve. Car wreck."

"Oh, I'm so sorry. How awful that must've been."

"Yeah," he said. "I felt so guilty when I finally realized I'd never see her again. I loved her, but I'd always took it for granted that she'd be around, you know?"

"I guess we all do that," I replied. "As kids, I mean. But that's so sad. It makes me want to stay here with my mom."

"I'm not trying to talk you into staying longer, but I understand if you do."

I cleared my throat. "I can't believe you lost her so young? How did you cope?"

"My dad," he said. (I imagined him shrugging and pushing his glasses up.) "He's the best person in the world. Plus, my grandparents helped—at least until I got older."

"Sounds like you had to grow up quickly." I glanced at the bathroom and tried to decide how much to tell him about my life. "I had to grow up pretty quickly, too." I bit my lip. "Never knew my dad—my grandparents also helped out a lot. Until they moved to Oklahoma, then it was just Mom and me, and later, Joe." I couldn't help smiling when I said his name. He'd almost blotted out the stain my so-called father had left on our lives. "Good old Joe, he treats my mom like a queen. She's so lucky—I want a love like that someday." I stopped talking, mortified I'd said so much. "I-I'm sorry. All this wedding stuff. I got a little carried away."

Reece chuckled. "Did you forget? You're talking to your soulmate. You can say anything—"

"Reece—"

"No, don't argue, and don't apologize—just hurry back to me."

I smiled and reassured him that I would. And then I hung up and dialed the hotel concierge. He was able to get me a ticket for a flight leaving in a matter of hours. I wasn't sure how these things worked, but I knew I could grow to love it. This must be how the other half lives. Anything their hearts desire, anytime they want it.

I called Reece and told him the news.

"I'll be waiting," he said. "I'm glad you'll be home tomorrow."

We hung up and I propped the bathroom door open with a chair (so I wouldn't have to wonder if anyone was in there when I got up again) and packed quickly. Then I set my bedside alarm for six. The concierge had arranged for a car to take me to the airport at seven. I hated having to wake Mom up to say goodbye (the old John Denver song "Leaving on a Jet Plane" went through my mind) "All my bags are packed, I'm ready to go... I hate to wake you up to say goodbye."

I shushed it and began writing a note on hotel stationery. Now that all the arrangements had been made, I couldn't imagine not going. My mind wandered back to Reece. "I'll be glad when you get home," he'd said. I liked the sound of that. To paraphrase Paul Simon, "Houston seemed like a dream to me now."

A sigh escaped my lips. Why had I changed my mind so quickly? Was I letting a man change my mind? No. No. It was my decision, pure and simple. I wanted to get on with my life. Not put it off a minute longer.

I lay back on the pillows fully clothed. I didn't expect to sleep but I must have. The purr of the alarm woke me gently right on time.

After brushing my teeth, I smoothed my hair and zipped my backpack. The bathroom door was open. The chair had stayed put. Everything seemed just the way I'd left it.

The hard part came next. I had to call Mom and tell her I had decided to let her and Joe have their house-hunting honeymoon without me. "Just be sure my Houston room has some sort of bed and a window," I joked.

Mom mumbled how much they would miss me, then the phone went dead and she was knocking on the connecting door again. We hugged tearfully. "Are you sure you can't go with us?"

I shook my head. "I'm so glad I got to be a part of the wedding. I really loved it, but I'm making a life of my own in California." I hugged her again. "I can't wait to visit Houston when y'all are settled—after my next SCA assignment."

She hugged me and kissed me on both cheeks. "You grew up so quickly, kiddo. I'm having a hard time catching up."

"Oh, Mom..."

We hugged once more and I pushed her back to her side of the door. "I'll call when I hit LAX."

Mom nodded. "Take care, baby girl. And if things don't work out, you *will always* have a place in our new home."

"Thanks," I whispered. She made it very difficult to close that door, both literally and figuratively. "'Bye, Mom," I murmured. Then I grabbed my pack and rushed for the elevators before I could change my mind.

As the concierge promised, a small, neat sedan picked me up and delivered me to the airport. The driver didn't act surprised that I had nothing more than a backpack for luggage—even though I had just exited one of the most luxurious hotels on the strip.

In less than two hours my plane touched down at Los Angeles International Airport. I never thought Reece wouldn't be there to pick me up, but when I saw his tousled blond hair and black-framed glasses as I came through the doors, I felt a huge sense of relief. Not knowing what to expect, I approached him with a smile.

He had no problem with public displays of affection. As soon as he spied me, he pushed his way through the people and swept me into an all-out embrace. "There you are." His whispered words made me feel like he'd been waiting a long time instead of a few hours.

I wrapped my arms around his neck and allowed myself to be lifted off my feet. My backpack slipped off my shoulders and I heard it hit the tile floor with a dull thud. I didn't care. Reece felt the way I'd known he would, all hollows and planes and solid lanky muscle. I gripped him tightly; the brakes on my own emotions wearing dangerously thin. I squeezed my eyes shut and held on. I never wanted to let go. But, of course, I did after a while.

"So glad you're back." He released me, grabbed my pack off the floor, shouldered it, and ushered me through the busy airport with practiced ease. I was glad I'd been allowed to carry my pack on board this time rather than having to check it in baggage.

He hurried me to a pale blue and white VW van with surfboard racks on the roof. I couldn't hide my smile, but if he noticed, he didn't comment.

Once he'd stowed my pack and me inside the passenger compartment, Reece strode around the front and climbed into the driver's seat. "Come here," he said. His voice was different than I'd ever heard it. "I missed you."

I leaned across the gap between the buckets and found my face clasped firmly between his large hands. In the privacy of his van, in the heated interior ripe with the summery smell of sunscreen and saltwater, I gave in. This moment had been building since the day he first walked into our camp on the mountain.

"I wasn't sure you were coming back," he said. His skin was as warm and fragrant as the inside of the van. The smell evoked everything I loved about Big Sur and my California experience.

"I almost didn't." I pressed my lips to his. I wanted to drink him in, inhale his scent, his taste, his very essence. Reece. My soulmate.

He pulled me across the awkward gap and onto his lap. "What changed your mind?" His hands began to explore the contours of my body.

I knew we were visible, in the bright daylight of the open airport parking lot, but somehow, I didn't care. "You," I said. "You brought me back, California boy."

He groaned and laughed at the same time. That got me giggling. A family with two elementary age children hurried by giving us the evil eye.

Reece grimaced comically and physically placed me back in the passenger seat. I rearranged my rumpled clothing as he started the engine and pulled out of the parking space, headed toward the exit.

"How far to your place?" I asked.

He signaled for a lane change that put us into the queue to pay out. "Not far," he replied. "Once we get on the freeway, that is."

It seemed to take forever to get out of LAX. To me, it was like a small city and even though I'd been there a couple times already, it still intimidated me.

But Reece knew his way around. I tried to pay attention in case I ever had to navigate it on my own—the way we'd been taught to notice everything in the forest in case we got lost—but it was too much, too fast. Finally, I allowed myself to sit back and enjoy the ride. He punched a button on the ancient dashboard and the radio blared to life.

"Sorry." He turned down the sound. Prince's "1999" faded softly away.

I gazed out my window, nostalgia washing over me like a bitter wave.

Reece kept up a steady stream of questions, asking me about the wedding, about the casinos, about The Bellagio, about everything in Las Vegas. If he noticed my reluctance to discuss parts of my trip, he didn't mention it.

After about an hour, we made it to Northridge.

By the time we got off the freeway, my mood had lightened.

Time to start a new chapter. I couldn't help what happened after prom. But a new question nagged me. Should I call the authorities and tell them I may have been the last person to see Rose before she went missing? I wasn't certain it was me, but should I check?

I vowed to try calling Asa again. He'd know if she'd been seen again after I left. At least I thought he would.

"Almost there," Reece said. "Can't wait to get you moved in." He pushed his glasses up.

I wanted to tell him I hadn't decided where to "settle in" yet. I had some money in my college fund, but I'd always intended to live in a dorm, not an apartment. I had no money budgeted for off-campus living. I opened my mouth to protest.

Reece held up one hand. "Just look it over before you say no." He signaled a turn. "Here it is."

Palm trees surrounded a stucco apartment complex. Each unit had a wooden balcony facing a huge open courtyard with an immense pool and hot tub combination. Tennis courts lay off to one side, a basketball court on the other.

"There's also sand volleyball," Reece said. "We're number 1116." He glanced my way. "It's just around the corner here, second floor."

I laughed weakly. "Where's the beach?"

Reece shrugged and pointed westward. "About half an hour. Depending on traffic of course."

I stared the direction he pointed. For some reason, I assumed he lived nearer the water.

"I did have a beach shack at one point," he admitted, seeming to read my mind. "But the drive to school was just too far. And then the job began to take up so much of my surf time it seemed the logical move."

Sounded to me like he simply grew up. But I didn't want to say that. It felt like something my mom would say. "Sounds like the best of both worlds." I grinned, hoping it didn't look like a grimace. Was I really thinking of moving in with this guy? I barely knew him. Pushing up my glasses, I observed him from the corner of my eye. Today he wore an aqua tee with a pocket. It looked every bit as worn and soft as the white ones he'd worn on the trail.

This wasn't some *guy*. This was Reece, my soulmate.

We backed into a parking space. Bougainvillea dripped from every trellis and many of the balconies. The fuchsia blooms hung down and met the same color flowers on the azalea bushes planted at the base of every building. I'd never seen such an oasis of color.

Reece laughed at my expression.

"What? Desert rat here, remember?"

We took a short walk up to his second-floor apartment. All the doors faced outward toward the massive pool. My head swiveled this way and that. I wanted to see everything at once.

"C'mon in." He opened the door and stood aside. "Phone's on the table there." He smiled. "I figured you'd want to call your Mom since I rushed you out of the airport."

I nodded and slipped my pack off my shoulder before placing a collect call. Reece disappeared into another room to give me some privacy. I reassured Mom I would come to Houston for a visit after they found a place. She seemed to understand when I told her I might be rooming with Reece, but she also seemed to think it was a co-ed dorm situation or something. Maybe I should be ashamed, but I didn't correct her thinking. Plenty of time for that later, if I decided to stay with Reece.

I hung up and glanced around. Neat. No clutter anywhere. Nautical blue curtains adorned every window, some half-opened to let in the light. Nubby, oatmeal sofa and a red canvas sling chair made up the small living area. A red and yellow surfboard stood in one corner beneath a shredded section of old fishing net hung with starfish and bits of green and blue sea glass. The small coffee table held the phone and a woven basket full of jade. I picked one up just as Reece came back. "From Jade Beach?"

He nodded and leaned against the doorjamb, one hand on the lintel above his head. My heart fluttered as I took in the way his lanky frame filled the doorway.

"How'd your mom like her jade?"

"She seemed suitably impressed." I'd had the date of the wedding engraved on it in the gift shop at Lucia Lodge. Then they'd mounted it on a beautiful teak base. The final effect had reminded me of a green dorsal fin breaking above black water.

Reece laughed. He sounded nervous. "Well, this is it. Think you could call it home?"

"Home?" I rolled the word around in my mouth a bit. "I'm not sure." I looked around the small rooms. "Where would I sleep?"

Reece grinned and indicated a short hall. "The grand tour."

He opened the first of two doors. This first one was obviously his bedroom. A clear-blue Macintosh computer adorned an otherwise bare desk, and a beat-up guitar stood on a metal stand in the corner. The blue bedspread sported a white sailboat in keeping with the nautical theme throughout the apartment. A navy throw rug lay beside the bed on the tile floor.

Down the hall, the second door led to another bedroom, quite a bit smaller. The room held a narrow bed and a small dresser.

"It's a little stark, I know." Reece pushed his glasses up and fidgeted in the doorway. "You can add your own stuff, of course."

I laughed. "It's perfect, Reece." I turned to him. "All I have are my backpack clothes, my other stuff is going to Houston. Joe's company is moving everything for them."

"Even better." He pulled me close as if not holding me made him anxious. "I know we have to keep this secret for a while, until our upcoming assignment is finished, but after that, we can be ourselves." His face neared mine, but I had to air a few things first.

I pushed him back, gently. "But what happens if we don't get along or something? Then I have no home."

An expression of pain crossed his face. "I know it's quick. But I've told you over and over you're my soulmate. Nothing will go wrong." He looked away, then back. "You don't seem to believe me, but I've been waiting for you."

"Waiting for me?" I'm sure my voice sounded as confused as I felt.

He shrugged, pushed at his glasses even though they hadn't slipped down. "I've dated a few girls—"

I'll bet, I thought, recalling the way his work-hardened frame had filled the doorway a few moments earlier.

"—but I've never lived with anyone. Never wanted to. Not even in those long weeks in the forest during assignments."

I didn't say anything. I couldn't say anything. When I'd taken the SCA assignment, I'd been running away—I knew it then, I accepted it now—finding another love had been the last thing on my mind. And I couldn't imagine living with someone I didn't love. At first, I'd thought it might be platonic, but not anymore. Not now, not after the way he'd greeted me at the airport. The way I'd felt when he pulled me to him.

But was it love? I studied him, standing there in a dust-mote filled shaft of sunlight. Yes. It felt like love. Not the way I'd felt about Matt—that seemed different somehow—but yeah, I looked forward to seeing him. I trusted him. And I couldn't wait to explore every inch of his lanky frame with my fingertips. That was love, right?

I led the way back to the living area. "Can we talk?"

He went to the tiny kitchen and got us both a bottle of water, then propped himself on a stool at the tall bar that separated the kitchen space from the living area.

I sat on the sofa and sipped the cold water. "I came back with the intention of sharing the apartment with you. Platonically." I let that sink in. And then I felt a little nauseous. Reece was my only L.A. connection. If he didn't like what I said, I'd be out on my ear. I could try to find an apartment on my own, but I didn't even have a car to get around, much less a bank account. Besides all that, I'd never rented anything or entered into any sort of contract in my life.

On the other hand, Mom would send me a plane ticket to Houston in a heartbeat. She'd made that abundantly clear. I could always sleep in the airport if necessary.

Reece threw his head back and laughed. "I'm sorry. You're right. It's too fast. I keep saying that and then I keep rushing you." He fiddled with his water bottle. "You must think I'm crazy."

"Well . . ." I took another sip.

Reece flopped down on the opposite end of the oatmeal sofa and held out his right hand. "Friends first," he said.

I placed my hand in his. We shook in agreement. "That's a deal." I stood, picked up my backpack, and started down the tiny hall toward the smaller bedroom.

"Hey, friend," Reece called softly.

I turned.

"Spare sheets and blankets are in the bedroom closet."

I smiled.

"But you're welcome to take my room . . ."

"I wouldn't dream of it," I said. "And once I get my own bank account, I fully intend to share the expenses." I hesitated. "Once I get a paying job, I mean."

Reece ducked his head, probably to hide a smile. We both

knew my next assignment was a volunteer position. I would have to get my grandparents to wire me the money from my college fund before I could pay anything. Then I would be job-hunting as soon as possible.

"Don't worry about a thing," he said. "To prove my intentions are good, I won't charge you any rent—"

I laughed. "And no 'special chores' or anything like that?"

He raised one eyebrow. "Now hold on a minute. We may have to do some negotiating on that."

I felt my cheeks grow warm, but it felt good to be back on joking terms again. Things really had been moving too fast.

20

I retreated to my room and searched the closet for the sheets and blankets. I had my camping pillow in my pack. It would do until we made it to a store. There came a knock on my door. I dropped the linens on the mattress.

"You might need this." Reece held out a regular size bed pillow. "There should be a clean pillow case there somewhere." He smiled.

"It isn't your only pillow is it?"

He shook his head and ducked out of the room. Then he turned back. "You hungry?"

I thought back to the package of peanuts on the plane that had served as my breakfast. "Starved."

He grinned and my heart stuttered.

"Lunch will be ready in five." He winked and closed the door.

I quickly finished making my bed and dashed across the hall to the bathroom with my brush and mirror. When I couldn't put it off any longer, I steeled my nerve, opened the door, and stepped out into my new life.

The unmistakable smell of frying bacon made my stomach

rumble. Reece looked like a natural at the stove, just like the first day in camp when he'd cooked our pancakes.

"Smells good, but where's your French maid outfit?"

The back of his neck turned red, but when he faced me he wore a huge, lopsided smile. "It's at the cleaners, darn it."

I sat at the tall bar, my feet on the rungs of the backless stool. "Can I really trust you?" The words just popped out.

He held up three fingers. "Scout's honor."

I breathed a sigh of relief. Stupid, I know. We'd had almost the exact same conversation when he first offered me a room. "I guess I'm a slow learner," I said. "I just keep asking the same questions over and over, don't I?"

Reece shrugged. "Doesn't bother me. I know I rush things. I've always gone after what I want." He placed a plate of bacon, lettuce, tomatoes, and avocado on the bar in front of me, and then pulled slices of golden bread from the toaster on the counter.

I took it upon myself to retrieve mustard and mayo from the fridge.

He took a butter knife from a drawer beside the sink and laid it next to the condiments. "Here's another shocker." He bowed his head and gave thanks for the simple meal.

I followed his lead and bowed my head. Afterward, I said, "I didn't know you were Christian." I spread the mustard on my bread. "I don't recall you saying grace before."

He shook his head. "Can't mix religion with government-funded programs like SCA." He slathered his own bread with Dijon on one slice and mayo on the other. "I don't think of myself as solely Christian, anyhow." He stacked lettuce, tomato, and avocado slices on his bread, and then placed the strips of crunchy bacon just so. "But you can call me Christian. I do believe in the teachings of Jesus. But most of all, I believe there's a Maker somewhere that caused all this."

I laughed at his choice of words. "Caused it all, huh?"

He shrugged. "I just can't get behind the whole 'beautiful accident' theory." He took a huge bite, chewed, and swallowed. "Or maybe I just don't want to."

I mulled it over as I built my own sandwich. "In other words, you choose to believe—"

"Right." He pointed his sandwich at me.

I took a bite. "I guess I'm the same way, to an extent."

He got up and poured our bottled water over glasses of ice. "To an extent?"

Now I shrugged. "I believe in a force somewhere, but I don't know if it's anything our tiny minds can comprehend."

"You mean like a universal force?" He sat back down. "Like *Star Wars*?"

I sipped, shrugged again. "Maybe. Something running the universes, holding everything together, but I have trouble comprehending it all."

At last he came around the bar and took the stool beside me. "That sounds a bit random."

"Yeah, maybe. I mean Mom raised me Christian, but I sometimes have doubts."

He nodded vigorously. "Nevertheless, I like a lot of the teachings in the New Testament—"

"Me, too! Love thy neighbor and all that—"

Reece grinned. "Yep. And all that."

We finished our lunch in a more comfortable silence, and then cleaned the kitchen together.

"C'mon," my new roomie said. "Let's get down to the campus and get those catalogs."

"Yes!" I washed my hands. "Thanks for lunch, by the way. I was famished."

He poked me in the ribs. "I could tell!"

"Oh you . . ." I smiled, embarrassed, but it didn't matter. By this time, we'd made our way down to the parking lot where Reece stuck his key in the door of the old van and tucked me inside again.

He went around, hopped in and turned the air conditioner on high. That took the place of any conversation for a while. Once the inside of the van had cooled, he turned it down and told me to choose the radio station. "It's not too far," he said. "I usually ride my bike, but it isn't built for two."

I liked the idea of bikes. I could easily imagine myself riding alongside this blond boy through these colorful streets. We passed row after row of pastel homes and campus-close apartment complexes. "Do the flowers bloom all year?"

Reece looked around. "Yeah, something blooms all year long. Not the same ones, mind you, but different ones." He gave me that lopsided grin again.

I looked out the window at the vast campus we were approaching. "Do you believe in ghosts?"

Reece laughed. "Where'd that come from?" He backed the van into a parking space near the administration building.

Stupid me. That *was* out of the blue. "Just wondering." I fiddled with my hair. "We discussed religion already, I figure we can get all the important stuff out of the way today." I made my voice light, joking.

"In that case, yes. I think anything is possible." He cut the engine. "How about you?" He sat with one hand on the door handle waiting for a reply.

"Nah. I don't really think they exist. Although I'd never rule out the possibility." I hopped out to cut off the rest of the conversation. When we met in front of the van I said, "And by the way, why do you always back in to parking spaces?"

"Just safer to get out," he said. "I backed over the little ol' lady from Pasadena one time." He grinned. "Don't want that to happen again."

I rolled my eyes and giggled. "So, you're the one they wrote about."

He shrugged and pointed me in the direction we needed to go.

The administration building hovered large and imposing and suddenly I felt like the eighteen-year-old high school girl on her way to register for college. Not exactly the way I envisioned it all happening, though. Had I slighted my mom again? When I called to let her know I'd arrived, I hadn't even mentioned the possibility of registering today. No time to worry about it now. Reece stood waiting for me inside the vestibule.

I registered for Composition and Rhetoric, Algebra I, Psychology 101 and History 1301. I filled out a work-study application and an application for grants and scholarships. Reece glowed when I wrote my GPA. "I knowed you was a smart one," he drawled.

The counselor thought I had a good chance for scholarship based on my need and my good grades. "And I like the fact that you took the summer to volunteer with SCA." She looked at me over the top of her half-moon glasses. "Mind telling me why you waited so long to register for classes? Most kids choose their college when they're juniors. Not the summer after graduation."

"Family problems," I replied. I prayed she wouldn't ask me to elaborate. I could feel Reece's gaze on my skin.

"And you're doing another SCA program before the fall semester?"

"No, I think that start date is too soon. Maybe mid-winter?" I glanced at my roomie and mentor. "We thought we could fit in one more assignment. I'm kind of thinking I might make it my life's work."

She nodded and wrote something on my app. "You're going to do fine," she said. "Just fine." She smiled and something inside my chest loosened.

I never thought it would be that easy.

We made our way to the bookstore where I used the voucher the counselor had given me to purchase my four textbooks. She'd told me I was a genius to have a copy of my transcript, but I didn't feel genius. I felt like an idiot. I'd fully expected to skip the basics in Math, English, and History. I'd been taking college credit classes in high school, after all. But that was Texas. This was California. Not all my credits had transferred.

Steeling my resolve, I didn't let on to Reece how it disappointed me. I just tried to go with the flow telling myself I might be able to test my way into a higher-level class once the semester began.

Reece squeezed my shoulders as we made our way back to the van. "Easy-peasy."

I allowed him to pull me to his side. "Surprisingly easy."

He nodded. "We've even got time to stop by the beach on the way home if you'd like."

"That's such a funny thought . . . stop by the beach." I grinned up at him. "I'd love to." I thought about the empty roof rack. "Will we go back and get your surfboard?"

Reece shook his head. "Nah, not this time. I just want to show you one of my favorite spots."

That made me happy. I saw him push his black frames up on his nose and I caught myself touching the nosepiece of my own glasses in subconscious imitation.

21

It took almost an hour to get to the beach. It seemed packed.

Reece parked under a row of immense eucalyptus trees. "This is Surfrider," he said simply. As we exited the van, he plucked a fragrant eucalyptus leaf and held it to my nose.

I inhaled the sharp, tangy fragrance and resisted pinching myself to make sure this was real. As we made our way across the highway toward the beach, the cool sea breeze lifted my hair and caressed my senses. Reece grabbed my hand and all my worries fell away.

We headed toward the water. The beach was crowded with people lounging on blankets. Short-legged beach chairs littered the sand and shortened versions of swimmers and surfers littered the cold, shallow water. A hundred yards out, serious surfers sailed the waves, sometimes riding all the way to the long pier jutting out over the water.

"It's perfect." I breathed the salt air and knew I'd made the right choice in staying. Suddenly, I couldn't even imagine tripping around hot, humid Houston in search of a new home for my newlywed parents.

Like a couple in a beach-blanket movie, we strolled down the beach hand in hand.

"Wow." I turned to Reece. The rugged hills behind his head made as beautiful a backdrop as the waves. "This is amazing. I'm so glad we came."

Reece wrapped his arms around me. "Gabi Kelly, this is your life." He unwrapped one arm and swept it across in front of us dramatically.

My eyes took in the wide expanse of ocean and I knew in my heart I'd truly found my way home. It made me briefly consider past lives and reincarnation.

"Hey, bro!" A big guy with bleached-out hair and sky blue eyes appeared from behind us and grabbed Reece in a bear hug.

"Joshie! Dude! Where you been?"

The man called Joshie held up his wrist. It was sheathed in a highly autographed and decorated cast. "Hawaii," he said. "Almost healed. Be hanging ten again soon." He grinned and his teeth nearly blinded me. I could easily imagine him surfing a big wave, grinning the whole time.

Reece grabbed him and shook him in another bear hug. "Joshie, I want you to meet my new roommate, Gabrielle." He beamed at me. "She's a lot prettier than you ever were."

The big guy hooted and enveloped me in a brief hug. "You've certainly improved your outlook, man. No doubt about that." He slapped Reece a high five. "So, what's keeping you busy? I lost track of you even before Hawaii."

"Trail work up the mountain," Reece replied. "SCA. That's where I met Gabi. We're going back next week."

Josh swiped his crinkly hair back dramatically. "Dude, you're one crazy mother. I wouldn't go up the mountain right now for *any* amount of money."

Reece and I looked at each other. "Why not?"

"You don't know?"

"We've been at CSUN ever since Gabs flew in this morning. What's happened?"

"Wildfire, man. Could be arson, could be lightning." He looked up at the clear blue sky. "They don't know for sure. Big fire though. Hope it wasn't your area."

Reece grabbed my hand. "Thanks, dude. We've got to go check this out."

I thought it endearing the way Reece slipped into surfer-speak with his buddy. It added one more dimension to the trail guide I'd first met.

In no time at all, we were back at the apartment where he phoned headquarters and got the scoop on the fire. All SCA crews were being evacuated and the secretary said our assignment had been cancelled, but if we wanted to come and help with the evacuations, we would certainly be welcome.

Reece turned on the TV, which he apparently never watched, and there it was. I couldn't believe we hadn't known about it. Reece went to the closet, pulled out his backpack, and took out a pair of binoculars. We walked out to a rise behind the complex and sure enough, with the aid of the field glasses, we could barely see the smoke. It was just a haze above the horizon, but it was there. And with the close ups on the news, I had a good idea of what was going on.

"I've got to go." Reece's whole demeanor had changed. Gone was the surfer dude; gone was the college boy who had given me the campus tour. Here was the man I'd met in the forest. The guy everyone could depend on to get them home safely.

I didn't like the look of that fire on the TV news, but I wanted to show Reece I could be of some use. I went to my room and got my own backpack, which I hadn't even unpacked yet.

Reece grinned. "They might not let you go up the mountain

with me. The U.S. Forest Service is in charge when it comes to natural disasters. It will be up to them."

"It's okay. I'll do whatever they need. Fetch and carry, office work, whatever." I felt a huge sense of relief when he nodded and continued packing his own bag.

In moments, we were back at the van. Before we started, Reece leaned in my passenger window and kissed me quickly. "I had wanted to discuss our *situation* over dinner on the pier." He caressed my cheek with his thumb. "The Malibu Farm Pier Café has the best grilled salmon around." He laughed. "The crab cake bites aren't bad, either."

Before I could think twice, I pulled his face close and kissed him back. "I can't wait to go there," I whispered. "I've never even had grilled salmon."

Reece grinned against my lips. When he sauntered back around the front of the van, he actually whistled a tune.

All the way to the staging area, forty-five minutes away, Reece kept up a steady stream of conversation about another fire he'd helped with last year. It made the trip go faster, and it made me respect him even more.

The minute we entered the forested area, we began to encounter emergency vehicles and park patrol units. Reece showed his identification and we were allowed to go through the temporary barriers and up the park road to headquarters.

At the makeshift office, it appeared to be controlled chaos. Reece squeezed my hand and whispered that we had to keep our relationship to ourselves a while longer, and then we climbed out of the van and walked into the melee.

Lucy was there, loading drinks and protein packs for firefighters. She gave us both a quick hug and put me to work packing the bags while Reece went to find the crew leaders who would be driving up the mountain to the firefighters' base camp.

We worked through the night and into the next day, and when I looked out the window and saw Reece and the others returning from the mountain, it was further affirmation that I'd found my niche.

22

That night, we all sat around the long conference table eating sandwiches and talking about the fire and the work it would cause. "It's only fifty percent contained at this point," Reece said. "Bill Cryder, my immediate supervisor in the Forest Service, went back up with another crew. I'm going back in the morning." He looked directly at me. "We can stay here overnight, or I can take you home before I come back in the morning."

I nodded toward my pack. "I've got everything I need right here." I didn't intend any double meaning, but when I looked up, Reece wore a tired, dirty smile. Once I thought about what I'd said, I realized it was true.

We stayed that night and two more. The fire crews then had the blaze fairly well controlled. It was a strange and wonderful interlude. Strange because Reece and I had to keep things secret, wonderful because I got to see the serious side of him that let me know what a good human being he truly was. He cared for other people, he cared for the animals being killed and injured by the fire, and he cared for the environment itself. And he made it all look easy.

Finally, being in the midst of Reece and the others just like him, I once again began to feel as if I'd left the past behind. And since there were always people around, and I was so exhausted, there were no bad dreams, no flashes of guilt waiting to ambush me.

When I realized how normal everything had been, albeit hectic, crazy, and over-the-top busy, it made me stop and think about everything that had happened before.

I needed to talk to Asa, to find out if there had been any news about Rose. I had a feeling all my bad dreams and paranoid fears would disappear once I knew she had been located. Chewing my lip, I thought of my conversation with the housekeeper. Had she given him my message? Wait—had I told her we were moving?

Crap. He had no way of getting in touch with me. I didn't even know how I could contact my mom in Houston until they got settled. Of course, I could always call Joe's company to get a message to them in case of emergency, and I had given *them* Reece's phone number. But apparently there would be no way for Asa to get in touch with me now. Not until I called him back —or the housekeeper—and left Reece's number with them, too.

What a mess.

But I didn't have time to dwell on it. It was time to help wrap up the temporary headquarters and head back to town. Now that the fire was mostly contained, a new headquarters camp was being created nearer the burned area. It was time for cleanup to begin.

We said goodbye to the volunteers at the staging area and I knew I'd made the right decision. I wanted to be a part of this life. The entire time we'd been there, I'd been itching to get up on the mountain and actually do some physical work.

I told Reece how I felt on the way home. He smiled and

reached across the seat-gap for my hand. "It's getting in your blood, too, isn't it?"

I nodded. "I think so. No, I know so." I squeezed his hand.

We stopped at In-N-Out Burger on the way home. Reece ordered two burgers for himself and one for me. We pulled into the parking lot and had an impromptu picnic in the van.

"I'll be working with the replacement fire crews for the next couple weeks," he said around a mouthful of fries. "Do you want to volunteer to help, or would you rather try to get a jump start on your work-study at CSUN?"

I thought it over as we finished eating. "I would rather go up the mountain with you."

His eyes shone. "I hoped you would say that—"

I held up my hand and swallowed the bite I'd just taken. "But to be honest, I need to start earning some money."

Reece nodded. "I understand." He seemed to think it over. "You'll need wheels to get around while I'm in the back country."

"I was thinking about that. Maybe I can get that bike before you leave."

"Good idea," he agreed. "You could always use mine, but I think it would be too tall for you."

I laughed. "Ya think?"

"You can deposit me at the new headquarters and then bring the van back and use it. I'll put you on the insurance."

That last statement caught me totally by surprise. "You will?"

Reece balled up his red and white paper burger wrapper, but not before he held it up and showed me the Bible verse notation stamped there: Revelation 3:20 "Behold," Reece recited from memory, "I stand at the door, and knock: if any man hear my voice, and open the door, I will come in to him, and will sup with him, and he with me."

"Wow." I was impressed not only that the verse was notated

on a burger wrapper, but also that Reece actually knew it by heart.

"Look." He held up my soda cup. Near the rim, a different verse was noted. John 3:16 "Even I know this one," I said. "For God so loved the world, that he gave his only begotten Son, that whosoever believeth in him should not perish, but have everlasting life."

Reece nodded. "That's only one of the reasons I like this company. Even though the verses aren't written out, I like the way they put their personal beliefs into their work." He sacked up our trash and opened his door. "That's the only thing that bothers me about SCA, we can't fully be ourselves with the kids. A lot of them might benefit from knowing their mentors believe in a higher power—"

"But we aren't allowed to say anything?"

He stepped out of the van shaking his head. "It's highly discouraged, although if the kids ask us, we can answer honestly, of course." He tossed the bag into the trash receptacle.

It cracked me up to hear him refer to my peers as kids. But I had another question for him. "Would you proselytize, if you could?"

Reece started the engine. "Not at all," he said. "But I would be more open in my own prayers and beliefs."

I rode in silence, thinking about what he said. Was it a good thing the government prevented mixing religion with trail work? Or was it the suppression of a basic human right, to worship? I tried to recall what the Constitution said about the separation of church and state.

It was a new wrinkle in the already rumpled page of my new life.

"Does it bother you," Reece asked.

I looked at him, not understanding.

"That I pray and worship?"

I laughed out loud. "Bother me? No. I love it." I rolled my window down and let my hand trail in the slipstream. "So far this is what I know of you." I held up my forefinger. "One, you're a trail boss who loves Mother Nature." I held up my second finger. "Two, you're a surfer dude who can't keep his glasses on his nose."

He laughed and pushed them up self-consciously.

"Three," I held up my ring finger. "You're a practicing Christian and a great cook—oh, wait, that's two in one, isn't it?"

He nodded. "But I like it."

I giggled. "Four," I held up my pinkie. "You're a very good-looking Christian surfer trail boss . . ."

His cheeks reddened slightly.

"And last but not least," I held up my thumb. "You're my soulmate."

A wide grin split his face. He reached across the gap and took my hand again. But this time, he brought it to his lips. "I am," he replied. "I am."

THAT NIGHT, after we unpacked and showered, we sat on the balcony looking down on the pool.

"I'm thinking about a swim." I still had my suit balled up in the bottom of my backpack. We'd all used them on the trail when we came across a good spot for swimming.

Reece grabbed my hand. "That's an excellent idea."

He ducked into his bedroom and I ducked into mine. When I emerged a few minutes later, he waited for me on the balcony. His board shorts were almost as colorful as a sunset.

"Ready?" I felt a bit self-conscious in my old black one piece, but it would have to do. I removed my glasses and laid them on the dresser.

Towels in hand, Reece gave a low wolf whistle. "Looking good, Gabs!"

I rolled my eyes and started down the stairs ahead of him. "Not bad yourself, Reece."

He laughed. Since I walked in front of him, I couldn't see his face. We arrived at the pool and I immediately slipped off my sandals and dove in. The water was so cool on my skin. It gave me a moment to collect myself before Reece dove in beside me.

We both came up smoothing our hair off our faces. At first, I wasn't sure who was near me, and then I realized he'd removed his glasses, too. With the slicked-back hair, his face became a study in cheekbones and blue eyes. I'd never realized how thick his brows were.

"Hey." I studied him from a few feet away.

He bobbed nearer, treading water. "Hey." He reached out to touch my long hair. His fingertips brushed my temple.

"This feels great."

He rolled his shoulders and I realized he'd been up the mountain, engaging in physical labor while I'd been down in the office making copies and fielding phone calls. "Especially after the last few days."

"Turn around." I took him by the arm. "Let me rub your shoulders."

He did as I said and I dug my thumbs into the hollows between his shoulder blades. For a minute, I pulled and kneaded to my heart's delight. He stretched his arms over his head. There were a couple of other swimmers at the opposite end of the pool, but it felt as if we were completely alone.

He caught my hand on top of his shoulder and turned to face me. This time, his face was much closer. "Thank you, that feels good." He pulled me against his body and I felt the distinct evidence of what my innocent massage had caused.

"I'm sorry, I didn't mean—"

He stopped my words with the broad pad of his thumb. "Don't be sorry. Soulmates, remember?"

I wrapped my arms around his neck and he pushed me into the side of the pool, his body pressing the length of mine. "I want you," he said.

His outspoken desire took me by surprise. With Matt, I'd felt the teenage rush of hormones, slightly clumsy, breathy, all in good fun. At prom, as much as I'd wanted to continue our passionate kisses in his old truck, I'd known, deep down, that nothing would come of it. I hadn't been ready for anything more than a little heavy petting in the parking lot.

But with Reece it felt much different, more real, more possible, more likely. In fact, nothing stood in the way of our passion except a few dozen steps back to his apartment, and a couple layers of wet fabric.

I let him kiss me in the water. And I kissed him back at first timidly, then more passionately. As he continued to press against me, I felt my doubts return. What were we doing? Wasn't it too soon? We hadn't even spent one night in the apartment yet.

"Reece, I—"

He pulled away before I finished my thought. "I know. I know." He began to stroke across the pool, then turned and came back for more.

I slipped out of his long reach and ducked under the water. He lunged for me, laughing, but I made it to the other side and climbed up the ladder to the deck. I could feel his gaze following my every move. I grew bold and walked back to where he still lounged at the side, looking up.

Once again, I dove into the deepest part of the pool and surfaced beside him.

"Remember the whale we watched off the deck at Lucia Lodge?"

I splashed water his way. "Are you saying I remind you of a whale in the water?"

He grabbed my waist and pulled me under for a kiss. I'd never been kissed under water before. We both came up spluttering.

And then something yanked me back down, this time all the way to the bottom of the pool. When I looked up through the swirly sparkles of sun, I could see Reece's long legs treading water above me.

I kicked down, hard, and my feet met the rough cement and something more, something extremely cold, like a rough patch of ice. Looking down, my chest beginning to burn, I was shocked to find myself staring into a flat, black nothing.

No, my brain screamed. I kicked down again and felt the same roughly surfaced resistance beneath my feet. But I didn't surge upward the way I should have. No matter how hard I pushed, I didn't move at all.

"Reece!" I screamed, but the sound was only in my mind. My lungs burned for oxygen. My chest felt puffed to bursting. I wanted to open my mouth and breathe, I wanted to open my mouth and gulp, I wanted air but the air was so far above the sparkling water—I knew it would be suicide.

I couldn't help myself.

I opened my mouth.

Strong hands grasped my outstretched ones, yanking me upward into the light. I breached like the whale, splitting the surface of the pool with the top of my head, gasping, coughing, choking.

Water streaming from my face, I blinked and stared up at the blessed light even as the blackness beneath me renewed its icy grip on my legs, threatening to drag me back down into the impossible nothingness.

Reece climbed out and dragged me onto the pool's concrete

apron. I felt the energy of others surround me. I felt their eyes, their stares, their disbelief. How can anyone even come close to drowning with no reason I heard them ask.

"Did you see it? Did you see the darkness?" I tried to form the words, actually felt the shape of them in my mouth, but they never came out, the gurgling water Reece forced from my lungs obscured them. "Hurts!" I managed to yelp as he continued to push down on my chest with both hands.

He let up and rolled me to my side. I vomited a stream of foamy water onto the cement. Oh my God, how embarrassing. I closed my eyes and wished I'd never left Texas.

"She's okay." Reece murmured. "She's okay."

I felt the others move away. "*Are* you okay?" His voice beside my ear.

"Yes." I began to cry, my shoulders shaking. "I don't know what happened." I opened my eyes and struggled to sit up. "Something was down there, holding me down."

"The drain," Reece said. "There must be something wrong with the drain."

Feeling like an idiot, I allowed Reece to help me up and walk me past the onlookers, my towel wrapped firmly about my shoulders. I raised my hand in a gesture of thanks, and to let them know I was truly all right. A few murmured Thank God. A couple of people actually clapped.

In the apartment, Reece hovered outside my bedroom as I stripped off my suit. The chlorine had been strong in the pool. I wrapped my towel around my body and cracked open the door. "Mind if I rinse off before I put on my clean clothes?"

Reece shook his head, but he didn't step aside. Instead, he pulled me into his arms. "That scared me," he whispered into my wet hair. "It really scared me."

I allowed myself to be comforted. "I'm sorry." The cold darkness at the bottom of the pool resurfaced in my mind and I shivered.

He held me tighter and his breathing quickened. I raised my chin to look at his face. He pressed his lips to my forehead and released me with a little shove toward the bathroom. "How about a margarita? I think we deserve one after the week we've had."

I mumbled, "definitely," and hurried on into the small bathroom. I half expected something to be leering at me out of the old-fashioned medicine chest mirror, but it was clear. I dropped my towel and reached into the tub to turn on the shower. A feeling of vulnerability washed over me as I stepped inside. I pulled the shower curtain closed, hoping that would help, but the metal rings created such a raspy jangle as they slid across the metal bar, it was like beach sand on raw skin.

What's happening to me? The question bounced around in my head as I let the warm water sluice away the chlorine from my thick hair and chilled body. Am I going insane, am I being haunted? I'd heard stories about poltergeists and evil spirits attaching themselves to people, especially people going through a lot of stress. *And people living with a lot of guilt.*

The water suddenly ran cold and I squeaked and reached down to turn it off. Too many showers today, I thought, recalling how we'd both showered before heading to the pool. I squeezed out my dripping hair and wrapped my towel around my body again. I hadn't thought to bring my clothes into the bathroom, but my room was just across the hall.

I wiped steam from the metal mirror and stood, perplexed, for several seconds. Then I realized the problem. The mirror was blank. It showed no reflection at all, as if I'd gone vampire beneath the warm shower spray.

For several seconds I stood, dumbstruck, waiting for something to appear, and then I realized the mirror wasn't simply blank, it was black. The entire room had gone as black as the underside of a storm cloud.

Reece knocked politely. "Gabs, everything all right in there?"

The darkness began to recede like water pulling away from the shore. Little by little my face emerged in the cloudy mirror. My eyes were wide, wild, terrified. I could feel my heart pounding in the back of my throat. "Yes, I'm coming out."

"Good, drinks are ready. Got some nachos in the oven."

I closed my eyes and willed my body to calm down. I could feel the remnants of stress eating away at my insides. Once, during one of our lowest times, my single mom had developed a severe gastric ulcer. The doctor said it was nothing but stress. I felt my own stomach churn in response.

———

23

"The nachos were amazing, and so are the margaritas." I could feel the effects of the alcohol before I'd reached the bottom of my glass.

Reece poured himself another, and then tilted the blender toward me. "You are twenty-one, right?"

I laughed, the tensions of the day fading away. "You're so funny sometimes."

He looked at me earnestly. "No, really." He set the blender down and took a giant gulp from his salt-rimmed fish bowl shaped glass. "You have to be twenty-one." He slapped his forehead with the heel of his hand. "I know you aren't twenty-one. What was I thinking? You just graduated high school!"

"Oh, c'mon, you aren't serious, are you?" I sipped the last dregs of my drink.

"I am serious." He plopped down beside me. "I just gave alcohol to a minor, my intern at that." The knowledge of what he'd done, what we'd done, etched his features with horror.

"It's okay," I soothed. "I promise I won't tell. I mean, sheesh, I drank champagne with my own mother just a few days ago."

Reece slumped backward into the sofa cushions. "I could

lose my job, be banned from the SCA altogether. What was I thinking?"

"You weren't thinking, besides, we uh. We aren't exactly sticking to protocol by living together anyway." I let my voice trail off to soften the truth of the statement.

He still looked stricken.

I placed my glass on the table. "Okay, fine. I'm done. I won't have anymore. Better?" I held my empty hands up in a placating gesture.

"I failed," he muttered. "I failed. Just because I fell in love with you, I let all my good sense go right out the window. I could jeopardize my whole future with the organization. Both our futures." He dropped his head into his hands as if in agony.

I sat up straighter and looked at his golden curls. "What? What did you just say?" Everything I'd been through lately made me question whether I'd heard him correctly.

He raised his head, a strange look on his face. "What did I say?"

No way I was going to repeat what I thought I'd just heard. I'd had too many close calls lately.

"I said I could jeopardize both our futures with SCA." His eyes were as transparent as the lenses in his frames. Windows to the soul indeed.

I nodded. "I – I thought you said something else, something more."

Reece threw his head back. "Did I say it out loud?" He raked his hand over his head. "I didn't mean to blurt it out like that."

I noticed he didn't repeat it though.

He took off his glasses and polished them on the bottom of his shirt. "I just don't seem to have control of my mental faculties anymore."

When he looked at me without the specs, his eyes seemed so vulnerable, his face so naked.

He continued speaking. "When I yanked you out of that pool ... when you couldn't seem to come up on your own..." His voice trailed away. "I felt something tear inside my chest." He put his glasses back on. "If anything happened to you, I couldn't take it."

That short declaration said more to me than even those three magic words he'd spoken earlier. "I'll find my own place as soon as possible," I murmured. "Maybe it isn't too late to get into a dorm."

Reece shook his head. "No, that's not what I want. I offered you a place to live—"

"Wait! What are you worried about? Our assignment got cancelled—I'm not even a volunteer anymore. There's no reason we can't live together now. Right?"

Reece 's mouth fell open and he smacked his forehead with his palm. "You're right! I'd gotten so used to you being a part of the work, I forgot you weren't yet getting paid. And now... you're right, you're no longer under my command."

I laughed at that. "Your command, huh?"

He blushed. I loved the way his skin showed his every emotion.

Just as I prepared to rub it in a little deeper, make him really squirm, someone knocked on the door.

Reece jumped up to answer it. "Mr. Crown," he said. "Come in." He stepped aside and a balding, middle-aged man strolled in and stood near the table.

"Reece, right? You're the one who called about a problem with the pool drain?" His voice was dry as toast. He sounded in a hurry.

"That's right." He glanced over at me. "This is my friend, Gabi. She got sucked down to the bottom of the deep end and couldn't surface without help."

The man shook his head. "Drain's working perfectly. I just

came from the pool—nothing wrong. If you have any more problems, let me know." He turned and strode back to the door.

Reece looked at me. He clearly wanted to say more.

I shot him a look to let him know I didn't want to make a big deal out of it. Regardless of what he thought, I wasn't certain it had been the drain that held me to the bottom of the pool.

He allowed the man to leave.

"It isn't right," he said. "I saw what happened. You were stuck down there. What if it happens again, to some kid maybe?"

I shook my head, an echo of the superintendent. "I really think the man is right. It didn't feel like the drain. I mean, I wasn't right over it, you know." I glanced down at the floor. "Maybe I had a panic attack or something."

"Has that ever happened before?" Concern laced his brows together.

"Maybe. I mean, what else could it have been?" As strange as it sounded, I almost had myself convinced. I thought about taking this opportunity to tell him about the other strange occurrences, like the frightening telephone call in Vegas, but I couldn't bring myself to do it. It seemed like too much. Maybe tomorrow. When this wasn't so fresh.

Fighting a yawn, I leaned back and closed my eyes. "I think I need an early night." Maybe it was the margarita making me so drowsy. Not to mention the stress of almost drowning.

Reece clamped his lips together. It was obvious he wanted to say more, but he didn't. He simply said good night and waited for me to go to my room.

I wished the superintendent hadn't interrupted Reece's accidental declaration of love. I really wanted to see if he would repeat it.

In my new little bedroom, the sheets I'd smoothed onto the bed were old and soft. They held the fragrance of salty ocean spray that made me think he'd had them when he lived near the beach. I inhaled their soft scent and buried my head in the poufy pillow. The pale blue curtains filtered the light coming in from the well-lit parking area.

A light knock sounded on the door.

"Gabs?" Reece's tentative voice.

I turned over and faced the door. "Yes?"

"Just checking to make sure you found everything all right."

I smiled. "I did. Everything is great. Thank you." I hesitated to see if he'd say more, when he didn't, I said, "I'll see you in the morning."

The sound of his bare feet padding down the hall comforted me. Maybe things will be all right. Maybe there won't be any more odd happenings once we get everything settled. I drifted off to sleep wondering if Rose had surfaced yet.

It seemed only a few minutes had passed when I felt Reece sit down on the side of my bed. Had I been crying or moaning in my sleep? I'd been dreaming about blackness, as if an abyss had opened up under my bed. I rolled onto my side, toward the door. I could barely make out his silhouette in the filtered moonlight. "Reece?"

A cold hand caressed my bare arm.

I drew in breath to scream, at the same time pushing myself as far away from the shape as possible. "Reece!" I yelled.

Pounding feet followed by a sudden slash of light when he flipped on the switch. "Gabi? What is it?"

"I - I thought you were here—"

"I am here." He sat on the bed and scooped me into his arms. "You're shaking."

I buried my face in his bare chest. "A nightmare." I hesitated, debating how much to tell him. "I thought, I thought you came in my room and sat on the bed, but when you touched me, your hand was icy cold."

"You've been through a lot." He lay down beside me. "I'll stay here for a bit, you go back to sleep."

I didn't argue. The fact that he didn't question my nightmare made me trust him even more. Strangely enough, I went immediately back to sleep. I really *was* tired. When I woke again, we were in exactly the same position we'd been when he first lay down beside me. Soft light touched the wall opposite the window. I thought it was morning light. It seemed more natural than the big arc lights from the parking lot.

"G'morning," he mumbled when I looked at his face.

I covered my mouth in case of morning breath. "Hi." I snuggled under his arm. "Can't believe you stayed all night." And didn't molest me.

He gave me a little squeeze and locked his hands together across my body. "Always," he said. "Anytime you need me."

I sat up, still in the circle of his embrace. "You know you're kinda scaring me with all this talk like we're going to be together forever."

He grinned. "Soulmates, remember?"

How could I forget? I lay back down, cradling my head in the hollow between his shoulder and his throat. The necklace Matt had given me draped itself across his chest. Stiff golden whiskers drew my fingertips to his jawline. "Scratchy."

"Want me to shave?" He tucked his chin down to feel them with his own fingers.

"Not until I do this." I placed my lips against the edge of his jaw. "And this." I planted a few more light kisses on his chin.

He made a sound of pleasure in his chest. It reminded me of the purr of a big cat—a leopard or a tiger. His body became as still as a wax figure.

When I glanced at his face, his eyes were closed, but his lips were turned up at the corners. I touched one corner gently.

He took my hand and turned the palm to his lips. Then he

opened his eyes and looked into mine. "I meant what I said last night. Even though I didn't mean to say it like that."

I wanted to say I loved him, too. But something wouldn't let me. Instead, I pulled myself up to his face and pressed my lips to his. "I think I—" My sentence was cut off by the slam of the bedroom door. I jumped and yanked the covers up to my chin.

Reece sat up, eyes glued to the door across the narrow room. "What the hell?"

That chilled me more than anything. For the first time, someone else had experienced the same thing I did.

He pressed his index finger to his lips and rose from the bed.

I watched him measure his bare steps toward the door. Had someone come in the apartment while we were sleeping? His tan skin glowed in the morning light. I suddenly wished for some sort of weapon, a baseball bat or something, but the only thing in the room besides the bed was the low dresser against the opposite wall.

Reece didn't seem worried about that, though. Before I realized he was even there, he had reached out and grasped the doorknob. I thought he would turn it slowly and quietly the way he'd stood up from the bed; instead, he gave the knob a hard turn and yanked the door open wide.

No one stood there.

Reece rushed into the hallway and I heard him make his way through the living room and back. By this time, I was out of the bed and peering down the hall, watching him. He never said a word, just ducked into his bedroom. I heard him fling open the closet door and shove aside the metal hangers on the rod.

"Nothing," he called.

I let go of the breath I'd been holding and grasped the buffalo nickel lying cold against my skin. My fingers rubbed and rubbed but after a few moments, I realized what I was doing and made myself stop.

The nickel felt like a piece of ice.

Reece strode back into my room and gave my closet a cursory going through. He closed the door carefully. "That was intense."

I glanced toward the open bedroom door. "Did you check the bathroom?"

He turned and took me in his arms. "I checked everything. It was just a fluke. Maybe a tremor. We're directly over a fault line here, you know."

I nodded. "But wouldn't we have felt it?"

He shrugged. "California shakes and shivers from time to time, we're all used to it. You'll get used to it, too. In time."

Chewing my lip, I stepped reluctantly out of his embrace and opened the dresser drawer. I pulled out my clean shorts and tank top. Reece took the hint and went back to his room. I've got to send Mom my new address, I thought. So they can send my clothes. I can't keep wearing these same three sets of clothing over and over. School will be starting in a couple of weeks.

Brushing my hair in the mirror, I studied my face. Maybe it had been a tremor. Not related to me at all. Not related to Rose or what happened at the pond. And the near drowning? Not because of Rose, either. Just my bad luck. Or a panic attack like I'd told Reece. We'd been so close to something physical there in the water, something so adult. Maybe my subconscious had panicked.

If only I had Asa to talk it over with. From the kitchen, the blender roared to life. Margaritas again?

"Breakfast," Reece called.

I took another quick look in the mirror. That boy seems to be on a mission to fatten me up. A vision of his golden chin whiskers and sleepy eyes flashed across my memory. Is he for real? Seems too good to be true. Could he be an illusion like all the other things?

I stepped into my flip-flops and walked to the kitchen. Reece stood at the bar pouring strange blue-green liquid from the blender into two tall, frosted glasses.

"Super smoothies," he said when he saw my expression. "Bananas, blueberries, kiwi, and honey."

I took a suspicious sip and began to smile. I'd never tasted anything so delicious. "Wow—you continue to surprise me."

"Only the beginning, baby." He tilted his glass toward mine for a toast. "Only the beginning."

We clinked our drinks together and the world fell back into place. While I finished my breakfast, I called Joe's new office number and left a message for Mom, telling her my new address.

She called me back in just a few minutes, informing me that all my things were in boxes but as soon as possible, she would sort out my clothes and send them to me.

I bit my tongue. That could take forever. "Thanks, Mom, no rush. I think I'll go and buy a few new things to tide me over."

"Great, honey," she replied. We chatted about the apartments they'd seen and the townhouse they were almost certain was the one they wanted.

She ended by saying, "Have you got plenty of cash? I'm sure you transferred your bank account already, right?"

"Doing that today," I said. "And then I'm going to ask Gran to transfer my college fund also, at least part of it. For this first semester, you know."

"Of course," Mom said. "Just make sure you don't spend your class money on other things."

I laughed. "I understand. It would be easy to do, but I've already signed up for work-study so I think I'll be okay with my savings and stuff."

Mom sighed. "You amaze me sometimes."

That little statement made me feel ten feet tall. I wondered if

I would always seek my mother's approval like this? At least it seemed she didn't hold a grudge for all the times I'd hurt or disappointed her. It must suck to be a parent sometimes. Would I ever experience those feelings? Would I ever want to? For some reason, the question nagged at me. It seemed important somehow. Maybe because of Reece's silly "forever" talk.

"What do you think about children?" I blurted as we drove to the bank.

Without skipping a beat, Reece replied, "I think they are crunchy and good with catsup."

A bit slow on the uptake, I sat there with my mouth open for a couple of beats. Then I punched him on the shoulder. "Oh, you."

He grinned and pulled into the parking lot. Inside, we waited our turn at the window where I opened my checking account with twenty-five dollars—pretty much the last of the cash I'd brought back from Vegas. Then the clerk had me fill out the form to close my account in Live Oak and transfer the balance. Once again, I felt so grown-up I couldn't stop smiling.

"Now I can call Gran and ask her to transfer some of my college fund here, too."

Reece high fived me on the way back to the car. "Do you have a favorite shop you want to visit, or should we hit the nearest mall?"

"The mall is fine, as long as there's an Old Navy or Gap, I'm good. Heck, even J.C. Penney's will do for my taste."

"That's my girl," he replied. "Shorts and T-shirts, what more does a body need?"

"Bath and Body Works come to think of it. Thanks for reminding me. I'm low on shampoo and crème rinse."

Reece laughed. "Midtown Mall, here we come." He got back on the freeway and we were there in no time.

The entrance led directly past the food court. "Food first, or food last?"

"Last," I laughed.

He nodded. "While you're shopping, I've got a couple of errands to run, too. What say we meet back here at Giovanni's Pizza in a couple of hours?"

"Sounds good to me." I smiled up at him and he leaned down and dropped a sweet kiss on top of my head. My heart thumped. I felt silly. It wasn't as if he'd kissed me on the lips. "See you soon." I walked quickly away.

I didn't turn around to see where he was headed, and I didn't even ask what errand he had to run. I was too busy trying not to fall off my flip-flops as I felt him watching me walk away. When I got to the corner—where I could unobtrusively look over my shoulder—I didn't see him anywhere.

24

At J.C. Penney's I scored another pair of shorts, another skirt, and a simple pair of super soft jeans. I also bought a frilly turquoise top and two short-sleeved shirts that were a little dressier than tank tops and T-shirts. I even managed to find a pair of leather sandals on sale. I still had the fancy ones from Mom's wedding, but I couldn't wear them every day.

Reece said it would soon be sweater weather, but I didn't feel the need at the moment. I could always come back later if the weather did, indeed, turn cool.

It was in the lingerie department that I began to waver. I ran my fingers over silky high-cut panties and lacy bras imagining how they would look on my new lean body. Wondering how I would appear in Reece's eyes. How the fabric would feel beneath his fingertips. My face flamed and I grabbed a delicate peach colored set before I could lose my nerve. For good measure, I picked up a six-pack of all cotton bikini panties and two new bras.

I felt positively brazen when I added a leopard print teddy to my pile of clothing on the checkout counter. Good thing the bank issued me a new bankcard and assured me all my previous funds had been transferred. I'd been saving that money—little by little—since my very first paycheck as a waitress back in Live Oak.

Fortunately, Bath & Body Works was near the pizza place. I stopped in, grabbed only the things I really needed (very hard to do), and then hurried back to Giovanni's.

Reece sat there, long legs stretched across the aisle, resembling a model for California Lifestyle magazine. Except for the Buddy Holly glasses. But even those didn't spoil his appearance; they simply lent him an air of *sophisticated* beach bum.

I dropped my bags into the booth. "Been waiting long?"

He shook his head. "Just got here. You hungry?"

"Ravenous," I said. "Shopping is such hard work."

Laughing, he directed me to the pizza buffet where we both chose our slices and our salads. I got a Diet Coke and he chose a giant iced water.

I bit into my slice of mushroom and pepperoni. "This is good."

Reece plowed through his veggie slices and glanced at my shopping bags. "It appears you were successful."

I nodded hoping he wouldn't take it upon himself to investigate. "I made quite a dent in my new bank account."

He raised one eyebrow.

"But I needed some things to tide me over until Mom ships my wardrobe. Especially if I'm going to start working soon."

"No argument here." He crunched ice cubes nervously.

"Everything okay?" I'd never seen him so antsy.

He nodded and favored me with a smile. "I've ummm, I've got a surprise for you after we eat."

"Really? For me? What is it?" Dumb question I know, but it just popped out, even though he'd just said it was a surprise.

"Ask me no questions, I'll tell you no lies."

Okay, so now I couldn't wait. I blotted my mouth with my napkin, took a huge gulp of my drink, and gathered my bags.

Reece cracked up. "Ready?"

"I can't remember the last time I had a surprise. I may have been eight years old."

"That can't be right. You should have surprises every day."

I ducked my head, delighted by the sweet affection.

We walked out of the mall side by side. Reece took my bags and carried them, and with his free hand, he reached for mine. I glanced up then, and immediately thought about running the backs of my fingers along his jaw to see if it was as smooth as it looked. I wondered when he'd had time to shave. Instead, I swung our hands back and forth, happy as that eight-year-old child I'd just conjured. "So, where are we headed?"

He grinned. "The van."

"Smart-aleck." I bumped him with my hip and he let go of my hand and pulled me into his side.

His voice was low, almost a whisper. "It's a surprise, remember."

He stored my purchases in the back of the van and peered at me with a glint of mischief in his eye. "Trust me?"

"Of course." I surprised myself when I answered without hesitation. I do trust him. I trusted him as much—or more—than anyone in my whole life.

"Good—it's time you learned to surf."

"Seriously? I thought surfing was done early in the morning, like your buddy, Joshie, said."

Reece laughed and kissed me quickly. "Yeah, that's a good time for sure, but to learn, early afternoon is perfect." He pointed to the roof of the van. "I even snuck my old board on there for you. Afterward, we can have dinner at Malibu Farm like I'd intended last week, before the fire took us away."

Adrenaline began to course through my veins. "Umm, Reece,

you do know I've never even been out in deep water, right?" I pictured myself riding a mammoth wave on my belly. "And after what happened in the pool, maybe I shouldn't—"

"No worries." He looked at me with a serious expression. "I think getting back in the water is exactly what you need. Like getting back on the horse that bucked you off."

We rode in silence for a few miles and then we appeared to be nearing the turnoff for Surfrider Beach. I recognized it from before. "Maybe you're right. I really am a good swimmer. At least, I used to be."

He smiled. "It was a fluke, a panic attack like you said." He made the turn.

"Here we are. This will cure you. We'll stay close to shore and I'll be beside you the whole time."

I tried to relax. "One more thing..."

"I know what you're going to say." He pulled a brown paper bag out from under his seat. Inside was my black bathing suit. "I snagged it from the bathroom when you weren't looking."

My eyes felt as if they might pop out of my head. "Wow. You really do plan ahead." But that hadn't been what I was going to say. I intended to say what if something grabs me and pulls me under the water again? What if it happens out here, in the ocean?

"I hope you don't mind." He kept his gaze on the road. "I just, well. I want today to be special."

Something let loose inside me. Nothing bad will happen today. I won't let it. My nervousness gave way to cautious excitement. The sight of the eucalyptus trees fanned my adrenaline rush and I had trouble sitting still. Reece squeezed my hand, and I squeezed back. Then he pulled into a parking spot and stopped.

"You can change into your suit in the back of the van." He

leaned over and pulled a curtain across the opening between the driver's compartment and the rest of the van.

"I never even noticed that," I said.

He leered at me comically. "I have zo many tricks up my zleeve."

Laughing, I stood and made my way into the back of the van with my suit. "This isn't a Chevy van, is it?"

Silence for a few moments. He must not have heard me. Then the CD player began playing the classic 70s rock song "Chevy Van" by Sammy Johns. I couldn't believe he'd picked up on my little joke so quickly.

"I love it," I said. "Even though I know this is really a Volkswagen."

"You're too observant," he said. "One of my favorite classic rock songs, though."

That led us into a discussion of all our old favorites, many of which just happened to be on the mix-CD he'd popped into the player. Jim Croce's "Operator" came on followed by "Please Come to Boston" by Dave Loggins, and by the time Jimmy Buffet's "Come Monday" played, I was changed and ready.

"Those songs," I said. "My Mom loves that music. She played them all the time." I stepped back through the curtain and took my seat in the passenger side. "I see you changed, too." He had on his board shorts and white tee.

"I had them on under my jeans. Brought you something else, though." He held out a second white T-shirt. "It's one of mine. You'll want it after we get out."

I held it to my face. "Mmm, smells like you."

He uttered a short laugh. "I hope that's a good thing."

"Sun, salt, and sand, with a hint of bonfire from the trail." I held it to my nose a few more seconds. "I love it. You may not get it back."

His expression was unreadable. "You can have anything I've

got." He opened the driver's door and stepped out into the perfect afternoon.

The weather surprised me. What had seemed warm back at the mall now felt rather cool. The ocean breeze I supposed. "Is the water cold?"

Reece handed me a couple of beach towels, then led me to the back of the van where he climbed up and handed down the boards. "It can be. If it's too cold, we'll come back and try it with wetsuits later."

I hefted the bulky board. It was much lighter than I'd thought it would be. We dropped our towels on the beach and hit the shallows. Reece took a few minutes showing me how to sit on the board and how to paddle. It seemed like second nature to him, but I was shocked at how quickly my arms and shoulders gave out.

"Ready to try a wave?" Reece stood and walked out a little further.

"Sure." I put on a brave face and followed him into the sun. The water grew colder the deeper we went, but the energy of paddling warmed us quickly. I surprised myself when I managed to catch the very first wave that came. I rode it—sitting on my knees—right back to the shallows where we'd started. When I glanced back, Reece lingered directly behind me. He wore a smile as big as Texas.

"Awesome!" He beamed. "How'd it feel?"

I gave him a thumbs up, turned my board around and started paddling back to the small swells. I couldn't believe I'd caught the very first one.

My luck ran out. Even though the swells were constant, and I did everything the same as before, I couldn't seem to catch any more at just the right moment. Twice I was left floating as the breaker went to shore without me, and a couple more times I actually managed to let the growing swells flip me over on my face.

Reece laughed as I came up spluttering each time. And just as I was on the verge of giving up—citing beginners luck on the first one—he pointed to a beautiful wave headed our way. "Let's go." He knelt on his board and paddled for all he was worth. "Stay with me, now!"

I stayed with him as best I could, but he left me behind and went past that wave toward the one behind it. He glanced back once, and I gave him another thumbs up. He met the second wave, dove under it, and waited on the third. He spun his board around and sat astride it, getting ready. Even from my vantage point I could tell the coming wave was different, stronger.

Sure enough, just as it broke behind him, Reece stood up, took control of his board, and rode it all the way in. When he passed me, I got brave and turned my own board to catch the gentler edge of it. I didn't attempt to stand, I simply knelt and held on, and it worked. Right before the shore, I stood up on trembly legs and flashed another thumbs up and then fell on my face.

Reece cracked up, and then hauled me, shivering, to the beach. He unhooked my ankle strap from my board and wrapped me in a giant towel. "You did great," he said. "I don't think I've ever seen anyone get to shore twice on their first time —except for me, that is." He chuckled again. "You're a natural. Are you sure you're a desert rat?"

I rolled my eyes and dragged myself to my feet. "I'm already feeling the burn," I said. "You didn't tell me it was such a workout."

"Where'd you think I got these?" He ran his hand over his six-pack abs jokingly. Then, to my dismay, he slipped his dry shirt on.

He gave me my shirt, and my glasses. He'd had them both

tucked away inside his towel on the sand. I pulled his T-shirt over my head, grateful for the delicious sun-warmed fabric.

"Hungry?"

I thought it a ridiculous question. Hadn't we eaten just before we came? "Actually, yeah. I feel like I've never eaten a meal in my life."

Reece looked at the westering sun. "It's late. Hard to believe we've been at this for hours, isn't it?" He picked up both our boards.

"Hours? No way. Seems like we just got here."

He laughed and told me to stay there and dry off while he carried our boards back to the van. "Then we'll go and grab a bite at the café."

I wrapped myself in both towels and sat on the sand, my knees drawn up to my chest. "I'll be right here," I said, exhausted.

With a nod, he trotted back the way we'd come, hauling both boards as if they were nothing.

I think I dozed.

In moments, he stood beside me. When I rose, he wrapped his arm around me and we strolled down the beach toward the pier. "You were right. I did need to get back in the water."

Reece slung his towel over his shoulder. I'd wrapped mine around my waist, sarong-style. Beside us, the sun gilded the waves. I suddenly understood why California was known as the Golden State.

"I'm glad you feel that way. I couldn't live without surfing now and then."

We made it to the long pier and took our time strolling to the Malibu Farm Pier Café at the far end. We sat on stools along the edge of the pier right over the ocean. The breeze cooled us and I felt completely out of place in my T-shirt, bathing suit, and towel, especially after I noticed some of the patrons were quite well dressed. But it didn't bother Reece. In fact, the chef came out to greet him as if they were long lost friends.

"This is so beautiful," I murmured, taking in the strings of twinkling lights adorning the café and the white outdoor table umbrellas. Wanting a bit of warmth, I ordered a caramel macchiato. "Mmm. That's wonderful." I sipped the steaming coffee carefully. "I can feel it warming me right to my toes."

Reece tipped his Beach House Ale toward me in a toast and we clinked the edges of our mugs together.

He ordered the crab cake bites. They were the perfect appetizers. For an entrée he ordered the Portobello burger and I got brave and ordered a tofu dish called Vegan Coconut. I'd never in my life eaten tofu. "I don't think tofu is even legal in West Texas," I muttered. But it surprised me. I loved it.

Reece laughed and ordered another ale.

The best part of all came when the sun began to sink below the horizon. The rich golden hues topped by the soothing white caps of the rising tide made my mind water for more the same way my mouth watered for the delicious food.

"This is amazing." My fork stopped halfway to my mouth as I realized I'd spoken aloud.

Reece sipped the last of his ale. "I've lived here nearly all my life and I never get tired of it." He held his empty bottle up so the last rays of the sun shone through it. "One more," he told the attentive waiter. "Need anything, Gabs?"

I shook my head. "No thanks, I'm too young to drink, remember?" I smiled. "Besides, I'm stuffed already." I liked the way he shortened my name. It gave me such a sweet feeling of belonging. But it surprised me when he drank a third bottle of ale. "Do you drink all the time?"

I hadn't meant the question to sound quite so blunt, but there it was. First the margaritas at home, and now this. Somehow, the third beer seemed excessive. Maybe surfing worked up a tremendous thirst—wait a minute, I'd worked every bit as hard attempting to surf. Was this a red flag as my mom would've said? Should I worry that he might turn out to be a lush? I'd over-heard Mom tell her friend Carla on the phone that my absentee father (she referred to him as the sperm donor) had turned out to be a lush. I'd thought it a funny word then, but it had stuck with me all these years. I also wondered how she knew he had become a lush. Had she been in contact with him without telling me? Or was it simply one of those grapevine things? If so, what else had she learned? She'd always told me she had no idea where he was.

Reece swigged from his new beer, a sardonic smile on his face. "Not to worry, Gabrielle." He took another quick drink and saluted the near darkness. "I'm not going to turn into a stum-bling drunk on you. I just feel the need for a little liquid courage right now."

Liquid courage? Seriously? "Wh—"

I wanted to ask why, or what for, or something along those lines, but he stood suddenly and motioned for our check. The chef waved to us from behind the counter, and then we were off, Reece practically sprinting down the pier toward the beach. It took all my remaining energy to keep up with him.

Did I say something wrong? Maybe his drinking *was* a touchy subject. Big red flag. Huge.

After attempting to match his long strides, I gave up and lagged behind. The coffee had warmed me, but the darkness had cooled the sand and my T-shirt, slightly damp, chilled me all over again.

It only took a few more steps before Reece realized I wasn't beside him. He immediately slowed and turned to face me. In the silky darkness, his expression appeared blank. Far down the beach, a bonfire bloomed, a distant flower blazing against the night sky.

Reece faced me, walking backward, a breeze blowing his unruly salt-water hair forward across his glasses. When he turned his head a bit, the tiny flame became visible through his lenses. It made him appear to have fire in his eyes. The effect took my breath away.

"Beautiful night, isn't it?"

"It is," I mumbled. It would be a lot more pleasant if we weren't running, I thought.

Seeming to read my mind, he slowed and allowed me to catch up at a normal pace. He slipped his arm around my shoulders as I shivered unexpectedly.

He pulled me closer, took a deep breath, and turned me to face him. Salty foam churned up the sand and washed over our flip-flops all the way to our ankles. It got deeper with each frothy wave. I pulled my towel more tightly around me. A few stars peppered the night sky, begging to be noticed and named.

"Gabi." His voice sounded serious. He hesitated, then cleared his throat and dug inside the waistband of his board shorts. I heard a tiny zip, and then he dropped to one knee in front of me.

Dumbfounded, I watched the inky silhouettes of several people moving around the flames of the bonfire over the top of his head. To my right, the dark ocean washed the sand with white spume that crushed a million ancient shells and crashed against the pilings of the pier behind us.

"Reece?" He probably couldn't even hear me over the sound of the surf.

He took my hands in both of his and I could feel something small and circular in his palm. "Gabrielle Kelly, I think you know how I feel about you." He waited a beat but I couldn't respond.

All I could do was nod at him in the scant light of the rising moon.

"I think you feel the same way about me." He turned my left hand up so the palm faced the sky. "I can't believe I'm doing this, it seems I'm always rushing you, or trying to." I saw the flash of his beautiful white teeth as he placed a delicate ring in my grasp. "I want you to marry me, Gabi. Will you?"

I closed my fingers over the ring and felt a tiny gemstone dig into my flesh. "Are you kidding me?"

Reece chuckled and I looked down at him still kneeling before me on the wet sand. The surf had re-soaked the hems of his board shorts. Something I couldn't believe I could see, much less take time to notice.

From down the beach the sound of music reached us. The bonfire party seemed to be growing louder. Every breeze brought a tiny snatch of "Margaritaville" to our ears.

I dropped to my knees, too. "I never expected—"

He took the ring from my palm and held it up to the moon-light. "It's not fancy," he said. "But it belonged to my mom."

I took the ring and turned it this way and that, admiring the classic pear shaped diamond set onto the fine band of gold.

"Try it on," he urged, taking it from me and waiting for me to stretch my ring finger toward him.

It fit perfectly. "It's beautiful," I breathed. "Did your dad give it to her."

Reece nodded. "Engagement ring. I left the wedding band at home, afraid of jinxing myself by assuming too much."

That made me giggle. I still couldn't bring myself to accept that this was happening. "Are you sure?"

"I've never been more certain of anything."

I looped my arms around his neck and pressed my lips to his. Our knees dug trenches in the wet sand. The waves reached halfway up my thighs as I whispered, "I love you, Reece Anderson."

"Will you?" he asked again.

I nodded, my breath trapped in my throat.

Reece leapt to his feet pulling me up with him. Our towels fell into the water, which was nearly to my knees even when we stood. All of a sudden, he swept me off my feet with a hand beneath my legs and one arm behind my back. I wrapped my arms around his neck and held on.

He walked us further into the water until the waves lapped at our waists, and then he set me down and devoured my lips with his kisses. It took me right back to prom and the memory of the white-hot lust that had enveloped me on the stone picnic table with Matt.

I didn't even notice how cold the water had become, or how the people at the bonfire were suddenly whooping and hollering. It wasn't until we waded out and headed down the beach in their direction—wringing our soaked towels out the best we could—that I realized the guitarist was strumming "The Wedding March."

I felt my skin glow with embarrassment, but Reece hugged me and on cue we bowed together, holding hands, as we passed the fire. A girl and a guy dashed out and dragged us to the party. It didn't take much to convince us. The flames danced across smiling faces and half-naked bodies and it warmed me almost instantly. Even the cold ice-chest beer cans they pressed into our palms couldn't dispel the wonderful heat from the fire.

Everyone offered congratulations and then the guitarist, who looked like Sammy Hagar, started strumming, "I Want You," by Bob Dylan.

Reece looked at me and once again the tiny flames danced in the twin lenses of his glasses. In the firelight, I could feel the promise of all the coming years with this tall, lanky man. And it was good.

Suddenly, I couldn't wait to start my life with him.

As if reading my mind, he pulled me to his chest and kissed

me ravenously. We broke apart and I couldn't resist holding my new ring up to catch the reflection of the flames.

Another round of raucous applause broke out and I tucked my left hand into Reece's palm, my own glasses salty and blurred.

Sammy Hagar strummed harder and sang even louder, sending the words "I want you," blasting across the waves and down the beach and I looked at these kind strangers and realized they were somehow Reece's people.

I'd definitely found my way home.

25

After a few more songs—not all of them devoted to us—the fire began to die down as couples broke away and waved goodbye, meandering down the beach toward the free street-side parking. Reece and I said our farewells and retrieved our towels from the forked sticks stuck into the sand near the fire. Dry and warm, we wrapped them around our shoulders, and strolled back to the van.

We took our time climbing the stairs to the apartment, stopping to kiss at one point, our breathing growing heavier, our towels slipping down, our T-shirts pulling up, our bare skin flaming where it touched, the cool air a balm when we broke apart. Suddenly we were laughing and chasing each other up the remaining steps and the lock wouldn't turn. "Open you slimy bastard," Reece cursed, and it was too funny because I'd never heard him say a bad word, ever.

The lock sprang open and we burst into the muted moonlit living room, pulling our shirts over our heads, falling onto the sofa on our towels. Our suits offered little resistance as we made love tenderly and hurriedly, the muffled moonlight setting the homey room aglow.

And it was wonderful right up until the moment I staggered into the bathroom and the shadow in the corner wouldn't be dispelled even when I turned on the bright overhead light. I began to think something—or someone—resented my happiness.

I closed my eyes and willed it to be gone, but when I opened them again, the thing stood shivering like dark static on an old TV. I opened my mouth to call out for Reece, finally getting up my nerve to let him in on my little problem, but the thing dissolved like black sand falling down the wall into the base of an invisible hourglass.

I waited a moment to make sure it was gone, and then I exhaled, quickly took care of my bathroom business, and dashed across the hall to his bedroom where my fiancé waited patiently.

He held one side of the sheet up so I could slide in beside him. "Come here, my soon-to-be wife."

I melted into his side and wrapped myself around his strong core. "I didn't know it could be like that," I murmured. My only other sexual encounter—which was my first and only—had been rough and quick and I'd regretted it even as it was happening. It *had* convinced me to get on regular birth control though. That was the only good thing about it.

"I knew it would be like this," he replied. "With you." He cuddled me closer. "I knew it the moment we met in camp."

I pulled myself up to him and kissed him lovingly, lingering over his face, examining every line and every lash.

He smiled slowly, eyes closed, and I kissed his lids, reveling in the smooth, velvet texture. When he opened them, I fell in love with the color of the sea all over again. "You're so beautiful."

He smiled and closed his eyes again. "More," he said. "More, and more, and more, and never stop."

I resumed my kisses, laughing each time he begged for more.

Eventually, I fell asleep on his chest, my ear pressed to his skin, our heartbeats somehow becoming synchronized until we both fell asleep.

Thank God there were no shadows, no pounding footsteps, no slamming doors. We slept straight through the night and when we woke, the sun poured in around the edges of the blue curtains. It striped the wall opposite the window and the honey-gold color reminded me of my new ring. I held it up in front of my face and the entire magical night seemed to exist in the multifaceted depths of the perfect diamond.

"Morning." Reece's voice vibrated beneath my ear.

"Morning," I replied. "Is it all true? Everything?"

He laughed. "I feel like we're in a fairytale. One of the good ones."

I sat up, trying not to think of the odd things that kept happening. Maybe they were from one of the bad ones, I thought. "I feel like we're in a fairytale, too." I wanted to ask what came next, but I didn't want to burst this sweet bubble of newness by forcing us to a different place. "I want to call my mom."

"I want to meet her," he said. "And you have to meet my dad."

Nodding, I held my ring up again. "Did he know you were going to give me this?"

"I told him when I called him from Lucia Lodge. He can't wait to meet you. Said he's always wanted a daughter."

Surprising tears sprang to my eyes and slipped over my bottom lids. I sniffled, trying to get them to stop.

"What did I say?" Reece's voice held a note of alarm.

I shook my head. "No, it's not that. It's just... my own father didn't want his daughter." For some reason, I couldn't say he didn't want ME, I had to refer to myself in the third person. "I've never had a father, except for Joe, and I never let myself think of him that way just in case it didn't, you know, work out between him and my mom." I wiped my eyes. "Sorry. I didn't mean to blurt out my whole life story."

Reece turned me onto my back and hovered over me, supporting his weight on his elbows. "I want to know everything about you, not just the good stuff, *everything*. We've both got history. I told you about my mom—" He broke off midsentence, then continued in a softer voice. "I sure wish she were here. You would love her and she would love you, too." He kissed me so gently, like a butterfly landing on my lips. "Just like I love you."

This time, the tears that ran from the sides of my eyes to pool in my ears were not entirely sad. They were happy tears, but with a touch of melancholy. Yes. It was time to call my mom. But would she be pleased, or would she worry we were rushing into things? Was it stupid to get engaged to someone my mom had never even met?

"I wonder if I should invite Mom and Joe to visit us here, and then tell them about this." I held up my ring finger. "I'm afraid it might come as a shock to her since we haven't known each other that long."

Reece chuckled. "How will she feel about us living together?"

My heart thumped. "We'll just pretend we sleep in separate rooms?"

"That could work. Maybe my dad can come down, too, before the wedding, I mean."

He lay beside me and I snuggled in under his arm again, my new favorite place. "That's an excellent idea. Speaking of the wedding... do we want to talk about the date?"

"Tomorrow's fine with me."

I elbowed him in the ribs. "I think we need to get to know each other a little bit while we're engaged." I giggled and held my ring up to his eye level. "I absolutely love this ring. Did I tell you that?"

"Not in those exact words." I heard the grin in his voice. "But I'm glad you do. Now, what do you want to know?"

I took a deep breath. "Kids," I said. "I know you love kids. You work with them on the trail, but—"

"I'm going to be a great dad. I can't wait to have little ones running around. We'll go to Magic Mountain and I'll have them out on the water as soon as they can walk and we'll surf together and—"

I interrupted him with a sigh. "You will be an amazing father. But I haven't had that much experience with little ones."

"You're a natural nurturer," he said. "You'll be a great mom."

I thought of the recent odd happenings, the panic attacks, and I wondered. Could I be a mom? Or would the stress cause me to have a nervous breakdown? I was beginning to doubt myself in ways I'd never done before. In my heart, I knew it was guilt over Rose and, to an extent, Matt, that was causing me to experience all these weird things. Yeah, but what about the sounds Reece also heard my mind whispered. What about those? And that slamming door, that was very strange.

Coincidence, I whispered back. Just coincidence.

"What?" Reece asked.

I shook my head. "Oh, nothing. Just thinking out loud. Anyhow, I don't think I want a family right away. We have to get our degrees first, right?"

"Right," he agreed. But I got the impression if it happened tomorrow it wouldn't bother him.

I sat up suddenly. "Hey, I left my new clothes in the van. Remember, I stuffed them under the seat when we got out at the beach?"

Reece yawned. "Give me fifteen more kisses and I'll go get them for you."

I heartily obliged.

It wasn't until he stood, in all his naked glory, completely unself-conscious, that I really got a good look at my new fiancé. I'd known he was all lanky muscle and golden tan, but I had no idea about the rest of him. Wow. Did all men look like this? I had no real experience with the male anatomy other than what I'd seen in Asa's medical books and the one sordid backseat encounter. But I didn't count that, not at all. And last night it had been quite dim...

Reece yawned and stretched and caught me looking. When I grinned, he slowly pulled the sheet back and let his eyes drink in every inch of me in my natural state. I shifted my legs to a more modest position and I saw the effect it had on him. He sat on the edge of the bed and drew his fingertips up the length of my body, beginning with the bottoms of my feet and ending at my lips. The process took several minutes as he followed his fingertip trail with his mouth.

By the time he got to my lips, I couldn't take anymore. I wrapped my arms and legs around him and drew his tongue into my mouth determined to never let him go. When he entered me this time, it was even better than before.

26

We fell back asleep draped across each other like exhausted puppies. Every time I stirred, he pulled me to him. But at last, hunger drove us to the kitchen.

We sat at the bar, me in his T-shirt, him in his boxers, and we ate cold cereal and drank wine. I wondered if I was the one who would become a lush, but I didn't care. I'd never been so happy.

I got Mom on the phone and invited her and Joe to come out and visit while we were on a break.

She saw right through my charade. "What's the big secret?" she asked. "That you two are living together?" I couldn't tell if she disapproved or not.

"Well, we share the apartment," I said. "I'll be paying my share of the bills, too."

"Uh huh." Her voice sounded flat.

"You're going to love him, Mom. He's the best person I've ever met. Ever."

That seemed to appease her. "I knew there was something special about him just by the way you mentioned his name when you were here." She took a long pause and when she spoke again, I could hear the tears she tried to disguise. "I can't wait to meet him."

I gulped. I hadn't expected her to get weepy. "You're going to love him," I repeated. I smiled at Reece sitting on the sofa with the remote, pretending not to be listening. "I'll see you next week. Love you."

"Love you, too, baby." She blew me a kiss and broke the connection.

Reece called his dad next, and that conversation seemed much more joyous. Of course his dad had a bit of a heads up that my mom didn't have. After he talked for a few minutes, Reece held the receiver out to me. "He wants to say hi."

I'm sure my eyes were like saucers. I took the phone. "Hello? Mr. Anderson?"

"Gabi! May I call you Gabi?"

I liked his voice. It was similar to Reece 's jovial tone, but even deeper. "Yes sir, of course you may."

"Then you just call me Archie, or Dad, whichever you prefer."

I looked over at Reece; certain he could hear each booming word. "Okay... Dad." That didn't feel quite right. Would I get used to it? Reece leaned over and hugged me sweetly. "I can't wait to meet you."

After that Reece talked to him a few more minutes—it turned out he couldn't wait to visit us and get in a little surfing. That surprised me. I tried to picture my mom or Joe out on the waves, and I couldn't do it. Of course, we'd never lived near the ocean, or any body of water. If we had, that might've made a difference. Come to think of it, they were going to be living close to the Gulf Coast now.

Next, I tried Asa. I couldn't wait to share my news with him, and to find out what was happening in his life. It seemed I hadn't seen him in years instead of just a few months. Sometimes my old life, the one I'd shared with him, felt as if it had belonged to someone else entirely.

The dorm phone rang and rang, and just before I hung up, a voice answered. "Stangel Hall."

"Umm, hello. I – um, I'm looking for Asa Letter." I hated sounding so timid. I didn't know why Asa had fallen out of touch so abruptly.

"Don't know the name. You sure he's in this dorm?"

No, I wasn't sure at all. "I thought he was. I know he's pre-med."

"Hold on, let me check the roster."

He put the phone down and went away. I could hear movement in the background. Doors opened and closed. Footsteps pounded up and down stairs, and someone yelled, "Bring that back!" And then the voice returned. "Okay, here it is. He stayed here for a couple of weeks, and then he moved out and left Tech altogether."

"What?" I couldn't believe my ears. "Why would he do that?" I didn't really expect the guy to answer; I just couldn't wrap my head around what he'd said.

"Says here he transferred. International."

Now I was really confused. "International? What does that mean?" I didn't care if I sounded like an idiot.

"International, you know, to another country." He waited for me to reply, and when I didn't (because I didn't know what to say), he continued. "Lots of people go to international schools for their medical degrees, usually in Central American countries, but this one is a little different. Looks like he transferred to Bern, Switzerland." He chuckled.

"Switzerland? Seriously?"

"I wouldn't lie. Would you like the forwarding address? Oh wait, here's an actual phone number. Will wonders never cease?"

He seemed to be enjoying digging through Asa's file. I had to wonder if it was legal, him giving me—a perfect stranger—all this personal information. I wasn't going to look the gift horse in the mouth, though. "Of course, that would be great."

"Got a pencil?"

I grabbed one off Reece's end table. "Ready," I said.

He rattled off a long string of numbers and I wrote them on Reece's little spiral bound notepad beside the phone. "Wow." I'd never made an international call in my life. I didn't know there were so many digits. "Thanks so much. I – I appreciate it."

"No prob," the guy said before breaking the connection.

Reece told me to call it.

"It will be expensive."

"Then you'll just have to make it up to me later." He waggled his eyebrows and pushed his glasses up. The effect was comical.

I leaned over and kissed the tip of his nose. "Anything you want," I whispered.

That seemed to give him something to think about.

I quickly dialed the number and after a few very strange rings—it sounded like one long ring from far, far away—a male voice answered, "Grüezi."

"Umm, hello?" I took a breath and rushed on. "I'm looking for Asa Letter. Is he – is this his number?"

"Asa?" the man answered in perfect English. "One moment, please." Something about the voice suddenly reminded me of someone from high school. There'd been a foreign exchange student, very quiet, kept to himself. Had he been at prom? Or wait, was he the one driving the silver Audi that night at the pond? I hadn't seen his face, but...

I held my breath. In the background, I heard faint conversation and then Asa came on the line.

He sounded wary. "Hello?"

I couldn't contain my excitement. "Asa?"

He exhaled as if he'd been worried about who might be calling. "Gabs? Honey, is that you?"

"It's me!" I squealed. "I'm engaged, Asa! I couldn't wait to tell you." I stopped to take a breath.

He sounded truly excited to hear from me, just like my old Asa. "Engaged? Who? Is it someone I know?"

"No, I met Reece through SCA up on the mountain. We live in California, I'm going to go to CSUN and work for SCA, too. I tried to call you at your dad's house."

Asa laughed jovially. "I know, Maria told me. I tried your house and the phone just rang and rang and rang, not even an answering machine—"

I groaned. "Mom and Joe went off on a three week cruise. Then they got married last week, in Vegas. Now they live in Houston. Actually, I tried to call you from Vegas, too." The memory of why I'd tried to call came flooding back. "That's when Mom told me about Rose going missing."

"I heard that, too." Asa's voice fell into my ear like a stone into a well. "She must have hightailed it out of there when Matt was transferred to Fort Worth."

A weight fell from my shoulders. "So you *did* know. Mom was on the cruise when it happened, but she found out when she got back. Apparently his brain injury was just too severe. He has to relearn everything. But I guess you already knew all that." Which reminded me. "Just what the heck are you doing in Switzerland anyway?"

Asa cleared his throat. "I came to Bern to be with Sven. His dad was killed in a car accident and he had to come back to help his mother. We live together, Gabs. He's, well, he's the best thing that ever happened to me."

"Awww, Ace. That's great. I'm so thrilled for you. Sven is the foreign exchange student, right? I vaguely remember him from school. I don't think we ever had any classes together or anything. But please give him my sympathy for the loss of his father. That must be so hard."

"Yes. He is struggling with it. He's quiet, you know. Back in Live Oak, he kept to himself most of the time. Didn't trust people. It's so much more relaxed over here, Gabi. I think Sven was in complete culture shock in the States. Anyhow, I couldn't tell you about him. I couldn't betray his confidence. Not even at prom that night."

"Wow. I had no idea. Well, I was going to invite you to come and visit me here in sunny California, but I guess that's out of the picture, huh? I mean, you are going to medical school, right?"

"Oh yes, well, I will be as soon as my transcript clears. They said I will be on the fast track once all the paperwork is in order." He stopped talking and began to cough. "Sorry," he said after a moment. "Picked up a little cold here in the Alps. Imagine that."

"I hope you feel better soon—"

"Oh, I feel fine," he interrupted. "It's just this nagging darn cough."

"Have you got back on the old wacky weed?" I joked. Neither of us had been able to see the attraction so many of our class-mates had for smoking marijuana. It had been a running joke between us ever since we'd tried it together on his roof one night.

"Oh, definitely," Asa played along. "I'm a regular pothead now."

I laughed. It felt so good to laugh with my friend again. "Well, I have to get off the phone. I can only imagine what this is going to cost," I looked over at Reece who made an imaginary hangman's noose around his neck.

"I understand. Hey, when's the wedding? Maybe we can get over there somehow—if it isn't too soon—"

"We haven't even set the date yet. We just got engaged last night. Oh, it was so romantic, Ace. But I can't talk about it now. We'll be on here all night. I'll write you—"

"I just had the most amazing idea," he said. "Come *here* for your honeymoon. I don't want to brag, but we have a huge home that's been in Sven's family forever. We've got plenty of room."

"Oh, Asa. That sounds too good to be true. I'll talk to Reece. You will love him, by the way, did I say that already?"

He sighed. "You did, and I know I will. And you're going to love my Sven, too, once you get to know him." I sensed a bit of trepidation in that statement but then I decided he was simply referring to the fact that we'd gone to school together for a whole year without ever speaking.

"Hey, Ace. Make sure it's okay with Sven, too, okay?"

"Of course." I could picture him waving my worries away. "I know it will be, but we'll talk, don't worry."

"By the way," I said. "I thought Sven was blond and blue-eyed."

"Yeah, he is. Why?"

"Oh, I had sort of thought you were having a thing with that dark haired guy you were talking to at prom."

"Oh—Dillon Karson? No. His dad used to be a golfing buddy of my father's. But they had a falling out. Now, he doesn't like me. I was terrified he might say or do something to out both Sven and me."

I recalled the strange look Asa kept giving the thin, dark haired boy. Man, had I misinterpreted that. Well, at least it made sense now. We said our goodbyes with Asa promising to call me in a few days to set our plans after we'd both talked to our significant others. Of course Reece loved the idea of Switzerland for a honeymoon. "There's only one thing," he said. "We may have to tie the knot soon. During winter break at school. Unless you plan to make me wait until spring."

"Hmmm, we could wait. That wouldn't be a problem. I mean we're living together anyway, right?"

Reece nodded. "That's true. But if we're going to ski, and why visit Switzerland if we aren't going to ski, then we need to go before spring."

"Ahhh, now I get it. Always the athlete. And here I thought we were just going to sit by a cozy fire all day."

He grabbed me and swung me around in a circle. "We can have a cozy fire on the beach here every night if that's what you want."

"I do," I said. "Just like last night. Oh, I can't wait to be Mrs. Reece Anderson." I showed him my ring again. "I'm just following in my mom's footsteps aren't I? Moving near the ocean, getting married, starting a brand new life."

"Works for me," he said. "I told you we were soulmates the first time we met."

I laughed. "Did you really tell your dad we were going to get married way back when we were at Lucia Lodge?"

My fiancé flashed me a wicked smile. "Yes, I did. I told you I always go after what I want." His expression became serious. "I didn't mean to eavesdrop," he said, "but do you have a friend that's gone missing?"

I tried not to let the disgust show on my face. "Not a friend, it's a girl who came to our prom with her cousin. He had a wreck on prom night, and now he's been transferred to a rehab hospital in Fort Worth and she's gone missing." My hand automatically went to my old buffalo nickel necklace.

Reece touched my hand, the one holding the coin. "And did he give you this? The boy who had the wreck?"

Startled, I replied, "How'd you know?"

"You caress it sometimes." His voice was soft. "I knew it had to be from someone special."

I ducked my head so he wouldn't see the tears that surprised me. "He did. He gave it to me on prom night."

Instead of being jealous, Reece leaned down and kissed me. "We've both got histories," he said. "Nothing wrong with that."

But what if he knew the truth about Rose? What if he knew I'd hit her with the car and left her at the pond and she hadn't been seen since? Would that be all right, too? Or would he have second thoughts about the wedding?

I closed my eyes and willed away the worries. There was nothing I could do about it now.

27

W e got our license and wouldn't you know? One of Reece 's old surfing buddies was also an ordained minister. He agreed to perform the ceremony on the beach at sunset on any given day. It reminded me of the minister in Las Vegas.

I told Reece I was a little surprised he didn't want a church wedding, but he assured me that even though he practiced Christianity, he didn't feel comfortable in any particular church. "Remember what you said about the forest being holy?"

I remembered.

"That's how I feel. Nature is my church, both the forest and the beach. It's been that way for a long, long time."

That didn't surprise me. It fit everything about him.

It felt right to me, too.

MOM AND JOE talked to Reece on the phone several times. Joe couldn't get away from his new job, but Mom flew down and spent a weekend. She insisted on getting a motel room nearby even though Reece offered to sleep on the sofa and let her have his bed. I couldn't tell if she really believed we were living together platonically, or whether she was simply resigned. At any rate, by the time she left, she seemed to have a genuine affection for Reece, and he for her. Which was good since we were getting married in a couple of weeks.

Once again, Mom and I went wedding dress shopping. This time, however, we hit the vintage stores on Rodeo Drive. She said she would never forgive herself if she didn't at least stroll the famous shopping lane while she was here—it was my idea to go vintage. I knew what I wanted. I had an idea of it in my mind. Hippie style from the sixties; long and flowing, like something you'd see on an old album cover. I'd be barefoot, of course, as would Reece.

The dress I found was simple ecru cotton with a bohemian lace overlay. Asa sent me a certificate for flowers, as many as we wanted, and for the bouquet as well. That was his gift to us since he couldn't be there. We'd already booked our flights for the honeymoon, though. I could not wait to see him—of course that wasn't the only reason I was excited about the honeymoon. Although, to be honest, it had felt like a honeymoon every day since I'd moved in.

The day of the wedding dawned overcast and gray. Mom and Joe were in a Holiday Inn nearby. Reece's dad stayed with us. He took the room that was originally mine, and the night before the wedding, he made Reece sleep in there with him because of that same old superstition that the bride and groom shouldn't see each other the day of the wedding. They planned to hit the waves early the next morning.

Suddenly I wished we had set the time for sunrise instead of sunset. How would I ever go a whole day without seeing him?

Mom to the rescue. She arrived at the apartment before breakfast, gathered up my dress, all my toiletries, and me, and away we went, back to her hotel via the scenic route. As she ushered me out the door of the apartment, I thought of one more thing. "I'll be done in five minutes," I said, pushing her toward the stairs. "I forgot something."

She urged me to hurry; she couldn't wait to see the coast up close and personal. I dashed back to our bedroom and pulled my tiny jade encrusted jewelry box down from the top shelf of Reece 's closet. He'd given it to me only yesterday. An early wedding present, he'd said.

With a twinge of trepidation, I pulled Matt's long chain up and over my head. The space between my breasts felt naked without the old nickel nestled there.

I tucked it down in the bottom of the felt lined wooden box and bit my lip. Today I would be married. I didn't think it right to wear the gift from my only other love—even though to remove it felt as if I'd given up on him. It would be safe here, and someday, maybe I would take it out again. When I had a chance to visit him in Fort Worth. But wearing it now was not going to help him. Even if that silly idea had lived in the back of my mind all this time.

I closed the lid and placed the little box back in the closet. Eventually it would have a home on my dresser, but for now, I liked knowing it was safe and out of sight.

Mom appeared to be champing at the bit when I dashed down the stairs and hopped into the car. Without another word, we drove out of the complex, took a short drive to CSUN so she could see it for herself, and then we hit the Pacific Coast Highway. We drove for miles and miles while Joe slept and Reece and his dad surfed.

The day with Mom turned out to be one of those memories-in-the-making. The rain came in bare spatters, keeping the weather cool and moist. We drove and talked, sharing childhood reminiscences and all our hopes and dreams, both the ones that came true and the ones that were still ahead. She finally gave in and told me all about my absentee father.

She said everything had started as the typical high school romance. But it quickly went south when his wealthy parents found out she was pregnant. His mother actually offered her ten thousand dollars if she would agree to give me up for adoption and never see their son again. Mom said she was so dumb-founded she ran straight to her boyfriend—my so-called dad—and begged him to marry her and start their life together. He coldly informed her he'd been accepted to Columbia, his mom's alma mater, and would be going to school early. He said he would pay for an abortion if she didn't want to put me up for adoption.

Mom freaked out, got back in her car, and just drove. Gran and Gramps tracked her down at a motel outside Abilene the very next day. They didn't even know what was going on, but when they found out, everything changed. They convinced her she would be able to make it as a single parent. Gramps even paid a lawyer to draw up the paperwork for the sperm-donor to terminate his parental rights.

Wiping a tear from the corner of her eye, she said, "I never wanted you to know what a jerk he was." She concentrated on the unrolling ribbon of highway. When I didn't say anything, she continued. "I blame his mother. She wouldn't accept it. Couldn't I suppose, and he'd never been allowed to make mistakes so he didn't know how to take responsibility for his—our—actions." She patted my arm. "It wasn't you. It wasn't even me. It was just them and their shallow morals and obsession with veneers. All they could think about was what would the country clubbers think, what would it do to his college fund, how would *their* lives be affected. They never once thought about you as a real baby, or about me as someone who might actually love their son." She wiped away more tears.

"He contacted me shortly after you started kindergarten. He'd got his law degree just like his mother and father had planned, and he was extremely unhappy. He wanted to know if you ever asked about him." She glanced my way for a second, and I favored her with a thin smile. "I told him no, that you knew nothing about him and never would. I went on to tell him we never wanted to see or hear from him again."

By this time, we'd driven all the way to Santa Monica. I'd wanted to go to Surfrider and take her to Malibu Farm Pier Café. I knew we'd probably see Reece and his dad—I guess I hoped we would—but at the last moment I decided to play it safe and stay away. Why tempt Fate? So we just drove and drove until we got to Santa Monica Pier and got out to walk.

We ate at a boardwalk hotdog stand but I was careful and ordered an avocado stuffed pita. I wasn't taking a chance on getting a bad hotdog on my special day. The weather had cleared, and the walk turned into a wade in the ocean. I enjoyed being with my mom so much, the time slipped by and suddenly we were laughing and rushing back toward the car. I didn't think it would take us that long to get back, but Mom insisted we leave at least a two-hour safety gap. "No way I'm going to make you late for your own wedding," she said.

To my delight, I soon learned the real reason Mom had made us start back so early. We stopped by LAX and picked up my dear grandparents who had made Mom swear not to tell me they were coming. I couldn't wait for them to meet Reece. My only regret was that they hadn't come down a day or two earlier.

I did have a couple of hours with them as we drove back to Mom's motel, where they had also reserved a room.

Suddenly, I had an attack of nerves. Time sped up and the final hours flew by in a blur. Then it was time.

Joe drove us the short distance to Surfrider where instead of simply spending the day surfing, Reece and his dad had been supervising the preparations for the ceremony.

I didn't see him when we arrived in Joe's rented limo, a very sweet touch from my new stepdad, but when they had me safely ensconced in the tent-like cabana, I peeked out and watched as he and his dad made their way through the guests to the archway. My knees went soft at the sight of him in his white board shorts and blue, white, and yellow floral shirt. The colors made his tan skin and blond hair glow against the backdrop of the ocean. I giggled when I saw that his dad was barefoot, too.

I studied the rest of the scene, trying to tattoo everything into my memory. The guests sat on white and yellow beach chairs facing a sky smudged with broad pink and yellow streaks on a soft background of cloudy blue.

In addition to my grandparents, Mom and Joe, Reece's dad, and all of Reece's surfer buddies, lots of crewmembers from SCA were also in attendance.

Lucy and Eduardo sat with Jerenda and Stephen. I thought I could see Aurelia, but it was hard to tell from the back of her head. I didn't see Nate anywhere; he'd said he had another assignment coming up and might not make it.

When our new friend, Robbie, the bonfire guitarist who looked like Sammy Hagar, began playing "The Wedding Song (There is Love)," by Peter, Paul, & Mary, Joe walked me from the cabana down a carpet of yellow and pink rose petals that perfectly echoed the colors of the coming sunset. As we neared her, I heard Mom tell Gran the yellow roses represented the great state of Texas. I had to cover my mouth to stifle a nervous giggle when I heard that.

Joe delivered me to Mom and she escorted me the rest of the way to Reece who stood with his dad. The white archway had been covered with cascading yellow and pink climbing roses. Twin torches burned merrily on either side of the arch. In front of Zack, the minister, someone had scratched the word SOUL-MATES into the damp beach sand.

I handed Mom my simple bouquet of baby roses and baby's breath, and she stepped back. Reece smiled, pushed up his glasses, and took both my hands. It surprised me when I felt him tremble with emotion. I turned loose of him just long enough to push up my own glasses, and that's when the twin torches fell against the wooden archway and set it on fire.

Reece and the other guys rushed into action yanking everything up and throwing it into the ocean where it hissed and fizzled and came washing right back to shore.

"Well," Joe shrugged. "That's the way to start a marriage, with a little excitement. Make some memories."

Everyone laughed. The sea breeze was such a constant, no one gave the little accident a second thought.

The ceremony continued. By now the incoming tide had begun to close in on our carpet of petals. But we'd counted on that. We liked the idea of the ocean taking them away. I hoped the foam would reach us before we were done.

"Dearly beloved," Zack began.

I took a deep, calming breath and squeezed Reece's hands. He returned the pressure and the pounding of my heart slowed to match the swooshing of the ever-present waves.

Thank goodness our vows were uncomplicated—we agreed to love and honor each other for all the days of our lives—I doubt I could've recited much more. When he asked us for rings, Reece's dad handed over the plain gold band that went with my engagement ring, and Reece slipped it on my finger. I'd bought him a narrow band of gold to match my own.

As soon as Zack pronounced us wed, we shared our first kiss as husband and wife. All the stress fell away and I knew without a doubt I'd made the right choice, even though it had been a whirlwind.

When we turned to the guests, Eduardo caught my eye and winked broadly. I grinned and winked back.

Now that the actual ceremony was over, we were able to relax. We strolled back to the bonfire where our new friends tended the food and drink. The photographer—Lucy's friend—took a million pictures, but my favorite one turned out to be right after the ceremony when we started back down the petal-strewn aisle and Reece's SOULMATES message was framed at our feet.

We walked back through the guests while Robbie played the full version of "The Wedding Song," and then belted out Dylan's "Forever Young." It sent chills up my spine and into my soul.

As the sun slipped deeper into the ocean, he began the unmistakable opening of Savage Garden's "Truly, Madly, Deeply." We came together shyly, holding each other close to turn and sway and glide through the flickering tongues of fire-light for our first dance as newlyweds.

Soon everyone was dancing and the music flowed as freely as the champagne and we traded partners so that it seemed we had at least a minute or two with every single guest in attendance. Every now and then I would be swept back into my husband's arms and we would laugh and nuzzle and kiss, and then another someone would separate us and send us spinning in opposite directions. Robbie made sure he included one classic after another so that before long everyone was singing along.

The reception dinner consisted of champagne, veggie and seafood shish kebabs, s'mores, and more champagne served on long white tables. When I threw the bouquet, Jerenda caught it and looked directly at Stephen, which elicited much teasing and caterwauling from the rest of the SCA folks. Robbie played Clapton's "You Look Wonderful Tonight," and followed it up with a medley of Beatles' love songs—"And I Love Her," "Something (in the way she moves)," "When I'm Sixty-Four," "All My Loving," and "If I Fell."

"Someone must've told Robbie how much I love The Beatles," I murmured when I had Reece back in my arms for a moment.

He just smiled and kissed me deeply.

At last, the fire died down and the dancers began to slow.

Robbie whammed the strings and broke into "I Want You," just as he had the first time we met him. That was the signal for us to catch our plane for the short hop to San Francisco where we would spend the night before catching our flight to Bern the following day.

After many rounds of tearful goodbyes and good lucks, I slipped into the cabana and changed into my own white shorts and floral shirt that exactly matched the outfit Reece wore. Mom and Gran stuffed an envelope full of cash into my pocketbook and told me to be sure and change it into francs as soon as possible. It seems they had set up a secret money tree that everyone knew about but us.

In the limo on the way to the airport, we snuggled and kissed and began to whisper the things we were going to do to each other as soon as we reached our honeymoon suite. I was thankful for the smoked glass separating us from our driver. We didn't actually make love, but we came close.

The nearer we got to the hotel, the more nervous I became.

Reece picked up on my nerves and pulled me onto his lap. "What, cold feet *now*?"

I shook my head. "I love you with all my heart. This is the happiest day of my life—"

He nibbled my neck and nipped at my ear lobe. "But?"

How did he always know there was a but? "But I feel strange. As if something is going to go wrong. As if some awful thing is waiting right around the bend, or over the horizon—"

"Or over the ocean?"

The voice of reason. "No, I've never been afraid to fly. It's, well, I—" Just then a car pulled out in front of us and the driver swerved, making me gasp as I peered out the window.

Reece followed my round-eyed gaze? "What is it? What's got you so worried?"

I shook my head. "It's nothing. Just silly nerves." That, and maybe a little superstitious feeling that I was so incredibly happy the other shoe was bound to fall at any time.

I closed my eyes, willing the anxiety to abate. When I opened them, Reece stared at me with an expression of deep concern. "Too much champagne. You'll feel better in the morning."

"Yes," I said. "I'm sure that's all it is." I took his hand and brought it to my lips. "I can't wait to begin our lives together."

Reece held me and kissed me tenderly. "You've been under too much stress. You left your home in Texas before you even graduated, and then your mom up and got married, selling your childhood home, leaving you rootless. Maybe things have been moving so fast you haven't had time to catch your breath." He stroked my hair and adjusted his glasses. "You don't have to worry anymore. I'm your home now. And you are mine."

I laid my head on his shoulder and breathed a sigh of relief. Jeez. We should have said that in our vows. It made me feel safe, and loved.

A cold spot the size of a coin arose between my breasts. I ignored it and concentrated on my new husband.

His golden-brown skin tasted like salt.

28

The honeymoon started with a bang. Although we were both exhausted and drained emotionally, we had just enough energy left to admire the gorgeous view of the Golden Gate Bridge from our suite at The Four Seasons. I'd never understood the big deal about a bridge before, but seeing it up close gave me a new appreciation. It was glorious. And when we learned that we had a trolley stop right outside the front door, we vowed to get up early enough to ride it before going to the airport.

We were sad to be done with our limo, the driver was so nice and the back seat so huge and plush (and inviting), but at least the hotel had an airport shuttle service so we wouldn't have to get a cab.

After making certain we admired the view from the room, the bellboy left us alone with our luggage and another bottle of champagne chilling in a silver bucket. Reece held it up questioningly.

"Why not?" I said. "Just a tiny glass. We can't let it go to waste, right?"

"Right." He poured it into the crystal stemware. "But only if we have some of this caviar to go with it."

I grimaced. "The way I feel, maybe I'll eat the crackers and you eat the fish eggs."

He laughed and raised his glass in a toast. "To us," he said.

I clinked carefully and added, "And to a million years together—soulmate."

He grinned and picked me up the way he'd done the night he proposed on the beach. Only this time, he laid me gently on the huge white bed. Honeymoon suite, all the way, someone had scattered rose petals here, too. They'd even copied our sunset wedding colors.

Reece undressed first, slowly. With great relish I sipped my champagne, nibbled my crackers, and watched him in the softly muted light from the rose-shaded bedside lamp. I'll never get tired of this, I thought. He is every sculptor's dream model, long and lean, all corded abs and thighs.

He removed his glasses and crawled up the bed to lie beside me. Taking my champagne glass from my hand, he tipped the remaining few drops onto my lips and kissed it away. Then he removed my glasses and laid them on the bedside table next to his. Our poor children will have severe myopia, I thought, but the idea was cut short as he began unbuttoning my blouse and shorts.

When I was naked he reached for the champagne bottle and rolled its chilled glass surface up the inside of my thigh making me close my eyes and grip the sheets with both hands. I opened my eyes as he dribbled a stream of bubbles onto my belly and breasts before slowly licking it all away. After that, things moved quickly to the incredible climax. Our pleasure lasted longer every time we made love. I vowed to myself to always be as generous in bed as he had proved to be.

"Husband," I breathed.

"Wife," he replied.

We fell asleep in a puddle of dampness that was only partially caused by spilled champagne.

The next morning, we bathed in the inviting heart shaped tub beneath the window overlooking the bay and the Golden Gate Bridge.

But since we'd slept in, we wound up rushing around dressing in layers for our trip to Bern. Asa had said the weather was already much colder than we would be used to, although I doubted he'd ever spent a night on the side of the Lucia Mountain Range in nothing but a sleeping bag and a tent.

Nevertheless, we knew what to do. With our fleece jackets tied around our waists, we caught the shuttle headed for the airport. I was only slightly disappointed that we didn't have time for a trolley ride after all.

My belly rumbled and Reece said, "We'd better get a bite in the airport before we board. Here," he pulled out a pack of Dramamine and offered me one. "Better safe than sorry."

I agreed. So much champagne the night before had left me more than a little queasy and fuzzy headed. "Thanks, hubs."

He just grinned and patted my knee.

THE FLIGHT WAS UNEVENTFUL, largely due to the fact that the Dramamine knocked me out and I slept the whole way. I felt Reece get up once or twice, and once he got a blanket from the flight attendant and covered us both. But I'm pretty sure he slept nearly the whole way, too, even though it was much harder for him to fit his long legs into the cramped space. When we woke, he had sprawled into the aisle without even knowing it.

"Glad we're here," I mumbled. "My first transatlantic flight, and I missed it."

He laughed. "Seen one ocean from thirty thousand feet, I guess you've seen 'em all."

We were spellbound by the Alps outside our window. "It's just like the pictures in all the books," I said as we oohed and ahhhed over the snow-capped peaks. "What an amazing landscape."

When we saw the horseshoe shaped Aare River, we knew we had reached our destination.

"I want to see the bears," I said, reminding Reece about The Bärengraben, the bear pit that had been around since the middle ages.

"It sounds sad," my new hubby murmured, "Tourist attractions."

I thought about it. Maybe he was right, but I knew I'd have to see them for myself just to say I did.

Then we were landing and my eyes were trying to take in everything at once while still watching for Asa, my oldest and dearest friend.

And then he was there.

He met us at the airport gate and walked us to the baggage claim. He looked the same, just a bit thinner.

I introduced him to my new husband and they shook hands warmly. Asa shot me an approving look and I nearly cracked up. On the way to the car, he never shut up. "I've got a whole tourist package thing for you two." He cleared his throat. "I consider Bern my home now. I want to show it off. And Sven, of course." He rolled his eyes. "You know him already, Gabs. Sort of at least."

I nodded. "Sweet Asa, I'm so thrilled you guys found each other. You were always my rock."

He coughed a few times, a deep, harsh bark. "Sorry," he said. "He would've been here with me to meet you, but he works full time at his mother's clinic. He's in the business side of medicine, although that may change if his mom has her way." He paused and took a drink of something in his cup holder, then continued as if he hadn't stopped. His excitement was evident. Or perhaps it was nerves. The smell of cigarette smoke hung heavy in the car.

"I can't wait to see your home and school, and the whole city —heck, the whole country!"

"Ditto that," Reece spoke up from the back seat. "We really appreciate your hospitality."

Asa waved his hand at Reece in the rearview mirror. "You're family now," he said. "I'll expect the same treatment when I come to SoCal to learn to surf." He smiled that sardonic smile.

Reece nodded and leaned forward to clasp Asa's thin shoulder. "Anytime, buddy, our casa es su casa."

I could see that Asa was a bit surprised at the complete acceptance from my new surfer husband. I think his history of forced secrecy led him to expect unkind treatment as a norm.

"So, what about school?" I asked. "Are they letting you in yet?"

His face told more than his words. That's when he explained that he was still waiting on his admission packet to be reviewed.

"Well," I finally said. "I'm sure it's so much more difficult to transfer internationally."

He didn't respond, instead pointing out interesting sights in the medieval looking old town through which we were driving. Then we entered the Nydegg Bridge over the River Aare.

"Oh, wow..." I couldn't keep the awe from my voice as we traversed the stone bridge that followed the curving river through the town.

"Look at these triple arches," Reece said. "Gorgeous."

"Wait until I show you Bern Bridge," he said. "Oldest bridge in Europe. In fact, it was the only way out of the walled city back in the seventeenth century."

He'd obviously done his history on his adopted city.

My eyes drank in the amazing sights. "How old is this place? Can we get out and walk?" I wanted to touch it, feel it, taste it, and experience it for myself.

"Of course we can walk. Some of these places were started in the twelfth century." He found a place to park and we all got out and stretched.

"The middle ages?"

Asa grinned. "Ain't it cool?"

We all laughed, and I linked an arm through both of theirs, locking us into a trio as we strolled along in the gorgeous alpine air. "This valley," I said.

"Yes," he agreed. "This beautiful, magical valley." We all looked up at the Alps in the distance and I think I actually sighed.

We wandered the cobblestone streets and Asa continued with his mini-history lesson. "The very first settlers here were from the Neolithic period."

I was astounded, but before I could speak, Asa stopped and began to cough. "Damn cold," he said when he could catch a breath. "Maybe the Alpine air isn't all it's cracked up to be. At least not for this old desert rat."

I hugged him tightly. "C'mon, sweetie, let's get you home. I'm beat anyway."

Reece took his arm and together we escorted him back to the car.

He took a deep drink of his bottled water, and then he actually lit a cigarette and stood beside the car for a few painful sounding puffs. In a bit, he felt well enough to drive us on through town to their house on the hill. I wanted to scold him for the cigarettes, but he'd smoked so long, ever since we hit high school, that I didn't bother to protest. I'd always thought it was just another way for him to get a rise out of his dad, until it had become an addiction.

Sven stood in the doorway of their home, watching for us, when we pulled into the circle drive. He hadn't changed since I'd last seen him. He still possessed a coolness that made him the calm to Asa's storm. I immediately sensed that they fit together as perfectly as any jigsaw puzzle.

"Gabi." He gave me a brief hug. "Congratulations." He turned to Reece and shook his hand. "So glad to meet you."

Reece shook and once again thanked them for their hospitality.

The house was a veritable mansion, a mini sandstone castle. I wondered if it was as old as the bridge, but I told myself it couldn't be. One thing seemed certain, though, Sven's mother appeared to be quite wealthy. Asa said she owned controlling interest in three clinics in the area, and divided her time between them. I took it that Sven was something of an apprentice in the business department of the Bern office, which struck me as a little odd. I wondered why he didn't follow her into medicine, but of course I'd never ask. It would be akin to asking Asa why his own father hadn't tried to convince him to stay and go to med school in the states.

On the other hand, with their strained relationship, he'd never planned on doing the alma mater thing anyway. He wanted to do everything on his own, always.

Once inside, Asa led us through the immense, tapestry-hung entryway and into the impressive book lined library. "When I get everything straightened out, and get my basics completed, Dr. Haag has promised to mentor me as I go through the various medical rotations. Right now, I'm leaning toward oncology."

"That is fantastic," I said. "Sven, your mom must be a very generous person. I hope we get to meet her soon."

He shook his head. "I don't think she'll be back in time.

Since my father's death, she's been extremely busy. Right now, she's in Zurich attending a conference."

I mumbled a "sorry we'll miss her," but in truth, I felt almost dismissed. I decided it was probably just me being a porcupine, letting my feelings stick out all over, and I determined not to let Sven's cool attitude ruin our visit.

Sven showed us to our room while Asa went to his to lie down for a bit. "This little respiratory infection is kicking my butt," he declared.

We unpacked our bags in a luxurious ivory and navy room fit for visiting royalty. The velvet spreads and drapes, the embossed wallpapers, even the ornate fixtures in the bathroom, all cried wealth—old wealth. "I'll bet she came from a long line of physicians," I whispered.

"Why are we whispering," Reece asked.

I giggled self-consciously. "I have no idea. I feel like I'm in a museum or something."

My new husband leered at me. "I can bring you back to the present."

I removed my shoes and crawled onto the bed, and then before he could attack me, I jumped up and pulled the blue velvet duvet from the four-poster and folded it neatly over the heavily carved blanket rack in the corner.

"Now," I said, running to jump on the bed.

Reece threw himself on me, covering me with kisses.

"Dinner in an hour," Sven called through the door. "I'm making Beef Wellington if you're hungry."

We fell away from each other like two kids caught playing you-show-me-yours by an irate mommy. "Did you hear a knock?" I mouthed.

Reece shook his head.

"Do you think he was eavesdropping?"

My new husband stretched himself out, hands behind his

head. His shirt and my bra hung from one of the thick bedposts. "Nah. Just a coincidence, I'm sure."

Feeling chastised, I called out that we would love Beef Wellington. I then went into the sumptuous bathroom to freshen up.

I opened the quaint wooden window shutters and my heart flip-flopped in my chest. Built near the top of the hill, the back of the house seemed to teeter on the slope. When I opened the window, the valley spread out below us like a green-velvet-lined jewel box. "Reece," I called. "You've got to see this view."

Sauntering in, my new husband surveyed the scene outside the window like a young lord. "I can dig it," he joked.

"I can't wait to get out and do some more exploring."

"And hit those slopes," he added.

I nodded and sat on the bathroom bench to run a quick bath. The flight had been long and cramped. A tiny soak, a change of clothes, and then we would be presentable for dinner.

"So- no fooling around?" Reece asked in an innocent voice.

I added a capful of vanilla scented bubble bath to the water and then glanced in as if measuring the volume. "I don't know... this tub seems big enough for two. Don't you think?"

Reece skimmed off his jeans and was in the tub before I could turn around.

We were both refreshed when we went down to dinner an hour later.

29

A sa sat at a massive kitchen island watching Sven prepare the beef for plating. I didn't want to admit I'd never seen Beef Wellington. The dish looked delicious and extravagant, especially when Sven plated it alongside fingerling potatoes with fresh herbs and wilted greens.

"You missed the fun part," Asa said. "He flambéd it and didn't catch anything on fire."

We both laughed and Asa rose and took us into the formal dining room. "Is this a hoot, or what?"

"It's gorgeous." I sat on the damask covered dining chair Asa pulled out for me. "You fit right in old friend. I'm so glad you found *your* soulmate."

He shoved the chair back under me, gently, and indicated a chair for Reece on the other side. "Thanks," Reece said.

Asa laid an envelope beside Reece's place setting before strolling back to the kitchen to help Sven bring in the meal.

"What's that?" I leaned over for a closer look.

Reece slid a finger underneath the flap. Opening the envelope carefully, he reached in and pulled out two all day passes for Gstaad Ski Resort. They were dated for the next day. Reece almost fell out of his chair. "Oh, wow," he said. "This is topnotch skiing." His eyes shone with awe.

I hugged him just as Asa and Sven walked in carrying plates and platters. Reece held up the passes. "You guys shouldn't have done this. It's too generous."

Asa beamed. "It's just our little wedding gift—"

"But you sent the flowers, and opened your beautiful home to us," I said.

My old friend waved his hand at me in a dismissive gesture. "Besides Sven, you're my best friend, Gabi. Not being there on your big day almost tore my heart out. Please, just indulge me these little luxuries."

I jumped up and wrapped him in a bear hug almost upsetting the plates he carried. "I love you, old friend. There was a huge hole in the big day without you there." I kissed him soundly on the cheek and then sat back down. "After we eat, I'll drag out the few pictures that we have." I laughed. "My Gran brought her instamatic camera and snapped away so we'd have some to show you."

"And I'm so glad she did." Reece looked at me. "I had the most beautiful bride in the world."

"Well," Asa said. "First, I want to hear all about the courtship." He placed the dishes on the table and passed the bread around.

Sven poured the wine and raised his glass in a toast. "Cheers to the newlyweds. Welcome to our home."

We clinked, and dined, and sipped our wine. Conversation centered on our wedding and on Asa and Sven's decision to relocate to Bern. "It was simply coming home, for me," Sven said, his voice soft, his accent even softer. "I miss my father, though. That's my one regret. I hadn't seen him since starting my exchange program last year, and then, poof! In the blink of an eye, he was gone." His gaze slid across the table to Asa who nodded but looked away.

We murmured our condolences of course, but in my heart I was glad he'd shared his pain. It made me feel better to know he actually had a heart. Because up to now, I'd heard the words he said, but I'd felt absolutely zero warmth from the man. In fact, I'd begun to think we were there against his wishes.

The meal was unbelievable and I complimented the chef liberally.

Sven accepted the compliments with nonchalance, but Asa let us know right away that cooking really was his partner's passion. "He's an accomplished chef already, and he wants to study at the Institute of Culinary Education in New York, or maybe Le Cordon Bleu in Paris." He shot Sven an unreadable look. "But his mom really needs him here now that his father is gone."

"Que sera, sera," Sven said. "One must do what one must do." He laughed a punitive little laugh and then beat a hasty retreat to the kitchen to get dessert.

I grasped Reece's hand on one side, and Asa's on the other. "Family obligations, huh?"

Asa nodded. "You know how it is."

"I have a lot of respect for a man who takes his responsibilities seriously. So many would just blow it off."

"You're so right, chickie. Sometimes I wish he didn't have such a strong need to please. I'm afraid he's sticking around here as much for me as for his mom."

"Can I ask you a question?"

Asa shot me a wary look. "Okay... but I may not answer."

I squeezed his hand. "I just wonder if Sven is the one who drove the silver Audi that night at the pond."

"Oh, God, no," he replied. "I wish he'd been the one. Things would have been so much simpler." His gaze flicked toward

Reece and he stopped talking abruptly, as if he realized he'd said too much.

I wanted to ask him what he meant, and whether he'd ever told Sven about Rose, but at that moment Sven appeared carrying a tiny wedding cake with a set of golden sugar rings intertwined on the top.

"There," Asa said, indicating the beautiful little cake. "Didn't I tell you he was an impressive chef?"

I couldn't believe it. I hugged Sven even though he didn't really hug me back. It surprised me, the fact that he would go to all this trouble for us, but when I tried to show my appreciation, he drew away. Either he didn't like physical contact, or my old friend had talked him into making the cake and opening his home to us.

I hoped it wasn't the latter.

We ate our cake and sipped our wine while we passed around the pictures of the wedding. But somehow things had changed. It felt as if we were suddenly only pretending it was another day in paradise.

I tried to discuss it with Reece later, but he didn't see a problem. The all-day ski passes had him stoked. His eyes gleamed every time he spoke of them. I tried to feel as excited, but Sven's mixed signals left me baffled.

We helped clear the table and then said our goodnights. "You guys have gone overboard for us," I said.

"Especially with these." Reece held up the gift envelope. "I hope you are joining us on the slopes."

Asa shook his head. "This respiratory infection has me wanting to crawl between the sheets and sleep all day, and Sven has so much to do at the clinic." He grasped my arm and herded me toward the stairs. "But we want you two to have the most amazing honeymoon possible."

I hugged him. It felt good to be hugged back. Reece gave him a hearty handshake and another thanks as well.

Asa pushed a note into his hand. "Just call this number in the morning, a car will come and take you to the train. Tell the driver what time you want him to come back and pick you up, and then we will see you guys for dinner tomorrow evening."

Reece shook his head. "This is too much. Just amazing. I can't wait for the two of you to come to Cali to visit. We will repay this royal treatment, I promise."

I laughed. "If you like camping it will be even better."

Asa rolled his eyes and smiled. "Girl, you know me better than that." He seemed about to say more, but a fit of coughing overtook him. After he caught his breath, he waved us toward our room with instructions to sleep as late as we wanted. "There'll be pastries and coffee in the dining room. Feel free to help yourselves." He smiled but it seemed pained. "And day after tomorrow, I've got a wonderful day of sightseeing planned."

I squealed and clapped my hands. "Asa, you sweetie. I've missed you so much." I don't know whose smile was wider, his, mine, or my new husband's.

After another round of hugs, Reece and I retired to our luxurious room.

Reece yawned and stretched. "It's a great honeymoon. Look at this." He pulled aside the drapes and revealed the valley below. Lights from homes were nestled in the bosom of the valley like tiny diamonds.

"Oh, it's even more beautiful at night."

Reece moved my hair and kissed the back of my neck. "Your friends are amazing."

"Even Sven?"

The kisses stopped. "Well, he's not quite as warm as Asa, but this house, that dinner, and the cake..."

"Yeah, I guess you're right. I'm probably just reading him all wrong."

"I want to hear more about what happened at the pond, though. If you want."

The kisses on the back of my neck sent good chills all over me. I turned to face him, and our lips met.

There was no more conversation about the pond.

I woke in the night clutching my new husband like a drowning victim. It took me right back to the evening in the pool at his apartment.

"Gabs?" He held me closely. "What is it? A bad dream?"

I nodded. "I guess so. I was under water, couldn't breathe."

He shushed me and soothed me, caressing my arms and my back tenderly. "It's okay. I'm with you. What are you worried about, skiing tomorrow? We won't go on any difficult trails. We'll stick strictly to beginners."

Snuggling deeper under his arm, I allowed him to think it was only the nerves of someone who'd never been on skis before. But it wasn't that. It wasn't that at all. It was a feeling of being held down, under water. Of not being able to breathe, or even scream for help. It was that same old feeling of guilt I'd been trying to ignore ever since Mom had told me Rose was missing. Did I leave her in the pond? *Did I?*

"It's going to be beautiful," Reece continued. "The snow in the Alps. I've only seen pictures. The Palace at Gstaad. Ski in/ski out. We can lunch there. Even the spa is open for day use if you want to do that."

"Asa said there's a horse drawn carriage ride, too." I smiled at the memory. He knew me well. "Can we do that, too?"

"Of course. We'll do anything you want."

"I don't want to keep you from the big trails, though. What did Sven call them, the black piste?"

"Yeah. Black diamond. But I'm not that experienced. I'll stick to intermediate instead. Or the beginners with you—"

"Nope. You've got to do some of the hard ones. When will you have this chance again? I'll be fine on my own."

"It's our honeymoon," he said. "I don't want to leave you—"

I put my fingers over his lips. "No. I don't want you to miss out. I don't want you to think—ten years from now—oh, if only I'd done that when I had the chance."

Reece smashed my fingers against his mouth and kissed them before pulling them away. "No, Gabs." He squeezed me against his side. "Haven't you got it yet? I'm not that guy. I'm your soulmate. Being with you is all I care about. You know, I fell for you before we even *kissed*. Something inside me yearned for something inside you."

I clutched him like a lifeline. "Are you sure? I – I don't want to disappoint you." I hid my face in his chest.

He lifted my chin with the tips of his fingers. "You're awfully hard on yourself, Gabrielle. The only way you could ever disappoint me would be if you told me to get lost."

He cradled me in his arms as if I were a child. It made me feel safe, safe enough to tell him the entire tale about Rose and the night at the pond.

"Now, do you see why I'm having all these horrid dreams and doubts?"

"I do." His voice was steady. "You found out she's missing when you were in Vegas?"

"Yes. I wanted to tell you many times. In fact, I tried a time or two and something always interrupted. I— I suppose I didn't try very hard. I think I hoped she would turn up and I'd never have to think about it again."

He paused, obviously thinking about something. At last he said, "How do you know she hasn't turned up? How do you know she isn't in Fort Worth with her cousin, or with his—I mean, with their—family?"

The logic of his question hit me right between the eyes. "Well. Hmm. I guess I don't. I mean, neither Asa nor Mom live in Live Oak anymore. I have a couple other friends I could call but that would seem a little odd after all this time, wouldn't it?"

Reece shrugged. "I don't know. I'm just thinking out loud. Maybe she isn't even missing anymore."

I thought it over. "You could be right. Oh, God. I hope you are." Little did I know, I would find out soon enough.

We drifted back to sleep holding each other tightly.

In the morning, we dressed slowly and walked down the hall toward the massive staircase. It was late fall and our time seemed to be flying by as quickly as if we'd entered a time warp.

Outside Asa and Sven's room, I hesitated, hearing noises of someone moving about. I debated knocking, but then Asa began to cough. It sounded as if he were dying. The cough turned into one long non-stop explosion that ended in huge sucking gasps for air. I imagined him red faced, eyes bulging, drops of blood flying like spittle.

Seconds passed like slow minutes and the coughing finally abated. I could hear Sven moving around, saying something about a breathing treatment. I pictured a pliable plastic tube attached to a mouthpiece. In a few seconds, all I could hear was the soft sound of a machine I assumed was a nebulizer. Apparently, this was nothing new.

I lowered my fist, glad I hadn't knocked.

Reece squeezed my arm and gave me a little push to get me moving on toward the staircase.

"That didn't sound like a little cold," I whispered.

Reece shook his head.

"What could cause that kind of coughing?"

"I guess you'll have to ask him when you get the chance."

I nodded, but a new mantle of worry settled about my shoulders.

In the gourmet kitchen, the huge silver cappuccino machine stood on the counter beside stacks of tiny foil-wrapped Swiss chocolate squares just perfect for melting in a mug. Knowing how much I loved cappuccino and chocolate, I had no doubt Asa had left it all ready for me. When I lifted the lid on a silver tray nearby, there was as promised, a beautiful array of pastries.

Reece grinned at the over-the-top show of affection. "I could get used to this," he said.

While the machine gurgled, I listened for movement from above, but the house was so massive I couldn't hear a thing. When the coffee was ready, we donned our jackets, picked up our mugs, and set out for a walk around the grounds.

The weather in Bern was moist and cool, so unlike the desert air where Asa and I had grown up. It was even moister and sweeter than our beloved Santa Lucia Mountains. I fell in love with the place and would've gladly made plans to visit again, soon. If I could be certain Sven wanted us there.

I decided to get Sven alone and ask him about Asa's health. Maybe that was what seemed to be bothering him. I wanted to ask Asa, but I didn't want to confront him if he didn't feel the need to tell me. I hoped the illness had come on suddenly, a temporary thing, or maybe even a leftover from a bout of flu or bronchitis. During our senior year, he'd had respiratory illnesses quite frequently—due to allergies, he always said, as if smoking a pack a day had nothing to do with it.

But *that* coughing sounded nothing like what we'd just heard upstairs. Back then it had been a nuisance. Now, it sounded grave.

"I've been thinking," Reece said. "As much as I'd love to get out on the slopes, I'm also wondering if we shouldn't just try to book a room at The Palace—for just today."

"Why?" I tried to hide the alarm in my voice. I didn't want to hurt Asa and Sven's feelings after they'd been so hospitable.

He laughed. "All morning I've been picturing you naked, on a bearskin rug in front of a roaring fireplace in our cozy little room at a ski lodge—"

"No, no, no," I interrupted.

He stopped.

I made a face. "Not bearskin."

From behind us we heard someone approaching.

"As a matter of fact, forget the rug altogether."

He looked at me in alarm.

"I may not know how to ski," I said, "but I can easily imagine you flying down the slopes with the wind in your hair—"

"Good morning," Asa said by way of greeting. "All ready to hit the slopes?"

I nodded and hugged him gently. "Thanks for the lovely breakfast." I held up a croissant and my mug. "You guys are really spoiling us."

He grinned. "That's my intention. I want you to feel as if you are at home here. Maybe you'll always come back to visit."

"Oh, Ace. That sounds wonderful."

Wrapped in our sweaters and fleece, the three of us continued our walk around the gorgeous garden. But we didn't get very far before the cough returned and we had to go back.

I helped Asa back to the house, my eyes welling up with tears.

Asa noticed. "I'll be fine," he mumbled as we mounted the steps. "I guess it's just a hanger-on." He struggled for a breath to finish his thought. "Just let me sit."

We got him installed in his recliner, a bottle of water by his hand, a blanket across his lap, and then I went in search of Sven. I wanted to know Asa's prognosis. But Sven had no time to talk.

He was on his way out the door. Apparently, he'd been called in to the clinic to straighten out some sort of billing snafu.

Reece met me in the kitchen. "I don't feel right leaving him alone like this." He took a pastry and a napkin to a small table near the bay window.

Asa must have heard him. "I'll have none of that. Sven is only a phone call away. I plan on going right back to sleep. Rest is what I need. And some chicken soup—which my man has promised to make for me this afternoon." His voice gave out. He didn't cough again, but I could hear him wheezing even from the other room.

I went back and knelt at his knee. "I'm with Reece. It seems so wrong to leave you—"

"Stop. I won't hear of it. I didn't invite you here to bedsit me." He waved his hands at me in a sweeping motion, like a broom. "Now, go. Have fun. You'll hurt my feelings if you waste this lovely day and those lovely lift tickets."

Reece stood in the doorway.

I shrugged. "Are you sure?"

Asa held up a cordless phone. "Got the clinic right here on speed dial, now go."

The driver waited for us at the bottom of the lane in a boxy, dark colored sedan. Asa had called him on the cordless phone. Apparently, he was Dr. Haag's driver and since she was out of town, he was available to us. What a lifestyle.

He took us directly to the train and instructed us on how to board and where to get off. His English was impeccable. We were surprised to learn that even the train was included in the ski package Asa had bought for us. The driver, whose name was Hans, told us that all of the ski resorts in Gstaad were available to us in our package, and each was connected by a bus or gondola. But in his opinion the best beginner's runs in the Bernese Alps were located on the family-friendly Höhi Wispile. It was one of the smaller hills in Gstaad.

"He's been so helpful," I told Reece when we boarded the train, "I think we should take his advice and start with Wispile, don't you?"

Reece nodded, but I had a feeling he was thinking of the larger hills, and runs.

All at once, we spied what appeared to be a castle on a hill behind a quaint village. "This is it," Reece said. "There's the Palace."

"Wow. I never thought it would look like this. I feel like we've gone back in time."

From the train, we walked all over the village. The weather was almost balmy. The high-end shops were quite eye-opening. "And I thought Vegas was expensive," I said, peering into the windows of the designer shops.

"We'll stop by on the way out and pick up souvenirs," Reece said.

Yeah, I thought. Very small souvenirs.

We continued down the promenade, stopping only to pick up super-expensive ski wear, until we came to the gondola connecting us to Wispile. We clothed ourselves and joined the group for beginners. I had a great time learning with other newbies, many just children, but I felt guilty that my sweet husband had to go through all of the basics this way—and then I looked up and caught him helping a little boy who seemed to be having difficulty staying upright.

Before long, Reece had the little one on his feet and skiing short distances. At one point I heard him say, "And if you ever come to California, I'll teach you to surf, too."

That made my heart melt.

Soon, I was able to make it down the short, gentle slope of the first run. "I don't mind if you want to try one of the longer runs," I called to Reece.

"Are you absolutely certain?" His face mirrored his conflict. I could see how much he longed to be on the higher runs, the blues and possibly even one of the blacks, but he just couldn't admit to himself that we might be okay apart for a bit—on our honeymoon.

"If you don't," I made my voice stern, "I'm going to sit down in the snow and cry. I can't have fun knowing you are bored." I shot him a deadly look. "And don't tell me you aren't."

He grinned and pushed his goggles up. "Okay, but maybe just one long run, maybe off-piste for a bit."

"What did you just say?" I joked.

"Off trail," he said. And then he realized I was joking. He swooshed over, planted a kiss on my lips—to which a couple of little boys whoo-hooed—and then he headed for the lift. I waved my pole at him and thought, yay! Now I can relax and really get the hang of this.

After a few hours, Reece was back. "Ready to try a bigger run?" His hair was a mass of blond corkscrews, his nose was sunburned, and his smile was as big as the mountain.

"I think I'm ready for that carriage ride to the restaurant Hans told us about."

Reece skied up alongside me and whispered. "And is there a bearskin rug in our future?"

I shoved him away. "I told you, no bearskin!"

We skied down the small slope together and returned all our gear. Being at the very start of the season, we were lucky there was any snow at all. But for my first try, I couldn't have asked for a better start.

"I loved learning to ski," I said as we made our way inside The Palace to the restaurant. "It certainly has made me hungry, though."

"I had a great couple of runs," Reece said. "The only thing is, next time you have to come with me. The lift was no fun at all without you."

In the restaurant, we dined on fondue with a hint of truffles, tasty slices of shaved beef, thin curls of Swiss cheese, and tender stuffed pasta shells in a fragrant red wine sauce. For dessert, there was—of course—an assortment of Swiss chocolates.

The carriage arrived and we got in and bundled up under a

mound of blankets. The sun was setting and the evening lights were popping on all through the village. The effect was that of a Currier & Ives print. My mom had one imprinted on a white china platter we only used for Christmas dinner every year. It showed a couple in a horse-drawn carriage being pulled through a snowy forest.

"This is so romantic," I said. "Such a wonderful honeymoon." My eyes were so heavy I dozed on Reece's shoulder. I'd never felt so tired, and so content.

We arrived back at the house via the car and driver just as Asa had promised. "Are we late for dinner?" I wasn't hungry, but I remembered our promise from this morning. What a day it had been.

"Of course not. Did you enjoy the slopes?" Asa didn't stand as we came in and sat down at the dining table.

"It was amazing," I said. "I'm so glad you treated us."

His smile was somewhat somber as he handed each of us an empty bowl from a stack near his elbow. "Here, have some of this delicious homemade chicken soup."

Sven passed the breadbasket, too. I noticed Reece had no qualms about having a bowl of soup with a slice of fresh bread. I nibbled at a slice and sipped at the delicious soup, too. I certainly didn't want to make Sven think we didn't like it.

"Well," Asa said. "I hope you two aren't too tired for a day of sightseeing tomorrow."

That got my attention. "I can't wait to explore this beautiful place."

After dinner, we had coffee in the library and regaled our friends with stories from Gstaad. As a native, skiing was second nature to Sven, but I'm pretty sure Asa enjoyed hearing about it. He and his dad often went skiing in New Mexico with his dad's friend, Karl Karson. It was my understanding both families had cabins there.

Sven busied himself building a fire in the massive stone fire-place, and Reece and I snuggled into the soft leather sofa.

I'm not sure who began to doze, first, Asa or me.

"I think I'd better get myself up to bed," he said. "The car will pick us up after breakfast in the morning."

We said our goodnights and headed toward the stairs. I hated to waste the wonderful fire, but Asa seemed even more exhausted than me.

For the first time since we'd said our vows, Reece and I went straight to sleep wrapped in each other's arms. So much for the bearskin rug.

Asa seemed much better the next morning. We met in the dining room and shared pastries and cappuccino just like the day before.

"Our driver will be here in half an hour," he said. "I've got one more surprise for y'all." His eyes gleamed.

We finished our breakfast, grabbed our jackets, and put on our most comfortable walking shoes.

The same driver met us at the car. He smiled and tipped his cap. He also seemed to have a genuine affection for Asa and addressed him as Mr. Letter even though he had to be at least a decade older.

"Are we taking a train today?"

Asa shook his head. "We've got a short ride, then you'll see."

In minutes, we arrived at our destination, the launch point for a river tour that sailed past the famous Rose Garden, Clock Tower, and Ogre Fountain. "We'll also see the Federal Palace, and the Einsteinhaus, where Albert Einstein once lived."

It was an amazing tour, so relaxing and informational. "I can't wait to go back and tour the Einsteinhaus and the Münster Cathedral. I hope my legs are up to climbing 344 steps after skiing all day yesterday." I grinned at Reece to let him know I wasn't serious. Nothing would stop me from going to the top of the cathedral. The tour guide said it was the only way to see the entire city at once.

"And in the Einsteinhaus we can do some simple experiments," Asa said. "I keep thinking if I visit there enough, I might someday understand his theory of relativity. That's where he came up with it, you know."

We all chuckled. Especially me. If anyone could understand it, Asa would be the one. He had the sharpest intellect of anyone I knew.

"The Clock Tower was fascinating," Reece said. "I can't believe it was built in the year 1530."

"I can't believe they've kept it working all this time. That huge figure of Chronos striking the bell is amazing. And I can't wait to go back and stroll through The Rose Garden. Was it really built on an ancient cemetery?"

Asa nodded. "Creepy, huh? But one other thing I want to do is to have a late lunch at The Granary. I want to take you there just to show off the ceilings and frescoes. Of course, the food isn't bad either."

"Is that the one that looks like a medieval church? The one he called Kornhauskeller?"

"Yes, it started life in 1711 as a granary to store grain for the entire city. The cellar stored barrels of wine that had been paid to the ducal rulers as taxes."

"Oh, I get it. A corn house." I laughed. "At least that's what it sounds like. And don't forget, I want to see the bears before we leave old town. The guide said it was an easy walk from the Einsteinhaus."

WHEN WE DISEMBARKED at the end of the tour, our driver was waiting. He told Asa Sven had sent word that he was needed at the clinic. That's when we noticed a cab waiting to take him away.

Later I discovered that the excuse was a ruse and in truth he simply had to go in to receive the results of some medical tests he'd had done.

Left on our own, we told the driver we would return in a few hours, and then we went on our self-guided walking tour, shopping the arcades for souvenirs.

I had looked forward to this all day, but the intrusive graffiti covering every vertical surface was such a disappointment, I felt secretly glad Asa wasn't with us, I think it would have diminished his new home a little bit. He had gone to such great lengths to show us the best of his adopted city. I didn't want him to feel disappointed. After that we went through Einstein's House—but we didn't do any experiments, not without Asa—and then we went directly to the deep, stone-lined bear pits. They were a bit depressing as well, just as Reece had thought they might be.

"Don't worry," the woman there told us in beautifully accented English. "The bears are getting a new home soon. More room, a hill to climb, access to the river and lots of green, green grass."

"That's wonderful. Thank you for telling me. I know they are a huge part of Bern's history—"

"Our namesake," she said.

I smiled. "Of course. Such a history."

Reece and I enjoyed hiking the historic cobblestone streets. After strolling through the Rose Garden, we made our way back to The Granary and had lunch.

"Asa was right," I said. "This is like stepping back in time." I laughed self-consciously. "I just keep saying that, don't I? But all this history. Medieval times, Reece. Can you believe it?"

We had just been seated in the restaurant. The cellar's high, curved ceilings did remind me of the ribs of an immense stone church, but the paintings on the wall and ceiling were anything but religious. In addition to traditionally dressed men and women depicted on the stone pillars, there were also paintings of the man in the moon, a mermaid, and a dragon.

"I adore this place," I said. "I think I've fallen in love with everything here!"

Reece laughed. "It's going to be a place I want to come back and visit often. Especially during ski season."

"I agree. I thoroughly enjoyed learning to ski, as much as I did anyway. I just regret that Asa had to leave so suddenly."

Reece nodded. "But after that coughing fit we heard this morning, I'm sure he wouldn't have been able to do all the walking we've done."

"You're right. I'm sure that's why he arranged that magnificent river tour, too."

After we ate, we considered going to the Medieval Market at Castle Lenzburg, but it was almost two hours away and we wanted to get back to the house and spend a bit more time with Asa since we would be leaving soon.

We walked all the way back to our prearranged meeting place and there was our driver. I wanted to ask if he'd been there all day, but I hated to sound ignorant, or nosy.

THAT NIGHT, after dinner, the four of us wound up staying in and playing Scrabble in front of the fireplace. I nudged Reece and whispered, "Well, here we are in front of a roaring fire."

He nudged me back. "Think they would mind if we…"

I blushed at the thought and tried to refocus on the game.

Asa won handily with his knowledge of Latin based words

from his medical library. But it didn't bother me. To be honest, I felt proud of his brilliant mind. He was still my best friend, always would be.

After the game, we went to bed early. Asa said it was because our car would be arriving at the crack of dawn to take us to the airport, but I'd seen him nodding, yawning. He was exhausted and obviously medicated. That worried me.

Reece and I enjoyed the last night of our honeymoon in our beautiful guest room making love slowly and tenderly in the big Swiss bed. I felt sorry to be leaving, but anxious to get home and begin our real life together. As man and wife.

AFTER THE CUSTOMARY breakfast pastries the next morning—and a quick stroll through that gorgeous coming-on-winter garden—the car arrived to take us to the airport. Asa grasped both my hands in his. He'd gone straight back to his chair, knees covered by a soft fleece blanket, after our brief stroll.

"I'm so glad I got you and your man out here to meet my Sven. I feel we killed two birds with one stone." He gazed up at me with a Mona Lisa smile that could have meant anything. "Now if I can just hang on long enough to see the two of you have children, my life will be complete."

I studied his weary young face. "What are you saying?"

"It's cancer," he said. "My lungs. I hate to break it so callously, just before you leave, but maybe I won't have another chance."

"Oh, honey." I fell to my knees beside his chair. "No."

He allowed me to envelop him in a hug and I was surprised at how his bones pressed themselves into my palms. Hadn't we hugged upon arrival three days ago? Had he been this frail then? I closed my eyes and said a silent prayer. When I opened them,

Sven stared at me from the doorway. The look on his face was dark, impenetrable.

All the way home, every time I dozed on the plane, I awoke with the memory of that awful stare. It reminded me of Rose for some reason. I know it made me feel guilty.

31

We had been home from Switzerland for a couple of weeks, just long enough for one short weekend camping trip before school was due to start on Monday. Our married life was everything I'd hoped it would be. We fit together as if we'd been married for years. When we were apart, I felt incomplete, lacking.

Our time in the forest had been just what I needed. Even though our newlywed life couldn't have been any better, Asa's news had left me reeling. I didn't understand how he could have lung cancer, even though he'd smoked for several years.

Some days I felt so empty and helpless that all I wanted to do was lie in bed and cry. That's one reason Reece insisted we go camping. When we arrived home, my dear husband decided he needed to go and wash the mud off the van. "I'll start the spaghetti," I said. We were both starved from our long hike down the mountain. Reece kissed me and told me he'd be home within the hour.

As soon as I walked in our apartment door, I noticed the little red light blinking on the answering machine. I pushed play on a message from three days earlier. "Call me, Gabs," Asa's voice said. "It's my dad. He - he had a heart attack. He's gone." The message cut off abruptly, but before I could call him back, a second message began to play. "Gabi, you must be up the mountain or something. I'm in Live Oak, at Dad's house... you can call me here." I automatically hit redial to call him back. The first call had been days earlier; the second was only an hour ago.

The phone rang ten times before someone picked it up. "Hello?"

I sank onto the sofa. "Ace?"

He inhaled carefully.

I wanted to ask if he had on some sort of oxygen mask or something.

"Hey, Gabs. Thanks for calling."

"Oh, Acie, I'm so sorry I wasn't here when you called. I feel terrible."

He didn't say anything, but I could hear his labored breathing. "I'm going through his things," he said at last. "I took his suit to the funeral home. The service is late tomorrow. I thought of burying him in his surgical scrubs, you know, since that's what he loved more than anything." He paused to catch his breath. "This is the time I really wish I had a sibling to share the burden. Or at least a mother." He laughed harshly. "At this point, even a wicked stepmother would do."

"You've got me," I said. "And Sven. But I know what you mean. I'm an only child, too." An image of me one day trying to plan my mom's funeral by myself entered my head, but the faces of Joe, and my darling Reece quickly displaced it. No matter what, I knew they would be there for me. "I'll be there tomorrow. I'll get there as fast as I can. I promise."

"That would be super, Gabs. Call when you get here, or better yet, just come on out to the house. We'll go to the service together."

"I will, sweetie. I love you." So, it was decided, I'd fly in and go directly to his father's home. I could tell the trip from Switzerland had taken a real toll on him. He sounded so much worse than he had when we were there. And that hadn't been very long ago.

When Reece got home, he stood in the bedroom doorway watching me pack. I'd given him the news in a nutshell.

"Should I go with you?"

I wiped my nose and shook my head as I shoved things into my bag. "You can come if you want, but I would understand if you needed to stay here."

Reece stepped up behind me and wrapped his strong arms around me.

I collapsed onto the bed with him holding me. The floodgates opened and I sobbed for my best friend and all that he must be going through. "He sounded so sick. This may be the last time I ever see him. I wish it wasn't for a funeral."

Reece held me and stroked my hair and rocked us back and forth on our wide, blue bed.

After a while, the worst passed and the tears dried and he ceased stroking my hair, but he never let me go. I relaxed into him and we stretched out, sideways, across the nautical spread.

His breath feathered the back of my neck. "I wish I could take away the pain."

I pulled his arms a bit more tightly around me. "You've already done that. You always do." I opened my eyes and drank in our beach-themed bedroom. I hadn't changed a thing. Even his old surfboard still stood in the corner. I adored that bright splash of red and yellow amidst all the blue.

A strong breeze fluttered the curtains and I imagined the smell of the ocean caressing my skin as Reece kissed my hair, my neck, and the side of my face.

I half expected him to continue with the kisses, but I didn't protest when he stopped and simply pulled me closer.

After spending a couple hours wrapped in my husband's arms, I'd awoken as the light was leaving the sky. The windows were painted rose tinted with gold. The color reminded me of the dress I'd worn to Mom and Joe's wedding. I rolled over and felt the warmth of the place where Reece's body had been.

"Reece?" My throat felt raspy.

"Right here," he replied. He stepped backward out of the closet with his own suitcase in hand. "Plane leaves at eight in the morning, right?"

I didn't reply but I was certain he could sense the relief that flooded my body. My Asa, having to travel all the way from Bern after just learning he has lung cancer. I couldn't really wrap my head around it. Lung cancer was an old person's disease, wasn't it? And now his father. How much could one person handle before they broke?

"Thank you, sweetheart." I pulled the spread up to my chin. "How did I get so lucky to be loved by you?"

He threw me a silly, lascivious, look and began to stuff underwear and shorts into his suitcase with abandon.

I laughed and crawled out of my warm spot. "Please, let me." I took the case from him and placed it on the bed. After fifteen minutes, he too was packed and ready to go.

We placed our luggage beside the door and went to take our baths and wash the smell of campfire from our hair.

I felt very blessed to have such a caring partner. In the back of my mind I couldn't help thinking how grateful I was that Asa had been able to know that same joy with Sven, too.

A few minutes later, the phone rang. Lucy needed to be helicoptered off the mountain. She'd been injured when a kid freaked out during a thunderstorm and shoved her as she tried to prevent him from heading down the trail in the dark.

Reece turned to me with a frown. "A broken ankle."

I hugged him and started unpacking his suitcase and repacking his backpack. "Don't worry, Crew Leader. You've got to go take her place. Those kids need you—and so does Lucy. I can just imagine how awful she feels."

"But you need me, too."

I knew he would tell the SCA to find another team leader to fill in for Lucy if I asked him, but he had just been made supervisor of the western range and I knew he would rather do it himself. It would show the organization they had made the right choice when they promoted him. I handed him his old backpack. "I'm fine. Just going to support my old friend." I stood on tiptoe and pressed my lips to his. "At least I don't have to go all the way to Switzerland."

Reece kissed me softly. "That was a great honeymoon. Maybe we'll be able to have Asa and Sven here to visit us before they go back."

Tears in my eyes, I turned away. He hadn't heard Asa's voice on the phone. I grabbed my husband's hand. "I just hope this isn't the last time I see him. He sounded horrible, Reece. Just awful."

"Maybe he sounded worse because of the circumstances. I mean he just lost his dad."

"Yeah. They were never close. The two of them had always seemed at odds. But maybe you're right. Maybe the suddenness of the old man's passing made him realize that now they can never make up for all that wasted time."

Since my flight would leave at eight the next morning, I would have to call a cab to get me to the airport by seven. Reece, on the other hand, had to leave immediately. He would take the van to base headquarters and then hike on up to the camp to meet the crew. It was about fifteen miles. He would have to start hiking at first light. The kids couldn't be left alone so that meant Lucy couldn't leave until he got there.

I envied him a bit. I'd much rather be heading back up the mountain with him than going to a funeral. But I would do it for Asa. It was the least I could do.

32

I flew into Midland International Airport and caught a puddle-jumper to Live Oak. My little hometown had only a county airport. From there, I took a taxi to Asa's country club address. The long wraparound drive took me directly to the massive front doors. The taxi driver brought my wheeled suitcase up the steps and I rang the doorbell. I couldn't keep my gaze from wandering up to the steeply sloping roofline. French doors in Asa's bedroom led directly out to the rooftop deck where we'd spent many a stray evening counting stars and drinking his dad's wine.

I was about to ring the bell a second time, but the door opened and there stood my dear friend. Our hug was sweet and careful. I didn't think it was possible for him to get any thinner, but he was little more than a skeleton with skin clinging bravely where fat and muscle used to be.

"I'm so sorry, Ace."

He shrugged. "I know. It's okay. I loved him as much as he would allow. But he never liked me as a gay person. I didn't tell him I had AIDS; it would've confirmed his opinion of all gays as perverts who deserved to get sick. I think he even said that to me one time—that AIDS was nature's way of cleaning out the gene pool—but it doesn't matter now, does it? He wouldn't even help me get into his alma mater. I was an embarrassment to him. Nothing more."

"AIDS? You have AIDS?" I know my shock was palpable. But I couldn't help it. That disease had never crossed my mind.

Asa nodded. "Full-blown. Thus, the lung cancer." He closed his eyes and gripped the doorjamb tightly. "It's funny. I could admit having lung cancer, but not AIDS. Not even to you, my bestie." He glared at me, daring me to chastise him. "Now, it doesn't seem to matter. I guess my father was right all along."

"Oh sweetie, I'm sure that isn't what he thought—"

"Yes, it is. He would've said I deserved this. Don't say otherwise. If it hadn't been for you when we were growing up, I don't know what I would have done—suicide probably."

I followed him into the house. He moved as if his spine was so brittle simply carrying his own weight might cause it to crumble. I wanted to ask about his prognosis, about chemo, radiation, but once again, he waved me off. "Let's go straight to The Skillet. I have a craving for extra sweet iced tea."

I nodded. "Should I change here? I came straight from the airport like you said, didn't even stop to reserve a room at the motel." I'd thought briefly of asking the cabbie to drive by my old house, but I decided a funeral and my best friend's lung cancer would probably be enough sadness for one day. Maybe tomorrow, if any cheer threatened to creep in, I could go by there and see where I'd grown up. See where I'd buried my kitten, Candy, beneath the old pomegranate tree. I swiped my eyes. What I wouldn't give to have a tall blond surfer-dude to hold me tight about now.

Asa trudged up the stairs ahead of me. His thin shoulders threatened to poke right through the soft fabric of his dress shirt. "We've got a little while to catch up before the service." He shifted his weight on the step. "You don't mind going to The Skillet?"

"Of course not. Whatever you want." I smiled to let him know I meant it. "Will Sven go with us?"

"Yes. He's finishing up in my old bedroom. I had a few mementos that I wanted to pack up and ship home. To Bern."

I nodded. I had to force my words around the huge lump that had risen in my throat. "This is hard, isn't it?"

He shrugged. "It would be worse without you and Sven. It would be a lot worse if I felt he'd ever actually cared about me."

That broke my heart. I didn't know what to say. The phone rang and saved me from having to say anything at all.

Asa's voice took on a sharp edge after saying hello. "No," he said firmly. "Don't come. We don't want you there. I don't care what people think." He clicked the off button and I realized he'd been carrying the cordless phone in his hand the whole time.

"Sorry. I've been expecting that call. Dad's old golf partner, Karl Karson. The one I told you about."

Once again, I didn't have a clue how to respond. I changed the topic by asking about his flight.

He laughed sarcastically. "I don't remember. I knocked myself out with anti-nausea meds. I would've made such a great physician."

"Oh Ace, you still will. You'll beat this thing and then you'll sail through med school and you'll come out with such a wonderful bedside manner—because you'll be so sympathetic to patients' feelings—that you'll have to close your practice to new patients after only one year."

"Rein it in, girlie. I'm not stupid. I'm terminal. Doc said I shouldn't have made this trip, but I couldn't stay away. Glutton for punishment I suppose."

"You just wanted to see me again. That's all."

"Right. That's it." He turned and enveloped me in another thin-armed hug. "Let me get Sven and we'll go. Would you rather change now or after we eat?"

I elected to change before we went to the restaurant. That way we wouldn't have to rush back to the house before the service.

Sven greeted me coolly. I got the distinct impression my presence was not welcome to him.

I ignored my doubts about Sven and we ate a leisurely meal —rather, Asa drank iced tea while Sven and I picked at our salads—and then we escorted him to the service. The First Baptist Church was filled to capacity. We were able to go in the side door so that Asa didn't have to navigate all those people. The doctor had attended Sunday morning services faithfully.

After a moving rendition of "Amazing Grace" by a soloist from the choir, the minister led us in prayer. Then he began to talk about what a devoted surgeon Dr. Letter had been, and what a tremendous addition he'd been to the community. He mentioned Asa's late mother in passing, and he mentioned that Asa was currently home from attending med school abroad. Then he began to preach a sermon intended to get folks to give their hearts to God.

Asa's elderly grandparents and his aunt and uncle sat on the front row beside us along with Maria, the longtime housekeeper, and her husband, Arturo. They deflected most of the hand-shakers during the procession of mourners. I tried to deflect them, too. I'm not a doctor, but I knew Asa shouldn't be exposed to all those germs in his weakened physical state.

His family wasn't close. They'd all flown in from Chicago where his dad was born. They were so different. I began to understand why Asa gravitated toward my mom and me. We were close.

Maria hugged and kissed me as if I were family, and I wondered what she would do now. She'd worked for Dr. Letter since Asa was a child. He told me she had been a tremendous help with the arrangements—just knowing who to call and what to expect—and that he'd even tried to convince her to come back to Switzerland with him and Sven. She had declined, of course, but she had promised to visit someday.

After the limo ride out to the gravesite, and a very brief prayer and the tossing in of handfuls of earth, the lot of us rode back to the church where several of the ladies had stayed to serve a buffet dinner in the fellowship hall. They had baked ham, roast beef, and three kinds of fried chicken lined up beside bowls of vegetables swimming in butter and potato salad with a base of homemade mayonnaise. I only knew that last part because a sweet little woman with lilac tinted hair told me she had made it herself. No wonder the man had suffered a heart attack, I thought, if they fed him like this all the time.

Asa tried to stay for the reception, but his strength gave out. He took one look at all that food and all those faces and that was it. He told us he was going home and we could come if we wanted. I was suddenly glad we'd had the foresight to eat something before the funeral.

At the house, Sven tucked Asa into bed in his old room and told me he would be out for the night. I got the distinct impression he wanted me to leave.

I called a cab and then crept back up the stairs and stood at the door, watching the rise and fall of my friend's thin chest. It was early, not even four o'clock yet, but I could see that Sven was telling the truth. Asa was out for the count.

I blew him a kiss so as not to wake him, and then I went downstairs. Sven was on the phone. He barely looked up when I went out to wait on the porch. I didn't bother to take the scenic route back. I didn't care to see any more of my old hometown. My best friend couldn't get out of bed. I gave the driver the name of a motel, and then I went in and took a long soaking bath, thankful the funeral was over and done.

33

I slept straight through the night, an amazing feat, especially since I'd become so used to sleeping wrapped in Reece's arms. When I glanced over the bed, I was surprised to see I had barely moved at all. At least there had been no nightmares.

In the back of my mind, a plan had formed. I'd go by my old house and see if anything had changed, and then I'd check on Asa, find out when he was flying back home. I even thought of going out to South Pond to try and get the memory of that night out of my head. But would I take a taxi there? No. That seemed downright ridiculous. I could've rented a car in Midland if I had thought of it, but our little county airport didn't rent cars.

I made coffee in the tiny pot provided, and then I showered and dressed and made my way downstairs. There was a small café next door called Allen's Galley. I'd been there once or twice with my mom, but it hadn't been one of our regular spots. Mostly it catered to guests of the motel and men and women on their way to work, needing early morning coffee.

Sitting alone in a booth, with the free newspaper they provided, I caught up on the local doings in my old hometown.

Not much had changed. Dr. Letter's obituary took up an entire page. Asa was barely noted as his son. I had to wonder who had written the damn thing.

After a short stack of pancakes, which reminded me of the first night Reece had breezed into camp all those months ago, I dumped three teaspoons of Coffee Mate into a white mug of steaming brew and wondered what my mom was doing this morning.

She had thought about coming in for the funeral, but she had been neither a friend nor a patient of Dr. Letter. I convinced her it wasn't necessary. She and Joe had found the perfect condo not too far from his new office. It even had a view of the Houston skyline—plus an extra bedroom and bathroom for me. They were in the midst of remodeling it so the floor plan would be more open. Every time I talked to her on the phone, she regaled me with talk of color swatches and hardwoods.

I'd never heard her so happy.

Across the dining room sat a woman who looked vaguely familiar. I thought she might have worked with my mom at one time, but I couldn't be certain. How odd to be back in my tiny town, where I'd spent the first eighteen years of my life, and I didn't seem to know a soul.

I never realized how thoroughly Asa and I had isolated ourselves all those high school years—mostly due to his big secret—and I had been just as diligent in keeping it as he had. Perhaps that was why he'd kept me around.

After paying my ticket, I left a tip and walked back to my room to call a cab.

The yellow taxi arrived in minutes.

The driver seemed surprised when I told him my destination. "Not many folks around here take a taxi to go sightseeing," he said.

"I used to live here," I said. "I should have rented a car in

Midland, but I didn't think I'd need one." I hadn't realized how incapacitated Asa would be.

The man adjusted his rearview mirror so he could see me better. "In town for a reunion?"

I shook my head. "For Dr. Letter's funeral, actually."

"Oh, I'm sorry to hear that. He operated on my Ellie when she had the gallstones." His voice held a note of awe. "Big loss for this town. Big loss."

Not wanting to lower this man's opinion—even if I could—I kept my mouth closed and simply nodded. Very few people knew how poorly the good doctor had treated his only son. But I did. And I had no respect for the man. None.

Five minutes later, we were on my old street. Some of the deciduous trees still held a few brittle leaves, but the live oaks stayed green all year. I'd forgotten how they shaded the entire neighborhood. It had been a good place to grow up.

The lump was back in my throat. Our small house had already sold to another family. Mom said it was a young couple expecting their first child. He had transferred into town with an oil company. No big surprise there. Oil was the lifeblood of the whole West Texas area.

"Stop for just a moment," I told the driver. "I used to live here, not very long ago."

He slowed the taxi to a stop, but there were no signs of life. The only real outward difference was a new SUV sitting in the driveway.

"Do you want to go in?" he asked as we idled at the curb.

I shook my head. "No, it's okay. You can go now."

"Where to?" His voice was kind.

I gave him the address of Asa's house and watched his eyebrows go up in the rearview mirror. "Country club?"

"Yes." I didn't take offense at his surprise. From seeing my little former home, the country club address was a huge change.

And in towns the size of Live Oak, the difference was like night and day.

He nodded and kept his questions to himself.

"Sir?" I tapped his shoulder.

"Yes ma'am?" He glanced into the mirror.

I hesitated for a split second, "Umm. Do you know where South Pond is located?"

His face split into a grin. "Of course. Everyone knows where the pond is. That's the place I first kissed my Ellie, way back in the day. Chuck Berry was on the radio if I recall. Or maybe it was Buddy Holly, that ol' Lubbock boy."

That took me by surprise. Buddy Holly made me think of Reece, and I wondered how he was doing. Up on the mountain, his only means of communication—besides the letters via horse mail—would be the satellite phone. Strictly for emergencies. "Could you drive me out to South Pond?" My voice sounded hesitant, even to me. "Would it be too expensive? I'd like to see it again, before I have to fly back to California."

"Good memories, eh?" The mirror showed his gap-toothed grin.

I didn't respond. Good memories? Not exactly. Should I go? What did I hope to find?

"I'll take you there, little lady. It won't be too much, it's not that far."

I sat back, a light film of perspiration coating the back of my neck. Why was I so nervous about seeing the pond? "Umm, sir?"

He glanced into the mirror again.

"I heard that a girl I used to know went missing. Have you heard anything about a girl named Rose Lintz? She only moved here last year."

The driver was silent for a moment. "I did hear something about a young girl who ran off with her boyfriend. My Ellie works in housekeeping at the hospital, you know. She said the girl had some connection to Matt Brennan, the boy who was paralyzed the night of prom. Real athlete, that kid. Saw his picture in the paper almost every Saturday morning during football season. Paper said he was going to play for Texas Tech."

I nodded. "Yes. That's all true." Tears clouded my eyes. "Matt was my friend. That's why I wondered about Rose. She was his cousin. I'd already left town when she went missing, but my mom told me about it."

"Well," he lowered his voice. "It probably isn't connected, but last week they found a woman in the pond." His eyes widened as if he'd just realized that's where we were headed. "Cops thought it might be her, but they had to send the remains to Austin. That's where they send off for autopsies, you know."

I shook my head. "What? They found someone's remains in the pond? Are you serious?" I couldn't wrap my head around that. "I can't believe I haven't heard about it."

"Oh, well. It's been kind of hush-hush. My Ellie was at work the night she was found. One of the cops brought in a drunk who fell and hit his head and Ellie overheard the officer talking about it on his radio."

"My God," I breathed. "Remains in the pond."

"Miss? Are you all right?"

My tone must've changed, alarmed him somehow. I met his eyes in the mirror. "I'm okay. Just shocked."

"Do you still want to go? There's nothing there now, of course. It's just like it's always been."

Just like it's always been? The last time I was there was a nightmare. I sure didn't want it to be just like that. Could the remains be Rose? If not her, then who?

I chewed my thumbnail, something I hadn't done since grade school. "Yes. Let's go. I don't know when I will ever be back here, and I'd like to see it before I leave."

"You got it," he said.

I can't believe I'm doing the very thing I said I wouldn't. Taking a taxi to the pond. We drove all the way through town and took the highway out the other side. In minutes, we were entering the loop that led to the parking area where Rose had accosted me.

"This good?" the driver asked.

I hadn't even noticed we'd stopped. Opposite the narrow neck of the water, where the weedy grasses grew waist high, remnants of yellow police tape fluttered listlessly. "Oh my God, is that where—"

"Yep."

It's real. Someone died here. Could it be her?

A hard rap on the window glass beside my head startled me. I jumped in my seat and turned to face the offender.

A man stood there, glaring at me, his face a study in impatience, his smooth mahogany head gleaming in the Texas sun. He wore a sport coat over an open-throated dress shirt. I could imagine him reaching up to that highest shirt button to unfasten it as the morning heated up. I wondered if he wore a suit jacket all year, even in summer.

The taxi driver lowered his window a few inches. To his credit, he didn't automatically lower mine, even though it was my glass the man had rapped on with those hard knuckles.

"Help you?" The driver's voice came out a little rough. I liked him more and more.

The man in the sport coat swept aside his coattail revealing a gold badge clipped to his belt. DET. CONLEY arched across the top of the badge. LOPD curved across the bottom of the badge. "Step out, please." He glanced at me. "Both of you."

All the blood left my head. My fingers fumbled at the door handle. Why was he here? The driver said the remains had been found a week ago. I opened the door and stepped out, shading my eyes with my hand.

The tall detective didn't back up an inch. I had to almost slither sideways to keep from bumping him as I exited the car. He didn't even allow room to open the door all the way. I didn't know what to say.

The driver stepped out. He had a bit more room to maneuver. "Everything okay, officer?"

"Detective Conley," the tall man said. He didn't offer to shake hands. "I'd like to know why you're here. At this crime scene." His words were directed at the driver, but his eyes were fastened on me.

I glanced at the driver unsure which of us should answer.

"My name is Rob Sosa, this is my cab." He didn't look away. "My fare is Ms—"

"Anderson," I volunteered. "*Mrs.* Reece Anderson."

The detective pretty much ignored the driver. "What's your first name?"

My heart began to thud. "Gabi. Gabrielle."

The detective reached into the inside pocket of his jacket, his eyes never leaving my face. With exaggerated slow motion, he pulled out a small spiral notebook, the kind that opened from top to bottom. Raising the no-nonsense cover with his thumb and forefinger, he made a show of slowly flipping pages until he found a blank. Then he held the notebook in his right hand while his left delved under his jacket—into his shirt pocket—to retrieve a mechanical pencil.

The late fall sun beat down on my bare arms as he clicked and clicked the end of the pencil until the perfect amount of graphite showed at the tip. Then, and only then, did he allow his eyes to look down at the page. "Gabrielle Anderson. Maiden name?"

My thumb found my new wedding ring and twisted it on my finger. "Kelly," I said. I almost told him my middle name, too, but checked my impulse at the last second.

He wrote my name in his book. "Gabi Kelly."

I noticed he hadn't written Rob Sosa's name down at all.

"You from around here, Ms. Kelly? Excuse me. I mean Mrs. Anderson?" His pencil remained poised over the page. He slowly raised his eyes to my face.

"I. Yes. I was born here."

He let his gaze drift to the taxi. "Car broken?"

It took me a moment. "Oh. No. Well, I don't live here anymore. Now I live in California. With my husband, Reece." I knew I was babbling. But I couldn't stop. "I'm in town for my friend's funeral. I mean, his father's funeral. I didn't rent a car. Didn't think I'd need to."

"Dr. Letter's funeral?"

If he hadn't interrupted, I would've kept talking. I inhaled through my nose, quietly, the way the choir teacher had taught us way back in middle school. "Yes." I straightened my spine, just a bit. "I heard about the remains in the pond. And since I'm not leaving until tomorrow—"

"You just thought you'd take a cab out here and examine the scene because, what? You've never seen the pond before? You thought we might've left a clue behind? You know something about it?"

His interruptions were so rude. And that last question really threw me. I tried to make my eyes blink, but my lids seemed frozen open. "What do you mean?"

Detective Conley held the notepad before him like a waiter in a restaurant. "You and the victim are about the same age. It's a small town. You must've known her. She'd been missing for a while. When did you leave Live Oak, Gabi? May I call you Gabi?"

My eyelids weren't the only things frozen. My tongue had turned to a useless block of ice, too.

"Excuse me," Rob Sosa said. "My meter is running. I don't think it's fair to expect Mrs. Anderson to pay—"

The detective didn't take his eyes off me. "Don't worry about it, Mr. Sosa. PD will cover the fare."

Rude, rude, man, I thought. But I still couldn't formulate a sentence.

"Well?" he asked. "When did you move away from Live Oak, Gabrielle?"

I shifted my feet in the dry grass. "At the end of the school year," I finally managed.

"After graduation," he wrote.

"Yes," I didn't want to lie. I was afraid to lie. "Ummm, just a couple weeks before, actually."

His eyebrows went up a notch. He stopped writing. "Why?"

"Why?" I echoed.

Voice even, not a sign of suspicion, he said, "Why would a small town girl suddenly leave town right before her high school graduation? Especially one who was born here? One who had probably gone to school with this victim for years, maybe forever?"

"Oh, no. Rose didn't go to Live Oak High—" I nearly bit the end of my traitorous tongue off when I realized what I'd said.

The big man stood like a statue, pencil poised, eyes on the page. He didn't seem to breathe. At last he said, "Rose who?"

34

Detective Conley folded his notebook closed. "I need you to come down to the station with me, Mrs. Anderson."

No more Gabi? Not even Gabrielle?

"Why?" I asked.

"I have a few more questions for you." He tucked the notebook away. "But I think we'll be more comfortable indoors, in the station."

"I don't have a car." I glanced at Rob Sosa, but he'd found something across the horizon that demanded his attention.

"Send the PD the bill, Mr. Sosa," Detective Conley said. "I'll make sure Mrs. Anderson gets back to her motel." He smiled and it was the smile of the Cheshire Cat on a dark night.

"Yes sir." Without another word, the driver got back into his taxi, fastened his seat belt, and executed a careful three-point turn. He never looked at me the whole time.

Without the taxi behind me, I felt completely exposed. I didn't know what to do, what to say. The weak sun grew stronger. Tendrils of sweat unfurled beneath my long hair. I felt sticky and unclean. My glasses slid down. I pushed them back up.

The detective indicated I should precede him. "My car is over there."

I began to walk, but I didn't see a car until we rounded the curve. This was where she ran at me. I'd backed into the turn-around. Asa's friend had been coming toward us, the big silver car hidden behind the bright headlights. Rose must've had her car around the bend like Detective Conley. That's why I hadn't seen her until she'd dashed out with the knife.

The scenes played across my mind like a home movie.

And then we were there.

His car was white, nondescript. Very little chrome.

He opened the back door and I got in. "Am I under arrest?"

He didn't answer. He'd already closed the door.

I saw nothing outside the car as we drove to the station. My vision had turned inward, back to that horrid night. Why had I gone back there this morning? Revisiting the scene of the crime? Didn't criminals always do that? I'm no criminal. I was the *victim*, that night. Now someone else is the victim—whomever they pulled from the water—it might not have been Rose. It could all be a huge coincidence. Except the detective had said the girl was about my age, and that I probably knew her. Why would he say that if they'd just sent the remains to Austin?

The brown sandstone police station was fairly new. It had been built just a few short years ago. Back when I was in middle school.

Detective Conley wheeled the car into the driveway behind the building. I'd never been back here. Apparently, this was where all the employees parked. Funny, I'd never even noticed it before.

We pulled into a shady spot and he turned off the engine. I tried to open my door, but there was no handle. That scared me.

I realized I was completely under his control. No one even knew I'd been brought here except for my cab driver.

I waited for the detective to open the door and let me out. He seemed in no hurry as he stood, adjusting his jacket, his belt, his I-don't-know-what. It occurred to me he was making me wait on purpose. Another deep breath didn't help. I could feel my nerves edging toward panic. I'd never been claustrophobic, but now my eyes searched the front doors to make certain they had handles, to make certain I could get out if I had to, even I had to crawl over—

"Mrs. Anderson?" Detective Conley had opened my door and I hadn't realized it. Get a grip, Gabs. Get a grip.

I stepped out, careful not to touch him as I eased past. I wanted to ask if I could call Reece, I really needed him, but I couldn't. Reece was in the backcountry. Satellite phone only for emergencies. Is this an emergency? No. Not yet. What would I say if I did call him?

"Am I under arrest?" The words tumbled past my lips like small stones. This time he answered.

"Of course not." He opened the rear door of the station— actually a set of glass doors with a keypad built into the wall beside them—and ushered me into a dim cool hallway. "I haven't read you your Miranda rights, have I?"

Hmm. Did that I mean I didn't have to be here? Didn't have to answer questions? What would he do if I refused? How would I get back to my room? I envisioned myself calling another cab to take me back to the motel.

With one hand beneath my elbow, he guided me down the hall past a series of doors. When we came to one with a sign plate that read INTERROGATION ROOM ONE we stopped. I wanted to ask if they really had more than one interrogation room here in tiny Live Oak, but I didn't think that would be in my best interest.

He opened the door, no keypad this time, and I walked in. The back wall consisted of a square reflective window, or maybe it was a mirror. It looked odd, but I couldn't say why. A gray metal table, paint nicked and pock-marked, took up the center of the room. Two chairs were parked on each long side, across from each other. The chairs on one side were straight backed, metal, no frills. The ones on the other side were plush office chairs on rollers. In the corner of the room, near the ceiling, a slim black camera appeared to be pointed directly at me.

The detective indicated one of the straight-backed chairs. I sat and placed my purse on the other one. When he was satisfied I was comfortable, he walked around the table and pulled out one of the office chairs. His large form dwarfed it and he made several minute adjustments. Each time he shifted his weight the chair squeaked and groaned. Each sound grated on my nerves.

"Thank you for coming in Mrs. Anderson," he began. "You don't mind answering a few questions, do you?"

"Of course not. But I still don't know why I'm here. Just because I visited the old pond?"

Detective Conley reared back in the office chair. For a moment, I thought he would go right on over, but he stopped at the apex and propped his right ankle on his left knee. His long fingers gripped the edge of the table lightly. "What made you leave town so suddenly, Mrs. Anderson?"

I sat up a little straighter. "I— um. I joined the Student Conservation Association. Went to California, to the Santa Lucia Mountains. I worked there all summer." I held up my left hand. "Met my husband there."

The detective remained quiet for a moment. Then he seemed to remember something. He let his feet hit the floor as he fell forward. "Are you always so impulsive?"

"Impulsive?"

"Skip graduation, move to another state, get married..."

For a moment, I didn't know what to say. Then it came to me. "I saw what I wanted, and I went after it. That's all." It's the same thing Reece said to me once.

He frowned. "You seemed to know the girl whose remains were found in the pond."

There it was. I'd screwed up.

"No. I heard it was Rose, a girl who went to the private school."

"So, she wasn't a friend of yours?"

"Me? No. I didn't really know her at all—"

"Who told you it was Rose?"

I shook my head. "The cab driver told me. He said his wife heard it at the hospital."

"So was that before or after you hired him to drive you to the pond?"

I didn't understand what he meant. "Well, I—"

He pushed himself back from the table. "Would you like a drink, Mrs. Anderson? Glass of water, a Coke, Dr Pepper?"

I nodded. "Yes, please. Diet Coke?" Anything to make him stop asking me questions.

The big man stood and started toward the door, then he turned and said, "Just one more question before I forget." He hesitated hand on the doorknob. "What was your relationship with Matt Brennan?"

My skin went cold. "Matt?"

He must've heard something in my voice. "Yes," he said. "Matt Brennan." He gave a hard small shake of his head, as if he'd thought of something but didn't want to divulge it, and then he went out and left me sitting alone with my thoughts.

When he came back in twenty minutes later, I started talking.

35

"We were in love," I said. "I know that's what teenagers always think, but in our case, it was true." I brushed my bangs off my forehead and took a deep breath.

The unsmiling detective simply stared at me and pulled out his little notebook. His burnished scalp gleamed under the fluorescents. I wondered if he shined it with a towel, maybe some wax like Reece and his surfboard.

And why wasn't he writing in that notebook anymore? He just held it, as if he found nothing I said worth noting.

The room grew cold and I shivered. Probably a tactic; turning down the temperature to make me uncomfortable. Just like his little waiting game earlier. Waiting me out to make me talk. I'd watched enough crime TV shows to wonder about these schemes. I took a sip of the Diet Coke he'd brought—to make me feel grateful, I suppose—and immediately regretted it because it made me need to burp.

I let the little bubble of gas explode in my closed mouth and began talking again to cover the sound. "We fell in love at prom. We were both with other people. I went with Asa and he brought his cousin, Rose." I sat up straighter in the hard-backed chair and hoped I'd said enough to placate him.

The detective sat motionless, one ankle propped on the opposite knee. I got the impression he might sit that way forever.

I started talking once more. I had to do something to make him stop looking at me as if he already knew everything and because yes, suddenly I *wanted* to tell him. I'd held onto the truth for too long.

I wanted to tell him everything about that night.

MATT STARTED out as my chemistry partner. He was so good-looking even the ancient teachers on the verge of retirement took a second glance when he walked into the room.

"What made him so attractive?" Detective Conley asked.

I figured he was simply feigning interest to keep me talking, but I didn't seem able to shut up now that I'd started. "Maybe it was his smoky blue eyes. Or those thick straight brows." I pictured Matt perched on a stool beside me in class, sunlight shafting through the Chem lab windows, illuminating that lush wavy hair the color of hard-shelled pecans, but I stopped myself from saying all that. Instead, I said, "He was the real deal. That's all."

"So, you had a crush on him?"

I thought of his yearbook photo, how I'd stared at it, comparing him to Johnny Depp and Jon Bon Jovi.

A crush? It *had been* a crush. Until prom. Then I'd found out he felt the same way about me and that's when I knew it was love.

I chewed my bottom lip. How much of that had I said? How much had I simply been reliving in my head?

I looked down at the surface of the table. The edge was worn smooth. I didn't want to think about why. Would I be shackled here once he knew the truth about that night?

A fluid image of Matt flowed across my mind. An image of him in Asa's side mirror as we drove away, one hand in his pocket, the other raised in a goodbye wave. Surprising tears stung my eyes, but I sniffled and willed them away. "He's in a rehab hospital in Fort Worth, you know. Had a wreck the night of prom. I think he was out looking for her."

"Looking for Rose? What makes you think so?"

I took a tiny sip. Swallowed. "She was supposed to meet him back at prom at one a.m. but she never showed."

"She got upset that you and Matt were together at prom?"

I hoped my face didn't show my shock. How could he know this? "I don't know. She seemed to. But I didn't understand it. They were cousins, not real dates."

"Were cousins?" He made a note in his little book. "Don't you mean are?"

Pushing my glasses up, I took another sip. "Detective Conley, I heard that Rose went missing over the summer. My friend Asa told me... or maybe it was my mom. I don't remember for sure. Anyway, when the cab driver told me about the remains in the pond, I just sort of assumed—"

He held up one hand. "Now why would a body in the pond automatically make you think of Rose?"

I sat back in my chair. I couldn't figure out what he wanted from me. Should I ask for a lawyer? If I wasn't under arrest, then I didn't need one, right?

"Do you know why I brought you in here, Gabi?"

Back to Gabi now? "Because I happened to visit the pond while you were there?"

"Yes, that's part of it." He smoothed his hand down over his bald pate and onto his forehead. When he got to his eyes, his long fingers rubbed gently across his brow bone as if he had a headache. "I go out there every day, you know." He rubbed his temples, too. "We don't have people go missing in Live Oak. Hardly ever. I feel a little guilty. I assumed Rose Lintz was a runaway. Her mom said it, her friends said it, everyone said it. Rose ran off with her boyfriend. An unsavory character who may or may not have sold drugs for a living."

I sat quietly.

"He left, too, by the way. But him, I was able to track down. He's in jail in Michigan. Said he hadn't seen Rose since the night of prom."

Once again, I didn't know what to say. I was afraid if I said the wrong thing, I might be stuck here all day. If I had my own vehicle, I could ask to leave—he said I wasn't under arrest, but I had driven my little Honda to my grandparent's farm. As far as I knew, it was still there.

"There's another reason I brought you here." He looked up at the large window-mirror on the wall and I quickly got the impression it must be one of those one-way things, or was it called two-way? The kind with a hidden room behind it, a spy room. I wondered who sat on the other side.

I soon found out when a woman I knew as Rusty Limon's mother walked into the room and handed the detective a laptop.

"Thank you, Junell." Detective Conley set the computer on the table and turned it so that he and I could both see the screen.

The woman he called Junell knew me. Rusty and I had shared the risers in choir all through middle school. We always saw each other's parents at concerts and fundraisers. I felt her gaze on me and I tried to smile, but it felt inappropriate, like laughing at a funeral.

She left the room without acknowledging me. I didn't realize she even worked for the Police Department. Was she an officer? I didn't have time to wonder, the detective reached over and tapped the space bar, bringing the laptop to life.

I gasped. The video appeared to have been recorded right here, in this very room. Sven wore a baggy sweater-jacket that had seen better days. I thought it might belong to Asa. As I watched, Sven pulled it around himself as if he were freezing.

Detective Conley cleared his throat. "I recorded this earlier today. I think you need to see it." He hesitated. "Listen carefully. You need something repeated, let me know." He pressed ENTER and the video came to life.

36

"How did they find her?" video-Sven asked.

Detective Conley leaned back in his chair. "Two kids out parking caught sight of her skull in the weedy bottom of the pond. Water level went way down over the last couple months—drought, you know."

On the computer screen, Sven nodded almost imperceptibly.

I cringed and sipped my suddenly-too-sweet drink. The aspartame seemed to coat the surfaces of my teeth. I wanted a napkin to polish them, get them clean, but even if I had one I couldn't do that without looking like a lunatic.

The detective's voice continued from the video. "Everyone, including me, assumed it was Addie Garcia from over in Odessa. She'd gone missing after a very public fight with her boyfriend." He leaned forward. "But it wasn't Addie. She turned up in El Paso. That left only Rose."

Video-Sven sat, immobile, wrapped in Asa's sweater like a mummy. I wasn't sure why he was even on the video. Was he a suspect? Was Asa a suspect? He'd been there at the pond, but not Sven. Or had he?

Detective Conley resumed speaking. "After we had the pond

dragged, the scuba divers recovered a large serrated knife. They also recovered a set of tire chains with a couple of ribs still tangled up in the links. Quite an unusual find in drought-stricken West Texas." He took out a light blue handkerchief and blotted his head. "Of course, some of our wealthier citizens have winter cabins at Ski Apache and Angel Fire so for them, snow chains make sense."

He thought for a half second. "Still, something about those chains stuck in my mind like a kernel of popcorn in an old man's dentures." He appeared to wait for Sven to acknowledge his remark, but Sven sat like stone. "Being the only full time detective on the force means that I see every single case that comes through the department."

Sven nodded. He seemed preoccupied, as if biding his time.

"I worried that piece of information all day long after the chains were pulled from the pond." He patted his scalp with the folded hanky again. "I knew there had been a case related to missing tire chains." He put the hanky away. "It just wouldn't come to me." He leaned back in his chair and stretched. "But then it did." He waited for Sven to reply.

At last Sven said. "Maybe it's different in your country, but it seems a missing girl should have been bigger news than missing tire chains." His soft accent kept the statement from sounding like an accusation. "I don't understand about the steak knife and the ribs, though. Was that from someone's barbecue or picnic?"

The detective didn't seem offended. "Well," he said. "Of course the missing girl was more important. But somehow, I knew those tire chains were big. A very big deal—if I wanted to solve the case that is."

Sven didn't comment so the detective continued.

"As for the ribs and the steak knife, no. Not a picnic. Not at all. Remember, I didn't even know Rose was missing until after the remains surfaced. That's when someone recalled how Rose had taken off right after prom. They called Rose's mama up there in Dallas. Then she called me. I interviewed her and Matt's parents along with a handful of her school friends—not you and Asa, though. Y'all were already gone to Switzerland.

Most of the folks I interviewed thought she'd gone to Michigan with her boyfriend, a couple said Montana. No one knew for sure until it was too late." He looked directly at Sven on the video. "That's why I came out to see Asa as soon as I learned the two of you had returned for his father's funeral."

What? The detective had been to visit Asa *before* the funeral? The knowledge made my blood boil. Asa had never mentioned it. Is that why he had taken such a sudden turn for the worse? No wonder Sven had acted even colder toward me.

The detective went on. "It was quite a surprise to hear from you today, Mr. Haag."

That seemed to get Sven's attention. "I wish I didn't have to be here at all. But after Asa fell into a coma, I could not rest until I told you everything." He looked down at his hands.

"I'm very sorry to hear he's in a coma," Detective Conley murmured.

Sven straightened his spine. His blue eyes were bloodshot. It was all I could do not to shake the computer screen. Asa in a coma? I knew he'd looked bad when I left last night, but I thought he was just exhausted from the trip and the funeral. A coma? Couldn't someone have called me at the motel?

And on top of that, what did he know that he hadn't told me? My mind filled with possibilities. Detective Conley looked at me to make certain I was paying attention.

"I don't know when the madness began," video-Sven said at last. "But I know when it ends because I'm ending it myself. Today. This is the end of it." He took a deep breath. His hands seemed to vibrate on the metal table. "I came here to tell you what I know because I'm tired of him covering for her." He glared at the detective. "He even left Tech to protect her. He was afraid that girl's body would be found someday. And I'm here to tell you Gabrielle Kelly did it. She knocked Rose in the pond when she hit her with her car. Then she drove it to Oklahoma and left it to hide the evidence." He huffed and dragged at the sweater stretching it all out of shape in his quest to comfort himself.

My heart fell into my gut like a dead weight. "I don't know what he's talking about. That's not why I went to Oklahoma—"

Detective Conley raised his hand, motioning for me to be quiet. "There's more," he said.

Sven started talking again. He didn't need prompting. "She took the best part of Asa, his loyalty, and she used it to save herself." His eyes welled up and he clamped his lips together. "He couldn't sleep, couldn't eat, smoked incessantly. I know that's why he got cancer; his conscience ate him up. Turned his insides black. My mother had him on a strict cocktail for the HIV. It wouldn't have turned to AIDS, wouldn't have let the cancer get in. He would have been fine if not for *this*." He swiped at his eyes. "But he wanted to protect her. Wouldn't take no for an answer." His voice trailed off. "We could've had it all. That girl ruined our lives."

His tears plopped onto the gray surface of the table. He didn't try to stop them.

On the screen, Detective Conley glanced away while Sven composed himself. "Take your time." He fingered the crease on his polyester slacks and waited.

After a moment, Sven cleared his throat and took a sip from the bottle of water sitting next to his elbow. I wondered if Rusty's mom had brought it to him the way she'd brought in the laptop. "I suppose you think I'm a monster," he continued. "Turning her in with Asa on his deathbed."

"Not at all." The big cop stared at Sven until their eyes met. "I think you are a good person who wants to do the right thing."

Sven grew softer, like a balloon with a pinhole leak. He broke down. His chin wobbled and his chest heaved and he inhaled deeply, shaking his head. Another tear darkened the battered gray surface of the table. "Asa said he was there that night. Saw the whole thing." He swiped at his eyes again. "He had to tell someone. So he told me."

Video-Detective Conley leaned closer as Sven continued.

"He said he took Gabs home after prom. She and Matt had danced together all night, and when they went outside to the courtyard, Asa said Rose followed them. She stood just inside the door for a long time, watching. He said he could see the anger rising off her like mist..."

I choked on the sip of Diet Coke I'd just taken. I didn't know she'd been watching us.

The taped detective sat forward. "What happened next?"

"She told Asa Matt called her right after she got home, and that she'd fallen asleep talking to him on the phone. After that, Matt went out looking for his cousin. Maybe she called him, I don't know, but that's when he had the accident. Gabi found out the next day, went to the hospital to see him, but couldn't get in because she wasn't family. She called Asa later. Said Rose accosted her outside the hospital, said she was pregnant with Matt's baby. Blamed her for his accident. Claimed if Matt had stayed with *her* at prom, the accident wouldn't have happened. They would have left together the way they'd arrived." He finished and looked away from the camera.

Detective Conley spoke again. "You really care for Asa, don't you?"

Sven bristled. "The same way you care for your spouse, Detective."

The big man shrugged and held up his bare left hand. "Not a

good comparison. She screwed me over—with my ex-partner. They took my kids and moved to Timbuktu. Cliché. To the max."

Sven smiled a tight little smile. "Sorry." He opened his mouth. Closed it. Dabbed his leaky nose with a Kleenex that had appeared from somewhere." Then he spoke once more, voice stronger than before. "I have to finish."

I heard the sound of his chair scraping the floor as he tried to get closer.

"The night after Matt's accident, Gabs got another call. From Rose, this time. She convinced Gabi that Matt had been released from the hospital and wanted her to meet him at South Pond."

"She told you this?" Detective Conley's voice on the video sounded cool, but he was obviously trying to make sense of it all.

Sven made a small noise of disagreement. "Asa was out with a friend when they spied her driving down Main, headed out of town toward the pond." He stopped talking, gauging his words perhaps.

The video-detective looked at Sven to see if he should stop the recording, but Sven shook his head. "He was with someone else. I wasn't there. It was the last time he was with that person. He said he ended it, for me."

I tried to imagine my friend confessing to all this and I came up with an image that was more audio than visual. I imagined the two of them in some bedroom in Bern, or maybe right here in Ace's old room. And I heard the sound of something indecipherable, lips on dry skin perhaps, or the soft whicker of a bleached white sheet sliding across thinly fleshed bone. Not a deathbed confession, exactly, but a terminal-prognosis confession at least.

Detective Conley studied the younger man on the video.

Sven held up one finger. "They followed her through town—she didn't even know it."

I couldn't believe it. If Sven wasn't the driver of the silver Audi, who could it have been?

"He said they followed her to the pond. She drove around and around, looking."

"What did she find?" Conley asked.

"She found Rose. Asa said the girl appeared near the edge of the pond where Gabi stopped the car and started to get out. That's when Rose ran at her, at the car. He said he saw the flash of a knife in the moonlight." Sven stopped talking and both the video room and our real room stayed perfectly silent.

Finally, after another moment, he went on, "He told me when she charged the car, she looked like a witch, or a demon, enraged. Gabi's windows were down. She jumped back inside the car and slammed the door. He said the look on her face was pure panic as she jammed the gear into reverse and tried to maneuver out of the parking area. But she couldn't manage it. She had to go forward again."

He closed his eyes and took a steadying breath. "He said Gabi didn't mean to hit her. He didn't think so anyway."

The detective leaned forward. "Go on."

Sven's voice echoed from the center of the table again. "When Gabi put it back in drive, the stupid girl ran in front of her. The car clipped her, and she flew through the air. Gabrielle hit the brake and staggered out—"

"Why did she stagger? Was she drunk?" The detective's voice grew sharp.

"Asa said she was just shocked. He swears Gabi was only trying to leave." He sniffed. "But then he always defended her, no matter the circumstance."

"What happened next?"

Another long bout of silence. On the screen, he tugged the sweater tighter. "Together they searched the area. He said Gabi was on the verge of hysteria."

"And the girl, where was she?"

Sven closed his eyes and composed himself. "They couldn't find her. She'd obviously got up and ran away. He said he made Gabi leave while he and his friend stayed to search."

Detective Conley spoke, "Did they find her? Did they find her and finish her off, attach the chains to her? Sink her in the middle of the pond? And how did they get her out in the middle, by the way? Was there a boat tied up nearby?"

Sven looked at the detective as if he'd suddenly grown a third eye. "Chains? What? No. Gabi hit her with the car. She flew into the water, probably unconscious. That's probably why she drowned." He shivered and pulled the sweater close again. "Asa said it was so dark, he and his friend left. They never found her."

Detective Conley shifted in his squeaking chair. "Well, someone found her. Someone found her and wrapped a set of snow chains around her body so she'd never leave the pond. The thing is, we can't tell if she was dead when they wrapped the chains around her or not."

Sven's face belied his shock. The iciness that usually masked his emotions was gone. It was obvious he did not know how the girl had been found.

"I didn't know all that," I said. "Are you sure it's even Rose?"

The detective pressed a key on the laptop and video-Sven was paused. "It's her." He stared at me. "I received official confirmation this morning." He continued to stare at my face. "That's why I followed you out to the pond."

"You followed me? But why?" Stupid, stupid question.

He tapped his ink pen on the table. "I knew you were in town. I watched all of you at the funeral. Asa looked bad." Tap, tap, tap with the pen. "When Mr. Haag came in first thing this morning," he tapped the laptop with his pen. "I had just received the Coroner's report. I went straight to your motel and waited." His smile was cruel. "I couldn't believe you took a cab to the pond. Why did you do that? What did you hope to find there?"

I looked away from that awful smile. "I don't know. I didn't hope to find anything. I only wanted to go by my old house. But then the driver told me about the remains and I just felt drawn." In the back of my mind a sudden thought arose. Hadn't I wanted to go back to the pond even before the cab driver mentioned the remains? Why did I keep telling the detective otherwise? Surely I could trust my own memory. I had nothing to hide, right?

He leaned back. "Murderers sometimes revisit the scene of their crime. Did you know that?"

I tucked a strand of hair behind my ear and pushed up my glasses. "Please, Detective Conley, I'm no murderer. It wasn't me. I've never even seen a set of snow chains. Besides, she's the one who had the knife."

"Ahh, so you *were* there."

Wait. What did I just do? Did I confess to something? Didn't he already know that part—after what Sven had said—oh, God. I just confirmed it. I closed my mouth, determined not to say anything else. "May I make a phone call?" I gripped the edge of the table. "I mean, you said I'm not under arrest or anything."

That got his attention. "Of course you may."

I pushed out my chair to stand.

"But wouldn't you like to see the rest of the video first?"

"There's more?"

"Oh, yes. So much more."

I fell back into the chair as if my bones had liquefied.

The detective tapped a key. Sven began to talk again. His voice had grown soft.

37

Detective Conley reached over and tapped another key to turn up the volume. "Karl Karson. That's who Asa was with that night. Mr. Karson has a cabin at Angel Fire."

"Karl Karson? Dr. Letter's golf partner?" I hadn't meant to blurt it out but I couldn't help myself. "Why was he with Asa at that time of night? Oh... my... God. Was he Asa's secret relationship? That old man?" I remembered about his son, Dillon Karson, at prom. How he had watched Asa, how Ace had later told me their fathers were no longer friends. They'd had a falling out. He'd said he was afraid Dillon was going to out him right there in front of everybody. Had he known about Asa and his father?

I hated to ask, but I had to know. "Did Karl Karson drive a silver Audi?"

"Oh yes." The detective's voice had taken on a gleeful tone.

I felt sick.

"Remember that burglary report I mentioned to your buddy there?" He indicated video-Sven.

"Yes?"

"It finally came to me... that report had been filed by Mr. Karson himself. He said someone at the garage must've taken those chains out of his trunk. Imagine that. A good way to cover your tracks, right?"

I shrugged. This was too much. I couldn't get over the fact that Asa had been having some sort of relationship with Karl Karson, a man who owned the only Audi dealership for miles around. Of course, in one way it made perfect sense. It would explain Asa's secret life, his lack of a relationship with his father, and of course, his father's falling out with his old golf buddy. Oh, what a tangled web, I thought.

"So, Gabi, did you hit her with your car that night?"

Bile rose in my throat. I felt the world go a little gray around the edges. "Yes." I could barely hear my own voice. "But I didn't kill her. She had a knife. She ran at me. My window was down. I only tried to get away from her. Away from there." I closed my eyes. "She ran right in front of me. There was a horrible sound. She flew up, over the car. Into the darkness."

"And then you and your buddies found her knife and finished her off. Took the chains from Karson's trunk and wrapped them around her body so she couldn't identify any of you."

My eyes flew open. "No. I left. Asa told me to leave, he said he saw Rose get up and run away. He said he'd make sure she was taken care of."

"Oh, they took care of her all right."

I shook my head. "No. My Asa wouldn't do that. And he can't even be here to defend himself." The thought of him lying in his old bed, in a coma, made my words all the more painful. "It had to be Mr. Karson. He must've done it and made Asa cover it up. He probably didn't want Rose to go back and tell everyone he and Asa were having an affair. Maybe he didn't want his wife and kids to know." It all made sense now. Asa got me out of there so I wouldn't see Mr. Karson. Did he know what they were going to do? Oh, Ace. My head began to pound. It was too much.

"You make a very strong case, Gabrielle. Can you prove she was alive when you left the pond that night?" He was like a bulldog. He just wouldn't let go.

I thought back to that horrific night. Could I? Could I prove anything? No, I ran. Ran like a rabbit. All the way to Oklahoma. All the way to California. I shook my head. "No. I took off. I was so confused, upset. Asa said let him handle it. He said he would take care of it. I thought it would all work out." That sounded lame, even to my own ears.

Detective Conley rose to his feet. He reached inside his jacket and pulled a set of handcuffs from his belt. "Gabrielle Anderson, you have the right to remain silent—" He walked around the table and indicated I should stand.

"Wait! You're arresting me? I didn't—"

"You have the right to an attorney." He continued reciting my Miranda rights as if I hadn't spoken.

"Yes. I want an attorney. Or... or at least my phone call."

"Cross your hands behind your back, please." He was all business as he clipped the cuffs on me.

I started to cry. "I can't use the phone with these on."

He picked up my purse and grasped my elbow. Then he finished reciting my rights and told me I was under arrest for murder. I couldn't believe I'd sat there and told him everything. I developed tunnel vision. The only thing I could see was whatever was right in front of me as he marched me down the hall to booking where Junell took me into the bathroom to search me.

Burning with shame, I closed my eyes and forced away the feel of her hard fingertips sliding inside the cups of my bra, the waist and legs of my panties, and I steeled myself, wondering what I would do if this was the place they did cavity searches.

But I was spared that indignity, at least for now.

As she patted me down, I pretended to be on the beach with Reece, waiting for the perfect wave. I hadn't quite got the hang of surfing yet, now I wondered if I'd ever have another chance.

After the humiliating search, I was un-cuffed, fingerprinted, and told how to stand for a mug shot. I tried not to sob as Junell stood me in front of the height chart and told me to give her "full face" and then "profile" while holding the plastic board with my prisoner number on it.

Everything seemed surreal. And yet all the officers acted like it was normal. For them, I suppose it was just another day. For me it was Alice down the rabbit hole.

At last I was taken to an office with a phone on the desk. I saw Detective Conley's name on the desk nameplate. As I sat there, hands re-cuffed—in front of me this time—wondering how to make a long-distance call (do I dial 9 for an outside line, or just push 0 for the operator?), the detective sauntered in with a cup of coffee.

"I need to call my mom in Houston," I said. "How do I do that?"

He reached across me and pushed a button. A red light lit up on the phone's base and a woman's voice came on the speaker. "Yes?"

"Shirl, get me a long-distance operator, Mrs. Anderson needs to call her mother collect." He looked at me. "When the operator comes on, tell her your name and your mother's name and tell her you are calling collect."

I nodded. My eyes burned from trying to keep the tears at bay. When Mom answered the phone, the operator asked her if she would accept a collect call from her daughter—me—at the jail in Live Oak. To Mom's credit, she barely hesitated. Of course she knew I was in town for the funeral, otherwise she might have thought the whole thing a joke.

"Mom?" As soon as I heard her voice I spilled out the whole sordid story. "But I didn't kill her, Mom—"

"Well, of course not," she said. "You would never do anything like that. You just keep your chin up. I'm going to catch the first plane, but first, I'm calling an attorney to come and get you out of there."

I burst into braying, donkey-like sobs of relief. Mom was coming. She would help. She would make them see I that I was innocent.

"Have you called Reece?" she asked.

"No, he's in the backcountry. They would have to call him on satellite phone. I can't stand the thought of everyone knowing this. Not yet. Maybe we can straighten it out before he gets home."

Mom remained silent for a moment. "Okay. We'll try that for now. I'll see you as soon as possible. Don't worry."

I told her how much I loved her and then we hung up. A uniformed policeman, whose badge read Officer Dunn, came and took me to a cell. He must've been standing right outside the door with Detective Conley.

I went into the gray cell without a bleat. An iron cot was attached to the wall and the springs were bare except for a rolled-up mattress on one end.

Junell appeared with an army blanket and a blue and white striped bed pillow. She handed them to me without a word.

I made up the bed and sat on it. At least the handcuffs were off. I'd had to stick my hands through a rectangular hole in the door and allow them to be removed that way. Another humiliation. As if I would turn into a raving beast and attack someone if they took them off before locking me in.

I pushed up my filthy glasses and rested my spine against the wall. I drew my knees up to my chest, wrapped my arms around my legs, and let the shakes come. For a few moments, I could do nothing but hold on and try to keep myself from flying apart. The caged light bulb in the ceiling threw strange shadows all around me. I squeezed my eyes shut and told myself none of it was real.

But Sven's last words on the video echoed in my head. "You know what Asa said to me after he told me all this?" Detective Conley and I had both waited to see what he would say. "He said true love is rare, but true friendship is rarer still." Then Sven swallowed audibly. "I think it's a line from some old poem or something. That's why he covered everything up, isn't it? Because she was his dearest friend."

That broke my heart. Was it true, did Asa and Karl Karson find Rose's body and sink it in the pond with the tire chains to keep me out of trouble? Or did he and his lover do that just to keep their dirty little secret? I know it couldn't have been anything worse than that. I know if she'd been alive when they found her Asa would have called 911. He would not have allowed Karl Karson to murder someone just to keep their secret, no matter how horribly the news would have impacted their lives.

Wait—

What if Karl Karson went back to the pond after he took Asa home that night? What if he found an injured Rose—or even her dead body—and sunk her in the pond all by himself? Wouldn't that absolve both Asa and me?

I assumed Asa wasn't in custody because of his health—I still couldn't believe he might be in a coma—but if everything I'd heard was on the level, then why wasn't Karl Karson in custody? After all, it was definitely his tire chains that had held Rose at the bottom of the pond all summer. Didn't that count for anything?

38

J ackson Peabody III arrived at the police station within the hour. I still had my head down and my eyes closed when Officer Dunn unlocked my cell door and let him in. When I raised my head, I recognized him right away. I'd seen him on the local news a few times over the years. He was one of Live Oak's most prominent attorneys.

Silver hair and ice-blue eyes, he carried a slim leather briefcase that probably cost more than my old Honda. He introduced himself and sat on the bed beside me.

"Your mother called me. I've known her for years." He grinned like a shark, showing all his teeth. "She's the only one I ever trusted with these pearly whites."

I had to smile at that. "Thank you for coming." I liked him now that he'd shown me his teeth. It felt like a connection.

He took out a fancy silver pen and a yellow legal tablet. "Give me the CliffsNotes on what got you in here."

I told him everything that had happened, including the video of Sven.

Mr. Peabody wrote in short jabs, chuckling when I asked if he knew why Karl Karson wasn't in custody yet. "He's in

Germany, at the moment. Big Audi convention I believe." He shook his head. "But don't worry, he'll be back. His company is here, his whole livelihood. He'll be back even if we have to have him extradited." He finished writing and glanced up. "And you really didn't do it?"

"No, of course not. I accidentally hit her with the car, but I was only trying to get away from her and her knife. Detective Conley said she had Karl Karson's tire chains around her waist." I assured him I hadn't even known Karson was the person with Asa at the time.

He didn't bat an eye, simply made another note on his legal tablet.

"Well," he said at last. "This is quite a tale, isn't it?" He returned pen and pad to his briefcase and said, "Wait here while I arrange your bail." As if I could go anywhere. He smiled, showing me his teeth again, making me smile in return. "In a few minutes, I'll have you out of here and we'll go to my office."

I watched him motion for the officer to let him out. I felt better knowing he was on my side.

After a while, Officer Dunn came back. His demeanor had undergone a decided change. He didn't say a word as he escorted me back to booking where Junell stood at the counter with my purse and its contents.

While I signed a form acknowledging the return of my belongings, I heard Mr. Peabody talking to Detective Conley.

"So let me get this straight." I saw him slide his briefcase onto the chest-high counter and lean forward slightly. "You arrested my client," he indicated me with a glance, "a girl who has never had so much as a *parking* ticket, on the basis of a second-hand confession from a man in a coma." He pulled his briefcase off the counter and held it at the level of his chest like a shield. "That about the size of it?"

Detective Conley opened his mouth, closed it, and then

opened it again. "She was at the pond the night Rose Lintz was killed. She admits hitting her with the car."

"In self-defense," Mr. Peabody said. "That's not murder." He indicated I should precede him to the door.

Detective Conley clamped his lips together. "Instruct her not to leave town," he said, getting the last word in.

Jackson Peabody held the door open.

I went through it into the bright fall day.

THERE WAS no sign of Sven as we crossed the sidewalk to the attorney's Range Rover. I couldn't believe Asa's man harbored so much resentment against me. He hadn't been there that night. He hadn't heard Asa order me to leave.

Mr. Peabody held the door while I settled into the front seat. "Do you really think they will arrest Mr. Karson when he comes back?"

"I'm afraid he may get out of it," he said. "Karl Karson is one of the wealthiest men in town. He'll bring in a battery of attorneys who will attempt to squash any evidence and convince folks his chains were simply stolen and used without his knowledge. He may even accuse your friend of stealing his car that night. Especially if Asa doesn't wake up. With him gone, there won't be any witnesses to say otherwise."

"What about me? I saw his car."

"Did you see him?"

I thought about that. "No. Never."

"He'll simply say he wasn't there. That it was only his car. Remember, he filed a stolen report about the chains before we even knew Rose was missing. His attorneys will insist his car was used and returned without his knowledge."

"But Sven will testify, about the affair, I mean. And the confession."

The august attorney shook his head and pulled away from the curb. "Without evidence, it's simply hearsay." He then asked if I needed to make any stops before we went to his office to have his secretary make everything official.

"Yes," I said. "If you don't mind, I need to go back to Asa's house to say goodbye. But I don't want to see Sven." The memory of our honeymoon in Switzerland burned in my mind. Now I knew why he'd seemed so cool. The whole thing had been Asa's idea. He had always been there for me.

"Let me make a call." Mr. Peabody picked up the receiver of his car phone and told someone to call Dr. Letter's residence.

Would Maria answer?

I glanced out the window at the leaves piling up in the gutters. Live oaks are evergreen. These leaves were falling from elms, maples, and other deciduous trees sprinkled throughout the area. Fall in west Texas is a very short season. Sometimes summer seems to bleed right into winter.

After a few moments, Mr. Peabody replaced the receiver. "No answer. Hmmm. I wonder..." he picked it up again and told the person on the other end, his secretary I assumed, to call the hospital and find out if Asa Letter had been admitted.

I crossed my fingers down beside my seat.

The phone jangled. Mr. Peabody picked it up and listened. Then he turned to me and nodded. "He's in ICU."

"Can I see him? I have to see him." Or would it be like Matt —only family? Would Sven let me in? Could I stand to look at him after he turned me in, tried to blame me for Rose's death?

"Is that wise? Going to the hospital? I thought his friend was the one who had you arrested."

"Yes, but this is Asa. He's been my best friend since we were in grade school. Even my husband doesn't know me like Ace." I turned to him, barely able to keep the tears at bay. "I have to see him, please. It may be the last time."

"I'll do my best," he said. "I promised your mom I would take care of you until she gets here. But I warn you, it could be ugly."

"Okay." I steeled myself for the possibility of a confrontation. "But you know what they say about friendship."

He glanced my way. "What's that?"

"True love is rare, but true friendship is rarer still."

39

I did make it in to see my Asa before it was too late. Mr. Peabody went in first and told Sven he had to talk to him about my case. I watched from around the corner as they strolled by on their way to the cafeteria. One thing about Sven, he never left Asa's side unless forced to do so.

When they were out of sight, I hurried to the Intensive Care Unit. The front of Asa's small room was glass. There was no privacy in ICU. Every patient was visible from the central hub of the nurse's station.

Through the glass, I saw him. A blindingly white sheet was folded down over his thin chest and tucked under the edge of the mattress all the way around. The silver bedrails were raised as well. He couldn't have gotten out of bed even if he had been able.

An IV snaked from a machine on a silver pole. The tube ended beneath a wrap on his left arm. An oxygen mask obscured almost all of his face except for his closed eyes. His lashes were dark fans lying on his cheeks. The planes of his face stood out in the soft glow of the ICU lighting.

My heart ached in my chest. It felt like the night of prom,

when I'd watched Matt grow smaller and smaller in the car's side mirror. I'd had the feeling I wouldn't see him again. Now, I felt the same thing about my dear friend.

No one questioned me or tried to stop me from going in. I pushed aside the curtain and tiptoed to his bed. "Oh, Asa. How can this be?" I laid my hand on top of his, curled my fingers into his slack palm.

I thought I saw his lashes flicker.

"You're a good friend," I whispered. "The best friend anyone could ever have." I thought about him telling me to take off, go home, that night at the pond. I'll take care of it, he'd said. And I wanted to believe he had done that for me, not just to keep his secret, but to keep me safe. To look out for me.

I know he wouldn't have been a party to murder no matter what. No one could ever convince me otherwise. But would he have helped cover up an accidental death? He might have, and if his conscience bothered him half as much as mine had been bothering me, it could have contributed to the downward spiral of his health. I believed that much was true.

On the other hand, I thought it entirely possible that Karl Karson had returned to the pond later, found Rose's body, wrapped his tire chains around her, and sunk her in the water all by himself. That was the easiest thing to believe. Why? Because he wasn't here. He wasn't here and he and Asa had made a complete break. Maybe it was for Sven (as Sven thought), but maybe it was that old conscience thing again. Heaven knows it had done a number on me.

Then another thought crossed my mind. If Karl Karson had given Asa this terrible disease, then perhaps he wasn't at an Audi convention at all. Maybe he was lying in a hospital somewhere. Maybe in Germany or somewhere else out of the public eye. Someplace where he could be treated without anyone knowing about it.

My tears fell onto the snowy sheet. So many wasted lives. I squeezed Asa's hand and leaned down to plant one last kiss on his smooth, young brow. "I love you, old friend. More than you will ever know."

His fingers curved around mine as if he'd heard every word. It wasn't my imagination. Beneath his mask, I'm sure he smiled.

My hand went to my throat, searching for the necklace Matt had slipped over my head on that fateful night. It wasn't there. It was in my little jade jewelry box back home in L.A.

I had a sudden need to see Matt, to give him back his necklace, to put an end to all that had happened, and to tell him what really occurred at the pond. But Rose was his cousin. If I went there, I might not be welcome at all.

Cut your losses, Asa's favorite saying echoed inside my head.

I squeezed his fingers. I hear you, old friend.

I hear you loud and clear.

MR. PEABODY KEPT Sven away for over half an hour, during which time I sat and held Asa's hand and watched his thin chest rise and fall so shallowly I often couldn't see it move at all.

When the nurse came in to tell me it was time to leave—I didn't realize ICU had such short visiting times—I leaned down and kissed his forehead one last time, certain I would never see my old friend again.

The nurse patted my shoulder. "Dr. Letter was a brilliant surgeon," she murmured. "We'll see that his son has the very best of care."

I nodded, but I couldn't say anything in reply. Sobs were building in my chest, making their way up my throat, preparing to explode from my mouth as soon as I could get out of that room.

In the restroom, I did my best to break down quietly, my fist shoved between my teeth. Everything felt so horrible, so wrong. And it was all beyond my control, just like that night at the pond.

Splashing my face with water from the tap, I yearned to feel Reece's strong, loving arms around me. The experience of having been arrested, searched, fingerprinted, interrogated, and then brought here to see my best friend lying silent and still at death's door, it was almost too much. I grabbed rough, brown paper towels from the dispenser and dried the water streaming from my face.

The detective had said not to leave town. What did that mean? I can't go home, I have to stay here in a motel? For how long? I needed to see Mr. Peabody, ask him all these things.

I turned off the faucet and the water swirling down the drain appeared to shimmer like pond water, green and slightly irides-cent. I closed my eyes and willed away the nonsense. When I opened them again, the water ran clear, normal. Examining my reflection in the mirror gave me chills, as if I were looking into someone else's brown eyes. Is it me? Am I in there, or is it someone else, playing mind games with me, driving me insane? How could anyone think I would be involved in murder? It was all just a freak accident. An accident caused by the victim herself. At least that's what I had assumed—until I found out about Karl Karson. Now, I might never know, especially if he is lying in a German hospital, at death's door like my Asa.

What if he died before he could be extradited? Someone would have to pay for this crime, for the remains in the pond. There would be no one to stand trial except for me. Would I become their fall guy, their scapegoat?

Shaking my head, I balled up the paper towels and tossed them toward the trash. Then I took a deep breath, opened the door, and prayed I wouldn't see Sven in the hallway. I'll scratch his eyes out, I thought. He's the cause of all this, him and that stupid videotaped interview. If not for that, no one would have even known about my trip to the pond.

He was nowhere to be seen. Only Mr. Peabody sat on a padded bench near the elevator, biding his time, looking over some papers from his briefcase.

"There you are." His voice sounded unconcerned. "Are you ready?"

I nodded and he pushed the button to call the elevator.

"Can I ask you a question?"

He glanced at my face. "Of course. Ask away."

"Have you seen the autopsy report on the remains?"

He patted the leather briefcase. "I have it right here. The good detective made me a copy while you were signing your release forms."

My eyes met his. "Have you read it?"

"Oh, yes. I glanced over it just now. It was definitely Rose Lintz."

When I didn't respond, he continued. "Was there something else you were wondering about, something in particular?"

I exhaled, and then plunged ahead. "She said she was pregnant. I don't suppose there was any way to tell if that was true. Since the remains were skeletal, I mean."

"Ahhh." The elevator dinged open and we got on. He pressed number one for the first floor. "Some of the internal organs were still intact." He glanced back through the report. "There was no mention of a pregnancy. And it's a routine test the medical examiner does on every deceased female when the death is suspicious or unattended."

"She told me she was carrying Matt's baby. I think that's why she ran at me with a knife out there that night. Insane jealousy. He'd said we were going to be together, then he had the accident."

Jackson Peabody remained quiet, seemingly deep in

thought. "But she wasn't pregnant." He drew a finger across his upper lip thoughtfully. "Just off the top of my head, are we certain Matt's accident was really an accident?"

The elevator stopped, the doors opened, and he stepped aside to allow me to exit first.

I turned his question over and over in my mind. If Rose had been jealous enough to lie to me about being pregnant, and then come after me with a knife, was it possible she could have caused Matt's accident, too?

Pretty farfetched? Maybe not.

After tucking me into the passenger side of the Range Rover, Jackson Peabody got in behind the wheel. After starting the engine and adjusting the AC vents, he opened his briefcase and pulled out a Nokia mobile phone. "Sorry," he said. "The office left me a voicemail earlier, but I was unable to return their call from inside the hospital."

I nodded, fascinated by the bright red phone with the black pull-up antenna.

When his call went through, he told someone named Senia —his secretary, I assumed—that we were headed to the office to sign the paperwork so he could represent me.

Whatever she said made his eyes widen and he turned toward me and held out the phone. "You've got a call from California. She had just answered it on the other line."

My heart leaped into the back of my throat as I pressed the red phone to my ear. "Reece?" Even though I knew it had to be him, my voice was tentative.

"Gabs?" He had to yell. "I'm on the SAT phone. Are you all right?"

I lost it. The braying sobs I'd stifled in the restroom earlier burst forth. "Oh, Reece. They think I killed Rose—"

"What?" His voice blared across the inside of the car. "That girl you said went missing?"

I swiped at the tears blurring my eyes. "Yes. They found her in the pond—but I didn't kill her—Karl Karson's tire chains were wrapped around her. He must have done it after I left that night. He and Asa were there, together. Asa is the one who told me she was okay. He said he saw her running away. But Karl Karson was married, with a family. He shouldn't have been out there with Asa—he was Dr. Letter's golf partner!"

"Oh, Gabs. I'll bring this crew down the mountain and get on the next plane. I can be there by tomorrow night—"

"Wait. Don't do that. They need you there. How'd you even know to call me here, on Mr. Peabody's phone?" The circumstances of the call struck me like a hammer. "How'd you find out?"

"I tried to call you at Asa's and the housekeeper said he was in ICU, so I called your mom and she told me everything. I was worried about you. Couldn't think of anything else..."

"Reece. I got arrested—"

Even over the satellite link, I heard him inhale sharply. "I know, honey, I know. That's why I'm coming. This is way more important that a few trails on a mountain."

"But the kids," I said. "They will have to—"

"They'll be reassigned to another crew or another crew leader can come in. I'm not worried about that. This is more important. You are more important."

I felt a weight slip off my shoulders. "I can't believe this is happening."

Reece said, "Don't worry. You'll be fine. Tell me where to fly in and what hotel you're at, then try to get some rest. Your mom said you have an excellent attorney. Just let him take care of everything." He hesitated and the line went so quiet I thought I'd lost him.

"Reece?"

"I said, how's Asa?" he had to yell again because of the connection.

"Not good. I saw him just now. Reece, he isn't going to make it. If he could talk he could straighten this out, I know he could." I wanted to go ahead and tell him Sven was the cause of everything, but that would have to wait until we were together, when I could get his input on it.

My senses still reeled every time I thought about how Sven was the one who had laid the whole blame on me. I couldn't understand it. Surely he could see that Karl Karson had to be the one who had sunk Rose in the pond. He had the greatest motive of all. He had to keep her from telling the whole town that he was having an affair with his golf partner's gay son—one who was technically still in high school. That would have been the end of Karl Karson and his fancy car dealership—at least in tiny Live Oak.

"Reece? Are you there?" The line had gone quiet again.

"Gabs? Gabrielle?" His voice was faint. "I think I'm losing the connection. I'll see you to—"

He was gone. I heard a loud click and the line went dead. But it was okay. He would come. He would be here tomorrow. Reece was coming. Everything would be all right now.

I tried to hand the phone back to Mr. Peabody but he didn't notice. He'd opened his briefcase and removed the autopsy report again, and a sheaf of other papers that appeared to be a transcript of Sven's taped statement. I kept seeing his name and Detective Conley's name written as dialogue tags.

Mr. Peabody must have felt me staring at him. "Sorry," he said, glancing up. "I couldn't help overhearing your side of the conversation so I looked back to check a few things." He held up the transcript. "You're right, you know. Karl Karson did have the best motive for wanting her gone. And Sven Haag didn't appear to know about the tire chains. It says here he thought you knocked her into the pond when you struck her." He tapped a line in the transcript with his forefinger. "The owner of the tire chains had to have attached them to her. He could have come back and done it, or he could have enlisted Asa's help after you left." He shrugged. "Who steals tire chains in the desert?"

"I'm glad you believe me."

He held up the coroner's report. On it I could see the drawing of a generic female body with certain areas marked with notes. "And then there's this." He pointed to a particular mark on the drawing's neck. "I believe this shows you are right. Karl Karson must have wrapped the tire chains around her and sunk her in the pond after he slashed her throat."

"What?" My mouth fell open in shock.

"Yes." He handed me the drawing. "I wondered about this mark, but I hadn't read the written report." He flipped up the drawing page to show the attached report. "Now I have. I glanced over it while you were talking."

"And?"

"It clearly shows serrated cuts on the victim's hyoid and clavicle bones." He looked at me closely. "Bones in and near the throat. Could you tell what sort of knife she was holding when she came at you?"

I shook my head. "Not at all. Just the reflection of moonlight on the silver blade."

"Well, too bad. I'll bet my eyeteeth if we could've searched her mom's kitchen before they moved we would've found a missing steak knife just like the one recovered along with her remains."

I let that sink in. "So you think Karl Karson cut her throat with her own knife and then tossed her body in the pond?"

He nodded, put all the paperwork back into his briefcase, and snapped it shut. "I'm almost positive. It's a long shot, but if luck holds, we may even be able to pull a few fingerprints off the knife."

"That *would* be lucky," I said. "After all this time in the water."

He laughed. "But if not, then our job will be a lot harder. In fact, without Asa, it will be difficult to prove Karson was even at the pond that night." He drove toward the center of town, leaving me to my thoughts.

Within moments, we pulled up to a turn of the century house that doubled as his law office. An ornate shingle hung from the craftsman-style porch. It read Jackson Peabody, Attorney-at-Law. "Are you certain Asa was in a coma?"

I nodded, but in the back of my mind I remembered the flicker of his lashes. "Actually, I'm not positive. I mean, I didn't ask. I just visited a while and left. He did seem to know I was there, though."

"Maybe I'll let Senia get your paperwork started while I make a call to ICU. All we need is a few words from him saying what really happened after you left." He walked me inside, introduced me to his secretary, and then pulled out his Nokia.

As he walked back to his office, I heard him say, "Dr. Guthrapalli? Jackson Peabody here. I need to know the prognosis of one of your ICU patients."

I held my breath.

He stopped in the doorway. "Is that right? Not a coma after all?" He turned and gave me a thumbs-up and a shark-toothed smile. "Excellent. My secretary and I will be there shortly. No, please don't tell him we're coming. We want it to be a complete surprise."

As soon as he pressed the END button on his phone, I jumped up and crossed the room. "Did he wake up? Is Asa awake?"

Mr. Peabody nodded. "He is awake and lucid." He turned to

his secretary. "I'll call Detective Conley on the way. He'll need to bring his video recorder. I'll need you to take Mr. Sven Haag down the hall and keep him away from ICU until we are finished."

I started toward the door, but Mr. Peabody stopped me. "Sorry, Gabrielle." He pointed toward the phone on the desk. "You will call a cab and go back to the motel to wait for us."

My mouth opened, but before I could say anything he continued. "My intern, Charlie, will be back at any moment so don't worry about locking up if he isn't back when you leave." He held the door open for his secretary who had grabbed her bag and stuffed a couple of yellow legal tablets into it. "Don't worry," he said to me, "I'll call you as soon as we are done. If he is as good a friend as you say, he will tell us what we need to know to have all charges dropped."

40

S o that's what happened.

I found myself sitting in an over-stuffed wing chair in my attorney's opulent office, waiting for another taxi to take me back to my motel where I would do some more waiting.

Not only was I praying that my best friend was feeling better —which would give me hope that there might be a treatment that could give him a few more years—but I was also hoping that he would come through for me and tell them the absolute truth about what happened that night at the pond.

My stomach churned when I thought about what it would be like if he decided to protect Karl Karson instead of me. Was that even a possibility? I didn't think so, but who knew? What if he really had stayed and helped Mr. Karson dispose of Rose's body? No. Not my Asa. That would make him an accessory to murder. And he could never do that, no matter what. It simply wasn't in him.

I took my cab back to the motel, thankful it wasn't the same driver from before, and then I sat right there in front of the TV in my motel room and waited. Just like Mr. Peabody instructed me to do.

REECE GOT in late the next afternoon. Mom met him at the airport. She'd arrived only an hour earlier so they both caught the same puddle jumper and came directly from the Midland International Airport to Live Oak.

When he came through that motel room door all wild blond hair and work-hardened muscle, I latched on to my husband and vowed to never let him go.

I felt terrible having caused him and Mom to come all the way to West Texas when it turned out I didn't need saving after all. You see, when Asa regained consciousness—it turns out he was basically weak and exhausted from the combination of his disease, the intercontinental travel, and the emotional stress of losing his father—he told the truth without hesitation even though it meant that his former lover would probably be extradited back to the states for murder.

It turned out to be almost exactly what we'd suspected all along. Once I'd left the pond that night, following Asa's orders, Karl Karson took Asa back to his car—at their regular meeting place, a back road rest area—and then returned to the pond.

Asa said Mr. Karson was so upset about the possibility of Rose telling his wife about the two of them that he had a feeling the man intended to return to the pond and look for her. So he waited a bit, and then followed him.

He got there just in time to see Mr. Karson swimming back to shore from the center of the pond.

I was used to seeing Karl Karson selling luxury cars on local TV commercials. I couldn't imagine him swimming across South Pond in his three-piece suit. The image was almost too bizarre to believe.

But believe it, I did.

Asa insisted he'd never seen Rose's body. Karson had

convinced him he only swam out to the center because he thought he'd seen something floating there in the moonlight. "But it wasn't her," he'd said. "It wasn't anything but pond scum. Green pond scum."

When I heard that, I thought of the greenish water that kept haunting me over the last few months. I think Rose may have been trying to tell me something.

"Isn't that odd," Reese said, when I told him about the green water. "She tried to murder you, but wound up murdered instead. Then her spirit tried to get you to help solve the crime."

Only my Reece could explain it all so succinctly. I know it was murder, no doubt about that, but after everything I'd been through, I found it difficult to process the details. I had the feeling I might still be processing them for years to come. The fact that Asa told the truth, and that he really did have a fighting chance at a few more years on earth, made everything okay for now.

Except for Matt.

He was still in the rehab hospital in Ft. Worth. There hadn't been much improvement, according to Mr. Jackson Peabody who called an acquaintance there and found out for me.

In fact, Mr. Peabody was convinced that Matt's accident investigation needed to be reopened, but I guess that would be up to his parents. I can't believe Rose would have caused him harm. She seemed so in love with him—but you know what they say about that proverbial line between love and hate. Maybe she was jealous enough to be that vindictive. But now that she's gone, I'm not sure it really matters.

We might talk to his parents about it, though, when we go see him next week. Reece brought me my old buffalo nickel necklace when he came to Live Oak to rescue me. Now I think it's time I returned it to Matt. He obviously needs all the luck he can get.

And my darling Reece will go with me. Not only is he NOT the jealous kind, he proved he is the forgiving kind when Sven caught me at the hospital and apologized for getting me into this mess in the first place. Sven said if he'd known the whole truth, he never would have mentioned my name. Of course I forgave him, too.

After all, true love is rare, but true friendship is rarer still.

MEET THE AUTHOR

Ann has been a writer since junior high school, but to pay the bills she's waited tables, delivered newspapers, cleaned other people's houses, taught school, and even had a short stint as a secretary in a rock-n-roll radio station. She also worked as a 911 operator and a police dispatcher.

Ann's stories began to win awards in her college days. Since then she's published novels, novellas, and short stories. But even if no one ever bought another book, Ann wouldn't stop writing. For her it's the cathartic pause in a sometimes-crazy world. Most of the time, it even keeps her sane.

We hope you enjoyed *THE REMAINS IN THE POND* by Ann Swann. Here is an excerpt from another of her books, *STUTTER CREEK.*

STUTTER CREEK

BY ANN SWANN

Amanda Myers was making a conscious effort to keep her heavy foot off the Toyota's gas pedal when she spied, what appeared to be, a small boy standing beside the road. An old- fashioned newsboy cap nearly obscured his tiny face.

Mandy hit the brake and steered the Celica toward the gravel shoulder. Even though she would be late for her evening shift at The Water House Bar & Grill, there was no way she could simply drive past a small boy standing beside the road.

With a practiced hand, she quickly texted her coworker, Myra, and asked her to concoct a cover story for her tardiness. She had intended to call her mom back home in Sunset, New Mexico and let her know how easy her college midterms had been. But that would have to wait.

The kid had seemed very small in silhouette—maybe five or six years old—and no house or vehicle in sight.

When Myra texted back to say the boss was on the warpath, Mandy replied, "Well, just tell him I stopped to pick up a boy on the edge of town. That should really turn his face red!" It was an inside joke. Everyone knew when the boss's face was red it was wise to give him a wide berth.

Myra sent back a row of question marks.

"L8R," Mandy responded. She looked all around. She had assumed the little guy would come dashing up to the car as soon as she had come to a stop. But even when she could no longer hear the crunch of her tires on gravel, he still hadn't materialized.

I didn't pass him by that much.

Craning her neck to see past the Toyota's blind spot, Mandy dropped the phone into the center console drink holder and shoved the gearshift into park. A thick stand of live oaks cast a deep shadow over the bar ditch. The setting sun made the trees appear as black-paper cutouts in a landscape collage.

After checking her mirrors to make sure no one was behind her, Mandy pressed the button to lower the passenger-side window.

It was almost all the way down when a man yanked open the door and exploded into her world like a tornado into a trailer park. Her hand flew to the gearshift, but she couldn't engage it. Even as her flight instinct kicked in, part of her mind was telling her this was almost certainly the same strange guy who had requested her section at the restaurant the night before. His eyes had seemed to follow her all around the crowded dining room, and his oily stench had made him stand out like a spot of mold on white linen.

Mandy drew in breath to scream; her hand scrambling across the console for her phone or the gearshift, whichever came first, but he was too fast. With lightning speed, he dove across the seat and slapped a rectangle of duct tape across her mouth. At the same time, he buried his free hand knuckle deep in the thick blonde braid at the base of her skull even as his other hand slid down to her windpipe and began to squeeze.

Mandy's fight instinct kicked in then, and she whipped her head back and forth in an effort to dislodge his hands. His stench, and the oily filth of his unkempt hair, was sickening. She clawed at his eyes, ripped at his skin, but it was no use. The psycho laughed and simply leaned his head back out of her reach.

That's when Mandy began to claw at her own face, attempting to scratch the silver tape off her mouth. It didn't matter. There was no one around to hear her scream even if she could have gotten it off.

She wasn't a quitter, though. Mandy did her best to get her feet out from under the steering column to kick. But he was pressing down on her with his whole weight. She was trapped. Calmly, the psycho took one hand off her throat, doubled up his fist, and hit her so hard the back of her skull struck the driver's side window with an audible *whap!*

Then, he went back to her throat. As his deceptively thin fingers crushed her windpipe, Mandy's grip on reality began to loosen. Tiny strobes flashed inside her skull.

He squeezed even harder; the tips of his fingers disappearing into the flesh of her throat.

At the last second, as her world began to grow dark, a memory flashed through Mandy's mind. She remembered how, as a small girl of six, she had begun to worry about running out of air because if you couldn't see something, how did you know how much of it was left? She *could* see balloons, though. So she had begged her mom to buy several packages of the colorful party staples, which she'd then blown up and stored in her bedroom closet. Her mom humored her. Her older sister, Kami, however, couldn't let a good thing like that go unnoticed.

She had waited until Mandy was out, then she'd tied all the balloons together and attached them to the stop sign on the corner. Mandy had felt so humiliated when she came home from school and saw them. She'd wanted to get them down and put them back in her closet, but she couldn't bring herself to do it. She would have let herself run out of air before giving her sister that satisfaction.

The balloon bouquet had wilted quickly in the hot New Mexico sun.

Now, even as she was dying, Mandy grasped the irony of that memory. She really had run out of air. Her last coherent thought —as the fireworks behind her eyelids exploded in the grand finale—was of those wilting, multicolored balloons.

OTHER TITLES FROM 5 PRINCE PUBLISHING

Wanderlust *Bernadette Marie*
Holiday Past *Jessica Dall*
Christmas Blitz *Amy Gale*
A Christmas for Chloe *Susan Lohrer*
Restored Hearts *Railyn Stone*
A Romance for Christmas *Bernadette Marie*
Saving Sarah May *S.J. Reisner*
Walker Pride *Bernadette Marie*
Abandoned Soul *Doug Simpson*